RHUGER'S PEARL

ORC MATCHED BOOK 1.0

CARLOTTA HUGHES

WWW.AUTHORCARLOTTAHUGHES.COM

First Edition
ISBN: 978-0-9893799-4-6 [EBOOK]
ISBN: 978-0-9893799-5-3 [PRINT]

www.authorcarlottahughes.com

For Connor.
Mo bhàrd gaisgeil.
Rìgh mo chridhe.

TABLE OF CONTENTS

Content Information

<u>Content Awareness:</u>

Please note that there are aspects of the story that may be upsetting to some. It is my responsibility as an author to be transparent with my readers so that they have a comfortable experience.

Chapters in the Table of Contents with an **asterisk*** are chapters that contain *explicit* sensitive content. For a full list of what chapters include what kind of sensitive content, please jump to the Content Awareness section at the back of the book. Please also note that I'm including *mentions* of sensitive content besides *explicit* scenes and they will be marked in the Content Awareness section, accordingly. A full list also exists on my website: *www.authorcarlottahughes.com.*

<u>Positivity Awareness:</u>

Fat body rep, anxiety rep, depression rep, healing trauma, ADHD rep, ASD rep

<u>Autism & Neurodivergent Representation:</u>

Amelia is a character who is autistic and has other neurodivergent experiences. I wanted to have a female main character who is autistic and neurodivergent because of the lack of representation in the romance genre. I am Self-Diagnosed with ASD and neurodivergent. Amelia's experiences are based on my own experiences and mental framework. These experiences do not reflect those of the entire spectrum of ASD and should **NEVER** be used to invalidate another person's lived experiences.

If you have questions regarding the validity of Self-Diagnosis for ASD, I highly suggest you read this paper by the University of Washington's Autism Center *https://tinyurl.com/yc7ukwjz.* Wherein they support self-diagnosis of autism as, most commonly, accurate.

<u>A Note On Orckin Culture:</u>

Because of the decline in the orckin species, their once broad and varied culture was significantly affected. Oral traditions and education were altered or eradicated to keep the wanted narrative. This occurred rather easily, as the orckin industry revolves around trades, and not all orckin are taught to read and write. Thus, some of their traditions passed from common knowledge entirely or were only mentioned in old tales.

This includes alternate forms of life paths for both males and females and gender identity outside of the binary. As the series progresses and humans and orckin find their cridhe mates with one another, the pressures of species propagation significantly ease, allowing for traditions, genders, and philosophies that were stifled to resurface. Especially with humans reintroducing similar concepts with their mates.

It is important to note that while it is not *required* for females in the orckin culture to produce orclings; it is an expectation by their society and often seen as an honor. Not all the five clans approach this in the same way, and often manipulation is used. Which, of course, is not completely informed consent. Consent is a big factor in this series, and occasionally a point of conflict, as they reestablish rules of conduct within their culture.

Overall, as the orckin revive their lost culture, there will be outdated modes of thinking, harsh punishments, misunderstandings, heavy conflict, and compromises.

Teanga Dhubh or Black Tongue, the primary orckin language, is loosely based on Scots Gaelic. A pronunciation guide and index exist at the back of the book. You can find voice clips on my website courtesy of *https://learngaelic.scot/*

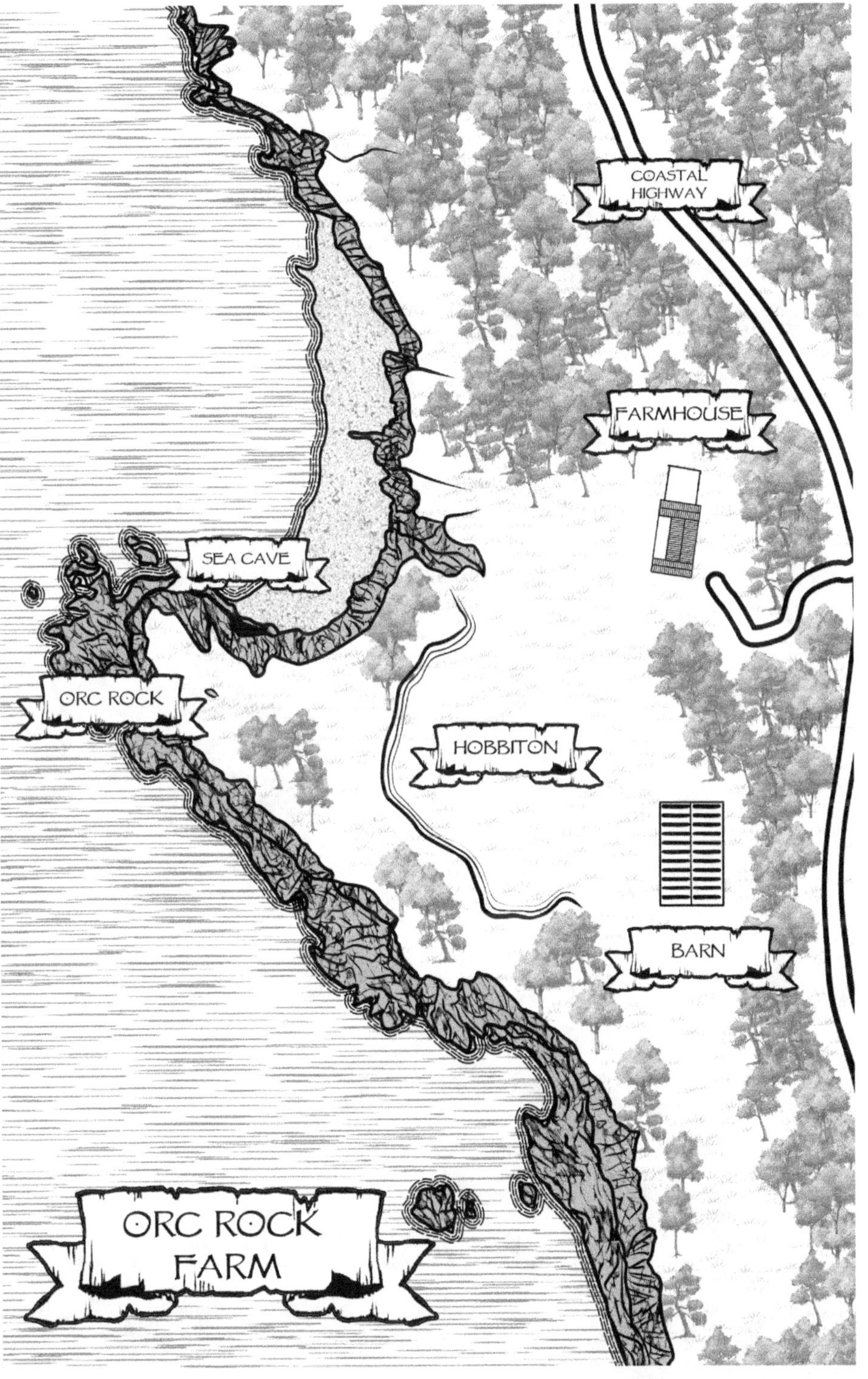

COASTAL
HIGHWAY
FARMHOUSE
SEA CAVE
ORC ROCK
HOBBITON
BARN
ORC ROCK
FARM

CHAPTER 01

AMELIA

Some relationships are a lot like an apple. Super shiny in the beginning, bursting with flavor and promise. But by the time you notice the rot in the middle, there's already a horrid taste in your mouth. My husband was that nasty grub rotting the apple from the inside out.

I didn't leave him. I escaped him.

It took months of planning, some scheduling gymnastics, the support of friends and family, and a big dose of sheer high-octane 'let this bitch burn' juice. I'd jumped into my packed rental car with my 3 cats—flipping the entire East Coast the bird as I drove over the North Carolina border on my way west.

I made it to the California coast in 3 days thanks to energy drinks, napping at truck stops, and code-red anxiety. The cats yowled me the song of their people the entire way and threatened to mutiny more than once as we drove through the Sierra Nevada Mountains. As I crawled through the winding switchbacks on Highway 1 along the coastline, my Grandmother Ruth's rough voice cackled through my car's speakers.

"You won't *believe* how these high-brow hipsters want to do *yoga* with *goats*. I've made so much money off of these idiots!" She crowed.

Yep. Grandma Ruth owned a small farm and bed-and-breakfast right along the cliffs overlooking the Pacific Ocean that specialized in... pygmy goats. For goat yoga.

The things rich people would blow their money on.

"How's Hobbiton doing?" I asked as I cranked the steering wheel through a tight switchback.

"Oh, you know, it's almost summer, so I've got people staying in shorts and tank tops. None of them have the good sense to check what the weather's like out here. They just see *California* and think it's going to be warm and sunny." She snarked, and I heard Totes McGoats, the father of the herd, screeching his agreement in the background. "The Goat Shire and Hobbiton Crew merchandise was a great idea, Eley! They're so cold from the fog, they buy whatever I have! I'm already out of everything thanks to this last cosplay group that came through for that convention in San Francisco."

I snorted. The fog is northern California's dirty little coastal summer secret. May to early June is warm. September is warm. Everything in between? Fog. Cold, damp, dreary fog. The rest of the year was always a toss-up.

So unknowing tourists just... don't think about bringing warmer clothes. And merchants make a killing off of poor saps like them each year. My grandmother now included. And I was guilty of helping her design her merchandise.

Because that's what I did. I helped create designs for companies for their products. It didn't pay a ton, but it had helped me when I was financially under my ex-husband's thumb. As it stood, I would now help my Grandma Ruth by taking over a lot of the upkeep for Orc Rock

Farm and its little side businesses. It was good to know that I had a future.

"The cats holding up okay?" She queried. Of everyone, she was the most worried for them and understood why I just drove without staying at hotels. I didn't want to stress the poor floofs out any more than they needed to be.

"Yeah..." Looking down, River snuggled in my lap, head nestled into my armpit. Jayne sat tucked as close to me as he could get on the console, and his sister Kaylee was hiding under a blanket. "We're almost to you now, so they'll be better once they don't have to be in the car anymore."

"I know your mother gave you a hard time about not getting hotels on the way here, but I know why you didn't. And I know you didn't want to leave a trail for him to follow." Him. My husband.

The emotionally, mentally, financially, and—once—physically abusive alcoholic narcissist. *That* husband—soon-to-be *ex*-husband if my attorney and I had our way. I became officially separated from the man the minute I'd fled.

He didn't know where my grandmother lived. I didn't tell any of our joint friends I was even leaving, let alone when or where I was fleeing to. I didn't want to have to get a restraining order, but I'd done it. After all, he could be a loose cannon and I didn't want to become a statistic.

As the number of miles between us grew, the more I realized how bad things were. How utterly *terrified* I'd been. All the time.

Let's just say that I'd already had a few breakdowns on my journey.

"Yeah, I just wanted to disappear," I replied thickly. Grandma coughed and tactfully changed the subject.

"How soon are you gonna be here, Eley?" She asked. For the millionth time in the last hour.

"I'm... actually here!" I chirruped and my grandmother gasped. The rough gravel crunched under the tires of the rental car as I pulled into her long driveway. The line went dead, and I chuckled.

The cats noticed the change in speed and anxiously started looking out the window at the wind-brushed hills. Cypress, pine, and eucalyptus trees grew bent towards the mountains thanks to the never-ceasing winds. Rolling down my window a little, I took a deep breath of ocean air tinged with the tangy scent of eucalyptus.

It smelled like freedom.

The mostly bare hills gave way to a curious copse of trees that almost looked sunken into the hillside. Orc Rock Farm spread throughout the windswept hills where the pygmy goats grazed, but the main house and Hobbiton were nestled into the bowl within the hills. Protected on three sides from the wind, it was a tiny wonder of a micro-climate.

Little hobbit hole cottages dotted the hills behind the main house, each set into the land and themed for Lord of the Rings fans. An outdoor bar called The Green Dragon boasted market lights and barrel seats. Herbs, wildflowers, vegetables, and dwarf fruit trees littered Hobbiton in a riot of color and scent. The entire scene was ridiculously idyllic and a permaculturist's wet dream.

Only made more so by the main house. A sprawling single-floor Craftsman with a tin roof and hand-hewn details. Stone walls cupped an overgrown garden, beehives snuggled up against the nearby treeline, and every inch of space was packed with trailing jasmine and tea roses.

And beyond the main house and Hobbiton, the Pacific Ocean glittered like a million diamonds sewn to a bolt of sea-green silk. White fluffy clouds passed overhead and cast shadows on the waters far below.

The sounds of seagulls and sea lions and crashing waves broke through the sound of the wind and called to some primal part of me that begged to explore the shore. To see what was on the other side of the horizon.

It was quaint enough to make you yack.

As I pulled up to the house, my grandmother was already in the driveway, high-stepping with her arms thrown wide in her excitement to see me. A grin pulled at my mouth for the first time in ages. I could almost feel the tendons in my jaw creak.

Grandma Ruth was pretty tall for a woman at five foot ten. Not as tall as I was at six feet, but close enough. She was plump like I was; her face lined with more smiles than frowns. She wore her wavy grey hair in a bun on the top of her head and her glasses were bright green. Ever the social and political advocate, she wore a Black Lives Matter shirt. Her green overalls were rolled up and her feet were in wellies— she must have been in the garden when I'd called.

She still wore her wedding ring on her left hand. A curious piece my grandfather had made her from a knife hilt. My heart swelled at that. Even after all these decades, she was still hopelessly in love with my late grandfather. She always said that my grandfather was an old goat, so she'd gotten Totes McGoats and started raising pygmy goats in his honor.

I threw the car in park and jumped out, closing the door quickly so the cats wouldn't escape.

"Come here, Eley!" Grandma Ruth hollered, with a grin big enough to split her face. She was laughing and giggling so much that it was infectious.

"Hey, Grandma." I swooped in for a hug and she threw her arms around my shoulders, rocking me back and forth and raining kisses on my cheek.

"How are you, honey? Tired?" She asked when she pushed me

out at arm's length.

"Yeah... I hardly slept on the way out here." I muttered. The fatigue finally hit me after three days of driving.

"Well, let's get your kitties inside and some of your essentials, and we can worry about the rest tomorrow. I'll make you some dinner and you can go crash. How does that sound?"

"Wonderful. Honestly, Grandma, thank you."

"Pish! You know you're my baby, Amelia. It's my life's greatest joy to look after my family." She flapped her hands at me, shooing me to go get my things.

The odd-sounding phrase made me pause. It was something Grandpa had always said whenever we thanked him. Shaking my head, I turned and ran my hand over my face. Being back here was making me nostalgic.

I walked towards the rear of the car and popped the trunk. Snatching the suitcase and toiletry bag from the stuffed trunk, I dragged them in behind my Grandma.

"The house has hardly changed since you were here last. Your room is still the last on the left down the hall. Do you need some help?" She called as she led the way into the lovely Craftsman.

"Nah, I got it. I'll be right back." I said, looking around. She was right, the house was largely the same.

The house screamed coastal cottage mixed with some industrial farmhouse. The place had warm oak floors, light grey walls with white trim, and white-painted built-ins in just about any cranny possible. And the built-ins overflowed with books and knickknacks.

She'd sprinkled lots of Tolkien memorabilia all over the house. Including Gandalf's sword, Glamdring, which hung in a place of honor over the stone fireplace in the living room. The entryway had a lovely little Tiffany flush mount light and an antique hall tree. Fresh tea roses spilled out of a vase and a doormat that said 'Bye Felicia' lay beneath my feet.

For as white as my grandmother was, she sure loved her gangster rap and Friday was one of her favorite movies besides the new LOTR and Hobbit movies, of course. She even had a painting from a local urban artist of The Notorious B.I.G. on the wall in her library.

My Grandma Ruth was not a woman to be pigeonholed for sure. She liked what she liked and her motto was 'Fuck the Aesthetic!'. I hoped I could give as few fucks as she did when I got to be her age.

The house smelled like fresh roses and weed, and I laughed, shaking my head as I made my way down the hall. It wouldn't be a trip to visit grandma without getting a contact high. But after my three-thousand-mile journey, I could use it.

Lovely stained glass transoms glittered high overhead, and they turned all light that hit them into a riot of color. The walls in the hallway held the usual family photos. I paused and smiled sadly at the aged photo of my giant grandfather as he held my much smaller, laughing grandmother in his burly arms. Gods, I missed him. My grandfather had been presumed dead—swept out to sea. My grandmother still firmly believed he was alive somewhere. But it had been twenty years.

He would have come home long ago had he been alive. Wouldn't he?

Smiling wistfully, I made my way to my old bedroom. It had a queen-sized bed with a matching dresser and desk. The all-wood furniture was carved to look like flowers and painted a soft grey. The walls were still an alarming shade of peach, from back when I'd been a teen and wanted to paint my room. I hadn't lived here full-time, but my grandma didn't mind. Claiming I was exercising my right to choose for my personal space.

I tossed my bags down at the foot of the bed and trudged back outside. Jayne, River, and Kaylee behaved themselves despite the yowling and mild kitty protest. It seemed they were as happy to get out of the car as I was. Slowly, I brought each of the cats into my old bedroom and shut the door so they could have some unwinding time. I brought their litter box, a covered one I'd strapped into the back seat, and food and water bowls in. Along with their toys and blankets and pillows that I'd flung far and wide inside the rental car.

Yeah, I did not spoil these cats at all.

After getting the three stooges all settled in, I closed my bedroom door and went to look for my grandma. I found her in the kitchen, barefoot, with a mixing bowl in hand. The timer dinged, and I watched with a bemused smile as she pulled out a batch of fresh chocolate chip and hazelnut cookies. My favorite.

"So, is this supposed to be dinner?" I laughed. Grandma whipped around and grinned at me as she shucked cookies off the cookie tray with a spatula.

"Well, if the witches in *Practical Magic* could have brownies for breakfast, I figure us plebs can have cookies for dinner." Her logic was about as sound as a loaf of bread. I wandered over past the farmhouse sink to where she was depositing the cookies. Snagging one, I stuffed it into my mouth. I rolled my eyes and groaned. No matter what, grandma cookies are the best cookies.

"SO good!" I melted and my grandmother whacked the back of my hand when I went for another.

"Don't ruin your dinner." She said with a poker face.

"Humor. Har!" I snagged another, and she grinned at me. I walked over to the back of the house. There was a beautiful view of Hobbiton, the Pacific with its slowly setting sun, and Orc Rock off along the shore.

It was blustery, but I went out onto the rear porch anyway. Stuffing the cookie into my mouth, I threw my arms wide as if to embrace the ocean herself. The wind lifted my hair back off my face and I breathed deep.

This must be what freedom felt like for a caged bird. Uncertain, exhilarating, and sad all at once. I couldn't fly yet, so to speak. But I knew I would again.

Grandma Ruth found me curled up in an Adirondack chair as the sun brushed the curve of the ocean. A lover kissing its sweetheart goodnight. She set a plate of cookies on the table between us and set a cup of steaming coffee next to me. She had a blanket draped over her shoulder that she tossed over my lap. A few minutes later we were both snuggled up under blankets watching the sunset with our *Practical Magic* dinner. I took a sip of the hot coffee and choked.

"Grandma! What did you put in this?" I coughed around the burn in my throat.

"Your grandfather's whiskey. What, you thought I'd have coffee and dessert for dinner and *not* spike it with the good shit?" Grandma Ruth snorted at me. I stilled as she took a long swallow of her coffee, eyes slipping closed as she hummed in contentment.

Grandpa had loved to distill whiskey. He made it every year, and it was often a gift he gave during the holidays. The work shed in the woods was where he'd distill it and age it. It was some sort of secret recipe and he kept the place locked up tight when he wasn't there.

When Grandpa had died, Grandma had stashed away all the remaining whiskey. Only doling it out on the anniversary of when he went missing or on very special occasions. She hadn't even broken it out for my wedding. The few tastes I had of it over the years were bracing. It was so strong and flavorful that it was like a punch in the throat.

I'd still never had better whiskey.

And that Grandma was willing to share it with me now… it meant something. It was a welcome home from my long-gone grandpa. I clenched my jaw and blinked back tears as I took a careful sip of the decadent drink.

We sat like that together for hours after sunset, the market lights switching on in the dim light of the crescent moon. It was the most peace I'd felt in forever. Just sitting with Grandma, each of us floating in our own memories, yet together.

After a time, Grandma Ruth turned to me and caught my eye. "I know things didn't work out with Adam as you'd wished. He mistreated you. I want you to know that you are home. This is your home. And it always will be. I've got you, Eley. You won't go through this alone."

I just nodded, a lump stuck fast in my throat. Grandma got up then and collected her things, a blanket wrapped around her rounded frame. She bent over and laid a sweet kiss on my forehead.

"Goodnight, Eley. Get some sleep if you can, sweetness."

"I'll try. Goodnight Grandma." She patted my cheek with such love and sadness in her gaze before she crept back inside her house.

I sat there on the back porch, staring out at how the moonlight danced upon the waves long into the darkest part of the night.

CHAPTER 02

AMELIA

Days had passed since I'd arrived at my grandma's farm. I'd spent them in my room. In bed.

All the depresso espresso.

I'd broken down the first night after I'd finally crawled into bed. The stress and anger and bitterness finally burst forth from me in a torrent of tears and snot. It was some serious ugly crying. My grandma had crawled into bed with me and held me until I'd fallen asleep.

She'd let me be, mostly. Of all people, I knew my Grandma Ruth understood grief. Because I was grieving.

Not grieving the loss of the relationship I had with my husband. No—I'd shed those tears long ago. I was grieving for myself. That lost innocence, loss of safety, struggle with betrayal, doing whatever I had to do to survive, to keep the peace—including lying. I grieved for the person I'd been before my ex-husband. And the woman he'd molded her into.

I grieved for the mangled wreck of a human being I'd become

in extracting myself from his clutches, too.

Days and nights blended into one. The cats were finally let out of my room to get acquainted with the house. They were happy to explore, done with my misery.

Grandma Ruth would bring me snacks and check on me. Brush my hair away from my face, sticky from the salt of my tears. I hadn't showered since before I'd arrived and I knew I smelled. It'd been days, after all. One morning, Grandma Ruth had decided I'd had enough of a cry.

"Alright, Eley. That man is as good as dead to you now. That no-good bastard is gone and you are free. Do you hear me?" She asked as she whipped the curtains open and jerked the window up so that the fresh ocean air swept out the stale stink of my room, cleansing it and leaving it fresh and alive.

How I hoped to one day be again.

"Yes," I mumbled and rubbed my eyes against the light.

"He's not worth your tears. Only your disdain. Don't let that fucker win! Now. We're gonna get you up, get you showered and clean, and then you're going to have breakfast." She reached down and helped me to sit up. "No offense, but you smell and you need to brush your teeth, sweetness."

I choked out a laugh.

"Thanks, Grandma."

"You're welcome. Moping in here will *not* make things better." She went to the drawers and pulled out some clothes I'd put away my first night back. "I've got a surprise for you, so let's chop-chop!"

I grumbled and sighed, shuffling my depressed ass to the bathroom. Getting my toiletries set up, I took a cautious sniff under my armpit and shook my head, eyes watering. Yeah, definitely ripe under there. I pulled my dirty clothes off and tossed them into a corner before I turned on the water to heat.

Glancing in the mirror, I froze. The woman who stared back at me looked... hollow. I looked at least a decade older than I was. I was only in my early thirties. But the bags, lines, and general weariness made me look so much older.

I took a deep breath, let it out, and lifted my chin. Adam couldn't touch me anymore. I was my own woman. I belonged to no one but myself.

So I'd take care of myself. My body. The body that, though chubby, had gotten me through the darkest part of my life. It deserved all the love and care I could shower it in. I would reclaim it one inch at a time.

Cutting hair was such an immediate change. One that I hadn't indulged in for a long time. Adam liked long hair. Had disdained any talk of me cutting it.

Snarling, I searched the drawers in the vanity and came up with a pair of scissors. A grin broke out on my face as I looked up and assessed my long, tangled, wavy brown hair. With a crack in my chest that felt oddly like a breath of freedom, I grasped one hank of my hair and cut. Locks fell to the floor around my feet.

When I'd cut away the last of my long hair, I set the scissors down and looked at myself. Instead of almost being down to my butt, my hair brushed my shoulders. I hadn't looked like myself in forever. But this was a step in the right direction. Next, I looked down at my body.

I touched and moved my body. Not sensually, but in an assessing way. Learning every curve, accepting them with all their imperfections, and giving them loving little pats. I was fat. And there was nothing wrong with that. No matter what he'd tried to make me believe, being fat didn't equate to ugliness.

I'd hidden my growing body from myself and my ex-husband. After he'd hurt me... I'd stopped caring. A part of me hoped that if I let myself go, he'd stop touching me. He couldn't touch me now. So I'd accept my body as it was and work towards being strong again.

Not skinny. Strong.

That mantra followed me into the shower, where I scrubbed away the last vestiges of my journey. Marking a line in the sands of time. I would be strong. Inside and out. I would be strong.

To hell with them all. I would prove it to myself if no one else. The one person who always got me up out of the shower after a crying jag or wiped away my tears when I woke up in the night screaming from a nightmare was... well, me. So I was going to spoil myself and honor that part of me that picked me up when I was at rock bottom. That part that got me out alive.

She deserved it.

I spent the next hour locked in the bathroom pampering myself, making noise so as not to worry Grandma by going quiet. I emerged clean, hair cut to my shoulders in damp waves, skin scrubbed and moisturized until I glowed rosy, and dressed in comfy leggings and an oversized t-shirt.

Following my nose, I found my Grandma in the kitchen. She had just placed some fresh fruit, scrambled eggs, and homemade sourdough toast with goat cheese on the table. She looked up at me and the changes she saw brought a smile of relief to her face.

"Come, Eley, and eat before it gets cold!"

"Smells good," I mumbled as I plopped down in the chair at the farmhouse table. Grandma set a cup of coffee in front of me and I smiled at her gratefully before I dug in.

It was delicious. And I'd forgotten how much I loved goat cheese. The sharp tang and spreadable creaminess of it had me groaning in bliss. Adam had hated goat cheese and refused to buy it. So I swore then and there that I'd have goat cheese every day if I could. Reclaim what I loved and enjoyed, one thing at a time.

"So what is this surprise?" I asked around a mouthful of fruit.

"It's hard to explain... but it's kind of a family secret. One I think it's high time you learned about." Grandma's tone was full of hesitation and she looked away from me.

"Oh?" That caught my interest as I shoveled the last of my meal into my mouth and gulped down my coffee.

"Get your hiking shoes on and I'll explain on our way." Grandma already wore exercise leggings, an oversized Notorious R.B.G. sweatshirt she'd gotten when Justice Ruth Bader Ginsburg passed, and hiking boots.

A few minutes later we were out on the back porch, tromping down the steps and into Hobbiton. The collection of hobbit hole cottages was just precious. We passed one called The Prancing Pony, one called Rivendell, and another one labeled The Lonely Mountain. I knew each was themed inside, with unique furniture, flooring, and decor.

Before I'd married Adam, I'd helped Grandma Ruth re-decorate them. She wanted them to remind her visitors of the new movies. We passed the bowl in the earth and climbed the berm to where she had a cliff-side area that was often used for marriage ceremonies. In the distance, we could see Emily with the goats.

Emily was Grandma's assistant. A quirky, grumbly, petite thing that would rather be with the goats and chickens than with people. She was splendid company, and it had been years since I'd seen her. I waved vigorously, and she waved back. Grandma tossed a small wave her way as she led me towards a trail that led down to the beach.

"Emily's still here?" I asked.

"Yep! She's a great help. I'm glad I'll have both of you around. She conned me into getting chickens. The audacity!" Grandma laughed over her shoulder, the ocean winds making our hair fly around our heads like fluffy halos.

I chuckled as I tucked my shorter hair behind an ear so I could see. Grandma had told me all about how Totes McGoats had taken great offense to the lead rooster, Foghorn Leghorn. Thus named because he was so *incredibly loud*. Loud enough that some local fishermen could hear him when they were out fishing off the coast.

Totes McGoats *did not like this*.

The Goatfather and Foghorn would get into minor scuffles. He hated the fact that Foghorn was louder than him. It was a common occurrence that McGoats would try to out-scream Foghorn at the break of dawn each day. Confusing the hell out of the fisherfolk and the neighbors.

"What about the bees?" I queried as we hit a sharp turn on the trail. The cliffs were easily a few hundred feet high from the shore and had many tight twists and turns, all leading down to the beach far below. It was risky enough that Grandma made sure everyone staying in Hobbiton signed a waiver.

"Mia's still around. She comes by to check on the bees and those cool new hives. They're great! Just have to turn a knob and viola, honey!" Grandma called over the brisk breeze.

Mia was a local beekeeper who tended to the hives on the various farms and properties in the county. She was a small thing at just five feet, smaller than Emily, but curvy instead of wiry. She adopted a lot of strays too and worked as a vet tech at the local animal shelter. Mia was a total sweetheart, and I was looking forward to seeing her again, too.

"I'll have to invite her over and we can all have midnight margaritas and hang out!" Grandma Ruth was always the partier and best believe there would be weed. Lots of weed.

"That would be outstanding!" I called, trying to keep my footing on the sandy trail.

And it would be, I realized.

Getting to enjoy myself in female company would be a blessed change. Adam had disapproved of a lot of my friends and had been controlling over who I invited to our house. I wasn't sure if I could calm my guard down enough to relax. Being on high alert had become second nature over the years.

But I'd try. And I knew they'd understand if I struggled. They were good people.

We finally reached the beach. It was a perfect crescent of grey and tan sand. I used to hunt for sea glass and pretty stones with holes in them here. Hag stones, they were called.

The waves lapped onto shore, the sea calm and the tide out. It surprised me how serene the ocean was today. Usually, there were whitecaps out on the vast expanse of blue-green with an overcast sky looming overhead this time of year. Instead, the sun glinted brilliantly on the surface of the Pacific.

The rough call of a raven had me jerking towards where they roosted in a cypress tree rooted in the cliff face. There were two of them. Both of them were eyeballing us as we passed beneath them.

"I didn't realize ravens lived here," I said. There had been one or two growing up, but usually, you saw seagulls, sandpipers, cormorants, and pelicans. Not ravens.

"They've been congregating at the shore for years now,"

Grandma called. As if on cue, ten more ravens flocked to the tree in an eerily quiet swarm. The chilly recognition of why a flock of them were called a 'murder' crawled up my spine. A full dozen of the birds now watched us with curious intent as we stood looking up at them.

"Strange." Grandma Ruth squinted at the big, black-fletched birds. "Two is for positive change, ten is for a major event, and twelve is for the end of a journey—the finding of the answers to a soul's questions."

"That's not ominous at all, Grandma." I tried to keep my tone light as we moved away from the cypress tree and turned out onto the sand. Grandma had always believed in omens. I was too cautious to ignore it. Especially with how my grandmother's expression turned thoughtful.

Instead of taking off her shoes to enjoy the sand between her toes, Grandma led me towards the sea cave entrance at the base of Orc Rock. You know, the place that had *always* been off-limits. Curious, I followed her with cautious steps.

"What are we doing here?" I asked. "I thought you said the sea cave was dangerous and off-limits?"

There was a chain-link fence barrier with a posted sign that said it was treacherous to deter those who didn't find a legal waiver intimidating enough. Grandma had hinted over the years that she believed the sea cave had to do with Grandpa's disappearance. She stopped and used a galvanized key on the galvanized lock that kept the chain gate closed. Birds and fish could go in and out at will. Larger things would just get stuck and die.

Like people.

"There's a reason for that..." Grandma said as I helped her swing the door wide. She pulled two flashlights out of her sweatshirt pocket and handed me one.

I followed her inside. We watched our feet as we climbed around tide pools and sharp shelves of stone that the tide had yet to wash into pebbles. The cave wasn't wide at the mouth, but it became apparent that the cavern went deep into Orc Rock. I had to place my hands on the damp cave walls more than once, as kelp was slicker than snot on a doorknob underfoot.

"How far back does this go?" I asked, nudging a scuttling crab out of my way with the toe of my hiking shoe. Grandma said nothing and soon disappeared around a sharp bend in the cave. I could hear her ahead of me and fear riddled my gut.

What was such a surprise and a gotdamn secret that it needed signed waivers, a locked galvanized chain gate, and a posted sign to protect it? What the hell had Grandma Ruth been hiding all these years?

Swallowing around my suddenly dry throat, anxiety riding high, I cast my flashlight around the sharp bend and spotted my grandma standing in a shaft of light. She clicked her flashlight off and looked at me with an apologetic smile.

Why did she look so sorry? Why was she so damn sad-looking?

"You may hate me for this. And it's a lot to take in. But you need to know." She murmured, voice thick with emotion.

"How could I ever hate you?" I asked, dumbfounded, as I walked toward her. The light was blinding, so it took a moment for my eyes to adjust to what she lifted her arm towards.

The cavern was enormous. It was almost as if Orc Rock were hollow. Shafts of early summer sunshine sliced through the darkness and lit up the rocky walls from the floor up. The floor was smooth with only pebbles and sand.

Then I noticed it.

The back wall.

It was oddly flat, not curved like the rest of the cavern. Sunlight streamed from the ceiling to bathe a thirty-foot-wide carved circle with steps leading to it. The thing was stunning.

I stood completely shocked at what was before my eyes. Rings upon rings overlapped in perfectly carved circles. A carved tree lay over them, the roots curling and extending out along the stone floor, the upper branches curving in the rough ceiling above. But it wasn't just any tree. No, this thing had six perfectly carved wings. Each feather carved down to the minutest detail.

There were fourteen tiny glints of light along an archway set into the tree's massive trunk. There were two more placed vertically in the center of the archway. And an empty divot where a third should have gone.

"What in the name of Lovecraft is this?" I asked in a shocked whisper. "Did you make this?"

Grandma was crafty and *not* of the Christian persuasion. She was pagan and proud of it. There were various altars across the farm for various deities she honored. But something like this seemed beyond her.

"No," she said simply with a shrug. "I don't know how long this has been here. It was here before I bought Orc Rock Farm."

"What is it...?" I asked in awe as I walked up towards it, my steps cautious.

"Your grandfather said it was a portal. A gate or Geata."

"A *what* now?" I asked in shock, head whipping towards my grandmother. Short hair flying.

"A gate."

"A gate to *where?*" I demanded.

Grandma took a bracing breath and let it out in a rush. Shoving her hands into her sweatshirt pocket, she met my gaze.

"To a planet called Talam." She murmured, face wary and looking far older than she was.

Okay. So there was a gate to another planet in my Grandma's off-limits sea cave inside of Orc Rock on her small farm where she had a Lord of the Rings-inspired, Hobbiton bed-and-breakfast and she raised pygmy goats for goat yoga.

...

Of *course* she did.

CHAPTER 03

AMELIA

"Okay," I said, holding up my hands. "Let me get this straight. This is a gate to another planet. Like *Stargate* or something, right?"

"Yes."

"How do you *know this*?"

I was not ready for her answer. She looked me dead in the eye and the brutal honesty I saw there froze me in place. "Because your grandfather is not human. He came through this gate. He is from Talam." Grandma Ruth lifted her chin at me as she said this. Daring me to refute her.

My brain short-circuited.

"What do you mean, Grandpa wasn't human?" I demanded, shaking my head. "He sure as hell *looked* human."

"That was because of his chleoc ring," Grandma explained. "It was a ring that allowed him to look like us while he was here."

"A *what*?" I asked a little breathlessly.

"A chleoc ring." She repeated.

"And what exactly did Grandpa look like *without* this chleoc ring?" I dreaded her answer.

Grandma Ruth shrugged and lifted her eyes and arms, swinging them around at the cave at large.

Slowly, realization dawned on what she meant.

No.

"He was an..." I swallowed hard. "ORC?"

Grandma Ruth nodded and shrugged helplessly at me.

"Are you *insane*?" I asked, horrified.

I wasn't sure if I was asking if she was insane to think this whole situation was real. That Grandpa really was an orc or that this weird carving was really a gate to another planet.

Or if I was asking her if she was insane enough to boink an orc alien.

Of course she was.

"Okay, so why should I believe you?" I asked, feeling a migraine imminent. I rubbed the bridge of my nose.

"Think about it. How often have you been sick?" She tilted her head, already knowing the answer.

"Rarely."

"You heal fast, don't you? Your mother too? Like baffle-the-doctors fast." Grandma Ruth began ticking off fingers.

"Okay."

"And both you and your mother have always been crazy strong and tall. It's your orckin genes."

"Grandpa was over seven feet tall, Grandma. Of *course*, we'd get emotion, but not this easy openness. It was jarring.

"Okay… I'll trust you," I said dubiously.

It alarmed me that he could carry me so easily. And being handled by so… *much*… of a masculine person was just freaking me out. My ex-husband had been kind of a twig whereas Rhuger was a ripped giant. He just oozed rugged masculinity that made my female hindbrain bleat in panic. To compensate, I turned to snarkiness out of a misplaced sense of self-preservation.

"Though, if you'd feel more comfortable, you can get on my back?" Rhuger asked. I thought about it while he walked. My mind whirled through the variables and logical options in a matter of moments.

"I think that'd be the best option. You can still grab for your weapons if you need them and I can hang on for dear life." Rhuger paused as if surprised.

"As you wish." He said with a shrug and set me down gently. I stood on my good leg while he turned and crouched down a bit.

Leaning forward, I set my hands on his shoulders. Once I was steady, I gave a little leap of faith and flung my arms and legs around him all at once. I could hear the air leaving his lungs as I knocked him forward a little as if he hadn't expected my total mount.

His hands snapped up and grasped my thighs before he looped his forearms under my knees. He stood straight and gave a little hop to redistribute my weight. I clung on and did my best not to choke him. My hands ended up splayed across his chest, the breadth of his shoulders making it easy to plaster myself against his back.

He cleared his throat and strode forward. His ears and cheeks were that vibrant green again from what I could see. He *had* to be blushing.

"Are you sure I'm not too heavy?" I asked.

"I'm sure." His voice was steady as he began hiking up a trail, not even getting winded with the extra weight.

"How far do we need to go? I don't want to tire you out." I insisted.

"Oc'Dellor is two days out. We'll make it almost halfway by tonight if we don't run into any more problems. There's a cave we can spend the night in. It's safe, a hunter's cave that travelers often stay in. There, I can assess your ankle and we can decide what to do from there. Is it still hurting you?"

"It throbs, but nothing too bad," I informed him. "Let me know when you want a break, okay? And I'll get off your back."

"You seem to think I'm so weak that I can't carry you until nightfall." Rhuger's tone was both irritated and amused.

"Well, you'd have to be a Marine for that." I snorted.

"What's a '*ma-reen*'?" Rhuger asked.

"A Marine is an elite human fighter in my country," I explained. "The average person would need to rest often carrying me if they could carry me at all."

"Well, none of our orcs could fight if they couldn't even carry their gear all day." Rhuger snorted. "Are humans really that weak?"

"I guess so? You just seem crazy strong to me."

"I'll take that as a compliment."

"If you must." I chuckled. Rhuger just hummed in amusement. He continued on, steps surprisingly light for his size and with my extra weight to boot.

Before long, the companionable silence turned soothing. The

wind through the trees, the drone of insects, Rhuger's even breathing, and his rhythmic heartbeat wove together to lull me into a soft feeling, almost like safety. My eyelids slid closed as I leaned further into his warmth.

CHAPTER 08

AMELIA

"Hey, we're here." Rhugher's gravelly voice pulled me from sleep and I gasped awake. When had I fallen asleep?

Looking around, I realized it was dark. Two of the three moons were visible in the sky above us. I spotted a cave nearby. Nestled into a low cliff face, with a moonlit clearing in front of the cave that offered visibility in case anyone approached. The cave mouth was dark, so it didn't appear to be in current use.

Rhuger gently set me down near a pile of stones and held a finger to his mouth, showing I should be quiet. I nodded, and he shook out his arms, snagged a knife from his bandolier, and stalked toward the cave entrance. I held my breath, realizing he was going to inspect the cave, to make sure we weren't walking in on a wild animal. Or a trap.

I couldn't help but be impressed with how quietly Rhuger moved. His footsteps were silent, and he approached the cave in a partial crouch, lowering his center of gravity. He was graceful, each movement calculated, not wasting an iota of energy. Witnessing all that prowling masculinity in one person was making my heart flip-flop in my chest.

What the hell was wrong with me? I'd never been attracted to someone so instantly before. It made me uncomfortable. I didn't want to think of Rhuger as less than a person, as just an object of desire, but he was making it hard.

... PFFFT.

Wrenching my brain up out of the gutter was a pain in the ass...

... GOTDAMNIT.

I crossed my arms over my chest as I watched the giant kilt-wearing orc commando...

I just hung my head in defeat. Where the *hell* was this coming from? My brain was balls deep in the gutter and I just had to accept that my brain suddenly got swapped with that of a fourteen-year-old boy. Shaking my head, I looked back up in time to see Rhuger step into the cave mouth, knife at the ready.

I'd expected him to wave that all was good, for him to enter the cave, for him to shout if something was there. What I *wasn't* prepared for was the giant four-legged beast that lunged out at him from inside the cave. It hit Rhuger like a freight train and sent him sprawling onto the ground, breath whooshing from his chest, knife skittering out of his hand and out of reach.

Choking back a scream, I hobbled towards them. I don't know what I thought I could do against a giant beast that was at least four times Rhuger's size, but I wasn't about to let the only helpful person I'd met on this planet die without an assist.

Rhuger's laughter cut off my panic.

Wait, he was laughing? I paused my shambling, shook my head, and took in the scene again. The enormous beast was wagging its scaled tail almost like a cat or dog would when happy. I watched in frozen horror as Rhuger reached his hands up and started scratching the beast under its chin. A reverberating purr ripped through the clearing.

Rhuger was giving scratchies to a beast the size of a Corvette. A Corvette shaped like a leopard and a dragon had a love child. It had a huge wedge-shaped head, saber-tooth tiger-like teeth, scales, and fur. Its back rippled with black jointed plates along its spine, from its spiked head down to the tip of its sinuous tail. What little I could see of its belly was also heavily scaled. The rest of its body sported glossy charcoal-grey fur.

I watched, wobbling on one leg, as the massive cat-o-saur laved Rhuger's face.

"Och! Get off me, ya scaly fluff ball!" Rhuger laughed and shoved at the cat's face. It purred in response and sat back on its haunches. "You're acting like it's been weeks since you've seen me, not two days."

Rhuger got to his feet and dusted himself off. The giant cat thing had noticed me and was making a chirrupy noise in its throat, nose flickering as it scented me in the air. Rhuger noticed and turned, abs rippling in the moonlight, making me wobble into full-blown noodle legs. It was criminal how gorgeous he was. Were all orcs like this or just him?

Rhuger strode to me and the swagger in his step blanked my mind. Were hips supposed to move like that? Because they weren't lyin' about what they could do to a girl. I blinked, and he was at my elbow.

"What are you doing? I told you to stay by the rocks." He admonished me as he swooped down to scoop me up into his arms.

Panicking and blushing like mad, I flung my arms around his neck and clung to him shamelessly. My mind was still *thoroughly* in the gutter as his scent washed over me. That ripe pomegranate, spice, leather, and pure masculine scent of him made me light-headed.

"Oh, I dunno. I saw you getting mauled by a giant cat, and my body moved to help before my brain could catch up." I snarked.

"You sought to protect me against a nocrys while injured?" He asked, his tone oddly warm.

"I mean, you're my only ally on this planet. I don't want you dead."

"Och, pearl, I'm touched." His tone was warm and slightly mocking. The bastard sure was a flirt.

"In the head, maybe," I mumbled, and he tipped his head back and laughed. Dazzled, I shut my mouth and looked away.

How the hell could someone look so good laughing? It was positively criminal.

My thoughts derailed as we passed the giant cat thing—nocrys. Its intelligent eyes looked me over, interest piqued, nose twitching as it smelled me. Evidently, I passed the nocrys test because it followed Rhuger into the cave without a fuss.

The cave was dark. Little light from the three moons crept into the cave mouth. But that didn't seem to be a deterrent for Rhuger. He just walked over and sat me on a wooden bench I could barely see in the dark.

"Stay here and I'll get a fire going." He murmured a little too close to my ear. I had to repress a shudder at how his breath whispered over the sensitive skin there.

"Okay," I murmured. Rhuger's arms left me and I suddenly felt their loss like an ache. Weird.

I sat in silence and listened as he rummaged about in the dark. A few minutes later, he clacked two rocks together. Sparks flew from the impact and fell into a small batch of kindling. Something looking akin to fur. With a few breaths, Rhuger coaxed the kindling to catch alight and began feeding the small flame.

The contrast of light and dark that played over his form as he built the fire caught my breath. The flickering shadows and dancing light from the growing fire flitted across the hills and hollows of his body, enchanting me, and settling into my bones. His otherworldly beauty was stark and undeniable. I swallowed hard.

Shaking myself, I focused on his actions instead. He'd built the fire from stones that seemed like flint back on Earth. I couldn't say for sure if they were or not, but I could say they had a similar function. Watching, I made mental notes about his process and what he used for what steps. And tried not to get lost in him again.

It wasn't long before the fire was crackling merrily. My mind filed away what I'd learned from watching him. If I needed to—I now knew how to build a fire on Talam. I was just glad that they seemed to do it the same way we did on Earth. That they didn't rely solely on those sunstones.

Now that there was sufficient light, I cast about, taking in the cave. There were beds and benches carved into the stone walls and shelves perched on jutting stones. There was even a worktable in the very back with what looked almost like medical supplies.

Everything within the cave was orderly and well-stocked. There were baskets with dried tubairs and other foodstuffs. Stacks of blankets and clothes. It was a veritable storage unit, appearing to have everything a traveler might need.

The giant cat rose from where it had been sitting at the cave entrance and prowled over to me. Knowing the drill from having three cats of my own, I sat still and calm. It was still disconcerting to have a feline larger than a tiger stroll right up to you, focused on you.

Rhuger watched us from across the fire, not in worry, but bemusement. I took it as a good sign his cat wasn't about to gnaw my face off.

"Hello, baby." I crooned softly to the cat as it got within a foot of me, crowding my personal space as cats do.

"Hifasa, be gentle." Rhuger admonished from across the fire.

"Is Hifasa the cat's name?" I asked.

"Her name, yes. She is my nocrys. Both a friend and a steed." He replied.

My gaze went back to Hifasa, who was staring at me. As our eyes locked, I hummed and slowly blinked for the giant kitty. A sign of trust and affection.

"Hmm, hello Hifasa." I hummed at her and her body language immediately went loose. She slowly blinked back at me. Letting me know she liked me and trusted me and already cared. "Such a good girl you are!"

Hifasa purred and then head-butted me. Her head was so big that it nearly knocked me over and I had to grasp onto her to keep from falling off the bench.

"Hifasa! Suidh." Rhuger said, a note of alarm in his voice.

I was too busy laughing.

Hifasa was purring loudly and rubbing her face all over me like I had a secret stash of catnip. I sat back up. Then I scratched her cheeks and the weird scaled ridges on her nose and forehead. She kneaded the floor of the cave, wicked claws raking through the dirt and stones.

"Aw, Hifasa baby. You making me biscuits?" I chuckled. As I scratched under her chin, Hifasa looked up at me, her eyes glazed over. A big dollop of drool plopped onto my lap. "And some gravy, evidently."

"What are biscuits?" Rhuger asked.

"Oh... uh, a type of bread?" I replied, scratching Hifasa's cheek with both hands. Did they have bread here on Talam? I wasn't sure how I'd explain that one if they didn't. "You knead the dough before cooking, so when cats do this with their paws like they're kneading, humans call it 'making biscuits'."

"Ah, we have bread—we call it aran," Rhuger explained. "It's made from the same grain we make our uisge-beatha, our whiskey, from."

"Aran..." I repeated, absorbing the word the best I could past my exhaustion.

Rhuger got up then with fluid grace. He stalked over to me and my heart began a staccato beat in my chest. He was just so unmistakably *male* in a way that I was decidedly *not* used to, with a confidence and swagger that the human men I knew lacked. My heart was in my throat as he dropped into a crouch in front of me.

Rhuger looked at my hiking shoes in confusion for a moment but seemed to figure it out on his own rather quickly. Cradling my hurt ankle in one large hand, he gently undid the laces and removed my shoe and sock with the other. He set them aside as if they were precious instead of the smelly, soaked footwear they were.

His head was bent over my foot, carefully rotating and touching it with his thick fingers. I hissed when he moved and touched it in ways that hurt. Rhuger looked up at me from under his brows to assess my reaction.

Well, my reaction was pretty fucking turned on because the guy's face wasn't far from the apex of my thighs. I had to grip the edge of the wooden bench, my small claws puncturing the wood till it creaked. I watched in fascination as Rhuger took a hitching breath, the pupils of his eyes blowing out until only slim rings of silver glittered at me in all that black.

"I take it, it hurts when you hiss like that..." He choked out.

"Um, yep." I tried to laugh it off, but I knew my expression wasn't convincing.

"Stay here." He near growled as he stood swiftly and stalked away.

"Okay..." I replied weakly, letting out a shaky breath.

I watched as he rifled through some items stashed in the cave. He made quick work of gathering a small pile of items—lending me to believe that he used this traveler's cave often. When he returned, he sat cross-legged on the floor. He pulled my injured ankle into his lap with utmost gentleness.

I watched in fascination as he picked up a small crock jar from the small pile of items and opened it. A strange herby scent I couldn't place wafted from the jar. Rhuger stuck a finger into the ointment and brought out a dollop. Before I could protest or ask him what he was doing, he had rubbed the ointment into his hands and then picked up my foot.

Gasping at the heat of his hand on my foot, I didn't have time to squeak, let alone tell him to stop before he began to gently, yet firmly, massage my ankle. I let out an undignified groan as Rhuger's strong fingers slid along the sore muscles and tendons. Working out knots I didn't know I even had.

His dark, amused chuckle ran up my spine like a physical touch, and I shivered. Rhuger was trying not to smile as I continued to grunt at his ministrations.

"You're good at that." I grudgingly told him as his thumbs rubbed along the length of the bottom of my foot. I had to resist the urge to bite my fist. How could something like this feel so good on a physical healing level but also be so damn erotic? Because holy hell, watching his strong fingers on my much smaller ankle did... things.

Rhuger just smirked, as if he knew the effect he was having on me and kept rubbing. After a few minutes, the pain ebbed. He leaned over, still cupping my foot in one massive hand, and grasped a length of fabric. He began winding it around, splinting and stabilizing my ankle.

"Let me know if it's too tight." He rumbled. I just nodded. Rhuger paused and cocked an eyebrow up at me. "I need you to tell me if you understand."

"Yes. I'll let you know if it's too tight. Promise." I dunno what it was about that quiet demand for confirmation, but it was fucking hot. Maybe it was all the times my consent never mattered.

Well, that thought derailed my horniness. Rhuger had already returned his gaze to wrapping my ankle. That was good because I didn't think I could explain to him what it meant that he required my consent for even the littlest things.

"The salve will help speed up your healing. It seems there are only some strained tendons and not any broken bones, so you should be well after a good night's rest." He told me as he released my ankle. Standing, Rhuger gathered the items and returned what he didn't use. Then he rummaged around and found a length of wood and took it over to his spot by the fire.

"Thank you. For taking care of me." I said.

"You're welcome." Rhuger looked surprised at my thanks.

An awkward silence descended, and he pulled out a few sacks and what looked like a traveling pack. Crouching, he rummaged through them and began pulling out food. He pulled one of his knives free from the bandolier crossing his chest.

"I can help cook dinner." I offered. He looked up from where he crouched by the fire, knife already flashing in the low light as he diced up ingredients. There was a pot on a large hot rock at the edge of the fire.

"It's my honor to care for you until we get to the Oc'Dellor."

"What do you mean?"

"Well, you are female and you're injured." He shrugged as if that was explanation enough.

And maybe to him, it was.

To me, it was weird. Not being shown consideration like this had become a norm for me. It was almost uncomfortable being treated like this. Like I had intrinsic value.

"What are you making?" I asked, hoping to steer the conversation to something more comfortable.

"Stew. I have some dried meat from my pack." He explained, holding up some dried meat strips.

"It smells good." I ventured. It did, too. He'd already tossed diced tiùbars, the last of the nutmeat, and some other items he'd gathered before I fell into the stream. Rhuger flashed me a small smile as he tossed the meat into the pot. He scooped out some sort of grain from a sack and tossed it in after the meat.

The awkward silence calmed into something almost companionable. Hifasa lay out next to the fire, her paw on my good foot as if making sure I stayed where I was as she napped. I leaned back against the cave wall and closed my eyes. Tired and sore.

I jerked awake from my doze when Rhuger nudged my knee. Looking up at him, he held out a folded piece of cloth. I took it automatically, looking up at his dark gaze in question.

"I figure you might wish to change. My vest can't be all that comfortable." He murmured, eyes intensely focused on mine as if he was fighting the urge to rake his gaze down at how his vest hugged my chest.

"Oh, thanks," I replied. Rhuger then stalked away and turned his back to me. "Oh, you mean right now?"

"I wish you to be comfortable. I'll put your tunic out to dry once you've changed." Rhuger called over his shoulder. He crossed his arms and waited patiently.

He wanted me to be comfortable? That was thoughtful.

So I tugged at the laces on the vest and got them undone. I glanced furtively at where Rhuger stood, but he was stock still, honoring my privacy. Trying not to think about that too much, I shucked his vest and tugged the tunic he'd scrounged for over my head.

The tunic was long, made for a much larger person, but it was soft and well-made. I took a moment to roll up the sleeves. The tunic came down to my knees, so I figured now was as good a time as any to dry my leggings. I slipped them off, carefully around my wrapped ankle, and set them on a rock closer to the fire.

Making sure the tunic covered my thighs and panties, I coughed delicately, indicating that I was decent. Rhuger still stood facing the opposite cave wall.

"I'm done," I called, amused.

"Good lass," Rhuger said. That... well, that was very nice to hear from him for reasons I wasn't ready to think about. He turned and looked at me. He froze, evidently surprised I'd taken off my leggings too. Coughing, he turned and began doling out some of the stew into a bowl.

Slipping a spoon into the savory bowl of food, Rhuger passed it to me before sitting down and helping himself. We ate in companionable silence. The stew was excellent, and I was surprised at the complexity of flavor Rhuger could elicit with just a handful of ingredients. He was an excellent cook.

When I finally ate my fill and leaned back on the bench, rubbing my full belly, Rhuger broke the quiet.

"I'm going to go out and keep watch for a while. Please get some rest." Setting aside his bowl, Rhuger stood and headed for the supplies at the back of the cave. He returned and handed me what looked like a blanket and a pillow. And a crutch. "For you."

"Oh, thank you. I appreciate you helping me out so much." I offered him a thankful smile and his cheeks flushed bright green again.

"I'll be back later." He coughed, turning and striding for the cave entrance. But not before he scooped up his vest and gave Hifasa head pats, speaking low to her in that odd language. He cast a glance over his shoulder, nodded, and left the cave.

I shook out the blanket and placed the pillow on one end of the bench. Curling up under the blanket, I couldn't help but think how Rhuger was just a completely different breed of guy than I was used to. And for once?

I felt safe.

My eyes drifted close in a peace I hadn't felt in years.

CHAPTER 09[*]

AMELIA

I awoke in the night to an odd sound coming from outside of the cave. The fire had burned down to embers and a quick look told me that Rhuger wasn't in the cave with me. His nocrys, Hifasa, was curled up nose to tail, asleep. So I knew whatever was outside wasn't a threat.

I lay there and listened for a moment. The sound was rhythmic and almost wet sounding. For the life of me, I couldn't place what it was. Curiosity won out against my exhaustion and I got to my feet, using the wall of the cave to brace. My splinted ankle was tender, so I used the crutch Rhuger had given me to hobble quietly to the mouth of the cave.

Whatever it was, I didn't want to spook it.

I edged around the lip of the cave mouth and froze, a gasp caught in my throat.

Rhuger stood in the clearing near the far edge of the woods. And he was bare-ass naked. The light from the triple moons limned his muscles and the planes of his chest and thighs. A shimmering puddle lay at his bare feet. It took me a moment to register what he was doing.

He was jerking off.

Out in the open. In the moonlight. The sound I'd been hearing was his fist as it pumped over his shaft. I felt something tighten low in my belly and a throbbing began between my thighs. It was easily the most erotic thing I'd ever seen.

He held his massive cock in one hand, his long, thick fingers barely able to wrap around it. He looked different from a human man, but I couldn't make out any details at this distance. His other hand held something up to his face. It was his vest. The vest I'd worn all day after falling into the stream. He was smelling it and groaning into the leather, muffling his voice.

It *should* freak me out that this massive male was using the vest I'd worn all day, the vest that had been against the bare skin of my breasts, soaked in my scent, as fap material. But I wasn't. My thighs clenched, and I was so turned on that I was having difficulty standing.

As far as I was aware, I'd never been *anyone's* fap material.

Was I into this?

Rhuger's pace turned furious as his hips snapped forward to meet his clenched fist. The wet slapping and his harsh breathing made my belly clench in need. His rhythm turned erratic, and he sank his sharp teeth into the leather of his vest as he gripped the veritable war club of a cock in his fist, snarling.

Streams of cum spurted from his throbbing tip and he tilted his head back, hips rolling as he rode out his pleasure. The puddle at his feet was his cum. How many times had he jerked off so far? The thought burned like a brand in my mind.

I was definitely into this.

I could feel how soaked my panties were. Fuck, it was so hot to watch him like this.

When he returned from his high, he released his shaft and looked down at it. It was still as hard as a rock and straining towards his navel. He made an irritated sound, sighed, and took it in hand again. He used his cum as lube and rubbed it all over his shaft.

Was my scent making him have a jerk-off marathon?

I should be outraged. I should be protesting and offended and throwing rocks at him.

Instead, I was horny as fuck, riveted to the spot like a gotdamn perv.

I must have made some sort of small noise because he paused. His head turned slowly, eyes flashing silver in the moonlight, as his gaze met mine across the glen. An unreadable look suffused his eyes as he sniffed at the air, and I swear to my wet panties he *licked* that delectable full mouth of his with his *long black tongue.*

To my utter shock and embarrassment, he turned, tossed the vest aside, and put on a show for me. Rhuger's gaze burned from under his lowered brow, an undeniable predator, as he stroked and tilted his monstrous cock and balls this way and that for me. So I could see it from nearly every angle. Could see it bob and drip pre-cum like a busted pipe.

Rhuger tilted his head back, baring his throat to me, eyes reduced to slits. His braid slithered from his shoulder and swung between his shoulder blades. With a very slow, deliberate intensity, he ran his tongue up over his lips and teeth, as if imagining what I might taste like. And with a devastatingly wicked grin that just oozed sexual appeal, he worked himself for me, eyelashes fluttering and moans catching in his throat.

I couldn't draw in air, as he showed me exactly how he liked to be touched. His eyes never left mine as he stroked himself, twisting his wrists and flickering his fingertips along his sensitive crown. His breathing was ragged and his hips twitched and jerked. He bared his teeth in a hiss before biting down on his bottom lip.

Did I say that watching him jerk off repeatedly to my scent was the most erotic thing I'd ever experienced?

LIES!

Having him perform for me was the sexiest, most erotic thing ever. Hot damn, I didn't think I could survive him. My heart beat against my rib cage in erratic sputters like a demented hummingbird ramming the bars of a cage. It wanted to be free to go flop over to his feet.

I watched, transfixed, as he used both hands on his shaft. Then one hand slipped to fondle his sac as his hips undulated. He'd been trying to keep quiet while he'd thought I was sleeping. Not anymore.

Rhuger moaned and hissed and groaned. He would say things in some guttural, lilting language I couldn't place as he began snapping his hips forward, both hands back on his cock. One hand worked his shaft while the other played with his tip, thick thumb running over and under his slit and frenulum. It wasn't long before his breathing grew ragged. He was edging close to his release.

My mouth went dry, and I drooled all at once over how magnificent he was as he shamelessly sought his pleasure watching me watch him. I was a gotdamn perv. And he was getting off on that fact. His snarl of satisfaction ripped through the glen, and his hips bucked.

"Amelia…" Rhuger rasped my name like it was a gotdamn prayer and he was a wretched sinner. He cried out then and sprayed his cum from between his fingers. His drawn-out, gravelly moan made me clench down on nothing. This orgasm of his seemed to last longer, more cum raining down at his feet than the last round.

When he finally panted his way down from his high, he released his dick. It finally drooped to dangle between his powerful thighs. An obscene war club that held so much sexual promise, I couldn't help but lick my lips.

His gaze zeroed in on my mouth, his jaw slack. Still breathing hard and without breaking eye contact, he raised his hand to his face. Rhuger's tongue slipped out between his sharp teeth to lick his seed off his fingers.

Fuck.

Unable to take it anymore, I groaned in my throat before turning to beat a hasty retreat into the cave. His dark chuckle followed me inside, sending shivers up and down my skin in a silken promise.

I laid back down, but I knew I wouldn't be able to sleep. I refused to touch myself, to sate my throbbing desire, in case he came back inside and took it as an invitation. Because if he did, I would be helpless to resist him.

As if he knew, he never came back inside the cave.

And I laid there awake next to Hifasa until the suns crested the horizon.

RHUGER

It had been the best orgasm of my life. And she had been nowhere near me. Just watched me from afar as I sought my pleasure. Enjoyed watching my body as I relentlessly pursued my release.

I'd never intended to have Amelia find me like that. Cock in my hand, my vest drenched in her sweet scent between my teeth as I fucked my fist like an orc possessed. I'd just sought to ease the ache that had begun the moment I'd laid eyes on her. Trying to be quiet as she slept in the traveler's cave.

If I didn't know any better, I'd say I'd entered the mating frenzy. The time of heat orcs entered when they found their cridhe. Their one true mate. But we both lacked the cridhe marks, matching symbols that told all that we had found our one true mate and would have no other.

The scent of her arousal as it had perfumed the air had tipped me over into doing something truly stupid. Instead of being thoughtful of her, a being from another planet with a different people and culture, I brazenly showed her how badly I wished she would touch me. And exactly *how* I craved her to touch me. For gods' sake, I'd bared my throat to her for her to rip out if she'd wished for my rutting audacity.

Having her witness my lust for her and not having her run away or attack? It was like I'd drank a bucket of luibh gaoil. The herb-infused uisge-beatha we drank to induce a mating frenzy-like state to produce orclings with our chosen mates. It'd taken every ounce of will I possessed not to run to her and plant my cock so deep inside of her cunt she'd forget the existence of any other male.

Especially that damned ex-husband of hers.

But I would do nothing to scare her or hurt her. And I knew that kind of behavior would undoubtedly do just that. So I'd stood my ground and devoured her with my gaze instead.

I hadn't meant to moan her name on my release, but it had come out of my mouth all the same. And when I'd finally come down from my lust-fueled haze, her soft, wonder-filled expression had clawed at my heart. I was terrified she would fear me. Instead, her arousal filled my nostrils until my mouth watered.

She'd made a mewling noise and bolted for the cave, despite the crutch. And I'd let her go. Knowing if I returned to the cave, there wasn't a damned thing on all of Talam that would keep me from using all of me to wrench every breathy moan from that little pink mouth of hers.

So instead, I looked down at my finally soft cock and sighed. Just her eyes on me had edged me to the release I'd spent so much of the night chasing. Finally sated, I snagged my kilt and buckled it back on. A physical reminder to behave myself.

I'd need to let her know I wouldn't touch her without her leave. The last thing I wanted was for her to fear me. She would need someone she could rely on and trust when we reached Oc'Dellor. And I would do anything to continue to be near her.

Even if it meant denying my body what it raged for.

CHAPTER 10

AMELIA

I woke to Hifasa's head bumping my face and purring so loud it was like having a sports car engine rev in my ear. Grumbling and pushing her away, I sat upright. My joints protested, cracking as I stretched. The bench hadn't been nearly as comfortable as the mossy bed in the gàrradh.

"Good morning, pearl," Rhuger drawled. His voice cracked through my morning fog like a whip. Memories of the night before crowded in and I felt my cheeks heat so hot I wondered briefly if I could fry an egg on them.

"G-good morning," I choked out, wide eyes meeting his across the fire.

"You hungry?" He asked me, stirring the coals. It took me a second to realize he'd meant hungry for food.

"Um, yes actually." In more ways than one, damn my ovaries.

Rhuger pulled out a tiùbar from the coals and prepared it for me. He sprinkled something onto it and handed it to me. I took it, nodded my thanks, and tucked in. I still had the blanket wrapped

grin was absolutely wicked, doing things to my insides and making me blush beet red. Seeing my reaction, Rhuger erupted in laughter, almost falling over.

"You're an asshole," I muttered, looking away and trying to wrangle my burning embarrassment.

"Maybe. But now you won't be able to help yourself but compare every other orc cock you see to mine." He chuckled, that delicious mouth of his still lopsided in a grin, eyebrow now cocked at me as if I'd refute his claim. Why couldn't I stop obsessing over his damned mouth?

"You mean that war club?" I blurted before I could stop myself. This made him laugh out loud again, his grin breathtaking. Rhuger stood in one fluid movement that spoke of all the naughty things he could probably do in between the sheets. He offered me his hand and I couldn't help but blush hard again as he helped me to my feet. "You say that like I'll be seeing a lot of orc dick."

"We're not a shy people." He explained with a smile before slinging his pack over one tattooed shoulder. His vest was nowhere to be seen, and I wasn't about to ask about it. He'd been using it as jerk-off fodder, after all. "Change. I'll be out front when you're ready."

"So what, you're a nudist colony?" I was now curious about what I was about to walk into once we made it to the city. He'd been so willing to strip, so I didn't know what the rest of the population would be like. Rhuger paused before nodding his head from side-to-side non-committally.

"Not quite. More like there aren't many females, and well, we're not shy about pleasure-seeking." He strode for the entrance of the cave and stood facing the world outside.

Taking that as my cue to change, I shucked the shirt and tugged on my bra, t-shirt, and leggings. Then I somehow got my sore ankle in its wrap into my hiking shoe. Lacing them up, I took a breath before standing.

I put my full weight on my injured foot, but it was as if the sprain was a week old rather than a day. Smiling to myself, I folded the shirt and blanket and set them on top of the pillow. I didn't think I'd need the crutch, so I left it where I'd propped it the night before.

Walking gently, but with purpose, I reached the front of the cave.

"All done," I said and Rhuger jumped a little. I couldn't help but grin. Then I caught a whiff of my clothes. They... didn't smell nice. I pulled my shirt up and sniffed before my face scrunched up. "Ugh, I smell like swamp and barbecue."

"We'll get you some fresh clothes and you can clean up when we reach Oc'Dellor." Rhuger gave me a lop-sided smile. "It's better to only take what is necessary from the stores of the travelers' cave in case someone else needs the items more."

"That's what I'd assumed." I gave him a half-shrug. It didn't bother me any.

Surprise lit his features, and he chuckled. As if it was strange that I came to that conclusion on my own. He grasped my hand and led me from the cave. The warm, buttery sunlight took a few moments to adjust to.

"Where's Hifasa?" I asked. She'd disappeared after waking me this morning.

"Off to find her breakfast and then return home." He said. "I hadn't intended to take her with me. She'd stubbornly followed me here to the cave. I don't have her riding gear and it's very uncomfortable to ride a nocrys bareback. Otherwise, I would have had you ride her to spare your foot."

"Aw. That's sweet, but I should be okay. So... you said that your people are exhibitionists?" Squinting at him in the light, I followed him into the tree line. His hand enveloped mine, and I felt like he was leading me through the wilds of this planet like two dating high schoolers would walk in the mall.

"We're a lot of things." He grinned crookedly at me as he led me along.

"Can't be worse than Love Fest in San Francisco." I shrugged, remembering some of the racier things I'd seen. Once you've seen a carriage with a little person in leather BDSM gear cracking a whip at two BBWs pulling the carriage dressed up as horses, including horse's tail butt plugs... not a lot will faze you.

"You've taken part in such things?" Rhuger asked, surprise limning his voice as he helped me over some rocks and onto a worn game trail. I'm not sure why he looked so impressed as his gaze raked over me. I just knew I didn't want him to think of me in a way in which I wasn't.

"No... not actively. There's just a lot of queer events near where I'm from, so I've seen a lot of kinks on display." I explained simply.

"So you're a prude." His admonishment stung, and I jerked to a stop.

"No!" I smacked him in the arm and he laughed and faked fending me off. I stopped in my tracks and looked down at my feet. "I just... haven't had pleasant experiences all right?"

There was a pause of pregnant silence only broken by the twittering of jewel-colored birds overhead.

"Do you want me to kill them for you?" The question made me jerk, and I looked up at Rhuger. His expression was grim, forbidding. All the beautiful angles of his face suddenly were hard and sharp.

"You're serious, aren't you?" I queried in a whisper. No one had offered to kill in the name of my honor before.

"Yes. Females should be cherished by their mates, not abused. My clan has rigorous rules surrounding such things." His sharp teeth snapped, his lip curling in disgust.

"Idealism like that doesn't make it into reality back home. I... I just don't want to ever see him again... My... husband... wasn't kind." It was so difficult to choke the words out. But I knew they needed saying. For myself, if no one else.

"He can't find you here." Rhuger held out his hand out to me, waiting patiently for me to take it. "If he somehow managed it, it would be my utmost pleasure to rid you of him once and for all. I swear to you that none shall touch you without your consent while you are here. I won't allow it."

I swallowed thickly around the lump in my throat. If his weaponry and the fierceness of his expression were enough to go off of, I believed him. Strange to feel like I could believe, and trust, a man... Er, male... so soon after leaving my ex in my rear-view mirror for good. I hesitated before taking his hand. His fingers laced with mine and I had to fight a blush as he gave me a small nod of understanding before leading us on.

"Why are there so few females?" I asked him.

"Plague wiped out many of our females and so we had to change our ways. Now it is the females who lead and choose in mating. Our leader, Rìgh Thorn, was wise in this." Rhuger's tone was a little clipped.

"Rìgh Thorn?" The name was familiar and I couldn't quite place it.

"Hmm. When the last wave of the plague laid waste to our clans, he returned to us and united us. Helped develop fair new laws to help us survive. But our numbers dwindle regardless." His tone was heavy as we walked through the dappled sunlight.

"How come? Is the plague something that happens often?" I asked.

"Every few decades it reappears, without a pattern. We're not sure how or why. Other clans often war with the Oc'Dellor to take our females by force. And with each other, too. No one wants their clan to go extinct." The wry expression he sent my way said a lot.

"Sounds short-sighted if you ask me," I said. Rhuger looked at me and cocked an eyebrow, silently asking for me to continue. "Well, if the plague has decimated your numbers, the clans should look at themselves as *one* clan to ensure the best possible situation for the females and the fertility of your people."

"Beauty and intelligence." Rhuger smiled slowly at me. I just muttered something noncommittal and looked away, shyness overtaking me. "If only all the orckin thought the way you do. Our kind would have a far better chance. Alas, most want their ways to endure more than they want to collaborate for survival. Not all clans treat females well. So it would force them to admit their mistakes and reconcile with their females."

"Oh, boo-hoo." I snapped. Rhuger jerked his head to look at me, and I mimed a crying motion with my fist. He chuckled. "They dug that hole for themselves. They can go lie in it."

"I agree."

"Can you tell me about your culture? You've mentioned clans. How many are there?" I asked. Rhuger bent aside a branch blocking the path. A small eruption of flying insects that looked similar to butterflies but with leaf-like wings had me gasping in delight. Rhuger just shook his head at my wonderment and led the way onward.

There had been hundreds of such small moments in the last few days. I was a nature girl. I couldn't help but delight in the new alien world around me. Watching how the natural world here on Talam held to the same, yet slightly to the left, rules of the natural world back home on Earth was fascinating.

"There are five united clans and many other small groups scattered around our continent." Rhuger began, raising a hand to show all five of his thick fingers, tucking one down to his palm for each example. "The five clans are the Oc'Turin, the Oc'Dellor, the Oc'Veltas, the Oc'Sentan, and the Oc'Blyre. Each reign over a region. The Oc'Turin occupy the steppes, the Oc'Dellor the forests, the Oc'Veltas the coast, the Oc'Sentan the wilds and deserts, and the Oc'Blyre haunt our mountains."

"Who leads the clans? You've mentioned Rìgh Thorn of the Oc'Dellor?"

"Och. A Rìgh and his Banrigh lead each clan, and the title passes down through their offspring. Normally it is a male who rules with his Banrigh supporting him, though there are females who rule. A Banrigh rules over the Oc'Veltas." Rhuger's short version of his culture was intriguing, and I knew without asking that it didn't even scratch the surface.

"So your culture is patriarchal, then?" I asked.

"Och, mostly." He cocked an eyebrow at me. "Not all of us think that's wise, as females are the ones highest at risk from the plague."

"You think females should rule?" Surprise had me raising my brows at him.

"Well, they couldn't do much worse than our males. Oc'Veltas has definitely benefited from it." He gave me a one-shouldered shrug.

"They have?" My inner feminist was punching the air in victory.

"Och, they have advancements we couldn't even dream of. They don't share them, though. It is a sore point amongst the clans." His tone was a little frosty.

"Oh, okay." Great job, Amelia. Antagonize the giant alien hottie.

We hiked in companionable silence. The forest was alive with the noises of birds and small critters. It was all a lot to take in. He didn't seem like he was in a rush to dump his world's histories on me. And I was thankful he was giving me the time to process.

Until two days ago, life on other planets had been theoretical. Now it was a fact.

"How did you come to find me?" I asked, curious about how he'd known I'd be in the cave out in the middle of nowhere.

"I... dreamt of the tree. It was vivid in my mind. When I woke, I spoke to Ruksala, and she told me to come. Once I scented you, I hurried, knowing I wouldn't be the only one looking for you." His voice was soft as if the verity of his dream shook him. He was about to speak again when a voice rang through the forest.

CHAPTER 11

AMELIA

"Halt!" a thunderous voice called. Rhuger came to a stop. He reached out an arm and herded me behind him. "Is that you, Rhuger?"

"Och, it's me!" Rhuger called with a wave.

Two orcs seemed to appear out of nowhere from the trees on either side of the path. One was tall and slim and strode with a predator's gait. He had his hair loose, and it fell in black waves to his shoulders. His skin was a soft grey. He would have been handsome had he not been sneering.

The other orc was shorter, his skin a dusky green, and he carried a bow in one scarred fist. He still towered over me, but he wasn't nearly as threatening. He was quiet and watchful—his eyes bright and intelligent as they looked at both Rhuger and at me where I stood behind him. Curiosity flickered there for a moment before his eyes shifted to his partner—the angsty-looking orc.

"So you came back alive, did you?" The grey orc sported a kilt, like Rhuger, and wore a dark-colored shirt with a hooded jacket over the top. Sturdy boots helped keep his footfalls quiet as he approached.

"Obviously." Rhuger drawled, and I snorted.

That caught the grey orc's attention. His gaze snapped to mine, and I swallowed. His eyes were purple. It was so strange to me to see someone with purple eyes that nearly glowed in the black of his sclera. A flirtatious smile curved his mouth, and I did not like it.

"Och, what did you find out in the forest, Fògradh?" The grey orc attempted to look around Rhuger at me. I tried to hide further behind Rhuger, clutching at the back of the waistband of his kilt. I didn't feel comfortable with this guy looking at me like that.

"What a pretty pearl," the orc with the purple eyes crooned, eyes alight as they raked over my form.

"Don't call me that. And you can keep your damn eyes to yourself." I spat back, frowning. Rhuger seemed to swell a little, his chest puffing out slightly. Was he proud that I let him call me pearl but not this guy?

Dork.

"The lady told you to stop looking, Asterun. I'd suggest you plant your gaze elsewhere before I pluck your eyes from your skull for your impertinence." Rhuger drawled. His hand rose to rest on the hilt of a knife.

Okay, that was kind of hot.

Okay, I'm lying. That was *really* hot, and I was blushing like an idiot. Rhuger would do that so I wouldn't feel uncomfortable? Was calling out a guy for his creepy behavior? Where the hell had I ended up? Magical let's-respect-women-land?

The orc Asterun straightened and bared his teeth at Rhuger. I did not like that, and I was ready to go feral on his ass when the other orc stepped up.

"Let them pass, Asterun." The shorter orc had his black hair braided into dozens of small braids. His mouth was a firm, disapproving line. Until he turned to address me and his expression softened. "We are honored to have you here, lady."

"Oh, thank you?" I asked, startled that he'd addressed me so respectfully. He'd even bowed in a courtly sort of fashion.

"It is a blessing to have another female amongst the Oc'Dellor." Was his reply as he slung his bow over his shoulder. Then he looked at Rhuger with his green and black gaze. "You do our clan honor by bringing her here for shelter."

"Be aware, there was an Oc'Turin who had scented Amelia after I found her. I lost him in the forest, but he might still pick up her scent, Ophir. He's of Oc'Blyre ancestry."

"I thank you for the warning," Ophir replied and whacked Asterun on the shoulder. "We will let the other rangers and guards know of the situation."

"Also..." Rhuger began and Ophir paused. "I saw a dorcha'aon."

Silence descended. Not even the birds twittered.

"A dorcha'aon? One of those hasn't been seen in Noc'tal Forest in decades." Asterun spat.

"Regardless. It stalked outside the gàrradh between here and the Craobh na Beatha." Rhuger said. Ophir paled considerably.

"It dared come so close to the gàrradh?" Ophir asked.

"Och. Close enough that I saw its eyes." Rhuger's voice was low as if just by speaking of it, they could summon the beast. Was that why he'd been uneasy the other morning? A dorcha'aon had shown up? What was it if they feared it so? "I heard a second one's call. So they are returning en masse. What's left of them."

"We will alert the guard." Ophir nodded his thanks.

"Come, pearl. Let me take you to Ruksala." Rhuger turned and grasped my hand, courteously steering me around and away from Asterun before he took up the rear, keeping himself between me and Asterun's disconcerting gaze.

I could practically feel Asterun attempting to undress me with his eyes. The orc hadn't heeded Rhuger's warning, as if to spite him. As if he didn't respect him and now wished to focus on me. Like I was some prize to be won.

It made me want to falcon punch him in the dick.

"I'll see you again, pearl!" Asterun called to our backs.

"Don't call me that!" I snapped over my shoulder. Rhuger just chuckled.

"Why do you allow me to call you pearl and not Asterun?" He asked as the other orcs blended back into the trees. The heavy feeling of Asterun's attention finally faded to nothing.

"Because you've been nice to me and helped me. Treated me like a person. He was looking at me as if I were a piece of meat to devour." I grumbled. "I hate it when guys refuse to see women as people."

"Och, I can see how that would be offensive." Rhuger nodded solemnly.

"Plus, I just don't like the guy. I don't get a good vibe from him." I couldn't help but grump.

"Vibe?"

"Feeling," I said, waving a hand as we descended a small tree-covered hill to a gully full of funny-looking ferns. They weren't just green, but a riot of other colors. Dusky purple, pink, slate blue, and turquoise.

"Ah." was his only reply.

"He's rather entitled, isn't he?"

"Yes. He's an excellent warrior, but kind of an asshole." Rhuger rumbled.

"Why did he call you a... What was it?" I asked, casting back for the word Asterun had used. "A Fògradh?"

"Ah." Rhuger looked ahead, a self-deprecating smile twisting the edges of his mouth. "A Fògradh is an exile."

"Wait, why did he call you an exile and then let us into Oc'Dellor?" I asked, bewildered.

"Because I'm an Oc'Turin exile." His voice had dropped and softened, a heaviness seemed to weigh on him with those words. The bright silver of his eyes dimmed and his expression grew shuttered. My heart twisted to see him so hurt. "The Oc'Dellor were kind enough to allow me to join them. Though I'm not an official part of the clan."

"Why were you exiled?" I blurted before my brain could catch up to my mouth. I grimaced at my lack of tact. "You don't have to answer that—"

"I was kicked out because of who my father was." Rhuger shrugged as he cut off my backpedaling.

"That sounds like a dumb reason," I murmured and grabbed his hand, stopping us both. His expression changed then, his silver and black gaze sparking once more as he looked down at me. "I'm sorry that happened. It's not okay. I'm glad you've found a home here, though."

Rhuger just blinked at me as if I'd baffled him. Was he so unused to compassion and simple kindness? The twist in my heart wrenched further as I looked at him. Could almost see the echoes of his past behind his eyes.

about to press and ask him what the shadows were that lurked in his gaze. I'd faced enough of my own to know that prying was not okay. If he ever talked to me about it, I decided that the least I could do was listen. Rhuger was proving to be my friend in all of this. So I'd be the best friend I could to him in this outrageous situation we seemed to have found ourselves in.

RHUGER

Amelia wouldn't become what she'd called a 'broodmare'. I wouldn't allow it. I'd kill anyone and everyone who tried.

It was no lie that she was a prize. Not just for her rare beauty, either. Her heart and spirit were unmatched and deserved to be protected. I understood this and our varying orckin ways. Yet... her words set fire to my control. Because regardless, our dwindling population would force her to do just that—force her to be a 'broodmare'.

Just like it had for all the other orckin females, regardless of clan.

The dark wings of my past buffeted my mind. Black memories of unwanted hands. Scenes of what the cruelest of the Oc'Turin had done to the females they'd intended to sire orclings on haunted the backs of my eyelids each time I blinked. I had frozen, caught in the terrors of my past, my blood-lust surging in my veins, seeking to cut, dismember, and destroy those who did such terrible things to others. Twisted orckin who were far away from the peaceful lands of the Oc'Dellor.

Amelia's soft voice cut through it all like a whispering blade.

"Rhuger...?" Her voice and uisge-beatha eyes pushed the dark back like shafts of morning sunlight. "Are you okay?"

Her sweetness cut like the sharpest knife against my battered heart. Haunting in how it caressed the darkness there with sparks of pure light. I couldn't remember the last time anyone... *anyone*... had asked me if I was alright.

I hadn't been alright for a very, very long time.

And this little neamhnaid was breathing life into my being like some sort of long-forgotten magic. Her kindness, both the painful lancing of fetid wounds and the healing balm that numbed them away. She was pure magic, this female.

"That will not be your fate." I hissed between my clenched teeth, jaw aching, and fangs groaning from the pressure. "I will not allow it."

Amelia's expression turned to one of surprise, her pink full lips forming a perfect 'O' that made me want to see how they tasted. This female truly was dangerous. Inciting my emotions into a wild riot of possessiveness, awe, lust, admiration, and a keen heartache all within a few minutes.

I took a deep breath and forced myself to shake away the last vestiges of my conflicting thoughts. I didn't have the luxury of time to spend scrutinizing my emotions and how Amelia affected me. Getting her to Ruksala and then someplace safe to sleep was the top priority.

Because many had already seen her. That was an unfortunate inevitability. And her fate would be in question until Ruksala or Rìgh Thorn decided on what would become of her and where she would stay.

"Come, we must get to Ruksala's home tree. The suns are descending." I strode toward her and she stood tall once more. Head high and bearing regal. I smirked slightly, more like a twitch and less like a smile. She nodded and offered me a small smile of her own before I led her down the broad cobbled avenue that would take us to Ruksala.

And Amelia's future.

CHAPTER 12

RHUGER

Ruksala's home tree was a massive thing. Easily the largest tree in Baile Coille and one of the largest in all of Noc'tal Forest. The monstrous tree was ancient and gnarled. Not unlike the orckin female who called it home.

She was Rìgh Thorn's mother, a previous Banrigh who had led when her cridhe, Rìgh Tyras, had succumbed to the an'sgudal. Rìgh Thorn had been gone for decades and no one had thought he would ever return. But he had. Now she advised her son and continued to serve her people as Fear a Chì, as our spiritual leader.

Craobh Bean Glic was the name of the towering behemoth or 'wise woman tree' in Common. It'd been the seat of the female Fear a Chì of the Oc'Dellor for nearly as long as the clan had existed. If not longer.

The canopy of the Craobh Bean Glic was so high that it crested the sharp stone peaks of the Fàinne Sleagh that ringed Baile Coille. The base of the tree was nearly as wide as the entire stone keep. And the roots delved deep into the bowl of the earth within the Fàinne Sleagh. So deep that fire, hurricanes, blight, flooding, blade, and war hadn't killed it throughout its long life.

The only tree that I knew of that dwarfed the Craobh Bean Glic was the Craobh na Beatha. The holy winged tree Amelia had stumbled out of. They were not of the same species, that I knew for certain. But something had kept this tree alive when all others had died in ancient times.

Standing before such a massive living thing was daunting. Made even more so by the additions made to the tree for millennia. The tree, as it had grown, had slowly engulfed surrounding stone structures that were now simply a part of the inner workings of the tree.

The Oc'Dellor built large buildings into and around the trunk. Most were the homes of Ruksala's helpers. A few housed guards. Walkways connected the outside buildings, and all structures were well above the ground so the main stairs could be raised to make them inaccessible to attack.

It was a self-sufficient tree fortress.

Age and time had partially hollowed out the heartwood of the tree. The empty heartwood area housed the orclings. There were well over one hundred small home tree-like huts built into the interior walls for the orclings to live in. Dozens of plank and rope bridges crisscrossed the space above the open courtyard at the base of the hollow. Creating a web of routes for the young ones to take.

They set halls between the massive rings of the outer tree growth. Often repurposed old buildings that the tree had engulfed. Classrooms, kitchens, workrooms, training spaces. All were built into the massive home tree.

It was a small city here within Baile Coille.

Amelia and I stood before Craobh Bean Glic and I enjoyed watching her strange white and uisge-beatha eyes widen, devouring the natural wonder before her. Her mouth was open in awe and I couldn't help the pang of desire that swept through me when she darted her tiny pink tongue out to wet her lips.

"This is…" she began, shaking her head. But she fell silent.

"It is called Craobh Bean Glic. Quite a sight, isn't it?" I watched Amelia as she nodded vacantly. I chuckled and chucked her chin, her mouth closing with an audible click of her oddly blunted teeth. "Come, there is much we need to discuss with Ruksala. We can explore the tree more another day."

"Okay," Amelia whispered as she followed me to the tree and the tiny powerhouse that ruled it.

AMELIA

Rhuger gave me some time to absorb what I was seeing.

The tree had been like a slap in the face. It was so enormous and mind-boggling in its construction. Because it was a veritable tiny city built into a tree. It was as if they'd crafted the tree to their purpose over the long life of the plant. Adding buildings and interior spaces that the tree simply… *grew* around.

Buildings poked out of the trunk of the tree at varying heights and one was very odd-looking, rather similar to a longhouse from the time of the Vikings back on Earth. It was nestled high in the crook, between two gargantuan arms of the tree. It was the only building that looked that way, and I wondered if that was where Ruksala lived.

The orckin who walked the bridges that spanned around the tree looked so small, giving insight into the scale of it all. Most appeared to be adults—some were warriors bristling with weapons. But there were also plenty of smaller-looking people who must be the orclings Rhuger had mentioned. The wild little ones who had lost their parents and were under the wings of the good caretakers, overseen by the Oc'Dellor's Fear a Chì.

It wasn't long before Rhuger was leading me towards the giant tree and I had to fall back on my instincts to absorb and process later or go mad. I'd barely even registered the countless lanterns and banners that fluttered in the breeze. Not to mention the strange platforms I could partially see between the branches of the canopy above that I couldn't fathom the function of.

"This way," Rhuger said, herding me towards a broad set of stairs that curved up the trunk. I was in an awed daze. The stairs had chains attaching the bottom stair to a winch above, explaining without words that this tree wasn't just a tiny city within a city, but a fortress just as imposing as the keep I'd caught glimpses of.

Poor Rhuger gently nudged me when I lingered too long, staring at the texture of the bark of the tree, how the orckin had attached their platforms to it in such a way that wouldn't impede its growth, the sheer brilliance, and engineering that had to go into creating such a marvel.

"Who's that?" A small voice rang out, snapping me back into the moment.

I looked over, and there was an orcling about the size of a human seven-year-old. He was pointing at me while looking at an older female orc dressed in a dusky purple dress. They stood in front of one building that ringed the trunk.

That's when I realized. All the orcs and orclings had stopped to stare at me. Again.

"Och, Rossi, that's rude." The older lady told the orcling in a hushed tone, attempting to push his arm down.

"Hi!" I called, waving. "I'm Amelia!"

The female's papery grey skin paled a few shades, and she bobbed a small bow. She even tugged the orcling into the motion. To the utter confusion of both myself and the orcling.

"No need for that," Rhuger said, taking a casual step towards them. They stepped back. There was an awkward pause.

A toddler appeared in the doorway behind the older female and the orcling Rossi. She was an adorable little angel with plump cheeks, a cupid's bow mouth, and soft black hair that curled gently at the ends around her pale green cheeks. Her eyes were huge and full of wonder as she tottered forward.

She stumbled over her own tiny feet, and Rossi reached out to catch her in time before she fell. Dropping her toy, it rolled toward me and bumped against my hiking shoe. She made distressed noises, a full-blown cry imminent.

Without thinking, I knelt and picked up the toy, some kind of puzzle ball, and dusted it off. I looked up at the small one. Her poor eyes were enormous black pits with rings of gold for irises, tears threatening to spill as she watched me handle her precious toy.

"Here you go," I murmured to her and held out my hand, proffering her toy with a soft smile. The little one stuck her whole fist into her mouth, eyes wide, staring at me.

"Peety." She whispered when she finally removed her tiny fist.

"So are you, sweetness." I chuckled, and she shyly stuck her head under Rossi's protective arm.

"Take it, Mira." The older lady said, placing a hand on little Mira's head, her purple skirts swishing in her wake. Rossi nudged her and little Mira bravely stuck her plump little arm out and grabbed her toy.

"T'ank you," Mira mumbled, clutching her toy to her chest.

"You're welcome, Mira," I murmured with a smile to her, Rossi, and the lady. I stood slowly so I wouldn't scare the orclings before I looked to Rhuger. There was a fleeting look on his face that I couldn't place before his expression changed.

"We need to go, Amelia. Ruksala awaits." He nodded to the gathered orcs and took my elbow, steering me toward the next flight of stairs.

"Why did the lady bow at me like that? She looked scared. Was it me?" I asked when we were out of earshot of the orcs, worried that I might have inadvertently offended them.

"You look slightly different from an orckin. Also, you are a neamhnaid." Rhuger shrugged one shoulder as he led me away.

"Again with that name!" I froze and panic began pounding in my veins. I hated it. To be thought of as a prize, an object, some rarity that had to be caged, was not something I wanted. Adam had done that to me... the bars of my cage, his years of mounting layers of control and gaslighting. I could almost *feel* the mental bars of the prison I thought I'd escaped, narrow against my mind. My breathing turned shallow and quick.

"Ruksala will help us understand why you have royal coloring despite your human heritage," Rhuger murmured gently, attempting to calm my distress. He caught my eyes and the sincerity and steadiness in his gaze eased those bars back. It worked. Releasing a panicky breath, I nodded to him, showing I would be okay, and he flicked a smile my way. "Good lass."

My blood started pounding for an entirely different reason then, with just those two words. *Fuck.*

I cleared my throat, and we continued up the next flight of stairs, growing nearer to that Viking-style longhouse. I followed behind Rhuger, who still carried his pack. It bumped against his heavily muscled and scarred back. A back that tapered down to a delightful dump truck of an ass.

Biting my lip, I wondered absently if his skin was as soft as it looked. And what it would look like with scratch marks crisscrossing the broad expanse of his back. Marks made by a woman in the throes of passion. I bit back a needy sound. My horny brain was going to break me if it kept up like this.

Before long, with me huffing and puffing and Rhuger not even breaking a sweat, we reached the broad platform with its large longhouse. I had to brace my hands on my knees as I caught my breath and studied it. It sat nestled between two arms of the massive tree with what looked like a pit or the empty center of the tree on the other side.

It was enormous, just like the tree. Like Viking longhouses, its overall shape was one long A-frame. It resembled an upside-down ship's hull because of the curved roof and spine. The spine of the roof had carved decorations embellished with colorful paints. The carved head of the spine that jutted from the front of the longhouse was the shape of a dark flying bird with its wings spread in protection over the building.

It almost looked like a raven.

Shaking my head at *that* improbability, I noticed that the roof, instead of being made of peat or shingles, was moss and some kind of creeping vine that seemed to anchor the building between the two broad arms of the tree. The walls of the longhouse were made of stacked logs, similar to a log cabin. At regular intervals along the sides of the building were pillars that helped keep the overhanging roof line stable. Each was covered in intricate carvings.

There were windows set into the log walls, with hinged hatch covers that were propped open to allow light and fresh air into the building. Smoke rose from along the spine of the roof, a clear sign that there was someone home, and that the building had good ventilation. The entrance was enormous and could have easily fit two nocrys side by side with room to spare. The exquisitely carved doors were wide open.

Almost as if Ruksala knew we were coming.

"How are you faring?" Rhuger rumbled, and I managed a shaky smile as I stood once more. The guy's concern over my well-being was, well, refreshing.

"I'm okay. I caught my breath. Not used to so many stairs." I panted. I hadn't *quite* caught my breath, but I would *not* be a baby about it.

"Hmm." He murmured noncommittally and looked me over with his brows creased. As if trying to find out the truth of it. He waited, and watched me as my breathing finally evened out. When he seemed satisfied, he tilted his head towards the open doors of the longhouse and held an arm out in silent invitation for me to go ahead.

"What's she like?" I asked, suddenly nervous. This woman was about to hold my future in her hands, after all. I strode forward towards the door, head held high despite my nerves. If I'd learned anything from my escape from Adam, it was to face my challenges head-on with determination.

"You will like her, I'm sure." Rhuger sounded amused as he followed close behind. Rhuger moved to knock on the door frame when we stopped before the open doorway. Before his knuckles could even skirt the wood, a strong female voice called out.

"Rhuger, what are you waiting for? Bring our guest inside! Stop wasting daylight!" The voice was warm and strong, yet rough with age. There was an edge of humor to her voice, as if all of life were her own personal inside joke.

I looked at Rhuger in surprise. He just cast me a crooked grin and shrugged with one shoulder. We entered, and I was astounded by how homey the space was.

There was a large rectangular hearth along the center of the longhouse with the recognizable sunstones giving off a pleasant warmth. The propped-open windows and the vent along the spine of the roof allowed for a lot of natural light to filter in from the canopy. Towards the rear of the building, there were rooms on either side of a narrow hallway.

Comfortable seating and tables took up various sections of the open area between the hearth and walls. Shelving lined the wall space, and they overflowed with books, jars, bones, pelts, and strange objects I'd never seen before.

And some human-made things that just about boggled my mind. I didn't know how a Da Vinci-style ornithopter had become an oversized coat rack on a planet in a completely different galaxy. I knew for sure I wasn't ready to hear about it.

"Come in, come in!" The warm voice called us further inside. I followed Rhuger, who took the lead, heading past the hearth towards the back rooms where a table and chairs covered in furs sat next to a U-shaped section of shelves stacked with books, scrolls, knickknacks, crystals, and everything from bowls of dead insects to honest to gods cogs. The low table seemed to be some kind of worktable. Or altar.

"Ruksala, I've brought someone to meet you." Rhuger rumbled.

"Yes, yes, Amelia, correct?" Called the voice from behind another shelf.

"You know who I am?" I asked, shocked, as we turned past a display of strange animal skulls and happened upon an old female orckin. The shock hit me anew. She was the tiniest orckin I'd seen yet other than the orclings outside. Barely five feet tall.

"Of course, I know who you are! Taobh A'Muigh, you were known to me long before you ever came through the Geata. Before this one ever came to Oc'Dellor, if I'm honest." The tiny female turned to look at me and I had to suck in a breath. She looked familiar in a way I couldn't place.

Ruksala squinted up at me before looking me over as she stood before us. Her smile was genuine if missing a few teeth, and the apples of her cheeks were round with welcome. Her black and russet eyes twinkled with keen understanding beneath a brow heavily tattooed with marks similar to the characters I'd seen on the portal back home in Orc Rock Cave. Ruksala's face was lined and papery looking, her skin tone a soft, pearly dove grey that nearly matched her white hair. She wore her hair in what looked like thick locs decorated with metal beads. Well-kept and loced because of the natural kinking in her hair rather than the matted locs worn by a lot of new age-y white folk back home.

She wore a dress similar to the other females I'd seen so far. A simple grey dress with a wide belt, dense with embroidery, looking like swirling mist. She wore a thick, long purple cardigan over her ensemble and it had an array of pockets stuffed with various items. Including what looked like a sleeping furred animal.

The silence stretched out between us for a minute as we stood studying one another. Ruksala gazed at me as if she'd known me my whole life. And strangely? It kind of felt like she did.

"Amelia..." Rhuger broke the silence.

"Och, she knows who I am already, Rhuger." The smaller orckin lady made a shooing motion at him. Rhuger just nodded respectfully. "Alright, lass. Let's get ourselves a seat and you can ask me what you want to know, och?"

"O-okay, Ruksala," I murmured, slightly shaken by her familiarity.

"Just call me Grammie, child." Ruksala waved over her shoulder at me as she tottered her way over to an overstuffed chair. Rhuger looked at me with his eyebrows up to his hairline in surprise. Evidently, people calling her 'Grammie' was not a common thing.

"Okay, Grammie?" I asked a little breathlessly as I followed her and perched on the edge of a chair. Rhuger stood, leaning against a bookshelf, having no business looking so damn good doing so.

Ruksala smiled at me and handed me a cup of tea. I nodded my thanks and took it in both hands. It smelled earthy and not unlike green tea. I took a careful sip.

"So how's Earth?" Grammie asked without preamble and I spewed the tea everywhere.

CHAPTER 13

RHUGER

Poor Amelia wasn't ready for Ruksala's humor. And *I* wasn't ready for the spray of tea from Amelia's lips when Ruksala asked her about Earth. As soon as Ruksala's question had dropped into the silence while Amelia sipped her tea, she'd immediately spewed the tea and began coughing. I knew I needed a bath after so many days out in the forest, but not like this.

Ruksala began cackling in laughter, eyes crinkling as she threw a rag at me. Unamused, I glanced at her after snatching it from the air. Fear a Chì came in two flavors, from my experience. Either onerous, self-aggrandizing doomsday criers or tricksters who occasionally pranked people with their foresight.

Ruksala was thankfully the latter.

"Oh *shit* Rhuger, I'm so sorry!" Amelia coughed and immediately set her cup down and stood. With a sparkle in her eye, Ruksala handed her another rag and Amelia snagged it with a quick word of thanks before rushing to me. "Here, let me help."

She looked so abashed, and it was such an endearing

expression, that it took me a moment to realize she was mopping at the tea dripping down my chest. I... was not prepared for her to be so close. Or for her to be touching me.

"Don't trouble yourself." I rasped as I attempted to back up, only to have the bookshelves behind me press into my shoulder blades.

"It's my fault. The least I can do is help." Amelia said, brows drawn in concern.

This... was *not* something I was used to. Being fussed over. Let alone by a female. Least of all by a neamhnaid beauty like Amelia. I felt my throat tighten, a flush brightened my skin, and my cock twitched to life all in a matter of heartbeats.

She was *too damned close.*

"Rhuger." Ruksala's voice cut through my haze of lust that made me feel like a gangly, untried youth.

"Yes, Ruksala?" I asked, attempting to dry myself off with the rag and keep Amelia from touching me too much in her sweet attempt at helping. All it was doing was making my skin hot and shivery.

"You will be Amelia's bodyguard. Even Rìgh Thorn won't gainsay me in this. You have long proven yourself as a warrior. Do you accept this responsibility, to watch over and ensure Amelia's safety?" Ruksala's gaze bored into my very soul and did not seem to find me lacking. I stopped attempting to dry myself off and even Amelia paused her ministrations to look between us.

"Och, it would be a great honor. I had already promised Amelia that I would keep her safe." I told her, straightening my spine.

"Good. Very good." Ruksala's gaze went hazy. As it always did when she reached out to the threads of the universe to seek its wisdom. To see what we could not.

"Go, prepare your house for her," Ruksala said to me in Black

Tongue. Her gaze was hard, demanding, and yet twinkling with wise mischief. She'd switched to Black Tongue on purpose, so Amelia would not understand us.

The thought of Amelia in the house I'd built for a mate I never thought I'd have sent a thrill down my spine. I wasn't about to gainsay the only person in Baile Coille who could rival Rìgh Thorn in power. If it meant staying near to Amelia, I'd do whatever Ruksala asked of me. Without complaint. She commanded that kind of trust.

So I nodded at Ruksala and bowed to her, hand to heart.

"As you command," I replied in Black Tongue. Then I turned to Amelia and switched to Common. "I will return for you soon. I'm going to prepare where you'll be living. You'll be safe here with Ruksala until I return."

"Okay. Be careful." Amelia said, eyes full of trust. Her worry for me struck a chord deep and sonorous in my soul. No one had ever told me to be careful before. Not even my Màthair, my mother.

Unable to speak, I just nodded and strode out the door of Ruksala's massive home tree. Amelia's words dogged my steps and echoed in my mind. Already, a crowd had gathered at the base of the Craobh Bean Glic.

I couldn't say it surprised me.

But it irritated me. It seemed to be mostly males. Males come to see the new female among their number. I snarled. She would stay in *my* house and would have *my* protection. Not theirs.

It was a cold sort of victory that sluiced through my veins. Because, though she would live in my house and have my protection, she was not *mine*.

Few of the orcs I passed seemed willing to ask me questions. My expression must have been more forbidding than usual. So it was with little fanfare that I stalked from the Craobh Bean Glic and down one of the many cobbled avenues that branched from it.

A few minutes later, I was standing outside of my home tree on the outskirts of Baile Coille near a stream that fed into the river in the town center. The house wasn't the largest, nor the best placed to be with the others. But I'd made it with love in my heart and it was peaceful here. Just how I'd always wished for my mate to be.

Forcing my thoughts away from such fancies, I stalked inside and began rummaging through my home—clearing out what was personally mine and readying it for Amelia's arrival.

AMELIA

"Well," Ruksala said as soon as Rhuger was out the door. "Now that it's just us girls…"

Grammie Ruksala gave me an exaggerated wink and pulled out a tin. Inside was a bunch of what looked like honest-to-goddess cookies. I couldn't help the involuntary groan and flood of saliva that came from seeing and smelling the little delights.

Full stop, I had one wicked sweet tooth. She snagged one and stuffed it into her mouth before proffering the tin to me.

"Take more than *one* now, child. If the Source has shown me truly, you've been through a lot in the past cycle."

"Cycle?" I asked, taking three cookies from the tin.

"Och, what humans would call a year. Here, it is not just the turning of the seasons, but one full dance of our moons. They align once a year." She set the tin on the table between us and nibbled a cookie with her remaining teeth.

"Oh. Is the alignment coming up or did it just pass? The three moons looked pretty close." I asked.

Ruksala beamed at me.

"Such a sharp one. I like that. Yes, the alignment is coming up. It happens every summer." She didn't elaborate, and I didn't feel comfortable asking about their traditions, so I just ate my cookies and drank my tea.

The cookies were good, almost nutty-tasting, with a hint of sweetness similar to honey. It wasn't quite like eating almond shortbread, but it wasn't far off.

"So, what would you like to ask me, child?" Ruksala asked, brushing crumbs from her dress. She pulled a strange-looking pipe from one of her many pockets and pulled out a small drawstring pouch from another, careful not to jostle the creature napping in a neighboring pocket. The pipe was short, almost like a weed pipe, and she began stuffing some herb into it from the pouch that smelled awfully familiar. Like Grandma Ruth's house.

"Is that... weed?" I asked.

"Hm?" she asked, packing the bowl with the herb.

"Is that marijuana?"

"This? This is what we call fighe inntinn bog. Or Soft Mind in common. It helps with pain and stress."

"Sounds like weed to me." I laughed. When Grammie Ruksala cocked an eyebrow at me, I grinned. "No judgment here. My grandmother smokes marijuana a lot."

"From what I understand, the plants are similar, but not the same," Ruksala explained. "I've never had marijuana, but I've heard of it. Fighe inntinn bog aids in healing and in connecting to the Source for my craft."

"You have?"

"Och, from others who have passed through the gate." She smiled at me then and lit a twig from a candle, bringing the lit end to her pipe and taking a few steady puffs. "But less on that and more on why you are here. What you've come to me for."

"Oh, right. I should explain…"

"No need. I already know how you came to be here." Ruksala waved a hand at me as she blew out her smoke and placed the pipe down on the table.

"Okay… I uh…" I mumbled, stumped. I thought I'd have to explain everything and plead my case. Not get right to the point. I looked down at my hands as I picked at my new claws. "Well, why do I look like this?"

"Isn't that obvious? You have orckin ancestry." Ruksala smiled at me kindly.

"Supposedly, my grandfather was orckin," I confirmed. "I just want to know where I can find my grandfather, how I can go home, and why I look like this when I looked, well, human before."

"Ah." She sat back in her chair, getting comfortable. I tried to be patient, I did, but my anxiety had a chokehold on me and wouldn't stop squeezing the daylights out of me. "These are easy to answer."

She paused for a while and her gaze went hazy.

"Are you alright?" I asked. It looked like she was high out of her mind. Ruksala rolled her eyes and looked at me sharply.

"Yes, I'm reaching out to the Source so I can *see*. Do you mind, child?"

"I'll be quiet, I'm sorry," I whispered and clenched my hands together, gaze turning down.

"That's a habit you need to break." Ruksala's mouth twisted in distaste.

"What habit?" The words tripped on my tongue as I registered her hard stare.

"Apologizing when you did nothing wrong. That ex-husband of yours train you to be that way?" She asked sharply. "Are you a hound to be trained to heel to your master's command? Or are you an infinite being, incapable of being shoved into a finite space? Are you a creator, a female, a mother, able to bring life into this world? Then why let a man, a male, control you and decide your fate?"

Her words were like whips against my psyche and I couldn't stop the tears that fell from my eyes.

"I'm trying to heal," I whispered, lips trembling.

"Och... I know Amelia." Ruksala sighed heavily and handed me a handkerchief. "Your ex-husband was intimidated by you. As well he should have been. You are far more than he was ever worthy of touching. You won't need to fear him ever again. This I have seen and can promise you."

Something cracked open in my chest and I pressed the handkerchief to my eyes, trying to press the tears and pain back behind them. The relief that flooded me at her words, each syllable a benediction and protective talisman for my soul. The truth shone brightly in her words, and I did not doubt them.

Adam could no longer hurt me. I was safe. I would *be* safe. Be *free*.

I felt a warm hand against my knees and pulled the cloth from my eyes. Ruksala was patting me affectionately, her face soft and understanding.

"You're safe. Rhuger will make sure you stay so." She grinned then. "He's a wonderful male."

"He's proven to be so, so far." I agreed, voice thick from fighting my tears. As if speaking of him summoned the orc, a knock came from the entrance of the longhouse. I looked up from Ruksala and caught Rhuger's silver and black gaze across the open space. His mouth fell into a hard line as he prowled towards us, at my side in a matter of moments.

"What's happened?" Rhuger asked, crouching down to look me in the eye. "What's wrong? Ruksala, what did you do?"

"Don't you sass me, you big glowering grump!" Ruksala scowled at him and Rhuger looked contrite, muttering something in that strange language. "Yeah, you'd better."

"I-I'm... Ruksala told me I'm safe. From him." I shuddered around the words as I choked them out.

"Of course you are. I'd kill him if he so much as showed his face to you." Rhuger murmured as he brushed away the traitorous tears that slipped from my eyes. I barked a rough laugh.

"Rhuger." Ruksala's voice snapped out with a sharp levity.

"Och, Ruksala?" Rhuger bowed respectfully to her at the waist, hand to his chest.

"If you do anything to harm Amelia, I'm going to skin your dick and use your scrotum as a rune pouch." Her face was deadpan, and I watched as Rhuger paled slightly before bowing again.

I couldn't help but clamp a hand over my mouth to keep from snorting and laughing. The relief of knowing that Adam would never touch me again was akin to being high. I wanted to scream and laugh and sob and take a nap all at once.

"Go on, take her to where she'll be staying." Ruksala made a shooing motion at us and Rhuger stood with fluid grace. "We'll talk again soon, Amelia. I'll be able to answer more of your questions later. Rìgh Thorn will be back tomorrow and you'll see him then."

I rose from the chair and ducked down to gather Ruksala in a gentle hug. She made a startled noise, then chuckled and patted my back. It seemed even wise women could be surprised. We said our farewells and strode out into Baile Coille, leaving the weight of my fears behind.

CHAPTER 14*

AMELIA

Word of my arrival had spread through the entire city. As we descended the stairs from Ruksala's abode and entered the main square, dozens of orcs were milling around that hadn't been there when we'd entered. The hubbub of conversation died as all heads swiveled in our direction.

Well. This wasn't awkward at all.

I longed to duck behind Rhuger and hide. But I refused to be a coward. For the time being, this would be my life—my people. So I had to make the best of it. And I knew better than to let a man catch on to my fear.

"Uh, hello?" I called out over the crowd. I offered a small wave.

The crowd comprised mostly males, with some females—most of them holding the hands of little ones or carrying babies against their chests. The air was heavy with their regard and I plastered on my best customer service smile. Rhuger stepped forward in the awkward silence that followed. He kept his hand at my elbow, as if letting everyone know I was under his protection. It helped to calm my shaking nerves.

"Folk of the Oc'Dellor." He called easily over the crowd. "This is Amelia. She will stay with us and will go before Rìgh Thorn tomorrow. Until she settles comfortably amongst us, Ruksala has charged me with being her guard."

There was some grumbling amongst the gathered orcs. Rhuger's fierce scowl silenced them.

"You will treat her with respect." Not a suggestion. Not a request. A demand. Spoken with the authority of a fucking king.

He looked down at me, his fiercely protective energy making my heart race. His gaze as it met my wide eyes burned with the promise he'd made me in the gàrradh and the one he'd sworn to Ruksala.

At that moment, a wail went up in the crowd.

It was a child. And that damnable motherly instinct of mine kicked in *hard*. I heard shushing and a male orc crooning to the child in Black Tongue as I scanned the crowd and spotted them. It only made the poor baby cry harder.

Without thinking, I moved toward the large, scarred orc, who was cradling a tiny bundle and attempting to feed it with a small leather bottle. Plump little grey arms flailed, fists clenching against the air in defiance. The other orcs stepped out of my path. As I reached the orc and the babe, he looked up at me, eyes wide. I just held out my arms toward the crying child.

"Let me try?" I asked. The orc looked between me and the small bundle before handing it over with heart-wrenching gentleness. It must be his.

"Oh, ho ho." I crooned as the orc placed the orcling babe in my arms. "It's okay now, I've got you."

The baby wailed its poor lungs out, clearly upset and unhappy. So I tucked the babe high on my chest so that it could listen to my heartbeat as I rocked it and pat its back in soothing circles.

"Shhhh, it's okay now, sweetheart. I know you're having a hard time. It'll be okay, you're not alone." I crooned and kissed the orcling's dark thatch of hair that lay in wisps upon its dark grey head. Its ears were so tiny and pointed and *adorable*.

It rubbed its face into my chest, hands grasping at my t-shirt. Its cries were heartbreaking and my mother's instinct was kicking me right in the ovaries. I'd always wanted to be a mother. Just not with Adam.

As I bounced and rocked the orcling, I sang.

"Smile, though your heart is aching. Smile, even though it's breaking. When there are clouds in the sky... you'll get by..." I sang softly, stroking the orcling's head as it quieted down. The old lyrics of my lullaby sprung forth from my lips—just trying to provide some comfort to this baby, the way my mother would comfort me. "If you smile through your fear and sorrow. Smile and maybe tomorrow... You'll see the sun come shining through... for you..."

The babe's wails died down, now listening to me and making mewling sounds. The eyes of every orc in the square were on me, but I refused to look up. Refused to acknowledge them. I wasn't here for them; I was here for the precious little one in my arms who just needed some snuggles.

"Light up your face with gladness. Hide every trace of sadness. Although a tear may be ever so near... That's the time you must keep on trying. Smile, what's the use of crying? You'll find that life is still worthwhile... If you'll just... Smile..." I finished the song, and the babe had fallen asleep. I couldn't help but smile to myself and place a gentle kiss on its downy head.

Looking up at the orcling's father, he looked... *devastated*. I paused. Vast tracts of tears were cascading down his craggy face, pooling along his scars and dripping off his chin to his tunic. He wasn't the only one crying, either. I look around and most of the orcs were shedding a tear or outright sobbing. The few females sent me broken-looking smiles of thanks through their tears.

I wasn't sure what to make of all of this.

"Your baby's asleep now," I murmured, moving forward to hand him back his child. The orc seems to shake himself awake and gently took the little orcling from me, tucking the bundle close to his heart.

"Thank you, Neamhnaid." The orc croaked, his voice thick with emotion. I wasn't sure why seeing me sing his child to sleep made him weep so. "You are a gift to our clan."

"Any time. Your child is precious. What is your name, and your child's?" I asked, curious. I'd happily snuggle that baby anytime. Damn my ovaries.

"I am Uther and this is my son, Nashton," Uther said, and I smiled at him.

"My name is Amelia. It's nice to meet you both."

There was a pause in the crowd, almost like everyone was taking a breath at once. Then it was as if they crashed around me like waves. Groups of orcs were crowding close, asking me questions about where I'd come from and how Rhuger had found me. I tried to answer what I could, but I was swiftly getting overstimulated. My ears rang, and it almost felt like the cacophony had unmoored me from my body.

I was close to dissociating completely. If I did, it wouldn't be good, and I'd end up unable to speak or do anything except function on autopilot. I cast around for Rhuger's onyx-and-silver gaze, his long braid, that sinful mouth. Instead, other faces belonging to people I didn't know swarmed closer. Offering to show me things, give me things, and share things. But I didn't want things. I'd never wanted things.

I wanted safety, freedom, room to breathe, care, and consideration. I wanted to be treated as a person, not an object. With honor, respect, dignity, and compassion.

I felt it then. Bubbling up from my stomach, muscles locking up and breath hitching. The inner scream that I could not let escape my lips. Panic delineated my nerves as my heart crashed inside my chest. If I couldn't find a way out, my inner scream would break free from the cage of my teeth. And I wouldn't be able to stop it once I started.

Catching a gaze through the crowd, I realized it wasn't Rhuger's. It shared his intensity, but the orc that stared at me devoured me with his gaze as if I was a commodity. Not unlike how that orc Asterun had ogled me. But this one was stocky, shorter than most of the other males. A desperate, oily gleam in his eye made me shudder and the hair on the back of my neck stand at attention.

Between one hitching breath and the next, tears gathering behind my eyes, a wall of green muscle cut off my line of sight to the creepy orc. He'd parted the tide of the others as if they weren't even there and his shadow fell over me, soothing, and bringing with it a familiar scent. Leather, spice, and something akin to pomegranate, but sweeter. My eyes snapped upwards and locked with the onyx-and-silver gaze I'd been looking for.

Rhuger's mouth was a flat line. His brow furrowed as his gaze raked over me, assessing me in a quick, almost clinical manner. The other orcs stepped back and the rising tsunami of panic within me paused. Their clamoring talk died out too, and I wanted to weep with relief at the cessation of sound.

"Come, we should get you to your new home." Rhuger's hand fell to my elbow, cupping it and sending a thrill down my spine, a breath of fresh air to my tight lungs.

"Okay," I replied, a little breathless. I politely waved goodbye to

Uther and Nashton and the other orc-folk in the square, allowing Rhuger to pull me down a lovely little side street.

He strode close to me, matching my gait, and kept an arm swept protectively behind me. As if wishing to screen me from the orcs in the square. Turning a corner, we passed between a few tree homes and out of sight of the others. Here, he came to a stop and turned to look me in the face.

"Are you alright, pearl?" Rhuger's deep rumble shook free some of the grasp the panic still held on me. I opened my mouth to tell him I was fine. My go-to response whenever this happened, not wanting to be a burden.

I shut my mouth and shook my head instead.

"What can I do?" He asked, concern for my welfare stark in his body language and eyes. Barking a surprised laugh, I felt some traitorous tears escape and brushed them away with shaking hands.

"You've already done it." My voice trembled as I stumbled over the words. My tongue felt heavy and unresponsive as I fought my instinct to go mute.

"You were feeling trapped again?" Rhuger murmured, and I nodded. "Why didn't you say anything?"

"Overwhelmed. Too many noises and faces. Too many people wanting something." I whispered. I hated to admit it, but I had a hard time processing too many stimuli at once sometimes. "Makes it hard to talk."

Rhuger surprised me then. He didn't tell me to get over it, that I was a baby or too sensitive. He didn't look at me with distaste or confusion.

"Okay." was all he said. "We will need to find a way for you to let me know when it gets bad like this again. So you're not overwhelmed to the point of silence. That way, I can help you."

"What?" I looked up at him, startled.

"What? Your well-being is my priority, pearl."

"You don't think... That there's something wrong with me?" I whispered in question.

"Something wrong with you? Och, no. Your needs differ from some, but there's nothing wrong with that. They should be respected so you can thrive." He cocked an eyebrow at me. I struggled not to cry. "Come, let's continue to your home tree. It's quiet there and you'll be able to rest in peace."

Baffled and shaken by his simple acceptance of my different needs as a neurodivergent person, I let him lead me on through the winding streets of Baile Coille. The number of occupied trees lessened, and I realized we were heading to the outskirts of the city. Wild critters chased one another around the trees and into the bushes along either side of the street. Hanging lamps of sunstones hung above us amongst the boughs to light the way when it got dark.

As we walked, the tension bled away from me and the tightness in my chest eased so I could breathe easier. My mind tumbled through the events of the day, sorting and processing, and absorbing as we continued in companionable silence. Something struck a chord, and I looked up at Rhuger.

"Why did Uther cry? Why did they all cry?" I asked. It was the strangest thing to me and I wanted to understand.

"His mate died giving birth to their son," Rhuger murmured as he led me over a small bridge that spanned a creek. The cobblestones along the street had moss growing between them and riots of flowerbeds lined either side underneath the towering trees. The area was still well kept, despite the fewer orckin living this way. It spoke volumes to the city pride of the Oc'Dellor. "I think you may have given him a glimpse of what he's lost."

"That poor orc and his baby..." I couldn't help the emotion that choked my throat. "I'm so sorry..."

"Are you a mother, then?" He asked me, quietly. I looked up at his face, his gaze shuttered. "You're so good with little ones."

"No. I've always wanted to be one, though." As the memories hit, my heart wrenched in pain. "I—When I was with my ex-husband, I'd decided not to have children. I didn't want them to grow up with a father like him."

It was the first time I'd said it.

And it was true.

I'd decided against children, claiming any and every reason I could think of. But I still wanted to be a mother. I just refused to bring any child into the world that would have a father that was narcissistic and emotionally abusive.

My father may have come out as gay and divorced my mother. But he still loved me something fierce and never let me forget it. My ex-husband couldn't even muster up the affection to pet my cats, let alone take care of them. How could I have trusted him with my child? What kind of mother would I be to stay with a man that would hurt my child emotionally and possibly physically?

I couldn't fathom it. And it was one of the many, many reasons I'd left him and filed for divorce. There were many things I could deal with and handle in a relationship—lack of love wasn't one of them. Neither was abuse.

"I'm sorry you had to face this." Rhuger's reply was guttural, his expression grim. "You would make a wonderful mother, should you choose. You are a brave and wise female to look to the care of children you have yet to bear."

I couldn't help the hard blush that rose from my neck and enveloped my face. My cheeks felt so hot. All I wanted to do was hide. Brave? Not really. Terrified, yes. I wasn't sure why, but having Rhuger look at me like that and talk about me being a mother made something flutter both in my heart and... lower.

CHAPTER 15

AMELIA

We reached the outskirts of the city. Here the trees were more gnarled with fewer tree houses. As if they were waiting for the population of the city to grow and build their homes amongst their craggy branches. There were fewer of the larger lanterns to light the path, too.

We crossed yet another small stone bridge that ran over a bubbling brook. Rhuger led me up a flagstone path towards a small knoll. An enormous tree had its roots woven over the knoll, disappearing beneath its mossy blanket with those lovely colored ferns growing in riotous clusters. A small stone-walled garden and one of those small huts curled around the base of the tree. Fading light from the twin suns filtered through the gaps in the canopy to bathe the garden in a golden glow. It was so beautiful and idyllic.

But that was nothing compared to the tree house.

It was like someone had taken every amazing cottage and charming home in fairytales and combined them into utter perfection. Broad steps curved around the wide base of the tree to a porch that extended out amongst the branches. A lovely railing with hand-carved details provided a measure of safety. There was an empty hammock hanging from two branches, and dozens of those odd lanterns swung gently in the warm breeze at varying heights.

Then there was the house itself. It was an almost square nestled at the junction of the tree's broad branches. The builder shingled the roof strangely in what almost looked like scales. An odd gutter-like system seemed to collect the rain and re-direct it to a water tank next to the hut close to the tree's massive roots. The roof had a decorative ridge that ran along the four eaves, and the carved whorls and creatures showed an excessive attention to detail.

They'd made the walls of interlocking boards, almost like shiplap. The windows were trimmed in more hand-carved designs and embedded with what looked like colored glass panels. The entire house was painted too, in lovely purples and sages, matching the blooming plants in the walled garden.

"Is this where I'm staying?" I asked Rhuger in a whisper, my mouth wide in awe.

"This home is yours." Came his soft reply.

"Mine?"

"Och. For as long as you want it." He said. Not renting, not visiting, not temporary, but *mine*.

"But... why?" The level of generosity bewildered me. The Oc'Dellor were extremely generous in their housing. People on Earth could easily learn a thing or two from them.

"Because you are a female and deserve your own home." Rhuger shrugged like it was the most natural thing in the world.

"But... I'm a stranger. I'm new here." I tried to protest. Being placed in a bunkhouse or some kind of inn was what I'd been expecting. Not staying in a house all to myself.

"Exactly." Rhuger arched his brows at me as if it were obvious why.

"Are all guests given a house?"

"No."

"Then why? Why do I get one?" I asked, confused by the orc before me and the jumble of emotions competing for the top spot. Irritation, awe, bafflement, and relief warred. Relief won.

"Because you need time to adjust. Ruksala was wise in this." Rhuger gave me a one-shoulder shrug and herded me to the stairs.

"Wait, where are you staying?" I asked, suddenly worried.

"In the hammock?" He was trying not to laugh at me as he pointed to the hammock swinging from the porch.

"Oh." I breathed and felt the surge of stress melt from me.

"Afraid to share a bed with me, pearl?" He chuckled into my ear and I could feel my face heat.

"More like afraid I'd be left alone. I'm glad you'll be here with me." That must have caught him off guard. Because he went still and when I looked up at him, his cheeks were that vibrant shade of green again.

He coughed and began leading the way up the stairs. He must have dumped his pack here earlier when Ruksala had told him to prepare this place for me because I could see it where it sat next to a trunk in the porch's corner.

Placing a hand on the railing, I marveled at how warm and smooth the wood was. The spindles were carved in such a way that they reminded me of curved feathers. Not unlike the feathers of the winged tree I'd come out of.

RHUGER

I watched as Amelia scaled the steps to the house I'd built with my own two hands. She marveled at every detail, from the carved spindles to how smooth the railing was, to the shingles I'd created from the scales of a giant wyrm I'd felled last year.

A giant reptile from the steppes, the wyrm had made its way to the forest to find food. I hated to kill the beast, but it had attacked orckin and nocrys. Old and sick, it had been incapable of hunting its usual prey. It was the same wyrm I'd created my clothes from and I still had a great store of leather and scales for the clan to use in the keep's warehouse. Felling it had earned me the right to build this house.

Amelia traced the ridges of the scales she could reach, as curious and awestruck as she'd been in Noc'Tal Forest. The colored glass in the windows in varying shapes and sizes had been the most costly of items added to the house. With how temperate the climate was in Baile Coille, most orckin went without window panes altogether. It was a sign of great wealth and status to have them, as the glassworks near the keep needed substantial amounts of sand traded for along the coast.

My cost came as slaying a nest of moileasgan near a coastal village. They were enormous, carnivorous mollusks that lay in wait under the surface of the sand, snapping closed their shells as soon as something edible moved above them. I'd harvested the royal neamhnaid from the slain moileasgan and given their meat to the village as it could feed many. Ridding the village of the monsters had garnered me the sand I needed. The meat bought me the colorants I'd wanted.

Before, I couldn't understand what drove me to earn the right to build a house, construct it, and give it the opulence it had. But now?

With Amelia admiring my hard work? It made it all worthwhile.

"Do you like it?" I asked. She turned to me, beaming a smile my way.

"Like it? It's *beautiful!* Whoever made it was incredibly talented." She said, and I fought the desire to puff out my chest and tell her it was me who had created it. She couldn't be my mate, so telling her I'd made it wasn't necessary. Nor was explaining the significance of her living in my house. "Can I go inside?"

"Of course," I murmured around the tightness in my throat. I reached the door just as she turned the knob made from a large, raw neamhnaid. The door, carved with water flowers, swung open.

Amelia gasped and wandered inside without hesitation. My heart lurched in my chest and it was suddenly hard to breathe as I watched her walk inside, shafts of fading light through the colored glass limning her curvy form. I knew every single plank and carving within that house. I was a part of every inch of it. Seeing Amelia within was like witnessing a goddess walk into my heart.

She whirled to me then, smile brilliant despite her blunted teeth, skin glowing with that neamhnaid radiance. That smile shuddered the very foundations of my existence. My hands twitched, wanting to cup that freckled face and kiss her with everything I had. But I couldn't draw in air to breathe, let alone get my body to move.

"It's magnificent!" Amelia cried. She spun and began her curious inspection of my house. Her hands caressed the woodwork and furniture, learning the heights and valleys of them with her fingertips. Most of the furniture I'd made myself. Her uisge-beatha eyes absorbed every detail. She spied a flaw in the table, a broad gouge from when I'd been deep in my cups one night, playing stupid games with my knife to keep the darkness at bay.

My muscles knotted until they screamed as tension ran over

me. Would she find the flaw hideous? Would she refuse to stay here if it wasn't perfect? Some female orckin did this, demanding perfection from potential mates. And rejected them outright if the home didn't meet their exacting standards.

But she just fingered the space where the wood was missing before moving on. As if the flaw wasn't a problem. I knew every error, every defect, every bit of shoddy craftsmanship in the entire house. And instead of doing what I expected, she just accepted them all as is. That, more than anything, told me that what she said must be true. That she was from another place through the Geata.

"You don't find an issue with the imperfections?" I asked as she inspected a chip in the stone sink in the kitchen area. I'd ground the sharp edges away, but it was still there. She looked up at me in surprise.

"No. Why would I? It gives this place character, doesn't it? I think it's charming."

"Charming," I replied, dumbfounded.

"Yeah. Houses are a lot like people. I've never liked perfect houses because that tells me they were never lived in, cold, empty. Fake. I prefer uniqueness, character, and quirks myself. Because it means they're full of stories." She shrugged one rounded shoulder, her odd tunic shifting.

What she said held a simple truth. Didn't mean that she hadn't just yanked the ground out from under my feet. I didn't like the feeling. Like I was losing balance, I shifted where I stood in the doorway. Did what she say mean that she'd accept someone's broken bits, their scars, fears, and trauma, as easily as she did my house's flaws? Did that mean that, perhaps, she could accept *me*?

"You should get some rest, pearl. The suns are setting." Was all I pushed past the lump in my throat. I reached for the knob and pulled the door closed. "Goodnight, Amelia."

"Goodnight, Rhuger." I heard her say, her voice soft and musical as the door closed with a click.

CHAPTER 16[*]

AMELIA

The night air was crisp, and it blew in through the open window. I was dozing, nearly asleep, as the sounds of the night insects and creatures washed over me in waves. It'd taken me so long to even get sleepy, having to adjust to the new nighttime sounds and the creaking of the tree house. The glowing bugs, reminding me of fireflies, flitted through the air while my eyes slipped closed.

The next thing I knew, a meaty hand clamped over my mouth. My eyes flew open, bleary from the short stint of sleep, and landed on a shadowy form on top of me on the bed.

I froze.

Memories, damnable flashes from the darkest recesses of my mind, paralyzed me. All the ways my ex-husband had hurt me replayed in fast forward. I couldn't seem to draw in air fast enough through my nose and I could feel myself hyperventilating.

I could smell the sour scent of the orc's sweat, hear his harsh breathing, and I fought the bile crawling up my throat. His foul breath fanned over my face, and I realized distantly that he had completely pinned me beneath him. His erection pressed into my thigh.

The orc, difficult to see in the dark, opened his mouth, about to whisper something.

He never got the chance.

A blade erupted from his mouth. He choked on it, eyes rolling wildly, as blood gushed between his shattered teeth and split tongue onto my face. His hand spasmed on my mouth as his eyes went sightless. His death rattle hissed around the blade.

Without warning, the blade was sucked out of the back of the orc's skull in a sickening, squelching noise. The body fell away, as did the hand. I scrabbled backward and swallowed a scream at the shadow past my bed, holding the blade in one hand, the hair of the orc who'd crawled atop me fisted in the other.

"Calm, pearl." Rhuger's voice rumbled in the quiet. I shook, tears spilling from my eyes as my hands fisted in the sheets. "I won't touch you. Please breathe."

I couldn't seem to gulp down air fast enough then. My heart beat wildly in my chest and I started sobbing aloud. Dry, rasping things that barked out from between my lips. Unable to get myself to calm, that blood-curdling fear of lack of control simmered in my veins. Darkness edged my vision as my chest heaved.

Rhuger was quiet as he slowly dragged the body of the dead orc out of my house. His nocrys, Hifasa, began yowling and chuffing at the base of the tree. That pried me from my fear enough that I noticed I still clenched my hands in the sheets. And that everything was covered in blood. That *I* was covered in blood.

Disgust and rage burned through the fear and ignited my limbs. Frantically, I began tearing off the bedding, sobbing and choking, until there was nothing left but the mattress, thankfully untainted. Looking down, my clothes were drenched in drying orc blood, too. So I ripped them off and began scrubbing my skin with a cloth from the kitchen, frantic to get the blood off me.

I ran to the small kitchen table and began pouring water from an ewer into a bowl with shaking hands. I dipped the cloth in it and wiped at my flesh again and again. Rivulets of watered-down blood sluiced off of me and onto the floor. Short, rough screams tore past my throat in bursts.

A loud scrabbling startled me from my frantic ablutions and my head snapped to the door, looking for the new threat. But it was Hifasa wriggling her long, lithe, scaled body through the tight doorway. I sobbed anew as she got herself inside and trotted over to me. She huffed and rumbled at me, bumping her head against my soft, naked stomach.

I dropped the cloth. Then fell to my knees and wrapped my arms around her, choking back my tears. Hifasa just licked me with her rough tongue, laving anywhere I hadn't been able to reach. Before long, I was covered in monster cat drool, but I was free of blood. Even my hair.

Shaking, I released her and got to my feet. I didn't want to be naked when Rhuger returned. So I snagged a clean tunic I found and tossed it over my head. Hifasa nudged me back to the bed, and I went on wobbly legs. I climbed onto the bare bed and she stepped up onto it and spun around before deciding on her spot, laying down right on top of me.

My sobs cut off as I grunted at her added weight. Her massive head rested on my entire torso while the rest of her curved between me and the door. She began a deep, gravelly purr that thundered against my chest. I petted her, running my tiny claws through the fur on her cheeks. Her eyes slit and her purr deepened.

Tears leaked from my eyes now, but I'd stopped sobbing. Kind of hard to do that with a giant rideable cat on top of you trying to press your soul back into your body. Rhuger tapped his knuckles on the doorway and I looked up. He dipped his head and walked over to gather up the ruined bedding and clothing. He slipped out silently.

When he returned, he had a large, well-worn blanket in his cleaned arms. He stopped a ways away from where Hifasa and I were on the bed and looked down at me with an altogether unreadable expression burning in his gaze.

"Why did he do that?" I asked Rhuger, voice cracking and betraying how close I was to breaking down again.

"Females are rare here." He said simply before looking down at his feet and letting out a heavy sigh. "Many died because of famine and war and plague. He was a fool and thought he could claim you while I just stood guard outside unawares with Hifasa down at the base of the tree."

"Claim me?" I croaked. Rhuger just cocked an eyebrow at me until I turned red in the face. Fear lanced through my veins again and Hifasa chuffed at me. "So he was going to rape me?"

"Claiming shouldn't be that. But he was desperate enough for a mate to try." Came his harsh reply.

"Then what is it supposed to be?" I asked, panicking even more.

"The choice of the claimed. There are few enough females that it's become their choice of who and when to be claimed and mated." Rhuger's tone softened, as did his gaze.

"Well, at least there's that. But how many orcs are going to be as desperate as this one?" I flung out a hand at the corpse that lay somewhere out past my door.

"Many. But no others will try this. They will see what became of him and will remember the laws." He lifted his tattooed shoulder in a one-armed shrug. "I'll make sure I appraise Rìgh Thorn of the situation when he returns tomorrow. He'll get everyone in line."

"What, and I should trust you?" The words tumbled out of my mouth and I felt sick with them.

"I've sworn to protect you. Your safety is my responsibility. That extends beyond just your life to the well-being of your heart and mind. He should not have gotten so close to you. The fault lies with me. I will not hide this when I tell Rìgh Thorn." The reply was smooth and open. It smacked of the truth and I couldn't taste a lie anywhere in his body language, tone, or gaze.

"And you can't be bought?" His face was so intense in the moonlight as he stared at me. As my question hung in the air between us like a fetid cloud.

"You are beyond price." He rasped, gaze going dark. I got an odd thrill at that. He bent and laid the blanket on the floor, within arm's reach, should I want it. "Get some sleep. You are safe."

He turned and stalked for the door and his hammock outside.

I may have had an orc on top of me, but Rhuger had made sure that he'd nothing more than breathe on me. And that orc had paid the ultimate price for that transgression. Rhuger had spared me from reliving my worst nightmare.

"Rhuger?" I called. He froze, looking over his shoulder at me with one arm on the door frame. "Thank you. For saving me."

He paused for a moment, then jerked a nod and slipped out into the night.

And somehow knowing he was there, and having Hifasa with me, kept the nightmares at bay long enough for me to succumb to oblivion.

RHUGER

Anger thrummed along my veins like lightning. Crackled along my nerves like wildfire. I was furious.

Tintain, the orc I'd skewered upon my sword as he'd attempted to force a mate bond with Amelia, was slung over my shoulder like a sack of nocrys shit.

My only regret was killing him so quickly.

I should have knocked him unconscious and dragged him out of the house—the house *I'd* built—and tortured him before disemboweling the cnuimh and stringing his intestines amongst the lower branches as a warning.

The soft thump he'd made when he'd bumped the table by the window had alerted me. He'd masked his scent and even somehow got past Hifasa. Rage burned in my chest. I wasn't just angry at this cnuimh, this worm of an orc. I was pissed at myself for letting him get past my guard.

Hifasa was with Amelia now. I knew she wouldn't let Amelia out of her sight. And would bite the head off of any other orc who thought to try his luck while I strung up Tintain.

Footsteps heavy and forceful, I took the path to the Traitor Tree. Craobh Brathaidh.

It lay on the outskirts of the keep upon a hillock. It was where we hung the dead who'd died for their crimes. Orc justice was swift and harsh. It had to be for a species on the brink of extinction.

Forcing a female, at least within the Oc'Dellor, was punishable by death. Not all clans saw it that way, though. The Oc'Turin weren't always so altruistic and rarely enforced such punishments. I snarled and gnashed my teeth to keep the memories that darkened the corners of my mind at bay.

This traitor had put me in a foul mood.

I climbed the hillock and flung Tintain to the ground. His corpse flopped like a dead fish. As I stared at his body, the memory of finding him sprawled atop Amelia, pinning her with his weight and muffling her voice with his hand rose behind my eyes.

Snarling at the memory, I roared at the lifeless corpse. I clenched my jaw as I knelt and began my work. I stripped him and grabbed a wooden board from the stack at the base of the tree. The dried remains of a few corpses swung in the night breezes, the ropes they hung from creaking in the dark. I wouldn't need any rope. Not for what I was about to do.

I pulled a knife from my bandolier and quickly carved his name and his crime upon the length of wood. Tossing the board to the ground beside Tintain's body, I prowled to the corpse and kicked him so he lay sprawled on his back. Crouching down, I gripped the knife so tightly in my hand that the handle nearly cracked.

With the cold precision I'd learned growing up amongst the Oc'Turin, I used the same knife I'd used to carve his crimes to free him of his malehood. His corpse was fresh enough that blood poured from the wound. Gripping his partially severed jaw, I stuffed his pitiful malehood into his mouth between his broken teeth. Teeth that had been so close to Amelia's sweet lips.

A surge of fiery satisfaction burned my blood to smoke in my veins. I'd never been this angry before in my life. If I could, I'd revive him, torture him, and kill him over and over and over again. *No one touched Amelia and lived. No one touched what was *mine.*

MINE.

The word echoed in my mind and in my bones. Made

something in my soul still. Like the sudden silence after torrential rain.

Pausing, I looked down at my blood-soaked hands, black claws glinting in the light of the three moons. A certain truth settled into my very marrow. I refused to think about it too closely. Amelia's welfare was my priority. Not my conflicting feelings.

Her haunted, terrified, and broken expression surfaced in my mind and a fresh wave of destructive, painful, and burning fury flipped that feral switch inside my mind that I kept such a close watch on. In a rush, I reached down and sank my black claws into his soft belly. The cooling flesh gave way beneath my hands like soft gruel as I shredded his abdomen.

Blood sprayed onto my face and chest. I dug my hands deep into his stomach and pulled out his intestines. It was slippery, but quick work to wrap his intestines around his neck and string him up from a low branch. I tied off his intestines before I hooked the plaque over his neck.

Stepping back, I surveyed my work. The corpse that swung in front of me looked like a dorcha'aon had ravaged it. Swaying with his guts hanging loose from his abdominal cavity, intestines dangling down to trail along the ground. I'd been so vicious with ripping him open that his upper and lower body were barely connected by his spine.

I felt no remorse for mutilating his corpse.

Baring my teeth, I turned and strode from the Traitor Tree down towards the baths. It wouldn't do to return to Amelia covered in blood. The last thing she needed was for me to show up covered in the remains of the male who'd nearly taken her. She'd endured enough.

I stormed into the baths and passed a handful of surprised orcs. None stopped me. No one asked me where the blood came from. They were smart. They'd find out for themselves when they passed the tree.

I wasn't sure if I'd be able to hold myself back if someone stood before me now. Not with this keen edge of madness skirting my rationality. Normally, keeping a stranglehold on my control wasn't an issue. So many years amongst the Oc'Turin helped hone that skill. But with Amelia threatened, that control was gone.

Towards the back of the cave system, there was a secluded spot I often used. It was blessedly empty. I stripped and strode down the steps into the hot water. Blood and gore slipped from my flesh to float toward the drains. I bathed quickly, not wanting to be alone with my thoughts for too long while in this mood.

And I had to check on Amelia. Make sure she was safe and let nothing hurt her ever again.

The flare of territorial demand that surged within my chest made me pause. Amelia wasn't my mate, my cridhe. So why did every part of me sing when she was near? Why was I so sure in my bones that she was mine?

Did the orcs who took mates feel this way?

Was it because she was mostly human?

She was like a drug. Like pure, unfiltered luibh gaoil and I was completely drunk off of her. I couldn't wait to get back to her. To see those uisge-beatha eyes of hers sparkle with joy. Or heat.

Groaning, the memory of her scent—so sweet and juicy, like ripe fruit and heady florals, made me stagger. The memory of how her scent deepened and blossomed like honey on my tongue with her arousal had my cock stiffening in the water.

I growled and shook my head. Now was not the time to succumb to some self-indulgence. And I shouldn't be thinking of her like that, anyway. She was not for someone like me.

Stalking from the baths, I swooped down and snatched my kilt and bandolier. They were clean and only needed a slight application of the cream made from a'crathadh cnòthan shells to clean the leather. Once dressed, I left the baths and headed back to my home tree.

Steps leaden, I paused at the base of the knoll. The windows were once again dark. The sunstone lanterns that hung from the branches cast a soft glow that made the home tree I'd spent years building with my two hands look like a slice of paradise.

Knowing Amelia was asleep inside made it even more like heaven. I liked that Amelia was in my home. Living there, sleeping there, as if it were hers. As far as I was concerned, it was.

Ruksala had suggested it, as I knew every splinter of the place, but I'd already hoped Amelia would stay. The dormitories, where unmated females lived if they did not still live with their parents, were no place for her. I knew, as if I'd always known, that she valued privacy and quiet. A sanctuary.

And it might be selfish of me, but gods how it sated some deep, primal urge in me to have her here. Knowing she was here, safe, granted me a measure of peace I'd never known. It made me... happy... seeing how she'd reacted when I'd brought her here. How much she loved the details I'd spent months carving into every surface of this home. Even if it meant I slept outside in my hammock.

An easy price to pay.

And now that Tintain had made his sacrifice, her safety here would never be in question again. A part of me was afraid she'd insist on moving now that he had attacked her.

It left me conflicted.

She'd be safest at Rìgh Thorn's keep. But something felt so right about having her here. I hoped she stayed.

With quiet footfalls, I made my way up the wide stairs to the deck. I peeked into the window near my hammock to check on Amelia.

I saw her sprawled upon my bed, Hifasa curled atop her. Hifasa's ears perked up and her eyes flicked to mine. Realizing it was me, she sighed and closed her eyes once more.

I released a relieved breath I hadn't realized I'd been holding.

Despite the long day of travel, meeting with Ruksala, taking care of Tintain, and the quick bath, I found myself unable to sleep. Too many memories from the past and the last hours warred within my mind. All haunted by Amelia's smile and horror-filled eyes. So I decided I'd make myself useful.

I grabbed my kit and my weapons and sat in front of the door and leaned against it. I placed my blades across my folded knees, removed a whetstone from my kit, and began sharpening them in the low sunstone lantern light. The shirring sound as the stone ground the metal down to a wicked sharpness filled the quiet of the night and warned all that I stood guard.

A deadly promise for those who even considered approaching.

CHAPTER 17[*]

AMELIA

The morning dawned bright and cheery. Trilling birds and the happy goings-on of the clan filtered in through the windows. Groaning, I pushed Hifasa off of me and stumbled to the toilet in a small room in the back corner of the house. Memories from last night came crashing back, and I shook from the force of them. Bile burned my throat as I bent over a stone basin with a drain that acted as the toilet.

I could feel the ghost weight of the orc, the rough texture of his palm over my mouth, and smell his foul breath. Every memory from the night before, overlaid with those from my past, battered my mind. Above that, behind my eyelids, I saw the orc's split face, spraying broken teeth and blood as the tip of Rhuger's wickedly curved sword punctured through his skull like a hot knife through butter. I lurched, stomach rioting as what little there was in my stomach splattered against the stone basin.

Rhuger's calm, patient face swam to the forefront of my memories and I felt relief uncurling those dastardly recollections hooked into me. My heaving stopped as my stomach emptied. I drew deep breaths of cool air as I wiped my mouth with the back of my shaking hand.

Rhuger had kept his word to keep me safe. He'd killed the clansman to protect me. And he didn't touch me at all in the aftermath. He'd been a comforting presence, a safe one, not demanding anything of me and providing me with what I needed. It was kind of him.

I got my shaking legs under me and stood with the support of the stone sink. The orckin had a simple plumbing system, and I was thankful as I pulled a small lever and clean water splashed into the sink. I rinsed my mouth out and washed my hands with what appeared to be some kind of soap. It was in a rough-cut block and smelled floral with a hint of citrus. It didn't foam but created a slippery film that rinsed everything clean.

A knock from the front door had me nearly jumping out of my skin and I dropped the cloth I was drying my hands with.

"Pearl? Are you awake?" the door muffled Rhuger's deep timbre.

"Coming!" I called, forcing my body, heart, and hands to stop shaking. Taking a deep breath, I strode to the door. Hifasa was sitting on her scaled haunches, beseeching me with her eyes to open the door so she could see her person.

Scratching her head, I cracked the door and peeked out. Rhuger's head snapped back to the door. His gaze met mine unerringly, and I saw his nostrils flicker. Could he scent that I'd puked my guts out? That was mortifying.

Hifasa, tired of my timidness, pushed her head around my legs and slithered her way out of the door in that boneless way cats had. But she wasn't tiny, and I nearly careened to the floor. I stumbled and caught myself as Hifasa vaulted over the railing of the porch, not even bothering with the stairs.

"*Nocrys sèididh.*" Rhuger bit out as Hifasa nearly bowled him over. "Are you alright, pearl?"

"I guess she got tired of me." I tried to joke.

"Och, no. It's breakfast time, and she's a glutton." Rhuger smirked. Then his face sobered as he noticed how disheveled I was. "How are you this morning?" He asked, tone gentle.

"Better. Still... shaky. But much better." I murmured. "Thank you again..."

"It was my honor. It should not have happened." His mouth pressed into a thin line. "I'll make sure I inform Rìgh Thorn when he arrives."

"When will he arrive?" I asked, suddenly nervous. I really hoped I could trust this Rìgh with my welfare like I could trust Rhuger.

"This evening." Rhuger nodded, then cocked an eyebrow at me, nodding towards the world outside my tree house. "In the meantime, would you like a tour?"

"I'd like that," I told him with a genuine smile. It seemed to startle Rhuger, and he glanced away. He held a stack of neatly folded clothes in his arms and a pair of boots.

"I've brought clothing for you. Your clothes are currently being laundered and I'm sure you don't wish to walk around so bare."

"Oh, yes, thank you," I murmured, entranced by the bright green color that nearly glowed high on Rhuger's cheeks as he looked everywhere but at me.

"I'll be outside when you're ready." He ducked his head and placed the clothing on a chair just inside the doorway and left, closing the front door behind him on quiet hinges.

"Heh, cute." I huffed with a smile past the brittleness I felt.

He'd been right about not walking around, barely clothed. I'd worn the tunic I'd found in the trunk, but the thing barely came halfway down my thighs. And after last night, I didn't want to show any more skin than I had to.

Pausing, I glanced down at myself, then at the door in bewilderment. Registering that I'd been standing there, in front of him, with half of my thick thighs just out in the morning breeze and didn't even notice. I'd *always* been self-conscious of my thighs, even when I'd been skinny. But around Rhuger? It was like that self-consciousness evaporated.

Unsure how to feel about *that*, I snagged the light tunic and pants from the pile and headed to the restroom, where I quickly shucked the tunic. It was then, as I looked at the tunic Rhuger had given me and the one I'd worn, that I realized I must have been wearing a male's tunic. Who did it belong to? Or had someone just left it behind?

With those questions churning in my mind, I attempted to wash up quickly. I still needed a real bath, badly if I was honest, but the house didn't appear to have a shower or bath. Weird considering how *clean* everyone had looked. So I made do with a sponge bath in the restroom sink. I didn't want to crawl into clean clothes smelling so ripe.

The tunic was cut to fit with short sleeves and slits along the sides at the hips for maneuverability. The laces at the neck were scratchy, so I tugged them out. It wasn't like the slit went down very far, anyway. The leather pants were like my leggings. Buttery soft with some give to them and lined in something fleecy that didn't suffocate. They were really comfortable.

As I looked through the rest of the clothing, I noticed some weird wraps, some light slips I assumed were nightdresses, a vest, and a pair of sturdy boots. The boots fit perfectly and the vest, once I figured it out, draped nicely around me. It even had a hood and pockets.

I stood and looked in a mirror, made of some reflective metal, and wondered how he'd known my size. The clothes fit perfectly and looked good on me. Then memories of how he'd held me when the womb-ripper orc had chased us and how he'd cared for my ankle came rushing to the forefront.

Oh. That's how. Well, hot damn. The guy sure paid attention to the details.

My face exploded with heat. I wasn't used to being taken care of so... completely. It made me feel awkward and, well, unworthy. I caught my gaze in the mirror again and I didn't like the woman who stood in front of me. And it had nothing to do with the physical changes that occurred when I came through the gate.

The woman before me stood hunched, shoulders rolled forward, chin canted down. A timid, plump thing forced into a smaller space than she could comfortably occupy. Shoved there by the opinions of others.

It made something flare inside my chest. Some small, defiant piece of me still existed like a lit match in the dark. So I fed it. Every insult, every comment on me being too much or too little, every sneer and insistence I diet and get skinny 'for my health'. Every time I was only fit to be touched in the dark.

I lifted my chin, stood tall, and squared my shoulders. It was then that a realization hit as my power-fueled reflection stared back at me. I wasn't too much. I didn't take up too much space. The woman who looked back at me dressed in garb from an alien world looked strong, commanding, and, I could admit to myself, pretty. The clothes seemed made for me, instead of made for a smaller body, so they accentuated my figure instead of damning it.

My gut roiled thinking of how many years I'd spent folding myself inwards to fit into the pigeonhole others had built for me. I grimaced and shook my head. How did I let others dictate who I should be? Why did I hand my power over to them? To my ex-husband? Let them take my kindness for weakness?

Fuck that noise.

I decided right then, marking a line in the sands of time. I was no longer on Earth, so Earth opinions meant shit. A new planet, new rules, the first being: no matter what, no matter how long it took, I'd feel unapologetically whole in my own skin. If mountains, oceans, and stars could take up space, then so could I.

Grinning at myself, feeling a weight falling from my shoulders, I grasped the tunic I'd slept in and strode confidently to the front door. I turned the pearly knob and pulled it open. Warm, buttery light blinded me for a moment as I took a deep breath. My eyes adjusted to the light, and I found Rhuger leaning against the railing with his arms crossed over his broad chest, watching Hifasa roll around on her back in moss and ferns below with a smile.

He turned his head to look at me and I could see his eyes dilate as he took in the outfit *he'd* chosen for me. An outfit I liked. An outfit I felt powerful in.

"I like the clothes. They're really comfortable, thank you." I said.

"You're welcome." He murmured, not blinking.

"Who's tunic is this?" I asked, holding up the garment in question. "I found it in the trunk last night and wanted to wash it and return it."

"It's uh..." Rhuger's cheeks turned bright green, and he rubbed the back of his neck, not looking at me. "It's mine."

"Yours?" I asked in surprise.

"Yes."

"Then, this house is yours?" I asked with dawning understanding.

"Yes." His blush brightened further, and he glanced at me then, eyes shining silver in the morning light. "We give females top priority for housing. There are no empty homes currently. It would be my honor for you to stay here until we could build your home. Or if you like this one, I can build another."

I was absolutely floored.

He'd given me his *house*?

I'd *worn* his *shirt*?

I'd *slept in his bed*?

And then I realized, what better place to house the one you're supposed to protect than the place you know the best? It made sense, but it didn't stop me from feeling guilty.

I'd *slept in his gotdamned bed.*

"Rhuger… I'm so sorry. Please, I can't take your house." I flapped my hands uselessly at the tree home behind me.

At the craftsmanship and love that obviously went into it. From the charming little flowers carved into the door frame, almost alive-looking in their detail, to the handpicked crystal knobs in the kitchen area. Whoever had made this house had been a master, and I was slightly shaken that this was *actually* Rhuger's house. He had *flowers* carved on his house, and it was so damn *endearing.*

His smile was near blinding. "It's an honor, truly. And I know every splinter of this place, so you will be safest here." He said, his words mirroring my own thoughts.

"But isn't it cold at night? You're outside in a hammock!"

"I run hot. And it's still the warm season." He said with a half-shrug. "It's no hardship to sleep out under the stars."

Why did that sound fucking romantic?

"Did Ruksala put you up to this?" I asked, crossing my arms. She'd spoken to Rhuger in that language so I couldn't understand her, and I had a feeling she'd insisted I stay in Rhuger's house.

"She was thinking far ahead of me, as is the wisdom of an elder. Had she not demanded it, I would have suggested it." His not-so-casual shrug showed how awkward he felt about the whole thing.

"I don't feel right kicking you out of your own home…" I looked up at him, picking at my fingers.

"You're not. Aren't I still here?" He waved out behind him where his hammock swung in the breeze.

"Well, if you insist. As long as you're okay with it and it's what you want, I'll stay." I gave him a small smile and handed over the tunic. He took it gingerly, as if it were diamonds instead of one of his old shirts.

"Now that's settled, are you hungry?" Rhuger asked over his shoulder as he stashed his tunic amongst his bags.

"Yes. Breakfast sounds wonderful." I replied when my stomach growled loudly. Self-conscious, I placed a hand on my tummy and Rhuger grinned at me.

"Come, the kitchens will be our first stop."

Rhuger took me back through the winding streets of Baile Coille to the keep, whose turrets pierced the sky. We passed orckin on our way, and they openly stared at me, but no one approached. The atmosphere was one of dour wariness as their gazes flicked between

Rhuger and me. I wondered if they somehow knew about last night.

We skirted the front of the keep towards one side where a smaller building jutted out from the stone and timber keep towards an open area with benches and tables. The aromas of cooking food hit me then, and I nearly drooled all over my new clothes. My stomach growled alarmingly and Rhuger fought a smile as we strode up to the building.

One whole side of the kitchens consisted of roll-up windows from which they were distributing food. Similar to a very large concession stand. Behind the wooden roll-up windows, a sprawling kitchen with many stone islands, multiple brick ovens, and even a whole roasting spit was laid out in meticulous practicality. Pots and pans hung from hooks in the ceiling to clear up shelving space. Bundles of drying herbs were in an adjacent wooden structure and a stone-lined room next to it housed root vegetables. Orcs bustled around the kitchen stirring cook pots and chopping ingredients. The smooth efficiency spoke volumes about whoever the head chef was.

"Sharn!" Rhuger called and waved, getting the attention of a tall female orc in an apron. She left her station, wiping her hands on a cloth, before making her way toward us. She eyed me with curiosity before looking at Rhuger. "Sharn, I'd like to introduce you to Amelia. Amelia is new here and she'll be meeting with Rìgh Thorn when he returns."

"Lovely to meet you." I bobbed with a smile. Sharn's face split into a grin and I paused. The orc female was beautiful. She was slightly taller than me and lithe, with toned muscle showing under her tunic and trousers. Her long black hair was silky, straight from where it fell from her ponytail. Sharn's skin was a lovely silver color. Her features were angular, almost sharp, but her soft mouth and sparkling blue irises in all that black made her stunning.

"It's nice to meet you too, Amelia." She reached out her hand and we shook. Her hand was larger than mine and covered in lots of small silvery scars. "Has this troublemaker been treating you well?"

"Um, yes, actually. He saved me and brought me here. Ruksala made him my bodyguard for now. And I'm evidently staying in his house." I don't know why I dumped all of that on a complete stranger. Maybe I was just desperate for female company. Someone who might understand what last night had done in shaking my faith in men... males... And offer some sort of emotional respite.

Sharn's eyebrows shot up.

"She's staying in your house, is she, Rhuger?" Sharn's mouth quirked into a lopsided grin, expression mocking. Rhuger turned that bright shade of green again.

"There are no homes available right now. She can stay there until we make other arrangements." He coughed into his fist and stared hard at some bread as if it could give him the answers to the universe.

"And where are you staying?" Sharn was practically shaking in laughter.

"In a hammock."

"And where is that hammock?"

"Would you stop it, Sharn?" His lip curled at her as he winced.

"He's sleeping on the porch?" I said, missing the joke. Sharn erupted in laughter.

"Are you guys friends?" I asked, confused by both their familiarity and yet the near-sibling vibe they were giving off.

"Och, yes, Rhuger has been a solid friend since he arrived here a few years ago." Sharn's smile was warm as she tossed one of the bread rolls at him. Of course, he caught it deftly and handed it to me. "Oh, she's going to be fed, Rhuger. That roll is for you to help curb your *hunger*."

Whatever the joke was, it had gone right over my head again. But it had made Rhuger turn a *vibrant* green in answer.

"You're as bad as Sigg, you know that?" Rhuger snapped, ripping into the bread with his sharp teeth.

"Hard to help when you got yourself into such a situation." She downright waggled her eyebrows at him.

"Is—is it okay?" They both looked at me. "That I stay at Rhuger's? I can stay elsewhere if it's a problem. I've camped before, so if I had access to a tent I would be fine."

"No!" Rhuger sputtered just as Sharn held up her hands and said, "No need, honestly." They looked at one another and Sharn took the lead.

"I'm just making fun of Rhuger. He's like a brother to me. And you're beautiful, Amelia. It's just so easy to poke fun at him." Sharn's smile was genuine and full of warmth.

"Oh, uh, thanks." I ducked my head, blushing.

"Come, we'll get you some breakfast and Rhuger can continue showing you around." She smiled easily as she led us around to the side of the building, where tables and chairs sat under the sheltering branches of a massive tree decorated with sunstone lanterns.

Rhuger and I sat down and Sharn brought us bowls of some sort of grain with a milky syrup to pour over it. Rhuger tucked in like he'd not eaten in days. I took a spoonful and gave it a tentative taste. So far, everything I'd eaten or drank had been safe, but you never know.

The flavors exploded on my tongue, and I groaned in appreciation. It was delicious. Like a less-mushy version of oatmeal, but nutty tasting. The syrup tasted close to coconut and had some sort of spice I couldn't place.

"It's so good!" I said around a mouthful. Sharn just grinned and handed me a roll.

"Let me know if you're still hungry and I'll grab you something else." She gave us a small wave and sauntered back to the kitchens.

"She's so nice," I said as I spooned the not-oatmeal into my face. I was hungry, I wasn't fat for nothing. Food had often been my vice, and I'd burned a ton of calories tromping through Noc'tal Forest with Rhugher.

"Sharn? Yeah, she's a great person." He nodded as he hoovered his breakfast.

"So are the kitchens for all the orcs, or only some of them?" I asked, honestly curious.

"They're for all, though mostly it feeds the mateless males." He mumbled around a mouthful of food.

"That's wonderful! I'm glad everyone's provided for."

For no one to go hungry? Even though the USA was *supposed* to be a first-world country, it was severely lacking in social programs that actually cared for the populace. Knowing this about the orcs, the Oc'Dellor, really warmed me towards them. Not a hard concept, feeding everyone. But one that people back home evidently thought was impossible. Yet here it was.

"One of the many reasons I joined the Oc'Dellor." Rhuger cocked an eyebrow before eating more.

"Oh? Do the Oc'Turin not feed their people?" I asked, curious and appalled.

"The Oc'Turin prize might and strength, power. Things are competitive and can be bloodthirsty. Even over something as simple as food."

"Oh, I'm so sorry."

"For what?" He paused, spoon halfway to that sinful mouth of his, his brow furrowing.

"Growing up in such an environment."

"If I hadn't, I wouldn't be the warrior I am now. And I wouldn't appreciate the Oc'Dellor ways. I'd take them for granted." He gave me a half-shrug.

"All knowledge is worth having, huh?"

"Exactly. Even the hard things. They give us clarity and perspective." His small, tight smile told me more than words could that this male had endured his own horrors. My heart ached.

"That's true..." I moved my porridge around with my spoon. I didn't have a clue yet how I'd gain clarity and perspective from surviving my ex-husband. But I hoped I did. Rhuger sparked a hope that I could.

When we'd eaten and left the kitchens, we passed a grass-covered knoll off in the distance. A large tree with twisted branches topped it. Nothing but stunted grass grew on that hillock. The ferns and other flora ended abruptly at the base. As if they knew better than to cross that threshold. A small group of orckin stood at the base of the knoll, looking up at what swayed from the branches in the breeze. Four large shapes hung suspended from its arms like nightmare fruit. Even from this distance, I could see that one wasn't as desiccated as the others.

A shudder ran down my spine as I realized it was the orc who'd attacked me the night before. The body swung in the breeze and the scent of death blew toward us. His innards spilled from his belly in a gory waterfall, his pants down around his ankles and his severed junk shoved crudely into his mouth. I couldn't read the sign that hung from his neck, but the message was clear, regardless.

Rhuger must have done this to the orc's corpse.

The thought should have terrified me. Revolted me. Made me run to Ruksala and demand that someone else be my bodyguard. Anybody else.

But all I felt was a grim satisfaction. I wondered if that made me a monster. I realized that if it did, I couldn't find it in me to care.

CHAPTER 18*

AMELIA

We walked towards a field that lay in sight of the keep, where a fenced-in area had stable-like buildings with oddly built structures that appeared to be an obstacle course. "You guys have horses?" I asked, confused.

"Horses? No. Nocrys. Like Hifasa." Rhuger's grin was bright. "My friend Sigg breeds, trains, and cares for them. It's a very prestigious position."

"I'd imagine so."

"They're difficult to tame, and a nocrys chooses its rider."

"It does?" I asked as we strode through the short grass toward a training corral. "So Hifasa chose you?"

"Yes, she did. See there?" Rhuger stepped close and pointed out a tall orc in the distance within the corral. I barely looked at the orc in question. Too flustered with Rhuger's nearness and how delicious he smelled. "That orc there is Sigg. He's allowing one of the younger kits to smell the orcs. See if it will bond with one of them."

"It's beautiful!" I gasped as I finally registered the scene. And the nocrys was exquisite. Instead of the black and charcoal of the other nocrys, this one was a pale grey, as if it had albinism. While it was lanky, still in its teen awkwardness, it was already growing into a powerful beast. Nearly as large as the others.

"Och. That one is going to make a fine sire one day." Rhuger leaned his forearms on the rail next to me and I murmured assent as we watched the kit meander in front of the orcs present.

Suddenly, the nocrys perked his ears and swiveled his head to look at us across the field. He tilted his nose in the air and sniffed, nostrils and whiskers flickering as he breathed in our scents on the breeze. I saw the other orcs look our way, including the massive Sigg. But before anyone could blink, the nocrys sprung, galloping full tilt towards us. And he was *fast*.

Rhuger shoved me behind him, already on alert. But the kit slid to a stop on the other side of the fence. He put his enormous head between the rails, looked past Rhuger as if he didn't exist, and began begging for my attention. All chirruping purrs and rough chuffing as he stared at me pleadingly with his warm, caramel-colored eyes.

Hesitantly, I stepped around Rhuger and reached out my hand, fist loose, and tilted towards the nocrys whose ears had immediately begun twitching. They were long, like Hifasa's, but they had tiny tufts at the end that were just *adorable*. When I was within reach, the mewling and chuffing ceased. He stood really still, allowing my hand to go right under his big velvety nose. With his whiskers flickering and nose huffing like crazy, he drew in my scent. I would bet good money he could smell my cats and that was why he was so interested. The thought of my three tiny hellions and this giant fur ball together made me grin.

A shudder rippled over the young kit and he went limp. He flopped to the ground and showed me his armored belly. He tucked his enormous paws, which he had yet to grow into, up under his chin. Lying there, he swiveled his head so he could look at me with imploring eyes.

"You can pet him." Came a deep timbre. I looked up and the large orc named Sigg was standing near Rhuger. Sigg was a few inches taller than him and had shoulder-length blond hair. A shocking difference compared to the black everyone else seemed to have. It was a striking combination with his grey-green skin.

"Looks like you've got yourself a nocrys, pearl." Rhuger rumbled with approval.

"Leave it to this vain little nocrys to decide to bond with the prettiest thing here." Sigg snorted and winked at me.

Rhuger scowled at his friend, and I had to laugh. I might be pretty enough, but I wasn't *that* pretty. I had pearly skin, a weird quirk of my genetics, nothing more.

"Sigg, this is Amelia. Amelia, this is Sigg." Rhuger introduced us.

"Nice to meet you, Sigg." I smiled.

"You as well, Amelia." Sigg gave me a graceful bow of the head and a roguish smile. Rhuger's scowl deepened.

"What's his name?" I asked as I bent over to reach the nocrys between the rails. The poor thing was so desperate for scratches that he'd plastered himself against the bottom rail, trying to reach me in an adorable wiggle.

Silence met my question, so I looked at them over my shoulder. And realized they both had their eyes riveted on my ass. Evidently, men and males were the same everywhere, even across the galaxy.

"AHEM." I coughed. That startled both of them. I pointed to my face. "Eyes up here, gentlemen."

"Och, can you blame us, Neamhnaid? You're new and lovely and we weren't expecting you to bend over." Sigg was blunt but, strangely, I didn't take offense. Probably because of his genial smile and easy-going manner. Rhuger just coughed and looked away, that bright green high on his cheeks again.

To spare us all, I knelt down and continued to rub the plated scales of the nocrys's tummy. Grunting in approval, the kit began a deep, contented purr that sounded more like a revving muscle car than a purr. His eyes turned glassy, and he started drooling from the belly rubs.

"He doesn't have a name. The rider names their nocrys." Sigg supplied as he watched me with the pale creature.

"I can name him?" I asked, pointing at myself like an idiot.

"Och, he's yours now, isn't he?" Sigg's bemused smile was quite the sight.

"I-I mean if you say so? I have nothing to pay for him with though..." It hit me then how dependent I was on the goodwill of these orcs. It didn't sit right.

"You don't pay for the nocrys, pearl," Rhuger explained. "They're provided to the clan. Plus, have you ever seen a feline alter itself once stubbornly decided on someone?"

"Nope. I've got three cats to prove it." I laughed.

"Cats?" Sigg asked, eyebrows going up in surprise.

"Yeah, they're *much* smaller than a nocrys, all fur, and no scales, but they're splendid companions," I explained as I shifted to scratch at the kit's cheeks.

"So, what will you name him?"

"Hmm... how about Luther?" I asked the nocrys who just

blinked at me in kitty bliss.

"Luther it is," Sigg said. "You might as well go!" He hollered over to the group of orcs who had gathered to watch. "The nocrys has chosen."

There was some grumbling, but most of the orcs just gawked at me. After last night, it made me nervous. As if my unease had summoned him, Rhuger stepped between me and the orcs, shielding me from their sight. Luther, already tuned into my feelings, rolled upright and hissed at them. Giant black fangs as long as my hand were a menacing deterrent. As if my bodyguard weren't deterrent enough as he glared daggers at them.

"What happened to the body of that orc?" I asked in a small voice as the other orcs dispersed. I knew, but I needed to hear it.

"He's hanging from the Traitor Tree," Rhuger growled, silver eyes almost feverish as his gaze met mine. "His crimes hang around his neck." I shuddered, and Luther shoved his giant head between the rails and into my chest, knocking me on my ass.

"Who is hanging from the Craobh Brathaidh?" Sigg's calm expression shifted into a ferocious scowl.

"Tintain," Rhuger growled the name like a curse. "He thought he could force Amelia as a mate. I split his skull with my sword for his trouble."

"Och, that stupid orc. Serves him right. Not to worry, Neamhnaid, no one else will attempt to harm you. Rhuger did his job well." Sigg jerked his chin at my bodyguard. "If anyone manages to get past him, Hifasa and Luther would shred them."

I just gave them both a shaky smile.

Determined to do his kitty best to soothe me, Luther bucked the top rail out of the fence and it clattered to the packed earth of the paddock behind him. He clumsily fumbled his way over the remaining rails and crawled as far into my lap as he could. Given that he was the size of a small horse, he didn't get very far. Luther began licking my face and hands with a rough, forked tongue. I laughed and attempted to push him off.

"Stop it, Luther!" I cried, falling onto my back as I fended him off. Luther just laid down on top of me. I fought to breathe.

"*Suidhe!*" Sigg said sharply, snapping his fingers and pointing to the ground. Luther looked at him lazily, like he couldn't be bothered.

"Luther. Listen to Sigg." I admonished and shook a finger at the giant cat who was attempting to press my soul back into my body. Luther just blinked at me. So I *pssst* at him and Luther startled. "You heard me! *Suidhe!*" I said firmly. When he hesitated, I made the *pssst* sound again, and he scrambled up and sat back on his haunches, bewildered.

So were Sigg and Rhuger because they were looking at me like I'd grown a second head. Getting to my feet, I looked down at my clothes and laughed. I was *covered* in really long cat hair. Looking at the confused males, I shrugged.

"I have three cats back home." I reminded them, brushing off my clothes. Once I was in order, I reached out a hand to Luther and began petting his ridged nose. Luther purred loudly, and I smiled. "That's right, good boy."

"You think you could boss me around and call me a good boy?" Sigg smirked at me and Rhuger smacked him.

"Do you mind?" Rhuger asked.

"No, but apparently *you* do." Sigg cocked an eyebrow and the slow smile at his friend's expense nearly split his face. The orc was handsome in a roughhewn, rugged way. Like the men on the covers of biker romance books.

"You guys like teasing Rhuger, don't you? First Sharn and now you, Sigg?" I chuckled.

"Sharn was giving you the business?" Sigg laughed. "What did this one do, Neamhnaid?"

"Gave me his house?" I asked, still at a loss over it.

"DID YOU NOW!" Sigg roared at his friend. Rhuger slapped a hand to his face and rubbed the bridge of his nose. His ears looked like they were glowing green.

"Do you have to keep telling people that, pearl?" Rhuger growled, and I pursed my lips, trying not to smile.

"Why? What does it mean that he gave me his house?" I asked Sigg.

"Well..." He grinned at Rhuger, taunting him.

"Don't you dare!" Rhuger snapped, but Sigg didn't look concerned in the slightest by the near-feral glint in Rhuger's eye. Training massive cats who could gut you with one swipe definitely made him immune to fear.

"No, tell me, please! I want to understand." I pleaded, and both of them looked at me with wide eyes. My expression must have looked a sorry sight, because Rhuger looked away, flustered. Sigg cast a mischievous glance at his buddy before smiling warmly at me.

"Amelia, it's a traditional mating gift for a male to gift a female a house. A place where she can raise orclings and care for her family."

"A... *mating* gift?" I asked, a blush burning fiercely up my neck.

"Och, I have no mate yet, and you needed someplace to stay. It's as easy as that." Rhuger wouldn't look at me and just gave me a one-shoulder shrug.

"If you say so." Sigg cocked an eyebrow at his friend, *clearly* not believing him.

It was as if that one little nugget of information was all it took to break me after days of rolling with the punches. This singularly outrageous gift and its far-reaching meaning knocked my feet out from under me. Setting me adrift with no mooring.

I stood there unable to move, my emotions a swirling vortex. In order not to drown in them, I pushed aside my pounding heartbeat, my running thoughts, and my raging hormones. Pushed them down and away so I could think, so I could breathe. So I could take stock of, well, *everything*.

I'd just escaped my marriage. Found out my *alien orc grandpa* was still alive somewhere in the universe. Worked a broken gate and got tossed face-first into the dirt of this planet. Met Rhuger, got chased by a monster of an orc, and got a crash course in Talam survival training. Had *way* too many close encounters of the horny kind with Rhuger. Got to Baile Coille, met a feisty wise woman, and was gifted a damned *tree house.* A giant, rideable cat that I didn't have to pay for choose me as his person. I was still internally quaking from last night's events and the Oc'Dellor's brutally efficient justice system. *Now* I find out the house Rhuger had given me was essentially a *mating* gift? But also *not*?

It was all just... too much. *Waaaayyyy* too damned much for a girl to take.

So I did what I always did when I felt like I was going to burst with my thoughts and feelings. When they overflowed the bounds of my being, out of my reach. I donned the pleasant mask I wore to hide my full self, letting it slip into place. I looked at Luther and gently petted him on his nose and forehead, seeking a modicum of comfort. A deep rumbling, stuttering purr was my reward as I fought to calm my whirling thoughts and the stuttering beat of my heart.

RHUGER

I could have gutted my friend for telling Amelia what it meant that I'd given her my house. Mortified, I both hoped she'd take offense and that she'd be pleased. Instead, she stood there, petting her nocrys Luther, seemingly unbothered by what Sigg had told her. But that serene expression conflicted with the warring, intense scents of her emotions that rolled off of her like a storm. They were so tangled I wasn't able to decipher them. To understand.

Did she care that I'd gifted her my house? It hit me suddenly that I wanted her to care. I wanted to see her blushing again and to see those uisge-beatha eyes on me, wide and warm. Welcoming. Not this lack of emotion that didn't suit her at all.

The want was a piercing ache I couldn't shove aside. What on Talam was it about this female that made me lose all sense? Made me care so damned much?

"Come, pearl. We should move on. You can visit Luther after we meet with Rìgh Thorn. We've got other stops to make."

"Okay," she replied in a singsong voice that wasn't quite right. Amelia bent and kissed Luther on the head before walking toward me.

I glanced at Sigg, and he returned my questioning look with a knowing one of his own.

"It was lovely to meet you, Sigg," Amelia said with a small smile. "I'm looking forward to visiting again and seeing Luther."

"Anytime, Neamhnaid," Sigg said with a nod of his head and a kind smile. A smile I suddenly wanted to smack right off his face.

"Shall we?" Amelia asked as she looked up at me. There was a blankness in her eyes that I couldn't place. It wasn't like when Ruksala slipped into the *other* to listen to the whispers from the Source. And it wasn't the flat, dead look I'd seen in one too many warriors' gazes. I couldn't place it and it was like claws raking stone in the back of my mind as we waved goodbye to Sigg and I steered us toward the market.

Amelia was quiet and distant as we walked. She didn't ask where we were going, didn't question me about the sights we passed. And it wasn't that companionable silence we shared, either. It was like she was here with me, but *not*.

A dark memory whispered past my mental guards and bloomed into a vivid image in my mind. It was my friend Kholt when we'd been on the verge of malehood amongst the Oc'Turin. When he'd returned, beaten and walking stiffly from the main hall with food for the both of us. I'd had my side split open and was unable to take the beating necessary to earn my food. So Kholt had done it for both of us. A price he'd paid that I'd never forget.

Kholt's gaze had been like Amelia's that day. And it had been that way every day afterward. I never asked him what had happened in the main hall. He'd never offered. I'd sworn that one day I'd repay the males who'd hurt him in kind. It was a vow I still intended to keep.

I nearly walked into a passing orc as the memory and the implications of how it connected to Amelia rattled me. Apologizing to the male, we made our way through the outskirts of the city along the cobbled avenues. My mind raced, and I stole glances at the female who I swore to protect.

Finally, I recognized her demeanor as one of survival. A blankness designed to slip through events as unscathed as possible, mentally and emotionally, if not physically. What had happened in her life to corner her into protecting herself this way? Had it been because of her ex-husband? Or did it go farther into her youth? Did *I* cause this somehow?

That question sat like a cold, slimy weight in my gut. I resolved then and there that whatever caused her to slip into this survivor's mask, I would face it with her. Exact vengeance like I intended to do with Kholt. Even if it meant facing myself.

Until then, I was committed to breaking her out of this haze. Bring her back to herself. I only hoped the market would revive her spirit.

"I've got a treat for you, pearl," I said lightly, cocking an eyebrow down at her as she looked up at me. Her expression was polite, gaze empty of that fire that normally burned so brightly. "This way," I told her as we entered the city center.

It was a ring of home trees with shops built below. This was where the tradespeople conducted business and trained their apprentices. There was the smithy, the glassworks, the tanners, the miller, the tailor, the woodworks, the bookkeeper, the jeweler, and more. In the center of this ring of trees was a shallow pool that the orclings often played in. Small bridges spanned over the streams that fed and released the water from the pool. Fish and aquatic flowers brought life to the space, and stone benches invited people to sit for a spell amongst potted greenery. The cobbles rippled out from the pool in a circular pattern, like the rings of a massive tree. Avenues and lanes branched out from it like roots while banners and sun-stone lanterns crisscrossed overhead. It was an industrious, lively, yet peaceful place.

We paused near the smithy and I waited as Amelia took in the sights and sounds. Glancing down at her from the corner of my eye, I could see a spark light up in those uisge-beatha eyes. It was a start. And a relief.

"This is the trade area. It's the city's center." I explained, bending towards her so she could hear me over the clanging of the smithy. "There are other tradespeople scattered throughout Baile Coille, but these are the first and oldest shops. Some have been here for a thousand years."

Amelia looked up at me, and like sunlight breaking through clouds, some of that blankness faded from her expression. Her brows rose and a look of awe suffused her features. Yet she didn't ask me any questions. So I told her about the center as if she had. The more I told her about each shop and the pool as we walked towards the market, the more she bloomed. It was like watching a flower slowly unfurl before my very eyes.

As we passed the pool, she stopped and stared at it for a moment, before sitting on a bench and taking off her boots. I frowned, my words petering out as I watched in confusion. Amelia set her boots aside and rolled up her pants, then stepped down into the pool. It came up to her shins as she ambled through the water. Light danced along the surface of the pool and outlined her curves. It stole my breath from my lungs.

Amelia stood and watched as the fish in the pool acclimated to her presence and swam closer. She bent over and it was a study in control to watch what she was doing instead of her generous ass. After a moment, I realized she was *petting* the fish in the pool. Huffing a laugh, I strode over to the bench and took a seat next to her boots, resting my elbows on my knees.

There was a gentleness, a peacefulness, in watching her slip through the water, brushing up against the sweet-smelling water flowers and petting the fish. All the while, the world bustled about around her. She seemed to exist with the world, indulging in the modest miracles of life in a way I'd never seen before. I wasn't sure I'd ever fully understand her, but I wanted to.

Eventually, she walked back, careful of the flowers and fish. She stepped out of the pool and sat down next to me, wiggling her wet toes in the sunlight. Sniffing the air subtly, I could tell that she was still a jumble of emotions, but calm was the most prominent of them.

"Did you have fun?" I asked, voice gone a little rough with the feelings she evoked in me.

"I did." She said with a small smile. A *genuine* smile this time.

"I'm glad," I said, and meant it. "Shall we head to the market?"

"I'd like that." She murmured as she put her boots back on, lacing them up quickly.

The walk to the start of the market avenue was short. There was a sharp bend to it, the elaborate shop of the glassworks jutted out and blocked the view. So you didn't see the vibrancy and the liveliness that gave the market its name right away.

"Welcome to the Eun'bogha-froise Market, pearl," I told her with a sweep of my arm as we turned the corner.

Her irises blew wide as the riot of color and life came into view. She came to a stop, taking it all in, her lovely mouth open in awe. I couldn't blame her. It wasn't named after the rainbow-fletched bird for nothing.

The open-air market wove along the sides of a broad avenue lined with stalls. Overhead, vast swathes of fabric in all the colors of the rainbow wove back and forth across the avenue between the canopies of the home trees. Helping to keep the powerful light of the suns or light rain from reaching the shoppers below, and casting the market in glowing color. Strings of sun-stone lanterns and fluttering banners, strands of chimes, and bits of sparkling baubles wove like a net beneath the colorful canopy. Even the cobbles were a colorful pattern, drawing shoppers along the avenue.

Each stall was built and decorated as the owner saw fit. Painted in every color imaginable with a variety of roofs and building techniques. The scents of food, incense, spices, and flowers wove their way to us, like a tantalizing siren as the voices of hawkers and the notes of a fiddle beckoned us forward. The pull was irresistible and I let

Amelia lead the way.

"This is nuts!" Amelia exclaimed as she looked around with wide-eyed wonder at the bustling stalls lining the avenue.

This was my moment. The chance to break the awkwardness between us. Hopefully, bring her back to herself.

"Och, but can it compare to deez nuts?" I asked. When she looked at me in confusion, I waved a hand at the front of my kilt, a cocky grin plastered on my face. Fiercely hoping she'd take the bait.

Amelia stood stock-still, blinked a few times, then slapped a hand across her face, groaning.

"Did you just?" She asked as she drew her hand down her face so she could eyeball me over her delicately clawed fingers. The tips of her ears were pink, and the sight made my heart soar. That indifference was gone like mist in sunlight, and she was my pearl once more.

I froze for half a breath. *My* pearl? Air hitching in my lungs, I expelled it in a rush and grinned roguishly at her. Placing my hands on my hips, I strode forward and bent down until we could see eye to eye. Attempting to cover up my internal battle.

My pearl.

"I just did," I said with a wolfish smirk. I cocked my head at her and my braid slithered over my shoulder. Watching those uisge-beatha eyes of hers track the movement, then dart back up to meet mine as her hand fell away, exposing those charming freckles and that damnable mouth that haunted my dreams.

My pearl.

Those two little words were like a chant in my mind as we stood staring at one another for one singular, infinite moment. Whatever she was looking for in my gaze, she found it. Pupils blowing wide, she gasped. Her scent shifted to that ripe arousal that made my eyes want to roll into the back of my head.

"We should check out the stalls," I said, breaking free from her gaze before she broke my control. I stood tall once more and strode past her. The merest brush of her arm against mine was a shocking jolt that nearly sent me to my knees.

My pearl.

She wasn't for someone like me. She deserved better. Yet that reminder was wearing thinner and thinner with each heartbeat. What the *hell* was she doing to me?

CHAPTER 19

AMELIA

Rhuger's flirting and the wide colorful market finally shook loose the remnants of my stoic mask. Letting it fall away like flaking ash. I wasn't blind. I could see how he worried as we walked from the nocrys stables. How he tried so hard to reach me. It was... sweet. Surprising. I wasn't used to this sort of attention.

He's your bodyguard, he's supposed to pay attention. He promised he would, didn't he?

The reminder that his interest was just part of his job kept complicating navigating this new world. And my war-torn heart. I was still in a wild tangle of feelings, but I resigned to letting them sort themselves out. Like allowing muddled water to rest while the sediment drifted to the bottom. To see clearly once more.

Rhuger pulled me from one outrageously decorated stall to the next. They were all different and delightful in their diversity. There were stalls filled with fruit, flowers, potted plants, finely wrought chimes, sunstone lanterns, spices, remedies, tasty treats, and tools for nearly every trade imaginable. It was so much to take in, as were the crowds of shoppers. The market was a bustling place, and it was the most orcs I'd seen in any one place in the city.

It should have overwhelmed me. But somehow, with Rhuger at my side, it wasn't so bad. I knew he'd help me escape if it got to be too much for me.

We were browsing in a broad stall overflowing with fabrics of all kinds. It was quiet in the stall, with only a few people milling about. The break from the swiftly moving crowds outside and the rich colors and textures of the fabrics gave me room to breathe for a bit.

"Tell me, pearl," Rhuger murmured as he leaned his elbow on the counter next to me. That lovely braid of his falling over his shoulder, his silver and onyx eyes drawing me in. Like they always did. I looked at him as my hands reveled in the textures of the fabrics in the stall. Some were soft, others rough, some slithered over my fingers like silk, and yet others boasted extravagant embroidery. The craftsmanship was remarkable.

"Hm?" I hummed at him and he cocked his head, eyes narrowing slightly as studied me.

"Was there something I said or did back with Sigg to..." He sighed and grimaced as he tried looking for the words. "...to make you uncomfortable? Feel unsafe?"

"No, why?" I asked, honestly taken aback.

"Because it was almost as if you became someone else. Like you'd donned a mask you wore like a fine dress. Made to please instead of just being yourself. I would hate to be the reason you felt the need to do so."

He noticed?

Of course, he noticed he's my damned bodyguard!

"Honestly, the only person I trust here is you," I told him, and he looked startled at that. "Well, maybe Ruksala too."

"Then why...?" He asked, brow furrowing. "Is it like when you had a hard time speaking? When you met Uther and Nashton?"

"Um, kinda?" I replied, flustered. Hesitating for only a heartbeat before the words slipped from me unbidden. "I guess it's because I was always told to calm down. That I was too emotional, too opinionated, too blunt, or rude. That my way of thinking bothered people. I got tired of the disapproval, of trying so hard to understand them when they didn't bother to understand me. So I created this pleasant mask to wear whenever I felt too much inside, so I wasn't a burden... so I wouldn't have to feel the pain..."

The words burned as they fell from my lips. An aching truth I'd kept close to my chest for so long that I'd learned to live with the sickness of it. I'd never felt comfortable enough to say this to anyone before, not even my mother. It rattled me that when Rhuger asked; I answered without a thought.

"Did your family treat you like this?" Rhuger asked with a quiet gentleness.

"Sometimes?" I shrugged. "I could be myself at home most of the time. But when we went out for social situations, or I was at school, I'd don the mask. It made life easier. Especially with Adam."

A clerk made his way over to us, eager to talk about his wares. But one cutting glance from Rhuger and the orc turned right back around and went to help another customer. I looked after the male for a moment, gathering my thoughts before I turned back to Rhuger.

"He didn't understand. And I didn't really either. He was normal, and I was... well, different." I sighed and rubbed a bit of cloth that felt like it was made of kitten fur between my fingers, trying to focus. "It made communicating difficult. Made seeing eye to eye hard, too. And in the end, he didn't trust me. Treated me like a child, a burden, and an idiot."

"You like to touch things," Rhuger observed after a long pause as his gaze regarded my fingers. He released his clenched fists. The only sign that what I said bothered him.

"Touching grounds me. Though some textures are a big *no thank you.* It helps me stay present and not fade back into the mask. Or go quiet." I murmured and let my fingers fall from the fabric. Self-conscious and a little unnerved by the vulnerability of the moment.

"Thank you for explaining this to me. For being honest with me. I appreciate it." Rhuger said with sincerity, standing upright. His tone shifted as he bent down to catch my gaze. "And I'm sorry that you went through that. That you were treated less than others. That you felt you couldn't be yourself. You deserved better."

Emotion blindsided me like a freight train and I gasped, pressing my lips together and wiling back the tears that now quivered along my lashes, threatening to spill over. He *saw* me. Saw me in a way I'd never experienced before. He didn't dismiss me, belittle me or judge me for just existing as I was. Why was he so good to me?

Because he's doing his job.

Rhuger's expression went soft, and he chucked me under the chin. "Aw, come on, pearl. No need for rain, och? It's a bonnie day, so let's enjoy it."

"Thank you," I whispered. "I really appreciate you."

Rhuger opened his mouth, closed it, and turned away, rubbing at the back of his neck.

"Shall we move on?" He asked, voice cracking slightly.

It was interesting to watch the exchanges between shoppers and the stall owners. They didn't exchange any sort of currency that I could see. Instead, the shoppers would hold up a leather thong with a carving on it. Some had additional beads. Then the shopper would be allowed to take what they needed. It seemed like a form of credit, but I wasn't sure how it worked without currency.

"Rhuger," I said, getting his attention as we loitered in a wind chime shop.

"Och?"

"How does buying and selling work here?" I asked, and he looked to where I was watching another shopping interaction inside the chime stall. This time, the shopper handed over one bead and walked away with an extravagant set of chimes that created its own symphony as he walked out with it. "What are those carvings? The beads?"

"Ah. Well, everyone within Baile Coille does their part to keep the city going. Each person, regardless of age or status, is given what they need, including food and necessities. Folk who work a trade, hold a station, or are a warrior receive a token." Rhuger rummaged in a small bag at his belt and pulled out a leather thong with a carved token that looked like a sword. He had the most beads I'd seen yet. "If you have a token, you're allowed to take a reasonable amount of goods from shopkeepers. It varies from shop to shop. Overall, it's a fair system."

I nodded my understanding as we watched passersby with their goods. Ruger paused and ran his fingers through a set of chimes. They tinkled a bright little melody that left me grinning.

"Some tokens are worth more than others. The greater the impact the orckin has on the community of Baile Coille, the greater the rewards."

"And the beads?" I asked, pointing to his. He shifted uneasily.

"The beads represent deeds of service or outstanding impact. They're used to purchase the best items, trade for large quantities of goods, or the ability to build a home. Only the Rìgh, his steward, or the Fear a Chì can grant them."

"They must be difficult to earn, then."

"Och, they are."

"How did you get so many?" I asked, and Rhuger's easy smile turned self-deprecating.

"When you're an exile like me, you have to work hard to earn the good graces of the rulers who allow you to stay." Rhuger sighed and tucked his token with its many beads back into his belt. "Sometimes, it isn't enough."

"That's bullshit." I snapped, affronted on his behalf. Rhuger glanced up at me, trying not to smile.

"You're adorable when you curse, did you know that?" Rhuger chuckled, and I felt it run over my skin like a caress. "I'm assuming 'bullshit' is a curse?"

"It is!" I scrunched up my face in my ire. "It's not fair that you've worked so hard and you're still not accepted! I can only imagine what it took to earn the right to build a house!"

"I slew a wyrm." He replied nonchalantly, amused at my indignation.

"A what?" I asked.

"A wyrm. It's a giant snake many times Hifasa's size. Its scales are the shingles on your house."

I paused, processing exactly *how* big that would be, and blanched. The wyrm must have been colossal to have scales that big. *Rhuger* had felled something that big?

"All by yourself?" I squeaked.

"All by myself." Rhuger's sinful mouth quirked up on one side. The effect it had on me was devastating. "It was old, though. Well past its prime."

"Still." I breathed in awe. Even if the beast had been *blind*, it would have been the challenge of a lifetime. That he was standing here, alive, shrugging it off like it was nothing, made me wonder. Exactly what kind of horrors had he endured to become the warrior he was today?

I wasn't sure I could stomach the answer.

"I want to give you a hug." I blurted.

"What?" Rhuger asked, voice cracking in his shock. His eyes went wide and that telltale bright green spread over his cheeks.

"I want to give you a hug," I repeated. "You've been through a lot, and it sounds like you need a hug."

"Alright." He murmured, hardly audible over the sounds of the chimes and the crowd.

I stepped toward him and wrapped my arms around his waist. Careful to avoid his sheathed knives on his bandolier, I placed my head on his chest and gave him a gentle squeeze, my hands spread flat against his back. Seeking to offer a simple comfort I'd always craved. I'd never hugged anyone this tall, and I absently noted how lovely it was. How it made me feel small, dainty even.

"I'm sorry," I mumbled against his pectoral. He smelled wonderful, but the lust I normally felt when I caught a whiff of him was tempered by the understanding that this comfort was *for* him.

"For what?" He rasped, unsure of where to place his hands. His heart pounded like a great drum under my cheek.

"For all that you endured, getting as strong as you are. It must have been so difficult. And lonely." I squeezed him a little tighter. Rhuger stopped breathing for a moment, then placed his hands on my shoulders.

"It's not your fault, pearl." He murmured and pet my hair. Gods, it felt so good to hug him. The tension and stress just melted away from both of us. It was simple, hugging Rhuger, easy. I liked it. "All of what I survived made me who I am. And it's worth it."

"It is?" I asked him, looking up to meet his silver gaze, gone soft instead of the sharp or molten I was used to. A smile quirked the corners of his mouth.

"Och. Got me a job protecting a strange human Neamhnaid, didn't it?" He ruffled my hair before pulling back. I let him go. All the good feelings slipped away with him as he sauntered out into the bustling avenue.

So *that's* how he saw me. Just a job.

RHUGER

Source preserve me. I would have happily traded all my beads for that one hug. That she gave it to me freely, and that I couldn't return it was equal parts ecstasy and despair.

She smelled like soap, sunshine, and the perfume she'd tried at a perfumer's stall. Heady, sweet florals like water flowers mixed with light, juicy fruit. The way the perfume had clung to her skin and blossomed her natural feminine aroma had made me bite back a howl. A bottle of it was now on its way to Amelia's tree home. I'd quietly shown the owner my token and paid the clips to have an orcling runner deliver it when Amelia wasn't looking.

Siren's Whisper had been the name of the fragrance. Gods be damned and my soul too, for how accurate a name it was. Especially when worn by the female who was slowly driving me mad. And here I was, encouraging that madness like a damned idiot.

I strode out into the avenue to gulp down the air in deep

breaths, hoping the whirling market scents would drive away Amelia's smell. It was a fool's hope, I realized, as her scent, and that perfume, were now seared into my memories. Along with her warm, soft body cradling the hard planes of mine, her sweet, trusting uisge-beatha eyes seeing into my soul. And her kind words.

Shaking myself like a wet nocrys, I turned to look back into the chime stall for my charge. She'd moved to the next stall. She was admiring the baskets of mounded spices that were stacked along the walls. Cloth dyed with different spices was draped along the roof and walls amongst dyed sunstone lanterns. The stall owner, an older female dressed in an elaborate dress dyed in all the colors of the cloth that decorated her shop, had come up to speak with Amelia about her wares.

I took an assessing turn, eyeing the sea of faces that blurred past, and the surrounding stalls. Tuning my senses to look for danger, I leaned against the post between the spice stall and a jewelry shop. I could hear the spice stall owner's robust sales pitch, an argument two stalls up about the quality of some leather. I could smell the bitter tang of fear and the burning metal stench of a lie weaving through the riot of scents in the market.

"Look, I'm not going to be purchasing these from you." The jewelry shop owner said firmly. I turned to keep an eye on what was developing next door. A male I'd never seen before was trying to sell a pouch full of pearls and not having much success.

"Please reconsider. I fought the moileasgan for these! Look at them again. They are of impeccable quality." The male pleaded, holding up one of the proposed neamhnaid.

Even if his tale were true, rare items such as neamhnaid were sold to the Clan. Then, once the best had been set aside for adornment for the royal family, the rest were given to tradespeople. Providing them with the resources to continue to create. Everyone knew this.

That he was trying to sell them directly to a shop owner was not only against the law, but it could also get both the jeweler and the orc selling them banished from Oc'Dellor.

I cast a quick glance into the spice stall. Amelia was still chatting with the spice trader. I hated to take my eyes off of her, even for a minute, but I couldn't let what was happening in the next stall stand. She was safe enough for a few minutes.

On quiet feet, I strode into the jeweler's stall. Pretending for all the world that I was shopping for a pretty thing to buy.

"Think of the coin you could save by buying directly from me!" the hawker insisted, desperation lining his words, his body language, his scent.

"Again, I will not purchase these from you. If you want to sell them, you have to go to Daingneach and hand them to the Steward." The shopkeeper said firmly, crossing his wiry arms over his narrow chest with an impressive scowl. "I won't risk my business on this foolishness."

The shopkeeper finally glanced up at me as I cast a shadow over them both. His eyes went wide as he recognized me. I held up a hand with a finger to my lips as I stood directly behind the hawker, blocking his exit. He was dressed in worn, stained traveling clothes. Not the clean, if occasionally patched, clothes offered to all residents of Baile Coille. Possibly from another clan, or even one of the minor clans in the outlying towns.

"What do we have here?" I asked in a rumble.

The hawker turned, eyes wide in his weather-worn face gone five shades paler green, and bumped into me. The pouch in his hands jostled, pearls spilling from it to fall to the ground. And shatter there. The jeweler and I shared a glance of understanding before I flicked my gaze back to the terrified hawker. He was looking at me as if I were a dorcha'aon come to devour him. He wasn't far off.

With a terrifying slowness, I looked down at the pouch of fake neamhnaid and plucked one from what was left. I raised my hand; the bauble held between my thumb and index finger. I glared at the con, his gaze was riveted on my fingers. With a squeeze, the fake pearl fractured and crumbled between my fingertips. The orc was sweating heavily, panting in fear, as I sprinkled the remnants of his attempted crime onto the ground.

The fake pearls had been made from formed glass. That someone from the glassworks might be involved in this little scheme was upsetting. I knew the apprentices and master well from building my house. I hoped they had no hand in this and he was from another clan. This... pissed me off.

"P-please Oc'Turin..." The hawker stuttered as he stared up at me, terrified. That this con knew who I was surprised me. It seemed my reputation had grown. Even the shopkeep had taken a step back at the scowl I cast at the con.

"Deceit will always return to force you to meet the truth." I hissed from between my teeth. The orc shuddered.

I snatched the bag of fake neamhnaid and grasped the orc at the scruff of his neck, steering him towards the avenue. Luck was with me. A couple of guards were passing by. Hailing them, they came over, frowning. One orc was Ophir.

"What's this?" Ophir asked, taking the bag of fake pearls from my outthrust fist.

"They're fake," I growled. "This one was trying to sell them to this jeweler." I yanked the orc in question out in front of me. He stumbled and only kept his feet because I held onto him.

"Was the jeweler going to buy them?" Ophir asked, flicking his green gaze behind me, face gone serious.

"No, he kept refusing," I replied. Ophir let out a breath of relief and motioned to the orc with him to take the trembling hawker from my grasp. The orc began babbling as the other guard grabbed onto his shoulder and hauled him over.

"That's a relief," Ophir said.

"No idea where he got the glass from. You might want to... ask him." I suggested. Ophir's gaze slid to the orc.

"You don't say." He said dryly. "Thank you for this, Rhuger."

I grunted in acknowledgment. "Any more sightings?" I asked. I'd been on edge the entire time I'd been back. Amelia was an effective distraction, but I wasn't about to pass up the chance to learn what the guard knew.

"You were right," Ophir murmured low, his hands on his belt. The other guard was having difficulty keeping his charge on his feet. "We've spotted tracks and heard calls in the night, but no sightings yet."

"Anyone sick?" I crossed my arms over my chest.

"Not yet. It's probably what's spared us so far." Ophir gave me a knowing look. *So far.* But the threat of both the dorcha'aon and the an'sgudal was imminent. "We're keeping it quiet. No one outside of the night guard knows about it. We're waiting for Rìgh Thorn's return."

"That's wise," I said. "I'll start carrying my bow. Just in case." I told him and he sighed in relief. Ophir knew of my skill with a bow.

"I'd appreciate that, Oc'Turin." He gave me a wry smile. His meaning was more of a nod to my training than to my actual clan. With a raised hand in thanks, he turned and strode off with the other guard and the hawker.

"Thank you, Oc'Turin." The jeweler said from behind me. I turned and the orc, bedecked in his wares, was bleeding relief.

"It's no problem. He should know the rules and abide by them as you do. You honored the clan today." I told him. He looked flustered at my words and looked about his stall.

"A gift for you? For your help? It's the least I can do." The shopkeeper said, sweeping his arms out at his wares.

I was about to refuse when a piece caught my eye. Reaching for it, I inspected its simple beauty. It was perfect. The shopkeeper nodded encouragingly at me and I took it in hand. I only hoped she liked it.

CHAPTER 20*

AMELIA

"Close your eyes, pearl." I heard Rhuger command from behind me, and I obliged, turning to face him. "Now stick out your hand."

"This better not be something gross." I frowned as I obliged. Rhuger's broad, warm hand cupped mine, his callouses scraping the back of my knuckles as his thumb rubbed a soothing circle in my palm. I felt that small touch as if it were everywhere.

Then, something cool slipped into my palm and Rhuger removed his hand in a gentle caress. "Open your eyes, lass." Rhuger's words were soft, and I obeyed, blinking up at him, then down at my hand. A strange necklace lay draped over my palm.

It was a simple design. A blade in shape the length of my palm carved of bone or tooth. One side was textured with a pretty pattern and the other was smooth. The blade split into two prongs at the top, and a metal bar went through both and connected to the leather cord on either side. Between the prongs, threaded onto the metal bar where it could spin freely, was a single pearl that nearly glowed.

I huffed a laugh as I realized he'd gotten me the Talam

equivalent of a fidget spinner. Grinning broadly at him, I slipped the leather cord over my head and the pendant settled between my breasts over my tunic. That he'd found something to keep me grounded I could carry with me was so thoughtful it hurt. My ex-husband had never done anything like this in all the years we'd been married.

"Do you like it?" He asked almost shyly from where he leaned against a post, even as he watched me like a hawk.

"I love it." I smiled warmly up at him as I grasped it and fiddled with the pearl, rolling it with my thumb. "Thank you."

"Good." Rhuger smiled softly before grasping my hand and pulling me away from the spice stall. "Come, let's get you something to eat!"

And boy, did we eat. There were decadent desserts made with something akin to honey and a type of pressed flower layered together. Various types of meat on sticks that I didn't bother asking about the species of, but tasted delicious. The herbs and spices they used had flavors I'd never experienced. I spied the dildo mushrooms and the vamp berries amongst the dishes. It comforted me to have something familiar in all of this newness.

We spent hours wandering the market stalls, talking to the shopkeepers, listening to musicians, and getting lost in the ebb and flow of the soul that was the market. All the while, an ache had lodged itself somewhere in my chest. But I kept reminding myself that this was enough. Being Rhuger's job, and possibly his friend, was enough.

The suns were touching the jagged stone spires that encircled Baile Coille when a rumbling noise rose beyond the market. Rhuger's sharp gaze cut across the avenue and he pulled me close and stepped us between two stalls as the masses pushed back to make way.

I couldn't make out the people who rode in on the group of nocrys. There were too many bodies blocking my view. Too many bodies pressed back and into us, jostling me. One orc stumbled back and bumped into me, hard. I lurched backward, eyes going wide with the realization I was falling.

But I never hit the ground. Fast as lightning, Rhuger reached out and caught me. Pulling me close as he maneuvered us up against one of the stall walls. Even as the crowd moved further back around us. A tree and barriers blocked the back of the broad space. I realized belatedly that we were trapped as the milling crowd quickly filled the short alley. Rhuger braced both arms against the stall, creating a small haven of space between him and the wall as the crowd broke around his powerful frame.

I looked up at him as he glared at the jostling throng, a snarl curling his lip. He was protecting me. I was so used to having to protect myself that I never really knew what it felt like to be protected. To have a safe space. It was nice.

Okay, it was *really* nice. Nice enough that I felt heat pool in my core as his scent invaded my senses. The memory of him acting all cocky after his 'deez nuts' joke, his gaze lancing straight into my very soul, and all the little moments since burned a brazen line of need along my spine as his body brushed against mine. An echo of when our arms had touched. When I hugged him.

The pushing finally stopped, the alley packed like a sardine can, and I knew when Rhuger caught my scent. He snapped his head down, gaze turning molten. But he wasn't the only orc to scent me. Heads turned in my direction and fear doused any arousal I had. Rhuger jerked as if he'd been slapped, then cast a glance over his shoulder, catching sight of the orcs who were still staring. Or making their way towards me through the crowd, their faces alight with interest. Rhuger hurriedly wrapped an arm around my shoulders, clutched me to him, and began moving us along the stall wall.

"Move!" He snarled and snapped his teeth more than once at

anyone in his way. He got us to the rear of the stall, where there was a gap between the wall and the barrier. Rhuger pushed me in front of him so I could go through first.

Only problem? I was a little too thick for it to work. Growling in frustration behind me, he grasped me around the waist and hoisted me. I wailed as I found myself flying through the air, scrabbling for purchase on something, anything.

Until my stomach connected to his boulder of a shoulder and all my air escaped my body in a rough *oof.* I was hanging upside down, staring at the mesmerizing muscles of his low back as they bunched and rolled under his lovely green skin as he moved. Dragging in a ragged gasp of air, I was about to berate him. I had my head turned, hood over my face, ready to give him a tongue lashing of a lifetime.

"Hold on," he growled, throwing one arm over the backs of my thighs, his broad hand gripping my leg close to my ass. His fingers dug into my thigh and hip in such a way that felt a little *too* good. He made an alarming roar of frustration.

My ire and the tiny pang of lust turned into confusion as I grasped onto the waistband of the back of his kilt and pushed myself up, shoving my hood aside so I could see. Then Rhuger *moved.* He stepped up onto a tree root, grasped a branch of the home tree with his free hand, hauled, and landed light as a feather on the barrier itself.

I gawked in utter bafflement as he walked along the narrow barrier between the back of the stall and the massive tree. He didn't even pause as he came to a low enough branch and grasped it, swinging us up onto the roof of another stall. He ran and jumped, vaulting over a narrow alley and onto the roof of the next stall along the avenue. I made an undignified squeal and clutched his waistband with both hands in mortal terror.

He threw my fat ass over his gotdamned shoulder! And now *he's doing fucking parkour!*

The roar of the crowd caught my attention, and I managed a glance toward the avenue we were running parallel to. It was like a small parade. The locals threw colorful flower petals and roared at the return of whoever it was. There was one orc at the center of the line of nocrys. He was massive and waved at the crowd with a broad grin. I was trying to focus on the guy's face, but Rhuger had other ideas.

Without warning, we were falling. Screeching, I panicked and wrapped my arms around Rhuger's waist upside down. Plastering myself against him, my cheek pressed up against those delightful muscles at the small of his back. We landed with a jolt. Rhuger stood tall and patted my arm where I'd flung it around him.

"You can let go now, pearl." He rumbled.

I made some sort of unladylike grunt in response.

"We're not clear yet, but I need to put you down now," Rhuger explained, voice tight and growly. "Unless you'd rather I keep carrying you like this? It might be a better idea. It'll be easier to spank you this way when you misbehave."

Oh, hot diggity dog.

My face exploded in a blush as my core clenched *hard* at *that* delightful scenario.

Rhuger stiffened, then barked a roar. He pulled my arms from his waist and I was suddenly flying through the air again, only to find myself back on my feet, staring wide-eyed up at a *very* pissed-off Rhuger. His lips pulled back as he bared his teeth at me briefly before snatching my hand in his and walking off, nearly dragging me behind him.

"Did you *have* to get aroused right then?" Rhuger snapped as we hurried down a side street and away from the throng in the market.

"It's not like I could help it!" I bit out, affronted. Not quite sure which time he was talking about since there had been a few instances in the last five minutes.

"You *need* to help it!" Rhuger whirled to a stop in front of me, releasing my hand, eyes wide and mouth pressed into a thin line of fury. "You do *not* understand what could happen if you don't learn to control it!"

"No! I clearly don't! Outside of what I'd have to fear as a human!" I cried, flinging my arms wide. "I'm not *used* to the people around me being able to *smell* it when I get turned on, okay?"

"Are humans so nose-blind they wouldn't be able to smell how absolutely *ripe* you were?" He laughed like it was unthinkable.

"YES!" I shouted, and he froze. "We've got pheromones, but it's not like we've got the noses of bloodhounds! We go off of visual cues for arousal!"

"So you don't smell it when I'm aroused. When I'm angry. When I'm happy." His words were more statements than questions.

"I mean..." I faltered and blushed, looking away. "You smell *good* to me, but I can't really pluck out your individual emotional scents out of thin air. I go off of your body language and facial expressions. I figured out that's what was happening on my own, okay? That you guys can smell... feelings. Boy, that sounds weird when I say it."

"I smell good to you?" He asked, the hint of a smile tinging his voice.

"Mmh," I grunted, refusing to look at him, and crossed my arms over my chest.

"Look, pearl." Rhugher began, calmer now. "I didn't realize you couldn't smell the same way us full-blooded orckin can. For that, I apologize." I looked up at him in surprise. He continued. "When I killed Tintain and strung him up from the Traitor Tree, it sent a clear message to everyone about what would happen if they tried the same. But that doesn't stop them from wanting to talk to you, court you. To think you're fair game. Do you understand?"

"Yes." I swallowed.

"When your scent..." Rhuger paused and wet his lips with the tip of his black tongue before continuing. "When your scent shifts... It calls to a primal part of us males that can be hard to deny. In close quarters like that, it becomes even *more* difficult."

"Because there's little air circulation?" I asked. Rhuger looked surprised at my blunt response. "I mean, it makes sense that with no airflow, no breeze, to dilute it, then it would be more intense."

"Such a sharp one." A small smile tugged at one corner of his mouth. A mouth no longer in a flat, angry line. "You know, each time I think I've got you figured out, you surprise me, pearl."

"Someone's gotta keep you on your toes," I smirked. Rhuger shook his head and chuckled. We both took a breath, the stress draining from us both, before we continued down the cobbled lane, leaving the market far behind us.

"I am serious though," Rhuger said, catching my eye once more. "Most orckin females can curb their emotions so as not to falsely lead a male on."

"But I'm not built that way," I whispered. And I wasn't. I never had been, even though I'd tried. I'd been slapped with enough disorders to prove it.

"Because you feel things so strongly." He murmured, putting two and two together. "Because *you* are used to visual cues, you developed that mask you wear when you're overcome or forced to become less to meet others' expectations. So you've never had to truly guard what you feel in the same way as full-blooded orckin females."

"Doesn't help that I tend to be more... 'emotionally sensitive', than other humans," I muttered. "But yes, visual cues I can adjust for or mimic to get by. But I've never been able to tame what lurks under my skin. Understanding it is an elusive, exhaustive task. If I *stop* feeling, it is a very, *very* bad thing."

I placed a hand over my chest. Something passed between us, an understanding that lit his gaze. If I stopped feeling, it meant I'd needed to retreat too far into myself to escape what was around me. And if pushed further to feel *something*, I'd feel trapped and then I'd do anything to escape.

Including taking my own life.

I'd stood at the precipice of *that* decision more than once before I left my ex-husband. And it wasn't a place I ever wanted to return to. Physically or mentally.

"We're going to need to figure out how to move forward with this." He said, brow furrowed in thought. "How to navigate the inevitable misunderstandings."

"I find avoidance to be a good method."

"Och, but then you'd never live freely. It's better to do at least one thing you're afraid of each day than to live in a cage made of fear." Rhuger's gaze was piercing. And full of a truth I was still learning. "You've already done many difficult things to break from your cage. Why stop?"

"Because he shredded my wings," I murmured. And it was true. Adam had systematically shredded my wings one cut at a time and cornered me in this cage of fear. Having busted the cage wide open, bars bent and twisted but still there, standing at the precipice of freedom, one question haunted me. "How am I to fly with no wings? I'll fall."

"Then I will catch you," Rhuger replied without hesitation.

"And we will fly together."

I'd clutch my pearls if I had any. I grasped the pendant he'd given me with its singular pearl instead. How the *hell* was this fucker so gotdamned smooth? I needed a hand fan to help me battle the fit of the vapors that overcame me as I stared at this determined, gorgeous alien orc. Who looked all the world like he hadn't just yanked my cracked foundations out from under me with ten little words.

Jesus Christ. He had this thirsty heathen praying for help from someone else's god. And here I stood, confused as fuck, because didn't he make it clear earlier I was just a job to him? Were we even friends? I squeezed the pendant in my fist, seeking the sense of pressure, a little pain, to center me. Bring me back to the present.

"So who was that? In the line of nocrys that everyone was cheering for. Was that Rìgh Thorn?" I asked, looking away.

"Och, that was him. We should head to Daingneach to request an audience." Rhuger replied. I could feel his eyes on me. Assessing. I wondered which of my emotions he smelled. Because I sure as hell couldn't pick one out of the turbulent storm in my chest.

"Daingneach?" I asked, struggling with the word.

"The keep, pearl." He explained.

I took a deep breath to fortify myself. This was it. I was going to find out precisely how kind of ruler this Rìgh Thorn was. Because my fate rested in his hands. Nodding to Rhuger, he led the way to Daingneach, his fingers once again laced with mine.

CHAPTER 21

AMELIA

When we came into view of the keep, Rhuger released my hand. I immediately missed his warmth. He led me towards the towering keep and I looked up at it as we approached.

The forbidding stone curtain walls were softened by creeping vines and moss that cascaded over its facade like a mantle. Warriors patrolled the battlements and the towers, and turrets pierced the sky like jagged teeth. The gatehouse was draped in banners in blue and purple that fluttered in the breeze. We passed through the gate with no problems, the guards nodding to Rhuger as we went. That was a relief, at least.

Once we entered the bailey, we strode down a cobbled path that led straight to the keep itself. Other paths branched out and gardens scattered inside the spacious bailey. I wondered if one of those paths led to the kitchens and if Sharn was there.

The broad cobbled path widened before the stairs that led to the massive doors to the keep. They were open and guarded by four orckin who stared ahead as if they didn't see us. The shadow of the keep fell over us as we ascended the steps and passed through the doorway. It took a moment for my eyes to adjust to the dimness within.

"This way, pearl," Rhuger murmured and tilted his head towards one hallway that branched from the entryway.

I followed in his wake, absorbing all the details of the interior. Tapestries with varying motifs hung on the walls, along with paintings, and niches held sculptures of all kinds. There was a lip along the top of the walls where they met the ceiling. Flames flickered there, lighting our way. It was a marvel and I couldn't fathom how they did it.

As we approached a set of double doors, I could hear voices. One stood out to me amongst the others. That voice... A deep rumbling brogue I hadn't heard in decades. The huge orc I'd caught a glance of at the welcome parade stepped out from the open doorway. He was accompanied by a knot of well-dressed orckin. They were talking in urgent, hushed voices as they turned away from us down the hall. My feet drew me to his familiar frame in a rush, leaving Rhuger to follow behind me.

"Grandpa Thorn?!" I cried, and the giant orc from the parade paused and turned to look at me. And holy shit. It was my grandpa! Older definitely, with silver streaks in his hair and beard, but he looked the same as the photo Grandma Ruth showed me of him in his orckin form.

He was huge, grey, an orc, and, well, *old*, but he had the same harsh manly planes to his face, his nose still slightly crooked from a mishap with a goat, his beard streaked with grey. He wore fancy regalia, a tunic the color of the California surf, dark wool leggings, and thick hide boots, all embroidered and trimmed in fur. Grandpa Thorn was fancy snazzy pants. And he was *alive*.

I staggered as the realization that he was actually alive sucker punched me in the chest. Relief and joy warred within me. The ache of his presence filled that hollow space in my heart. And it *hurt*.

Oh, *Grandma Ruth.*

She'd been right all along. He hadn't drowned. He'd left us, left *her.* My Grandma Ruth had never been the same afterward. She'd never taken a lover after that, either. Like a mourning dove who'd lost her mate. A bitterness over my grandmother's grief tainted the joy of seeing him again.

"Do I know you, lass?" He asked, his brows creased in confusion. As if I looked familiar to him, but he couldn't place me.

"It's me!" I cried, throwing a hand over my heart. I laughed as tears choked me. "Your little chestnut!"

"Amelia." Grandpa Thorn whispered my name, face gone pale, and before I could sob again, he pulled me up into his arms and swung me around the hallway, bawling into my hair. I clung to him and sobbed into his shoulder. His familiar scent soothed the jagged edges of my emotions.

When he set me gently to the ground, he tenderly pulled away and began brushing my wavy hair away from my wet cheeks with his enormous paws. I held his forearms clutched in my tiny clawed hands and sobbed hard. The old wound of loss lanced and cleansed with my tears.

"I missed you so much, Grandpa!" I wailed.

"Och, my little chestnut, I missed you too! Where's Ruth? Where's your grandmother, your mother? How did you get here?" He asked me, questions rushing from him like a flood as he looked beyond me as if searching for them. His brow creased in confusion as he took in the empty hallway behind me before looking down at me, eyes imploring me to tell him where our loved ones were.

"They're still back on Earth. I'm the only one who made it through the gate." I whispered.

My mountain of a grandfather swayed as if mortally struck. Devastation carved itself deep into his beloved, yet alien, face. I steadied him by gripping his forearms again. He looked at me with eyes gone hollow.

"Are they well? Happy?" He croaked. My heart bled for him.

"Mom and dad divorced, but they're much better off and happy. I got married and am getting a divorce." I swallowed, debating whether to tell him more about my situation. Deciding it could wait, I offered him a weak smile and continued. "Grandma's still feisty as ever, still running Orc Rock Farm. Still waiting for you to come home."

Grandpa took a deep, shaking breath, and tears spilled over his lashes. "She... she stayed true? All this time?"

"Of course she has. She's always loved you something fierce." I said with absolute conviction. Then I paused and met his gaze. "And you?"

I grew up watching my grandparents like they were the epitome of a fairy tale romance. Inseparable, doting, enduring, true. I already had my fairy tale ending shattered by a mockery, a dastardly sham, of what I always thought love was. If my grandfather hadn't been true to my grandmother, then... all hope for love was truly gone.

"Always." He said with feeling around the lump of emotion in his throat. "She is my cridhe and I have not had nor will I have another. I haven't been whole since I left all those years ago."

Relief was a trapped kaleidoscope of butterflies behind my rib cage. There was a heavy silence as we stood together in the grand hallway. The gathered orckin and Rhuger attempted to provide us with what privacy they could by looking elsewhere.

"Why? Why did you leave, Grandpa?" I asked, voice cracking. "We thought you died!" I sobbed. Suddenly I was just a kid again, finding out my grandpa was gone.

He rumbled something in that language and swept me back up into a crushing embrace. He just held me and rocked me as I cried it out. After a few moments, my blubbering faded and Grandpa Thorn set me back down on my feet. He pushed back my waves and brushed away my tears as they continued to spill from my eyes.

"I'm so sorry, chestnut." His voice was a desperate, pained rasp. "I would have come back to you if I could."

"Bullshit!" I choked, my indignation riding high.

"It's true, Amelia. Please allow me to explain. Just not here." His face was so grave, etched with sorrow. "Come with me to my study. I need to hear more about our family, too. There's a lot for us to catch up on."

I nodded shakily and my Grandpa Thorn... *Rìgh* Thorn turned to the small knot of orcs who waited patiently for their Rìgh. His bearing changed from doting grandfather to absolute power in the blink of an eye.

"We will continue our discussion once I've finished with my granddaughter." He said, voice commanding.

"But, my Rìgh..." One orc pleaded. He was well-dressed and, I assumed, was some sort of advisor. He looked at me with more interest than I was comfortable with.

"It can *wait*." Grandpa Thorn said, his tone forbidding as his gaze bored into that of his advisor.

"Yes, my Rìgh." He replied with a dip of his head. He and the other gathered orcs bustled off down the hallway, murmuring to one another and casting glances over their shoulders.

"Alright, chestnut, let's go get settled in my study and catch up, hm?" He asked softly, returning to my loving grandfather once again as he wrapped an arm around my shoulder. The man... Orc... Was giving me whiplash with how he switched between his two personas. His copper and onyx gaze flicked up to where Rhuger stood behind me. "What do you want, Oc'Turin?"

"He's my bodyguard, Grandpa," I said, and he jerked in surprise.

"Fear a Chì Ruksala appointed me." Rhuger explained, stepping forward.

"She did, did she?" Grandpa asked dryly. There was a pause as they looked at one another over my head. "Well, come along, Oc'Turin. I'd like to hear how you came to be my precious granddaughter's bodyguard."

Grandpa's voice held an edge to it that I couldn't place. Why would it be bad that Rhuger was my bodyguard? Grandpa Thorn steered me down the hallway and up a flight of broad stone stairs to the second floor. Rhuger kept pace behind us as we rounded a corner and approached a set of thick wooden double doors. They were carved with the lovely motif of the Craobh na Beatha, an echo of the gate I'd passed through. My grandfather had passed through.

Rhuger stepped around us and opened the door. I tried to catch his eye, but he had his gaze aimed downward in respect as my giant of a grandfather ushered me into the study. I looked around as Grandpa Thorn moved to his desk and Rhuger closed the double doors behind us, offering us privacy.

The room was big, with an enormous stone fireplace that was tall enough that I could step into it without hitting my head. Bookshelves made of lovely purple-hued wood lined the walls. Filled with leather-bound books, scrolls, knickknacks, and weapons. Where there were no shelves, tapestries hung to help stave off the cold. Comfortable-looking chairs were scattered around the place, along with tables laden with more books and maps.

Glancing down at the top of the nearest table, I noticed something that looked familiar. I picked it up, the vellum thick and durable, and smiled. It was a map of Orc Rock Farm.

"It took a while to get the map right." Grandpa Thorn said from behind me, voice thick.

"You did a great job. It looks perfect." I smiled at him and he looked like he was about to cry. "Oh, Grandpa, it's okay," I said, putting the map of his home back and going to him, arms wide.

"I can't believe you're here." Grandpa Thorn mumbled as we hugged. He pulled away, holding me at arm's length, his eyes glassy with unshed tears. "You look just like your mom. Like Ruth."

Oh, *Grandpa...*

"Now, you'll have to forgive this old orc. Please tell me how you got here. What happened?"

So I told him. I started by telling him about leaving my ex-husband, driving across the country, staying with Granda Ruth, and her showing me the sea cave. Of my finding the missing crystal acorn, of putting it in the divot. And having the gate come alive at my touch.

Then I shifted the tale to arriving on Talam, of Rhuger finding me moments after I'd eaten Talam dirt. And then of that womb-splitter-sized orc, Rhuger's swift action and our sprint to safety. Grandpa Thorn had frowned then, his copper gaze sliding to Rhuger where he stood nearby, leaning against the wall.

"We stayed at the gàrradh and the traveler's cave," Rhuger said, taking on the mantle of the story. "There's something you should know if you haven't been informed already." That caught my grandfather's attention, and he turned to give Rhuger the full bore of his regard and Rhuger pushed off the wall to stand tall before him. "The dorcha'aon are back."

"What?" Grandpa Thorn asked, voice deep and soft, even as I saw his hand shake before he fisted it at his side. "Are you sure?"

"Och. I stood watch while Amelia slept at the gàrradh. I heard them calling to one another in the night, like steel on stone. Then one came out into the clearing. Stared me down before running off after likelier prey." Rhuger explained. "I saw its six glowing eyes. Saw the tracks raked into the earth in the morning."

"Why wasn't I informed immediately upon my return?" Grandpa Thorn slipped back into Rìgh Thorn, his commanding tone skittering across my skin.

"I'm not sure, my Rìgh," Rhuger replied, thrown off. "I informed the guard as we entered Baile Coille."

Grandpa Thorn grunted and ran a hand over his mustache and beard. He looked down at me and, I swear, I saw fear flicker there before he turned back to Rhuger. Was he afraid for me?

"What else?" He asked, striding to his desk and taking a seat behind it.

"I brought Amelia to Ruksala in your absence. Ruksala appointed me her guard. She commanded me to ready my home tree for Amelia to stay, so I did while they spoke." Rhuger paused for a moment, taking a deep breath. Even as my grandfather eyeballed him like he wanted to skin him alive. "Tintain, an orckin of the Oc'Dellor, entered Amelia's home tree and attempted to force a mate bond with her."

"What!!" Grandpa Thorn roared, getting to his feet and knocking his chair back in a clattering crash. Startled, my shoulders tightened up towards my ears.

"He was dealt with, Rìgh Thorn. His corpse now hangs from the Craobh Brathaidh" It seemed to mollify my grandfather, who began to pace in front of the fireplace.

"I saw there was a new corpse. Was it you who dispatched him?"

"Yes, my Rìgh."

"And how was it that you were at my granddaughter's home?" Grandpa Thorn snarled.

"I was posted outside in my hammock. Hifasa was at the base of the tree." Rhuger explained, hands still clasped behind his back, spine straight, but body language resigned to whatever punishment my grandfather would dole out.

"And you did this, took on this task, without knowing who she was?"

"Yes."

"Why?"

"I was the one who found her in the cave by the Craobh na Beatha. She was alone and an Oc'Turin scout nearly had us. I felt it was my responsibility to continue to protect her until your return."

"And you sought nothing for yourself?"

The silence stretched between them, thick with a history I couldn't comprehend.

"Your ways are the right path forward, Rìgh Thorn. I don't pretend that I'm owed anything, least of all from a female." Rhuger's tone was self-deprecating, yet stark with honesty.

"Grandpa..." I ventured. Both males turned to look at me. "Rhuger's saved me twice now. He has sought nothing from me. Has done more than I could hope for regarding my well-being. He spared me from..." I swallowed hard. "From re-living the most horrible event in my life. He has my fervent gratitude."

There was a pregnant silence as both my grandpa and my

bodyguard took in that information. Grandpa Thorn took a deep breath, and a deadly surety settled into his stance. As if he were preparing himself for battle. He opened his mouth to say something when Rhuger spoke first.

"Who hurt you?" The words hissed out from between Rhuger's teeth like a quenching sword.

I looked at him, our gazes joining. The orc, who was so easy-going, so flirtatious, and in control, was practically vibrating with rage. It was clear the leash he kept on himself was close to snapping. I should have been afraid, terrified of his reaction. Instead, a sense of safety I'd never known wrapped around me like a blanket. He truly meant that he'd protect me from *anything. Including* my past.

"Who did such an unspeakable thing to you, my pearl? Tell me and I will destroy them and burn their world to ash." He growled, baring his teeth. Grandpa Thorn jerked his head to look at Rhuger with a scowl. When I didn't respond, Rhuger strode to where I sat, frozen, and gently grabbed my chin, tilting my face up to look at him. "I need you to use your words, pearl. Who?"

I gulped and tried not to react to the feel of his fingers on my chin, his nearness, and the molten intensity of his gaze as it bored into mine. The pure overwhelming power and masculinity poured off of him in waves, cascading over me as surely as his scent did. His face was so close that I could have kissed him. I wanted to kiss him.

"Adam." I rasped. "My ex-husband."

Those three words dropped into the radiating rage rolling off of Rhuger and my grandfather like stones into a deep well. Rhuger hissed and released my chin in a gentle caress before standing tall again. He broke our gaze and turned to stand before my grandfather. Their eyes locked, two powerful males sharing an unspoken understanding.

"If the Geata is ever fixed, I request the right to hunt this Adam and bring him back here to face justice at the Craobh Brathaidh. To string him up alongside Tintain. His crimes hung from his neck for all to see. His malehood impaled on his forehead with my knife." Rhuger near-snarled into the quiet, only interrupted by the shifting sunstones in the fireplace. Grandpa Thorn looked Rhuger over with a cold, assessing eye.

"Are you asking as a bodyguard or as a Leanabh Rìgh?" Grandpa Thorn's tone was regal, power incarnate. I did not know what a Leanabh Rìgh was.

"Does it matter?" Rhuger bit out fiercely, fists clenching at his sides. "I've already dispatched one male who thought to harm your granddaughter. I've proven myself to you countless times. For all the time I've spent with the Oc'Dellor at your discretion, I've rarely asked for anything." Rhuger let out a ragged breath, his posture releasing the rage that had a death grip on him. "I ask for this."

Grandpa Thorn squinted in thought and stroked his beard. Dragging out the heavy quiet as he made a show of contemplating the situation. I knew from experience that he'd already decided. But whether he'd reveal his decision or not, was another thing entirely.

"I shall think about this. And your request." He said, and I saw Rhuger's hands twitch in response. "Your last few days have been quite busy. You've earned yourself some time off. You're dismissed for the time being, though I expect you to be back at her home tree by moonrise."

"But, Rìgh Thorn—" Rhuger began, but my grandpa held up a hand.

"She's well guarded here with me, Oc'Turin. I'll honor Ruksala's decree for your role as Amelia's bodyguard. But I also desire a few hours alone with my granddaughter."

Rhuger paused and thought about it for a moment before giving him a nod and a curt bow. He turned to me then, gaze shuttered.

"I'll see you back at your home tree, pearl." Rhuger dipped his head, gaze smoldering with more than just rage before he turned on his heel and strode for the door. He closed it behind him so quietly it was alarming.

Grandpa Thorn turned his attention from the study door before releasing a breath. His shoulders slumped. That mantle of power slipped from him and he looked at me with such anguish in his expression.

"I'm so sorry, chestnut." He whispered. "I'm sorry I wasn't there to protect you."

Pressing my mouth into a thin line, trying to hold back the sudden sob that had lodged itself in my throat. I nodded, sniffing and holding back my tears with sheer willpower. I'd cried my last over my ex-husband. Over the husk of a woman he'd made me into.

"You should stay here in Daingneach. I'll get rooms ready for you and have your things moved. You'll be well protected here and I'll be close by." Grandpa Thorn said, recanting his previous acceptance of me staying in Rhuger's home tree. He nodded to himself and strode for the door.

"Wait!" I cried, holding out a hand. He stopped and looked at me. "Please. Don't."

"Why not, chestnut? I want you to be safe, and the safest place for you is with me."

"Because..." I began, casting about in my mind for all the reasons why my living in the keep was a bad idea. "Because you know I can't cope with a lot of noise. And Daingneach is always bustling, right? Rhuger's home tree is quiet and I love it. Grammy Ruksala put me in Rhuger's care for a reason, right? Had him prep his own home for me to stay in, right? And he's done his duty already. I know I'm safe there. And I'm a grown woman now. I should be allowed to make my own choice in this."

Grandpa Thorn looked at me for a long minute, assessing. He finally knocked his head back, sighed, and rubbed his face. I knew I'd won when he looked at me again, a wry smile on his mouth that curved his beard.

"Chestnut. You still know how to argue like your mom and grandma, huh?" He chuckled.

"It's why mom makes such a talented attorney, isn't it?" I replied.

"I want you to have the choices you can have here. You're right that Ruksala must have put you in Rhuger's care for a reason. I've always trusted in her visions and as *uncomfortable* as I am to have you live in the Oc'Turin's home tree with him just outside your door... He *has* proven to be trustworthy with your care." He sighed again. "If this happens again, if you've been put in danger like that again, I'm going to pluck you from that home tree and sequester you here in the keep myself. You are my granddaughter and it's been so long since I've been able to protect you."

"I know. Thank you, Grandpa. Can you tell me why you left? What happened?" I asked shakily. Desperate for a change of subject. I'd won for now, but Grandpa Thorn was notorious for talking himself back into something if left to ramble for too long. He pulled a cord along the wall. In mere moments, a servant appeared in the doorway.

"Bring in something for us to eat and drink." He told the servant, who nodded and left, closing the door behind him.

Grandpa Thorn waited where he stood by his desk. Staring at nothing as a heavy silence blanketed us. The servant returned a few minutes later with a tray of food and a pitcher with two cups. They set it on the low table near me and left on quiet feet, closing the door behind them. Finally alone, I waited for my grandfather's answer.

"I can." He sighed as he sat opposite me in the matching leather chair. We both settled in before he continued. "The night I left, I'd had a terrible dream. One I can only remember in bits and pieces. It was a dream similar to the one I had before I went through the Geata and met your grandmother. But this one... It was filled with fire and gnashing teeth. And screams."

Grandpa Thorn looked shaken, his face paling as his mouth flattened into a harsh line. I frowned. Very little ever rattled my grandfather and his words tasted of truth. The dream had been terrifying. He shook his head as if banishing the memories of it. He reached over and grasped the pitcher, filling a cup with a green liquid before handing it to me. I took it but didn't drink it as I watched him pour himself a cup and down it in two long gulps. He sighed, glanced at me, and refilled his cup.

"It's like wine." He explained, lifting his cup. Taking a hesitant sip, I found he was right. It was like wine but more floral with an aftertaste similar to peaches. It was good. I took a long drought of it, feeling the hint of alcohol burn its way down my throat.

"So the dream?" I prompted him.

"Yes. The dream." He murmured. "I've had dreams that have told the truth. Been prophetic. It must be a gift from my mother, Ruksala."

"Wait, Ruksala is your mother?" I asked, confused.

"Yes. She's your great-grandmother." Grandpa Thorn said with a hint of a smile. "Quite the handful, isn't she?"

I just nodded mutely. I hadn't considered that I'd find more family here on Talam than just my grandfather. Gods, it was a lot to take in.

"I was afraid," Grandpa said, staring off at nothing. "I knew I had to go to the gate. Ruth tried to stop me, tried to ask me what was wrong. But I wasn't even sure myself. How could I explain it to her?" He nursed his cup as if seeking courage from the burn of alcohol. "When I reached the Geata, the tide was already filling the cavern. I'd reached the Geata when I heard Ruth calling to me. I touched the gate, and it opened and pulled me through. But not before I saw the heartbreak on her face as she fought the tide. Fought to get to me. I realized too late what I was leaving behind. Who I was leaving behind."

There was a long silence as I absorbed his tale and he refilled his cup. I absently drank more and grabbed some of the food on the plate, fruit, something similar to cheese, and bread. Simple fare and blessedly familiar. I ate a vamp cherry, its tart juice jarring me awake from my stupor.

"I should have waited for her to reach me. I should have brought her here with me. But in the end, it was a boon that she didn't, och? I waited at the gate for her to come through. I waited longer than I should have. Eventually, I left." He took another long pull from his cup. His gaze, when it met mine, was full of anguish, bright with unshed tears. "When I arrived here at Baile Coille, it was to discover that my father had died fighting the dorcha'aon soon after I'd left, succumbing to his wounds and the an'sgudal. That my mother, Ruksala, had taken over command as Banrigh until either I returned or she passed. No one argued her reign.

"The an'sgudal had just swept through Baile Coille once again. And I arrived to the burning pyres of the dead, staining the sky an oily black. The dorcha'aon hadn't arrived this time. No one knew why, but it was a blessed relief. As was seeing my mother alive and well, if not full of sorrow. But that relief was short-lived." He rasped, his mouth flattening into a white line as he wrestled with his ghosts. "I'd just taken over as Rìgh of the Oc'Dellor when the outlying villages started getting raided. Their females and orclings were taken. So everyone rushed to Baile Coille for safety. The Oc'Turin were to blame. They'd made a pact with the Oc'Blyre to take those who were ours. It was years of fighting against them. The Rìgh of the Oc'Turin finally fell to the keen edge of my sword through his neck just a few years past. His despot son, Orok, took his place."

He paused then. Sighing heavily and looking into the flames that flickered in the fireplace. I waited, giving him the space and time he needed to process. To find his words.

"There has been peace since, as Orok still works to fill the power vacuum left behind by his father. The Oc'Blyre returned to their mountains and I've worked to rebuild our clan ever since. Worked to ensure that everyone is cared for and that our females are honored as they should be. Our numbers have swelled over the last few years, and I'm glad I've been able to do some good in all of this."

I reached across the space between us and placed my hand on the back of his where his scarred knuckles were pale grey from how hard he was gripping the armrest. His copper gaze snapped to mine even as his hand relaxed its death grip on the chair. Grandpa Thorn released a breath and cupped my face in one of his massive hands.

"I am so happy to see you, chestnut." He whispered. "I'd lost hope of ever seeing my family again."

"I've missed you." My voice cracked around the words. "I'm so sorry you endured so much since you got here. I wish I could have helped you."

"Och, no. I'm glad you were away on Earth. Safe from all of this." He gave my cheek a gentle pat before replacing it on his thigh. "I'm sorry I couldn't be there for you when you needed me most. You deserved far better than you got."

"Well, I'm here now. And Rhuger has done a good job of protecting me." Grandpa scoffed at that and scowled. "You don't like him, do you?"

"I don't have to like him." He grumped, and I wondered at the history that obviously hung between them.

"True. Still. I'm here now. You're not alone anymore."

"Oh, chestnut. Such a sweet lass, wanting to look after your grandfather, och?" He smiled and patted my hand, copper eyes warm and soft.

"It's my life's greatest joy to look after my family," I replied with a grin, repeating his old adage. He chuckled at that and we spent the next few hours talking about our family and what had happened over the last two decades.

CHAPTER 22*

RHUGER

With Rìgh Thorn's dismissal, I left Amelia in the capable hands of her grandfather and his guards. I was exhausted. But I was also restless. The leash of control I had on my instincts was so taut that one more irritation would cause it to snap. Source help whoever stood in my way then. With heavy steps, I made my way toward the training yards. If my mind wouldn't shut off, if I couldn't release this blistering anger, I'd have to work my body until I could.

The hatred I'd experienced when Tintain had touched Amelia was *nothing* compared to what churned and roiled under my skin. Fury at what she'd endured coiled in my stomach like a wyrm preparing to strike. The loathsome creature named Adam, her *ex-husband*, should have cherished her and protected her. Instead, he'd committed one of the *vilest* acts against her. Violated her body, her love, and her trust.

I hoped Rìgh Thorn said yes to my request. My instincts raged for vengeance on her behalf.

Uther was still in the training yard, even so late. The Master of Arms had decades of fighting experience. He'd led countless skirmishes against the other clans who sought to either steal our resources or our females. He was as honorable as they came and a brilliant teacher.

"Och, Rhuger, what are you doing here?" Uther called from where he stood by a rack of weapons, inspecting them. "Did the Neamhnaid tire of you already?"

"She's with her grandfather, Rìgh Thorn," I replied as I neared the rack of weapons.

"She's Rìgh Thorn's granddaughter?" Uther was shaken, surprised.

"Amelia is from the human lands past the Geata," I explained briefly. Uther was one of the few orcs I could trust with such information and one of Rìgh Thorn's councilors. If I didn't tell him, Rìgh Thorn would. "I found her and brought her here—evidently she passed through the Geata."

"So Rìgh Thorn was a little busier on the other side of the gate than he let on," Uther smirked, his deeply scarred face twisting slightly. He wasn't ugly by any stretch, but his scars often repelled most. His late mate Isa had seen past them and gifted him Nashton before she passed. The little orcling was strapped to Uther's back in a small harness, fast asleep.

"Mmh." I plucked a bow from a rack and tested the draw. The pull in my back as I drew the string tight felt good. Deciding that archery could help push away thoughts of Amelia, and could ease the burn of my anger, I grabbed a bucket full of arrows and headed over to the archery range.

"So why are you here instead of waiting for the lass?" Uther asked. "Aren't you still her guard?"

As much as I cared for Uther, I was trying *not* to think of the sweet female. Irritation flared, so close to my half-contained fury, and I had to fight not to bark at my friend.

"Och. Rìgh Thorn dismissed me for the time being and stated he'd send her back to her home tree with a guard. He gave me time off." I viciously whipped an arrow from the bucket, notched it, and sent it flying. It hit dead center.

"You mean to *your* home tree? Sigg told me about how you *gave* her your house instead of having her stay with the other females in their dormitory." Uther's cocked eyebrow made me see red. I'd never shown an interest in the females here at Oc'Dellor. Too many memories of my time at Oc'Turin kept me from finding interest in anyone. Now that Amelia had shown up and had invaded every pore of me with her sweet scent, I wasn't getting any peace from my friends.

"Damn Sigg! Look, Uther, I'm trying to forget about her, och? Yes, I gave her my house to use as she wishes until she decides what to do. I thought she'd appreciate privacy, and the dormitory is a far cry from that. She's beyond my grasp, och? I am an exile and I've sworn to protect her." I snarled at Uther while trying not to shout and wake Nashton.

"She's already gotten under your skin, wormed her way into your heart, hasn't she?" Uther asked quietly. I didn't need to reply to that. But I did sneer at him. He just grinned and unslung Nashton from his back, cradling the orcling to his chest.

Uther sat nearby with his tiny son while I released arrow after arrow into the target downrange. I grasped arrows one at a time, grasped them by the handfuls, and shot multiple arrows at once. All of them hit the target where I wanted them to land. But no matter how many arrows I shot, how much my back and shoulders and core screamed in protest at the exertion, I still couldn't get Amelia's uisge-beatha eyes and bowed mouth from my mind.

Every time I pulled the bowstring, the curve of my bow mimicked her lips. How they'd move when she spoke. Reminding me of all the conversations we'd shared, the laughter, and the light over the last few days. And the wicked little pink tongue that lay behind her blunted teeth.

Eventually, I stopped shooting and stood, breathing heavily and pouring sweat as I stared downrange. The target was bristling with arrows, some split or shattered by their fellows. My rage had quieted to sparking embers, finally. But the space the rage had occupied had been flooded with the female who drove me to madness.

Her scent had ripened into arousal when I'd gripped her chin in Rìgh Thorn's study. When I'd demanded who caused her pain. Her lack of fear at seeing my rage baffled me. Did she not see how dangerous I could be with these intense emotions I could barely harness? While she could smother hers with a mask, all I could do was find an outlet, *any* outlet, lest I destroy everything in my path.

"Still can't get her out of your mind, och?" Uther asked. I grunted my assent. "Go bathe and try to get some sleep. You don't want to reek when she comes back to your house. I'll take care of the targets. You're dead on your feet, anyway."

Head hanging, I gripped my friend's forearm before plodding my way toward the baths near the cliffs. The baths were inside a cave system that had been carved and molded over the centuries. There were steam rooms, hot and cold baths fed with water from different springs, stairs and lounging areas within the water and without, and even drainage to ensure the water stayed clean for the bathers.

Trudging inside, there was no one to be seen. So I wearily pulled off my clothing and tossed them in a pile nearby before stepping down into the hot water. Steam wafted from the surface and I sighed as the heat from the water soothed my sore muscles.

I dunked myself under the water and stood in a rush, water running from my skin in tiny waterfalls. Pulling my hair free from its braid, I grabbed some soap and worked up a good lather before I washed my hair and body. Once I'd rinsed myself off, I returned to the steps and sat in the quiet. Only the sounds of running water broke the stillness.

Alone in the baths proved to be worse for my mind than being in Amelia's presence. Because now it was just me alone with my thoughts and a raging erection. Sitting on the stairs at the far end of the baths, water shallow around my hips, I grimaced down at my groin.

I'd rarely been soft since I'd found her in the Craobh na Beatha cave days ago. She'd been so plump and disheveled and strange. Skin as luminescent as a neamhnaid, eyes the color of the harsh spirit we drank with a tongue small and pink and lovely.

Her scent had branded itself into my mind. I couldn't breathe enough of it in. It had been the most trying thing to keep from burying my nose in her neck every time she was near. And when her scent changed, deepened, turned immeasurably sweeter when she was aroused...

Snarling, I took my shaft in hand and gripped it hard. Slick was already sluicing down my cock to drift away in the water. With a twist of my wrist over the head, I took the slick and spread it over my twitching, swollen dick. My knot, the bulge halfway down my shaft, ached sharply. It was so full of seed I felt like I'd burst. Throwing my head back, I pumped my fist.

I'd never been with a female, only males. The only one I nearly mated with had chosen another in the end—so I didn't know what it would feel like. But that didn't stop my mind from conjuring up Amelia.

What she'd looked like drenched from the stream, that strange delicate garment under her shirt and how it cupped her rounded breasts. How she'd looked in my vest—all softness and curves and plump flesh—the laces barely containing her chest. What her face looked like as she caught me sating myself that night, her scent drenching my vest as I'd bit it, wishing it was her skin that gave way beneath my teeth instead of leather. I'd stood naked before her—showed her my body and cock—what I could do for her if she'd wanted. The scent of her arousal as it perfumed the air had sent me over the edge, cock spurting harder than I'd thought possible.

And since we'd gotten to Baile Coille? The female was an absolute menace. Answering the door in nothing but my tunic. That devastating hug I'd trade all my beads for. Those tiny touches that shook me to my core and left me wanting more.

When I'd slung her over my shoulder at the market to get her to safety, I'd grasped her thigh just below her ass. A small sin. And one that was rewarded with her ripe arousal right under my nose. I'd threatened to spank her like a misbehaving orcling and her body had responded so strongly that I'd nearly come undone with the need to plant myself inside of her.

My memories merged with the present and I looked down at my cock, pre-cum slickening my fist as I stroked it. Anyone coming to the baths would hear the obscene noises I made, but I was beyond caring. My mind was too full of Amelia and what she'd look like naked here in the baths with me. What that strange undergarment hid from view. How the water would cascade down her lush curves. What she'd feel like with her thighs wrapped around my hips, my dick buried inside of her.

Thoughts of her in my arms as I carried her to safety, the knowledge that she lived in *my* house and slept in *my* bed all blurred into a fierce need to have her be MINE. *My mate.* Pumping my cock harder, my hips jerked as I felt myself closing in on release.

Breathing ragged, I moaned as I imagined what her cunt would feel like as she came from my touch, coming undone beneath me as I took her in every way. I squeezed down hard, pretending it was her cunt, and roared. Cum shot out of my crown in thick ropes, plopping into the water. Panting as I came down from release, I watched my spend as it swirled away towards the drains that kept the baths full of hot, clean water.

And like before, my erection barely softened.

I swore to myself then and there. If I ever gained her favor and she invited me—an exile and from a rival clan—into her bed, I'd leave her the most satisfied female on Talam.

My cock refused to do otherwise, and so did I.

CHAPTER 23

AMELIA

Late that night, I couldn't sleep. I'd tossed and turned in my bed and couldn't seem to get comfortable. My mind wouldn't shut off either, too filled with the truths I'd learned. Too full of all that had happened, I decided to see if Rhuger was awake. Maybe he'd be able to keep me company. Tell me a story or two until I got sleepy.

I got up from the bed and walked to the door, snagging a shawl from the peg by the doorway and wrapping it around my shoulders before stepping outside. The sunstone lanterns were faint, having faded with the deepening night. Rhuger was asleep in his hammock, swinging in the evening breeze.

Approaching him, I couldn't help but smile at how he sprawled in the hammock. Legs splayed, one arm flung up over his head, eyelashes sinfully long against his cheeks as he snored softly. I noticed his hand fisted something near his face. Leaning over him, I noticed it was his old tunic that I'd worn. He was using it as a pillow; the fabric scrunched close to his nose.

"I guess you really like how I smell..." I murmured, bemused. There'd been a bottle of perfume I'd admired in the market waiting for me when I got back. I'd thought maybe I didn't smell nice, that it was a polite way of telling me I had B.O., but seeing Rhuger like this? Made me wonder if it was the opposite.

My smile dropped as I gazed at him. He was so handsome it hurt. Rhuger's features were soft with sleep and it took all I had to only push back a strand of loose hair from his face instead of kissing him.

I didn't know how he'd take it if I kissed him, and I hadn't asked permission.

Didn't negate how badly the urge hit me, though. I couldn't remember a time when I'd wanted to kiss anyone as badly as I wanted to kiss Rhuger. I knew I was catching feelings for him and no matter how hard I tried to just be friends; it kept slipping from my fingers.

I didn't know what drew me to him so inevitably. Why I reacted like this to only him and none of the other male orcs I'd met. It was like my heart, mind, and body didn't belong to me anymore. They were all his. And I wasn't sure how to proceed.

I didn't want to be any more of a burden to him than I already was.

I made to move back towards the door when his hand shot out and grasped mine in his sleep. Startled, I froze, my heart thundering in my chest like a storm.

"'melia..." He mumbled in his sleep, face nuzzling deeper into the tunic.

Fuck.

My heart nearly tore in half. A part of me desperately wanted to climb into that hammock with him. To have him wrap his arms around me and nuzzle against my neck. To feel safe for once as I slept tangled up with him.

I knew I was already lost. And so damnably lonely. But I

wouldn't invade his space without his consent. That wasn't right.

So I squeezed his hand, ignoring the impulse to kiss his scarred knuckles, and let go. He frowned in his sleep. I retreated to the door and slipped inside before I lost my control.

What the hell was happening to me? I'd never responded to anyone so strongly before. A jumble of emotions, I crawled back into bed and hoped sleep found me quickly.

"Good morning!" I called as I came outside. I'd risen early, only managing a few hours of sleep, but I was still full of energy. Rhuger was busy lacing his boots, and he shot me a small smile.

"Good morning. Did you sleep well?"

"Nope! Hardly slept at all."

"I'm so sorry. Any reason?" He asked, concerned. So stinking cute.

"No, it just happens sometimes." I shrugged. Then I grinned. "So, care to tell me how you can keep watch while sleeping?"

"What do you mean?" He frowned as he finished tying his boot and stood.

"Well, I came outside last night to check on you since I couldn't sleep, and I found you with the tunic I'd worn shoved in your face," I explained. Rhuger flushed a bright green that stained his neck, all the way down his tattooed shoulders. He mumbled something under his breath about 'scent' and refused to look at me.

"What was that? I only heard the word 'scent'?" I asked, confused. Rhuger cleared his throat and looked me in the eye once more, the bright green still riding high on his cheeks.

"We can smell more than just emotions, pearl. People have scents, and we're able to differentiate between them. So, any scent that wasn't mine, Hifasa's, or yours, I would notice and wake up. It was part of my training. And it's how I caught Tintain." A tick worked in Rhuger's jaw.

"Oh, so is that why you were using the tunic I'd worn as a pillow?" I asked. Rhuger went stock still and his eyes widened slightly. He looked like he was internally screaming and I had to hold back a laugh.

"Yes." came his strangled reply.

"Okay," I said, a small smile fluttering at the corners of my mouth. "Well, should we go get some breakfast? I don't know about you, but I'm starving!" I strode down the stairs, my soft leather boots making little noise as I descended. When I got to the base of the stairs, I looked up at Rhuger, who still stood there, as if stunned. I called up to him, "Are you coming?"

"Yes." He said hurriedly and strapped on his swords and axe. His long sword he left leaning against the house, as always. It seemed he only took it when he left Baile Coille, as the only time he wore it was when he'd found me. But he did snag his bow and quiver, putting them over his shoulder and across his body. Rhuger took the steps two at a time, meeting me stride for stride as I started walking toward the kitchens.

As was our habit, we fell into a companionable silence. I could tell Rhuger wanted to say something but figured I'd wait until he was ready to tell me. He proved me right as we strode amongst the home trees on the outskirts of the city center.

"About yesterday..." Rhuger began, and I jerked to a halt, memories hitting me like a wave. He stopped near me and I held my breath while I waited for him to finish. Terrified of what he thought. Of me. Of the remnants of who I'd been before Adam had broken me. Swallowing hard, I faced him. "... I wanted to apologize for my anger. I didn't intend to frighten you."

"You didn't," I replied in surprise, releasing my pent-up breath. Rhuger looked confused for a moment before nodding.

"I'm glad." He sighed heavily and ran a hand along his braid, looking me dead in the eye. "I can't tell you how sorry I am that you endured what you did."

Startled, I frowned at him. "Wait... Aren't I..." I began, trailing off before shaking my head and forging on. "Don't you see me as damaged goods now?"

It was like I'd slapped him in the face with a giant salmon. A look of horror suffused his features before a fierce scowl took its place. He stalked toward me, a predatory cadence to his steps. Rhuger grasped my chin gently and lifted it so I couldn't avoid his gaze. An echo of yesterday. Of his protective rage, and how it'd made me feel safe and turned on all at once. A fluttering began low in my belly at the memory and the rough tenderness of his touch as his thumb caressed the underside of my bottom lip.

"I will only say this once. So I need you to listen to me. To hear my words and understand them for the truth they are. Do you understand, my pearl?" He growled into the space between us. I nodded, too caught up in his scent and his nearness to form words. "I need you to say it."

"Yes." I breathed, a throbbing beginning in my core. Fuck, him saying such things turned me into a swooning mess. His gaze never wavered as he took a deep breath that suddenly hitched and stuttered in his chest. Rhuger froze, and I watched in fascination as his pupils blew out, turning the molten silver of his irises into thin rings of eclipsed suns.

"Good little pearl." He growled, his tone gone deep and sultry. I swear to all the gods, my pussy quivered and pulsed at his words as wetness flooded my panties. *Shit.* Rhuger visibly struggled to regain control, and when he did, he continued. "Hear me now, pearl. You are a person, not an object, not *goods, a person.* What you endured does *not* define you. Only *you* get to decide that. *He* does not get to dictate your worth, your value, as a person. He harmed you, but you are not damaged, not broken, only unaware of your own healing from the vicious wounds he left you with. Do you understand? Do not let him win."

I released a shaky breath as his words settled into my bones. Into the deep wound in my chest that Adam had struck with his words, his neglect, his gaslighting, his abuse over and over and over again until he'd laid my spine bare. Until my heart bled out, leaving me a hopeless husk. Until I'd somehow found the courage to leave.

Rhuger's nuggets of truth, understanding, and perspective eased into that wounded place like pure light, re-aligning my mindset. Softening those jagged edges that were slowly healing. Supporting the tangled wildwood my heart had become.

I would always carry those dark memories with me. It had happened *to* me; it *was not* me. A knowing settled over my shoulders, then. One that told me that the more positive memories I put between then and now, the duller the pain would be. The easier it would be to bring those two halves of myself back together, to stitch the wound closed and watch it turn into a scar.

"I understand," I whispered, the words slipping from my lips like quiet victories.

"Good lass." He murmured in reply. A proud smile bloomed on his mouth as he released my chin. I felt his touch as a ghostly echo against my skin as it slipped away. "Now, shall we go get some breakfast?"

"Sure." I coughed, trying to rein in my hormones and the sudden urge to cry. I followed Rhuger onto the winding streets of Baile Coille and held my head high. As if he hadn't just altered my entire world. As if he hadn't left me reeling from his touch.

Rhuger saw me. And that truth sang in my healing heart like the most brilliant of symphonies.

"What's going on?" I asked Sharn as we arrived at the kitchens. She looked exhausted as she shoved two bowls of the usual mash to us.

"Well, Rìgh Thorn requested we prepare a feast in your honor tonight." She smirked and winked at me.

"What!" I cried. "No, I don't want anything like that!"

"Too late!" Sharn laughed. "Everyone's excited about it. We love a party, us Oc'Dellor. There's going to be feasting and singing and dancing."

"Can I at least help?" I asked, flustered that an entire *feast* was being held in my honor. What?

"If you're anything like Rìgh Thorn and Ruksala, there's no stopping you if I tried." Sharn laughed.

"You got that right!" I chirped, grinning. "So, what can I do to help?"

"Eat your breakfast, then come back. You too Rhugher, you're not getting off the hook if Amelia's insistent on helping out."

Rhuger mock groaned as he scooped up our bowls and shambled off to one of the tables like he was put upon by the world.

"Poor baby has to help." I chuckled.

"Och, he's just faking it," Sharn said, and handed me a few rolls. "Go get some food in you. It's going to be a long day."

She wasn't wrong, either. After we ate, Rhuger and I were given different tasks. Sharn had to literally throw a pot at him to get him to leave the kitchens where I was helping. Insisting I'd be safe with the kitchen staff and her there. Reluctantly, he left with a crooked grin as I doubled over laughing.

He was sent out to haul kegs and casks, tables, and more. His size and height made him an ideal candidate to hang banners and lanterns the smaller females and shorter males couldn't reach. And each time he completed a task, he'd come back to the kitchens to check on me. It would've been sweet if it hadn't been annoying.

Meanwhile, I helped in the kitchens. Whatever needed doing, I did. From plucking game birds that looked like tiny ostriches, to chopping vegetables, to making pastries. Towards the end, there was a giant stack of pots and pans near the sinks, so I went over and washed them.

"Och, she can help in the kitchen anytime." I overheard the head cook say to Sharn in passing, elbowing her and pointing at me. I couldn't help the smile and blush that flushed my cheeks. Helping always brought me a measure of happiness. As did doing a good job.

"Time to rest, Amelia," Sharn said, patting my shoulder as I scrubbed a large cooking pot.

"But I'm not done..." I said, looking at the stack of plates and bowls, pots and pans that still needed cleaning.

"No, but you need a break. You're looking worse for wear and your hands won't be able to do much but stay in a fist if you don't rest them." She gave me a knowing look and took the scrub brush out of my hand and pulled me away from the sink. "You've done plenty and you need to eat."

My stomach rumbled then, and I realized I was actually rather hungry. Sharn glanced at me with her royal blue eyes and laughed. On our way out of the kitchens, she snagged us a couple of meat pies and a jug of that flowery wine to drink.

"Is it okay for us to do this?" I asked, not wanting to get into trouble.

"Of course, it is, silly. We need to take a break and eat. How else are we supposed to keep going?"

"I dunno, you just do?" I said, shrugging my shoulders.

"What do you mean by that?" She asked, alarmed, as we sat down at a table. I groaned as my tired body sank onto the hard wooden bench in grateful bliss. She handed me a meat pie and took a swig from the jug.

"Well..." I began, suddenly realizing that I wasn't in America where companies worked you to the bone. I was working hard here, sure. But I'd worked harder for far less than the Oc'Dellor provided. "Back home, our country doesn't treat their people all that great. No one is guaranteed food, housing, medicine, or anything, really."

I bit into the meat pie and the flavor burst over my tongue. Groaning, I dug in and soon polished off the hand pie. Sharn wordlessly passed me the jug of wine and I took a good few pulls on it to wash it all down. She tucked into her meat pie, thoughtful, as she watched me take another drink.

"Is your whole planet like that?" She asked finally.

"No, some places are better, and some are worse," I replied with a shrug.

"Sounds like it's pretty bad. Are females taken care of at least?"

I barked a laugh. I had to. "No. There are more females in my country than males, yet males make most of the decisions and have for hundreds of years. Until the last hundred years, women couldn't vote, have property, their own money, or get an education. That changed. But recently? It's all gotten thrown back by a small number of people in power. So those rights are being stripped one by one."

The dismantling of Roe v Wade was just the beginning. So much was changing, and not in a good way. But in the way that dystopian nightmare novels were written. That hinted at a post-apocalyptic wasteland where nothing grew and power was all that mattered.

"Things used to be worse for females here amongst the Oc'Dellor. Rìgh Thorn has made changes that his father Tyras refused to make. It's benefited us all greatly and we're now prospering in ways other clans and villages cannot." Sharn told me as she polished off her hand pie.

"I'm glad my grandfather did good," I murmured. "Pretty sure my Grandma Ruth would brow-beat him if he hadn't."

"Rìgh Thorn's Banrigh?" She asked, perking up.

"I guess so?" I replied. "They're married."

"Can you tell me about her?" She asked, her eyes bright sapphire blue like the summer sky.

"Sure," I said and as we stood and went back to work in the kitchens, I told Sharn and all the other orckin in the kitchens about Grandma Ruth, her Tolkien bed-and-breakfast, and her strange obsession with raising pygmy goats. They were all excited to hear about her and life on Earth, listening in with keen ears as work continued in the kitchens.

CHAPTER 24*

AMELIA

The suns were nearing the stone spires that ringed Baile Coille when Rhuger returned from helping with the feast. He strode up to the roll-up doors at the kitchens and called out to me where I was busy loading the last of some tarts onto a tray. I looked up and saw him and couldn't keep back the grin that spread across my face. I set the last few tarts down and hurried over to him.

"Rhuger!" I called as I wiped my hands on a cloth. "How was your day?"

"Hello, pearl." He said with a smile. "Busy. Have you finished?"

"Yes!" I replied as butterflies battled in my belly. How could he look so good when he smiled? "Um, what now?"

"Now it's time for us females to go get ready!" Sharn called as she threw an arm around my shoulder. Rhuger looked like he was going to argue, but she held a finger up to him. "I've got this, you mother nocrys. Go get cleaned up yourself. You smell!"

"Sharn..." He began, but she twirled me around and pushed me in front of her, back the way I'd come and towards the back door of the kitchens.

"See you at the party!" She cried over her shoulder.

"Sharn, do I really—" I started to protest, but she spoke over me.

"Yes, you really do, Amelia." She laughed. "We both need a bath, and I doubt you have a dress to wear."

"Um, no," I replied as she stopped shoving and grabbed me by the hand, leading me within the bailey of Daingneach. "Wait, there're baths here?"

Sharn stopped and looked at me with something akin to horror as I nearly ran into her.

"You... didn't know there were baths?" She asked.

"No?"

"How have you stayed *clean*?" Sharn's indignation was palpable.

"I've been giving myself sponge baths in the sink?" I replied. "I thought that's what everyone did, as there wasn't a shower or bath in the home tree."

"Uh, *no*, Amelia. That is *not* what we do and I'm going to wring Rhuger's thick damned *neck* for not telling you!" She cried as she grabbed my hand again and led me to what appeared to be a barracks. Once inside, it was clear it wasn't a barracks for warriors. It was full of females. "Amelia, welcome to the dormitories. This is where the unmated females who don't stay with their parents live."

The dormitory was a long hall with dozens of beds lining both sides and a large door at the back. Tapestries and high windows gave the otherwise harsh space some softness. Each bed had a trunk and the beds that weren't in use had their mattress and bedding folded at the top of the bed frame.

"Woah." was all I could manage as dozens of pairs of dark eyes swiveled to pin me to the spot.

"Everyone!" Sharn called, wrapping her arm around my shoulders again. "This is Amelia. Amelia, meet everyone!"

There was silence for a few heartbeats, and then suddenly there was an eruption of excited chatter. Some females came up to introduce themselves. Most of their names and faces I promptly forgot in the whirlwind. There were a few who stood off to the side, noses in the air as they whispered behind their hands. I knew that kind of behavior all too well. That was some high school bullshit.

"Alright, enough! We've got to get ready for the feast." Sharn said, shooing everyone back. "Does anyone have a dress Amelia could borrow?"

"I'd let her borrow mine, as we're of a similar height. But she's too *wide*." Came a snide voice laced with disdain. A hush fell over the room and everyone turned to look at the small cluster of orckin females who had been talking behind their hands. The one who'd spoken was the female in the middle.

She was stunning. About my height with a tight, trim body that models had and everyone else envied. Her high cheekbones, full mouth, and bright green eyes accentuated her copper skin tone. Her black hair fell in waves around her shoulders and down her back in effortless cascades that would do any hairdresser proud. Even her dress was a lovely peach color that guided your gaze to her like a beacon.

And I knew I stood there with my waves frizzy from the humidity of the kitchens, sweaty and smelly. With my dump-truck ass and chubby belly. Taking up space and looking like the Michelin Tire Man's little sister.

But I was hot, tired, and seriously *over* that shitty high school mentality, some people never grew out of. It hadn't been cute when I'd been a teen, and it *definitely* wasn't cute now. So I did what I do best when presented with this kind of shit. I strode over to her, the other females moving aside to make room. Her little gang jockeyed around her in a show of support for their tiny queen. I stopped just a few feet from her, looked her dead in the eye, and said...

"And?"

I held her stare and watched as confusion flickered behind those black and green eyes.

"'And' what?" She asked.

"I'm wide... And?" A hush fell as we all waited for the pretty peach princess to respond. When she didn't, I raised my brows at her and crossed my arms over my chest. A chest that was bigger than hers. Just like the rest of my body. Just like my attitude. "I'm wide, thanks Captain Obvious. I would have never known had you not spoken up. Also, there's nothing wrong with being big or fat or anything, for that matter."

"Who's going to want to be a mate to someone so physically unappealing?" She scoffed. "It's like Manira over there. Who's going to want to be a mate to someone so broad and muscular?"

I felt a disgusted look crawl over my face as I stared at her.

"Look, peaches." I began with a sigh. "I don't know what rock *you've* been living under, but it's different strokes for different folks out here and not everyone is going to want what you're offering, okay? Also, you have the personality of a turd. I'd rather have someone like me for who I am, not my body that's going to change over time. Making fun of how I look or Manira looks or anyone else won't win you any favors in the long run."

Her mouth closed with an audible *snap*. Fury burned in her expression as she turned an interesting shade of rust red. Murmuring and tittering began around me. And I realized *I'd* need to be the adult here. Fuck.

"I don't want a pissing contest with you. Just leave me be and don't be an asshole and we'll get on just fine." I turned and began walking towards Sharn, whose eyebrows had shot up into her hairline.

"At least I would look good standing next to Rhuger. You look like a pile of nocrys shit when you stand next to him." She called over the heads of the other females.

I stopped.

Those words might have hurt me once. Might have cut me to the quick and drastically hurt my self-esteem. But I'd survived worse than this from my ex-husband.

"Jealousy isn't a cute look for you, peaches," I called over my shoulder with a wave and kept on walking.

Sharn let out an indignant snort and slapped a hand over her mouth as she stifled her laughter. Other females either muttered disapprovingly or giggled. A big female came to stand next to Sharn as I approached. She was the tallest of the group, with a similar copper skin tone to lil' miss peaches. She was broader than Sharn and had a powerful physique.

"Amelia, what in the Three was that?" Sharn laughed as I reached them.

"What? I don't tolerate bullshit." I replied. "I'm allowed to take up space."

"You are something else." Sharn shook her head and placed a hand on the larger female's arm. "This is Manira, by the way."

"Thank you for sticking up for me," Manira said with a smile.

"No problem, Manira. No one deserves to be belittled about how they look." I replied with a smile of my own.

"Here." Manira held out a swathe of deep purple fabric. I took it from her and realized it was a dress. "You can keep it. It was never my color, anyway."

"Oh, Manira, thank you! Are you sure?" I asked, deeply touched by her gift.

"Of course. I've never worn it and the color would suit you, even if it's a little long."

"Can I give you a hug?" I asked, suddenly close to tears.

"Okay?" she replied awkwardly, and I gave her a big hug. My arms barely made it around her strong back and my face was just above her cleavage, but I made it work. When I pulled away, I beamed up at her and she returned my smile.

"We should head to the baths and clean up," Sharn said, turning towards the back of the room. I waved goodbye to Manira and followed Sharn through the door at the back. As soon as I passed through the doorway, chatter from the unmated females echoed in the dormitory behind me.

Sharn led me through a hallway, down some broad stone steps to another level. I could feel the humidity and temperature shift as steam floated in curling tendrils along the hall. Beckoning us forward with the promise of hot water.

The hallway opened up to a room filled with three pools of water that were lined with worked stone. Water cascaded down the walls at the back of the room, feeding the pools. Steam wafted off of them and I groaned at the sight. I was *desperate* to get fully clean.

"Over here," Sharn said and led me over to one side where there were benches, buckets, and what I figured were toiletries. "Put your clothes in a cubby!"

"Okay," I said and set the dress into one of the stone cubbies that were carved out of the cave wall. I took my lead from Sharn and stripped.

She paused as I unhooked my bra, brow furrowing. Sharn had a band around her chest, but it was a simple thing. Not the weird lacy under-wire contraption I'd put on to make myself feel more feminine that day I'd stopped moping at Grandma Ruth's house and taken a shower. When I'd sworn to love the body I was in.

It felt like ages ago instead of just a few days.

I finished stripping and put my clothes in the cubby next to my dress. I left my shoes under the bench. Turning, I noticed that Sharn was staring. Her vibrant blue eyes riveted on my body.

"Sharn?" I called in a singsong voice, waving a hand in front of her face.

"Sorry." She muttered, startled as she turned away, her cheeks and ear tips a bright silver.

She quickly finished stripping, stored her clothes, and grabbed a bucket and some soap, and something similar to a loofah. I did too, mimicking her. As we made our way to one pool, she refused to look at me. Was I so different?

Looking down at myself and then back at Sharn, all I could discern was that I was chubby and curvy, whereas she was willowy and sleek. That and our skin tones were different, but that didn't matter. Once submerged in the delightfully hot water, I let out a groan and sat down on one of the stone ledges under the water's surface. I let the bucket with my items float and relished the warmth as it seeped into my very bones.

"This is *wonderful*." I sighed and dunked my head underwater. Resurfacing, I wiped the water from my eyes and looked at Sharn. She still wouldn't look at me and she was awkwardly soaping her loofa. "Hey, are you okay?"

"I'm fine." She replied automatically.

"Really? Then why won't you look at me? Is something wrong?" I asked, suddenly worried about my new friendship being ruined by how I looked.

"No!" Sharn cried, finally turning to look at me as she pulled out her hair from its high pony. "You're so straightforward."

"Then what is it?" I asked, confused.

"I..." She began, then winced. "I've never seen a female so..."

"Fat?" I asked.

"I would say 'plump', but yes," she whispered, that blush high on her cheeks again. "You're really pretty."

...Well, then...

"Who or what do you prefer?" I asked her, reaching over and grasping her hand in mine. Her brows shot up in surprise before she gave me a sardonic smile.

"Not males, that's for sure." She murmured before patting my hand. The surprise must have lit my features because her gaze suddenly became guarded.

"Sharn... do you... like females?" I asked, openly curious.

"Yes," she said, glancing at me, then down.

"Oh, okay," I replied. She looked up at me, with her brow furrowed again. "I'll be honest, I'm not into females."

"Oh! Source no! I didn't mean to imply that I had any feelings for you other than friendship." Sharn cried with her hands up and a grimace on her face. "Truly, I'm not interested in you in that way, it's just..."

"You realized you like chubby girls?" I asked with a smile.

"Yes..." she replied, throat bobbing as she swallowed. "I've never seen a plump female before. Are all humans like that?"

"Humans? Oh, no." I said, waving a hand in dismissal as I reached for my bucket. "We come in all shapes and sizes. Are orckin females not plump?"

"Not that I know of." She replied, relaxing a bit. "Most of us are similar to me, stocky or muscular."

"Huh, that's interesting," I replied, reaching into my bucket and pulling out my soap. I dunked it into the water and started working up a lather.

"You're not... offended?" She asked hesitantly.

"Why should I be?" I asked back, adding the suds to my hair and scrubbing. Gods, it felt good, and I sighed.

"It's not an accepted thing. There are such pressures on us females to fight against the demise of our kind. We don't get to choose for ourselves." Sharn told me, eyes sad. "Not really."

"Well, if you don't have feelings for me and I don't have feelings for you, I don't see any conflict or problem, do you?" I asked after a pause. Gods, to have that kind of weight on your shoulders must be... agonizing.

"I guess not." She said, surprise limning her voice.

"Why should I be offended, then?" I asked, dunking my head back in the water and washing free the suds.

"So humans accept this? Females being attracted to females?" She asked, hope in her voice.

"Where I'm from, it's becoming more accepted for females to be together now. And males to be together too. It's not perfect and there are some places on my planet where it's still illegal. But the world is changing for the better." I explained.

"I wish I could live in your world." She whispered, and I looked at her.

Sharn looked forlorn. The raw hunger and longing in her gaze for what I was describing was heart-wrenching. What must it be like to be attracted to people you couldn't have? She must be so damned lonely. It made me want to figure out how to help the orcs so that they could live the lives they wanted instead of living one of duty.

"Well, if there's ever any hope of fixing the gate, I'll find you a nice girl, okay?" I said. Sharn smiled a little and then splashed me.

"Silly human." She chuckled.

"Not so silly! I'm serious. You deserve to be happy and love who you want." I replied, sending a splash her way. "Even though your kind is suffering, that burden shouldn't mean you can't find happiness."

We sat together in the softly steaming pool, quietly washing up. When we went to get out, I wasn't self-conscious in the slightest and Sharn didn't stare. We dried off with towels and set them in a basket. As we were quietly getting dressed, I was struggling with how the deep purple gown was supposed to go on.

"Here, let me," Sharn said and came over to help.

I relaxed and let her help me put on the chest band, then the underdress that was tied at the shoulder, almost like a Korean hanbok. The sleeves were short and light, the fabric soft against my clean skin. Then the overdress that cinched my waist and drifted in two panels, one in the front, one in the back, to the floor. Manira was over a head taller than me, so there was fabric pooling on the ground.

Sharn rummaged through a few baskets before she pulled out two brooches. She used these to help me pin up the extra fabric. If I were to have done it, it would have looked like a disaster. But Sharn somehow made it look like it was made to be that way. The female had talent.

"You're a good person, Amelia," Sharn said as she finished dressing in a similar dress that matched her blue eyes. "Thank you."

"You're a good person too, Sharn," I replied with a smile before hugging her. She stiffened for a moment, then relaxed and hugged me back. "Don't worry, I won't tell anyone unless you say it's okay."

"Come here, I need to do your hair." Sharn swallowed hard and pulled away, tears glimmering like stars along her lashes. So I followed Sharn out of the baths, smelly clothes in hand, and off to finish getting ready.

CHAPTER 25[*]

RHUGER

The suns were setting, their last flush of light painting the clouds overhead in a riot of pinks and purples. I'd cleaned up and changed into a leather kilt and black tunic tucked into the waistband. I kept my bandolier across my chest and my axe at my hip, but left my swords and longsword at the home tree. Tonight was a celebration, one that would be well-guarded by the sentries on patrol. And Amelia would be doubly guarded by Rìgh Thorn's personal warriors. So I could ease my guard a slight bit.

I knew that I could trust Sharn with Amelia's safety. I'd been training her for well over a year now as Uther wasn't officially able to. But that didn't ease the knot of worry in my belly that could not, would not, be sated until I could clap eyes on Amelia again.

I told myself that it had to do with her safety. Though, if I'd been honest with myself, it had more to do with wanting her near. Source, I couldn't get that neamhnaid female out of my mind.

Entering the great hall within the keep of Daigenach, I scanned the gathering crowd. Already orckin were getting themselves deep into their cups. Food was continuously being brought out and placed upon the long tables and benches that filled the great hall and on sideboards along the wall. The entire place was decked out in flowers, banners, and lanterns. All to welcome their new Leanabh Banrigh. Their princess.

My eyes searched the crowd for my charge. *My* princess. I spotted Sharn first across the hall. She was ushering a shy Amelia out from the side entrance. My heart near-faltered within my chest as I looked at her.

She wore a deep purple dress, the embroidered belt cinching her waist and accentuating her wide hips. Her hair was pulled back from her face in three braids, one at the crown of her head and two along the sides. The rest of it fell in soft waves about her shoulders, with little tendrils floating free about her cheeks. Amelia was, without a doubt, utterly enchanting.

And I wasn't the only orc in attendance who thought so.

Just like that, my mood flipped. Scowling, I swept my gaze over the gathered orcs who had seen my pearl enter. Kept a keen lookout for those who showed a little *too* much interest as my feet drew me ever forward toward my charge.

An orc had stood, staring at Amelia, as if to go speak to her. As I passed him, I let loose a possessive snarl that made him jump and nearly shit himself once he recognized me. And soon, others recognized me as well, quickly turning their gazes elsewhere.

As it should be.

Amelia might not have been mine, but she *was* my charge. She was also the Rìgh's granddaughter and Leanabh Banrigh. Not just some random female to be gawked at and wooed.

Sharn was attempting to herd Amelia toward the dais where Rìgh Thorn sat at the high table along with several councilors, the Master at Arms, Ruksala, and a couple of others. But Amelia was wide-eyed and adamant about not going up, about keeping out of her grandfather's sight.

Sharn caught my gaze as I approached them and let out a sigh of relief before turning Amelia around so she could see me. My steps faltered as I came to a halt before them. And gods, I'd thought she was stunning from across the room. She stole my breath up close.

The underdress and how it tied at her shoulder kept her outfit modest, but the rest of it? How the belt hugged her waist, and the skirts flared and were pinned up in lovely folds that accentuated the curves of her hips and thighs despite her being entirely covered?

It made me want to get on my knees and beg her. For what, I had no clue. But I'd take anything she'd give me.

"Rhuger!" She said my name like she was happy to see me. As she always did. Something I was struggling to get used to, as most people were *not* happy to see me. Ever.

"Hello, pearl," I murmured and plastered a jaunty grin on my face. I couldn't let her see how much she affected me. Though if the look Sharn was giving me was any sign, I was doing a shit job at it.

"You look so fancy, it suits you," Amelia said with a smile that I felt from my heart down to my groin. Especially as her scent and the hint of *Siren's Whisper,* the perfume I'd bought her, cut through the clamoring odor of hundreds of males.

"Thank you. You look exquisite." I said and nearly kicked myself. Was 'exquisite' a little too much? I should have said 'lovely' or some other, less personal word. Her cheeks pinkened regardless.

"Thank you. Manira gave it to me." She replied. "And Sharn did my hair."

"They did a good job helping you. I'm glad." I said, tossing Sharn a wink of thanks, and she grinned. Moving to stand at an angle, I gestured up at the dais. "Shall we, pearl?"

"Do I have to?" She asked in a tight, resigned voice. Her face slipped into that mask again.

"Unfortunately, yes," I said. "But I'll be with you."

The look she gave me then, Source, it struck me to the quick. Gratefulness mixed with determination and resolve. As if I not only protected her, but emboldened her. Helped her find her bravery when she faltered.

She took to the steps, and I followed her, moving without thought as my brain was distracted by all of her loveliness. As she took the steps ahead of me, my eyes riveted on the generous swell of her ass. I heard Sharn cough behind me and I startled, looking away across the crowd. But not before I caught Rìgh Thorn scowling at me. Fuck.

"Come here, chestnut." Rìgh Thorn called, patting a seat between him and Ruksala. The one normally reserved for the Banrigh. Uther sat on his other side, his son Nashton asleep in his arms. As we approached, I stepped forward and pulled out her chair and Amelia sat as I pushed it in for her.

"Thank you, Rhuger." She said with a smile, and I nodded to her before stepping back to stand at her shoulder. Ruksala was eyeing us all from behind her cup, a mischievous twinkle in her eye.

"Oc'Turin." Rìgh Thorn called over his shoulder, beckoning me to his other side. I dutifully went over and bent down to hear his words. "Enjoy the feast. My granddaughter is safe for now. And you'd best keep your eyes in your head before I remove them. You're dismissed."

Unease pulled at my gut, even as Amelia bent forward to glean what was happening. I'd fucked up. And that error had just cost me. Not to mention what it might cost Amelia if she struggled, and I wasn't there to help her.

But I could do nothing but nod to them both and back away. I strode down the steps and headed over to where Sharn, Sigg, Hisouk, and his sister Manira sat together. They quickly made room for me along the bench, Sharn moving to the inner side so I could have a clear line of sight to watch over Amelia from afar. Bless the female for being so sharp. I sat down at the end of the bench and grit my teeth.

As much as I enjoyed spending time with my friends and hated the spotlight, I'd rather be up on that dais, standing behind Amelia.

"Ooooh, someone's in trouble," Sigg said next to me and I glared at him. He laughed and punched me in the arm. "Couldn't resist staring at her ass in front of the Rìgh, could you?"

"Tell me you wouldn't have either in his position." Sharn pipped up and Hisouk chuckled.

"Och, but I wouldn't have acted like an orcling caught with his hand in the candy jar." Sigg laughed.

"You would have made it worse by being openly flirtatious." I bit out as my gaze nearly bored a hole through my friend's skull.

"Being overly flirtatious means everyone *expects* it from me. Isn't that right, Manira?" He asked, leaning over to nudge Manira in the shoulder. She turned a bright copper and nodded, even as Hisouk scowled at our friend. "So it's less of a problem than if my default expression was that of a territorial and foul-tempered nocrys."

"I'm not territorial." I bit out as I grabbed a dearc ruadh and popped the tart berry into my mouth. Needing to sink my teeth into something.

"Tell that to that orckin over there who you snarled at earlier. He had to *leave* to change his damned pants." Sharn snorted and shook her head at me. "At least you're keeping back the horde with your scowls."

"Only he doesn't scowl whenever Amelia looks at him," Hisouk said quietly next to Sharn. "He smiles and I swear, I even heard him *laugh.*" Sharn covered her mouth with her hand and eyeballed Sigg, who turned to me, waggling his brows.

"Does that sweet ray of sunshine get under that prickly exterior of yours?" Sigg crooned as he poked me in the side.

"Stop it," I growled, pushing his hand away and popping another berry into my mouth, hoping the tart juice would help me curb my irritation. It didn't.

"She's really soft, did you know that?" Sharn asked me with a crooked grin.

My mind blanked as I remembered all the times Amelia had been in my arms. Precisely *how* soft she was. And warm. I felt my cheeks burn.

"We took a bath together," Sharn said, cocking an eyebrow and giving me a knowing, taunting look. "I think I'm the first orckin to see her in all her curvy glory."

"Sharn. She is not for you." I snapped. Insanely jealous of my friend and trying to pretend I was Amelia's impartial guard instead of the obsessive green youth I felt like. How *dare* Sharn be the first to see her naked. I grabbed my cup and took a swig of the watered-down uisge-beatha.

"No, she isn't. But after seeing her, I can definitely say I now have a type. Not *her*, of course, but the pillowy softness of her?" Sharn put her fingers to her mouth and smacked a kiss to them, raising her fingers upward as if blowing a kiss to the gods.

Something snapped in my brain, and I saw red. My fingers squeezed the cup and the horn it was made of splintered in my fist with an audible *snap*, whiskey gushing out around my fingers to spill over the edge of the table and onto the floor. Everyone at our end of the table froze. Even those at nearby tables looked at us with eyes wide and full of fear.

But then I felt it, like a whisper, a pull, and I looked up at the dais. Straight into the uisge-beatha eyes that haunted my dreams. Her brows were drawn in concern as she looked down at my fist. She made to get up, but Rìgh Thorn held out a hand, insisting she stay in her seat, even as he glared daggers at me.

I broke eye contact and looked down at my fist. I eased my hand open and the sting of whiskey burned where the horn had sliced open my hand. Clinging to the pain, I grabbed a cloth napkin and wrapped my hand in it. The cloth staining pink and red with my blood.

There wasn't much damage and it would heal quickly, regardless. A quirk and a blessing from whoever my father had been. Some remnant of magic passed down through his line. Talk resumed around me, even as I moved aside the cloth so I could watch my flesh knit back together. Leaving pale scars in its wake.

I was made different. Made for war and destruction. Both by blood and by might.

How would Amelia look at me once she actually saw me in action? She'd seen me split Tintain's skull in half point-blank. But she hadn't seen me rip his corpse to ribbons. Had never seen me slaughter on the battlefield.

She was made different, too. Made with kindness, gentleness, and peace. A purity I could never hope to touch with my blood-stained hands. With a warmth I'd hungered for my whole life.

Memories clashed within my mind as I stole a glance at my charge. The bloody battles I'd fought, the lives I'd taken, warred with the image of Amelia as she stood in the pool in the city center, petting the fish. With her marveling over the smallest nuances of my world. The thousand smiles she'd gifted me and her face as I'd clapped eyes on her for the first time within the Craobh na Beatha.

Two vastly different paths for two souls brushing against one another in passing.

The understanding that one day, she would see that side of me, see the beast that lurked beneath my skin. And how the way she looked at me would change from sweetness to disgust? It slithered down my spine like ice.

AMELIA

I'd heard the snap of the cup over the cacophony of the crowd as orckin ate and drank and talked. I looked over at where Rhuger was sitting with our friends and saw his thunderous expression, and how his fist grasped the shards of what had once been a horn cup. Worry knotted in my belly, and as if he'd felt it, he looked up at me with those obsidian and silver eyes. At that moment, it was like there was no one else in the hall.

I made to get up. To go to him and make sure he was alright. But Grandpa Thorn put a hand out in front of me.

"Stay here, chestnut." He rumbled as he glared at my bodyguard. "He'll be fine."

"But Grandpa—" I protested, but his gaze slid to mine and I saw the keen edge of them soften.

"You're too kind-hearted for your own good, you know." He said as he pulled back his hand and grabbed a cup of that floral wine. "Believe me, that orc has been through far worse and come out just fine."

"That doesn't make me feel any better," I told him. "Just because he *can* go through a lot doesn't mean he should have to."

Grandpa Thorn paused and looked down at me thoughtfully before smiling at me. "See? Kind-hearted through and through. Still, chestnut, that's not how things work here, despite how it may seem. Outside of the stone spires, the Fàinne Sleagh, my reach doesn't go far, och? And there's only so much the other clans will do to change their traditions."

"Tradition is just peer pressure from dead people," I replied. Surprise lit my grandfather's gaze.

"You were always a sharp one. Couldn't get anything past you when you were little. It seems things haven't changed a bit." He reached over and patted my cheek affectionately. I winced, and he paused, then pulled his hand back. "Did he slap you?"

I didn't have to ask who he meant.

"No. But he'd punch things near my face, or threaten to." I murmured, trying to will my body to not spiral into the shakes.

"I won't do that anymore if it affects you so, chestnut," Grandpa said softly and I gave him a watery smile.

"I'd rather you didn't stop. You used to do that when I was little and I liked it. And the more pleasant memories I put between now and then, the less it will affect me." I told him, reaching out and grasping his hand in mine to reassure him.

"As you wish." Grandpa Thorn murmured with a soft smile. "Now, let's dig in and you can tell me more about when you were in college."

So we did. Grandpa had already introduced me to everyone at the table. I remember most of their faces from yesterday when I'd first reunited with Grandpa. Uther was there with Nashton and I was itching to ask if I could hold him. But instead, I told Grandpa Thorn about my time in college, what I'd done after, and anything else leading up to my marriage.

Throughout my time talking and eating, I could feel Rhuger's gaze on me. I knew others watched me, but he was the only one that mattered. It made me feel comforted knowing he was watching over me. When I could, I'd sneak glances his way, watch him as he ate, and scanned the crowd.

When we'd finished eating, my grandfather stood, raising his cup high. The gathered orcs all went silent as their Rìgh silently demanded their attention. Unease coiled in my gut as I saw the eyes of everyone assembled swing to land on me. The stranger in a strange land.

"People of the Oc'Dellor!" He bellowed beside me and I tried not to flinch. "This is an auspicious day. My granddaughter, despite all the odds, came to us through the Geata. Having her here is a blessing unlike any I've known in a long time. Please join me in welcoming her to our clan!"

Whoops and hollers followed his words, and the orckin were pounding their cups against the table tops. The cacophony slid that pleasant mask into place, and I could feel my ability to speak fly from me like a startled bird. I automatically pasted a pleasant smile onto my face and raised my cup to tap against my grandfather's before I raised it to the awaiting horde of cheering orckin.

As if he'd called my name, I looked at Rhuger. Saw him with his hurt hand fisted in front of his mouth as he scowled up at the dais. Saw how his eyes burned like flaming quicksilver.

But my attention was ripped from him as an attendant brought forward a pillow. And on it was a crown of flowers. Grandpa Thorn beamed down at me before he stood behind me and, taking the crown of flowers and raising it high to the cheers of the crowd, placed it on my head.

"Now!" Grandpa Thorn hollered over the crowd, and they calmed just enough for him to be heard. "It's time to celebrate! Out to the bailey, the lot of you!"

Cheers went up and hats were tossed as orckin got up from the dozens of long tables to head to the front doors, which had been thrown open to the crisp air of evening. They were laughing and singing, cheering and talking. Their voices echoed endlessly against the stone. But I couldn't hear them. A high-pitched ringing had begun in my ears and it felt like someone had stuffed cotton in them at the same time.

Mask still in place, I got up when Grandpa Thorn beckoned me and took his arm as we descended the dais. On the opposite side from where Rhuger, Sharn, and the others were sitting. I looked over my shoulder at them and only glimpsed them staring after me, as Grandpa's guard fell in behind us, blocking my view.

I don't remember much after we left the dais. Just snippets of conversation with various people who seemed important. The texture of my grandfather's tunic under my hand where my arm was looped with his. The smell of the flowers atop my head that shed petals as I moved. But I was on autopilot. Moving and smiling as I should, but inside I was curled up in a corner, waiting for it all to be over.

CHAPTER 26

AMELIA

Eventually, the gods must have taken pity on me, because Grandpa Thorn guided me out into the cool evening air. The change in temperature and fresh air was like a slap to the face, jarring me awake. The sounds of the partying orckin rose in the night like sparks from a bonfire, but in the open space of the bailey, it was easier to take. I was still overwhelmed, but at least the ringing was fading and I was more present.

The bailey was decked out with tables of food and drink, bonfires, and streamers. It was lovely to see the gardens and large central square alive with lights and people. It seemed that the party spilled out into Baile Coille as the keep's gates were flung wide and people were weaving between the garden paths towards the gates and beyond like a living ribbon.

Sparks from the bonfires danced into the sky and the scent of fire mixed with the heady scents of the garden flowers. Grandpa Thorn kept me latched to his arm, his massive hand clasped firmly over mine on his forearm as we continued to walk amongst the more elite of the Oc'Dellor. The guard stayed at our backs and I felt smothered. I longed to escape and weave through the crowd until I could find Rhuger and my friends. Find someplace quiet to enjoy the evening in their company.

"My Rìgh." A familiar voice called, and we turned to see Sharn and Manira standing nearby. "I was wondering if I could borrow Amelia for a bit? Introduce her to some of the females?"

My grandfather paused and I could feel that he was about to refuse, to keep me close and I couldn't stand it. I needed to breathe. I needed this out that my friends were offering me.

"Please?" I managed to say from between my frozen lips as I looked up at my Grandpa Thorn. Something must have shown through and reminded him of the challenges I had, even as a kid. I saw the realization, understanding, and even regret flicker there for a heartbeat.

"You'll keep your eye on her? Make sure she's safe?" Grandpa Thorn said over my head in a tone I'd heard before. I turned to see that Rhuger had joined Sharn and Manira. Relief burst through me and I felt my shoulders relax, my mask soften.

"I have sworn to do so, my Rìgh," Rhuger replied with a small bow.

"So be it." Grandpa Thorn said. He patted my hand to get my attention, and I looked back up at him. "Be careful, och? Stay close to Rhuger and your friends."

Still having difficulty speaking, I just nodded, and he released my hand. I let it slip from his arm and grasped my necklace as I moved away from the ring of guards and higher-ups. Nearly bruising my thumb against the carved surface of the rough side in a desperate attempt to ground myself, even as I reached out for my friends.

Rhuger's warm hand grasped mine as Sharn looped arms with me and they led me away, with Manira bringing up the rear. They blissfully steered me through the front gates and away from the partying throng in the market square, down one of the side streets to a lovely little garden. Somewhere we'd lost Manira. They helped me sit down on a stone bench and I sighed, leaning against Sharn's shoulder, and closing my eyes.

"Are you okay, pearl?" Rhuger's rumbling voice pierced through the relieved fog I floated in.

I opened my eyes, and they locked with his where he'd knelt in the grass at my feet. I raised my hand and shook it back and forth, trying to indicate that I was kind of okay, kind of not. Rhuger frowned, but his gaze softened when he realized I still clutched the necklace he'd gotten me. Was trying to ground myself with it.

"Is it okay if we stay here for a while where it's quiet?" He asked me, and I nodded. "Will that help you return to normal?" Again, I nodded. "Is there anything I can do to help?" I reached out to him and he took my hand. I grasped it tight and I could see an understanding spark in his gaze.

He sat down on my other side on the stone bench, lacing his fingers with mine. After all the times we'd held hands over the last few days, it felt so natural. His warm hand, long fingers, and calloused palm were so soothing and familiar. Rhuger began rubbing gentle circles in my palm with his thumb, petting the back of my hand with his other one.

We sat like that for a while. I felt the stress and overwhelm melt from me in the soft quiet of the little garden. Finally, I was able to sit up and open my mouth. My jaw cracked from gritting my teeth this whole time. Sharn looked at me, worry etched in her expression. I gave her a reassuring smile in return.

"Sorry about that," I said, my words a little slurred as my mouth remembered how to form syllables. "Thank you for rescuing me, you guys, I can't tell you how much I appreciate it."

"Did Rìgh Thorn not know about this?" Sharn asked me in confusion. "He helped raise you when you were young, didn't he?"

"He did. I think he just forgot. It's been a few decades, so I can't fault him for it."

"Still," Rhuger murmured, frowning as he held my hand in both of his warm ones. "This isn't something one should forget."

Just then, Manira appeared, balancing four cups in one hand and a basket of food in the other. Sharn got up and helped her with the cups. They sat on the bench opposite us and set up a little picnic. I leaned my head against Rhuger's shoulder and sighed. He was so calming to me. It was like with one touch, he banished all that stress and left me feeling calm, centered, and awake.

"I wish I could have been there for you on the dais," Rhuger murmured as Sharn and Manira chatted.

"It's okay."

"No. It's not." He said firmly, and I looked up at him. "Rìgh Thorn forgot and put you through hours of what must have felt like torture to you without any support."

Tears burned, and I blinked them back. I wasn't used to being *seen* and *understood*. He kept ripping the ground out from under me and steadying me at the same time.

"Well, I have the support now." I gave him a small smile and a bright green tinted his cheeks. Cute. "I'll have to sit down and talk to Grandpa about my limits. They've changed since I was a child, too, so he's really not at fault."

"Are you hungry, Amelia?" Manira asked. "You didn't eat very much when you were up on the dais."

"Yes, I am," I told her with a grateful smile as she passed me a cloth filled with food and a cup. "Thank you Manira, I'm truly touched that you noticed."

"Well, that's what friends are for, right?" She replied, her cheeks tinting copper. Manira was muscular, but she was also lovely with her strong cheekbones and full lips. I could think of many a short king who would fawn over her. And she deserved it, being an absolute sweetheart on top of her loveliness.

"Yes, you got it," I replied with a smile and dug in.

We ate and drank and chatted for hours as the party continued in full swing. Manira and Sharn wanted to hear about Earth, so I answered their questions as Rhuger sat next to me, his shoulder brushing mine as he sat in companionable silence. We could hear the revelers in the square as song after jaunty song wove through the boughs of the home trees, beckoning us to the square to dance.

"I don't know about you guys, but I feel better and I'd like to go dance," I said, standing up. "Would you like to join me?"

"Sure!" Sharn replied, standing up as Manira put everything back in the basket.

"I'm not a great dancer," Manira murmured.

"Who says you have to be?" I replied. "The whole point is to have fun. You've got the upper hand here because you know these songs and dances. I don't. Would you teach me?"

Manira's face transformed into a startled one of happiness. "Sure, I'd be honored to."

"What about you, Rhuger?" I asked, smiling down at him where he still sat on the bench.

"I'm not one for dancing." He replied. "I'll keep watch."

"Are you sure?" I asked, a tad saddened. A part of me hoped we could have a dance together. The thought alone made my heart race.

"I'm sure." He replied with a grin.

"Please, can I have one dance?" I asked, the words slipping from me before I could curb them. There was a pause as everyone waited for Rhuger's response.

"Alright." He managed. "One dance. You lassies go have fun, och?"

"Oh, we plan to!" Sharn said, grabbing my hand and Manira's. "Let's go!"

Manira and I laughed as Sharn practically hauled us behind her. I looked over my shoulder and Rhuger was following behind us. His gait was loose and easy in that way that screamed he was a predator. Predator to my girly parts. I blushed and looked away, desperate for him not to smell the shift in me.

Once at the square, I could see a ring of revelers circling the pool in the center where orclings played under the watchful eye of all. Brazers glowing brightly with sunstones ringed the outer edge of the square and musicians had set up out front of the glassworks.

"Come on!" Sharn cried and hopped to the ring of dancers and was quickly swept away. Manira and I looked at one another before we laughed and joined in.

Somehow, I managed to stay next to Manira as she taught me the steps to the dances while we twirled around the pool. This all should have overwhelmed me as I fumbled the dance steps, laughing. But for once, it didn't. Instead, I felt exhilarated for the first time in years. The beat of the drums, the resonant strings of the fiddle, and the trilling sounds of the flutes buoyed my spirit and my feet.

The music surged something within my chest that I thought long dead, making me want to run, gasp, and cry to the three moons that orbited overhead. Some primal need in me that could only be sated with the thunderous beating of my heart in my breast that matched my feet as they hit the cobbles and resonated with the beat of the drums. I tilted my head back and ululated like Xena, surprising Manira, who then joined in, the orckin near us doing the same until the entire ring of orcs were crying out to the stars above.

I caught sight of Rhuger then, on the outskirts of the ring of dancers. Saw as he moved over to the musicians and sat among them. He was quickly lost to me as we moved around the pool. But when he came back into view, he was playing something that looked like a mandolin. Lending a harmonic counter to the fiddle and the pipes.

Entranced I left the surging throng of dancers and found myself before him. He gazed up at me with an intense look I couldn't read. Then he grinned a devilishly wolfish grin that fluttered things low in my belly. Then he picked the not-mandolin in a flurry of notes, the other musicians pulling back in the song to allow him his solo.

Grinning so hard it hurt, I clapped along to his song. My feet moved and I let the music take me as I twirled and danced before him. Lifting my arms up towards the night sky amongst the fireflies that danced above us all like a churning sea of stars. My very soul lifted towards the heavens on the music he played. It felt so good it hurt, the sharp edges of it piercing, but I didn't care.

I was soon caught about the waist by someone and pulled back into the ring of dancers. The music changed and moved along with the orckin. I copied them, stamping my feet and swaying in time to the new song, learning the dance on the fly. Laughter bubbled up out of my throat as I attempted to keep up as the tempo increased.

Around and around the pool we danced, swapping partners and twirling until the rushes of air from our movements sent sparks from the braziers flying up into the night sky. But each time the dancing throng turned, and I danced the steps closer to the musicians, I would look for Rhuger. His eyes would catch mine, twinkling with something I couldn't name, and I'd smile at him before being whisked away again.

He was watching me dance. Watching over me.

I felt safe and happy. He wouldn't let anyone hurt me. I trusted in that.

The utter relief was giving me a head high, my endorphins pumping through my limbs as I danced with people that were... well, mine. Song after song had the orc-folk hurtling around the pool. I did my best to keep up with their endless energy.

But like everything in life, the jubilus dancing came to an end. Something wrenched in my chest as the music changed to something slower, more romantic. Orcs seemed to partner up or sauntered over to where food and drink overflowed the tables. There were both male-female and male-male pairings in those who were dancing slowly together now, sharing kisses or nuzzling one another. I stood there, trying to catch my breath as I watched couples dance together. That old ache throbbed hard in my chest. Tears slipped free, and it took a second to recognize why.

I was so happy. But I was also lonely. I'd been lonely for a long, long time. Even before the night my ex-husband hurt me. Everything felt so bittersweet at that moment it hurt.

A hand rested on my shoulder, and I whirled, looking up into Rhuger's handsome face. He'd apparently left the musicians, handing off his mandolin to someone else to pluck on for a while.

"Why are you crying?" Rhuger asked, concerned. "Did someone hurt you? Touch you?"

He was so protective; it was sweet.

"No—I just... can't remember the last time I was this happy," I admitted, rubbing my tears away with the heels of my hands. "It's been, well, years probably."

Rhuger's full, sensuous mouth thinned out in an unhappy

expression.

"You should always be happy. You glow like the neamhnaid you are when you are happy." He murmured, tucking some hair back behind my slightly pointed ear. I flushed, hard.

Hooo boy, this orc was definitely a smooth talker and a flirt. Yep. Wasn't affecting me *at all.*

"Why are you always so nice to me?" I asked suddenly. "I know you've basically volunteered to be my bodyguard, but why?"

"Because..." He murmured, gaze searching mine.

"Because isn't a reason, you know." I teased, trying to smile through the lonely ache in my chest.

"Because when I look into your eyes, I see my own cridhe looking back at me." The words were so quiet I barely caught them.

"Cridhe?" I queried softly. I didn't know the word. Didn't know Black Tongue.

He swallowed and reached up, about to touch my hair again, when my grandfather shouted over the crowd from somewhere near the tables of food. I looked, and he was actually *standing* on one table amongst some platters, crushing pastries underfoot. Weaving as if he were drunk as a skunk.

"To my gorgeous granddaughter, Amelia! She is a beacon of hope and has brought me great joy!" He roared over the crowd. The music went quiet and raucous shouts went up amongst the orcs. Rhuger stepped away from me as my grandfather looked for me in the crowd. He spotted me, flailed his tankard high, squinted at Rhuger, and scowled ferociously.

"To Amelia!" I heard Sharn shout and saw her arm jutted up out of the crowd near the tables.

"To Amelia!" Everyone else shouted in a boisterous chorus, everyone turning to me with their fists or cups high in salute. I just smiled and waved politely. Completely unsure of what to do in a situation like this.

Thankfully, someone herded my drunk grandfather off of the table as if he were an ornery cat. Sharn and Manira appeared and a cup of floral wine was shoved into my hand.

"Drink!" Sharn cried, even as she clunked cups with me before downing her own in deep swallows. I followed suit, thirsty and needing the buffer of alcohol to keep going. The wine burned a little as it went down and I sighed once I'd finished my cup and handed it off to someone coming by with a platter filled with empty cups.

Sharn grabbed my wrist and pulled me back into the dancing throng, with Manira close behind. Leaving Rhuger standing there, his hand outstretched as if he wished to keep me with him. But that was silly. He was just my friend... my bodyguard...

Wasn't he?

CHAPTER 27

RHUGER

The moons had all set by the time I could stumble tiredly away from the throng of celebrating orcs. Despite the evening chill, there were couples cuddled together in just about every quiet spot I passed. A pang of envy stabbed my heart as I saw their love for one another and knew it could not be mine, too. All the sharper for having witnessed Amelia dance and whirl to the beat of the music I helped create.

She wasn't mine. Couldn't be mine. I would be her bodyguard and her friend, no more.

Lies, all of them.

I knew I was lying to myself. But my exile from my home clan, my tentative acceptance amongst the Oc'Dellor, and Rìgh Thorn's menacing glower towards all who would dare look at his lovely granddaughter warred with my instinctual draw towards her. I'd proven myself a warrior and a reliable orc amongst the Oc'Dellor. I had yet to become fully one of their clan.

That wouldn't happen until I took one of their females as a mate. I couldn't bring myself to do it. Hadn't been able to these past years despite willing offers.

Absolutely wouldn't now that Amelia had appeared like a dream. She wasn't for someone like me. And I had to accept what she gave me and demand no more. Though I craved it with every fiber of my being, unlike anything I'd ever hungered or thirsted for before in my life.

Taking another female as a mate would be the right thing to do. To ease this gnawing need inside of me in the arms of a willing female. To forget Amelia and the effect she had on me. The mere thought made me want to vomit.

If Amelia were my *cridhe*, my true mate and equal, I would have a claim on her. But cridhe mates had faded from our clans in the past decades. A new cridhe pair not known to exist since Ruksala and Rìgh Tyras had found one another across the clans. The likelihood that she was my cridhe was so slim a chance as to be laughable.

I'd let the damnable word slip free when she'd asked me why I had been so willing to be her bodyguard. And why I had gone far and above in my duty. Thank the Source she did not know what cridhe meant.

I wandered aimlessly amongst the home trees, passing groups that were laughing and enjoying themselves. Even a few who were openly sharing their pleasure—some orcs stopped to watch in appreciation. I ignored them all. Lost to my own inner turmoil.

I suddenly found myself in a small garden with paved paths and a small meadow. Amelia stood there under the stars, sparkflies glinting around her and flowing in her wake as she walked amongst the grasses they called home.

She was swaying and moving her arms to music only she could hear. Her fingertips brushed the tops of the grasses and scattered the sparkflies that swayed with the stalks in the breeze. My breath caught in my throat and I froze.

Gods, she was so lovely. I couldn't breathe past the tightness in my chest. Every cell in my body screamed to go to her and worship her there in the tall grass. It took all my willpower to stand stock still at the edge of the meadow and keep watch over her.

As I'd sworn to do.

She turned, and I saw her small smile as her peach and pearl grey fingers skimmed the grasses, scattering the sparkflies in her wake and causing warmth to bloom in my breast. She noticed me then and stopped her dancing. I felt the loss of it, that beautiful moment, like a visceral ache.

"You found me." She smiled brilliantly, her small white blunted teeth flashing in the dim light of the stars.

"Och." was all I could manage. I cleared my throat and tried again, shifting on my feet. "The moons have set. Are you tired? Did you enjoy yourself?"

"I did!" She laughed and trotted up to me, her lovely face dotted with light freckles that mirrored the stars overhead. "It was so much fun to dance like that, to learn about my Oc'Dellor culture. And to hear you play! You're a wonderful musician, you know."

"Thank you, pearl." I swallowed, gobsmacked by her sweet loveliness. "I used to play often when I was younger. Haven't had the desire to play in a long time."

"I couldn't tell if you were rusty. Your playing was excellent!" Her praise and smile were like a caress and I shivered.

"Are you tired? You've had a long day."

"I am. My feet hurt."

"Your ankle? Is it still bothering you?"

"Only a little. It's why I'm out here. The soft earth doesn't hurt so much to walk on. And the fireflies are so wonderful! I'd missed them once I moved back to Grandma Ruth's farm in California." Her smile turned soft and wistful.

"You have sparkflies on Earth?" I asked, surprised.

"Sparkflies? Yes, not the exact color. Ours are a light green when they flash their butts. Yours are almost the same light blueish-white as stars. Fireflies don't live on the west coast where Grandma Ruth's farm is. They were my favorite part of living on the east coast. I o-oh!"

I knelt in the grass as she talked and reached out for her hurt ankle. She allowed me to pick it up, and she balanced on one foot. When she wobbled, I grasped her hand and placed it on my shoulder so she could balance easier. Smirking up at her, I tried not to let my gaze rake over her curves. She blushed again. I'd surprised her. It was then I could smell the faint sweet hint of her arousal on the breeze.

I froze. Inhaling deep, I drew her scent into my lungs. The roaring lust that took over me at that moment was hard to shove aside. My face was at the apex of her thighs and my mouth watered at the thought of what she might taste like. What she'd look like if I pulled her down into the grass and raised her dress up over her curves to bare her most secret place to my gaze. If I pulled her thighs wide and took her to my mouth, where I'd lap at her juices until she writhed for me and—

I shook my head sharply and jerked my gaze back down to her ankle.

She's not for me.

My wicked thoughts weren't helpful, and I wanted to hiss in irritation. I shifted instead, trying to ease the pressure on my straining cock beneath my kilt with as much subtlety as I could muster. Then I began examining her ankle, looking for swelling and tenderness. She hissed slightly as I gently pressed against her tendons with my fingertips. There was a small amount of swelling, but nothing as bad as when she'd initially hurt it in the stream.

"Your ankle looks swollen, but it should be fine." I couldn't look at her as I stood and turned back towards the path. "We should get you back home so you can put it up and get some rest."

"Wait! What about our dance?" She asked me. Looking down at her open, kind, accepting face, I felt that stab again. I shoved it down.

"Another time. It's late." I murmured and turned to lead the way to my house.

"No! I promised you the last dance." Amelia grasped my hand before I could walk away. My gaze snapped to where she clutched my hand. It was so small where it clung to my fingers. My heart thundered loud enough in my chest, I was sure she could hear it as I raised my eyes to hers. A daring spark lit me from within, and I twined our fingers together until our hands were tightly laced. Raising her hand to my face, I placed the lightest of kisses on the back of her knuckles.

"As you wish," I told her, voice gone deep and rough. Her face flushed that pretty pink it always did when embarrassed. Or aroused. Gods, how I wished for it to be the latter every time I saw her cheeks pinken. And that I was the reason.

I pulled her to me and tugged her hard enough that she stumbled a little and bumped into me. I relished the feel of her, however brief, against me like the Source damned wretch I was. She muttered something about being clumsy. I just allowed my free hand to drift to her waist, unable to keep my eyes off her.

She trembled slightly, but like the brave female she was, she placed her free hand on my shoulder. We swayed together, mere inches apart, under the starlight. Her hand in mine. The distant music wove to us on the air. Our movement scattered the sparkflies as we moved out into the meadow under the stars.

Amelia's heartbeat fluttered at her throat like a trapped bird. She wet her lips with her tiny pink tongue and I felt my groin tighten in desire. Whatever she was thinking about, she suddenly acted on it. With a step toward me, she wrapped her arm up around my neck and pressed her body close to mine. She placed her head against my chest and I kicked myself for being unable to control my body around her.

She'd hear how hard and fast my heart beat, feel how my erection strained against the heavy leather of my kilt, and push me away. My body betraying my oath to protect her from harm and to keep my hands to myself.

But she didn't. I almost blacked out with the sudden understanding that this dance was more than just two friends dancing to her. That, perhaps, she might feel a little of what I felt towards her. I wanted nothing more, and yet I wanted to rage against the constraints of our circumstances.

We danced like that for a time. I rested my head against the top of hers and sighed, hands clutching gently against where they lay on her body. She pulled me tighter to her. I wanted to weep at how good it felt to be held like that. To have someone hold me with such tenderness.

Without warning, she moved her head and looked up at me. Her face was so close to mine I could have easily closed the distance and claimed her mouth. Instead, I held still and let her do with me as she willed.

"Can I show you a human dance?" She asked me. I just nodded.

She spent several minutes showing me the dance. It was a simple thing, just a four-beat step pattern she called a waltz. Mind and body too full of her and the moments we'd shared kept me so preoccupied I stepped on her feet. More than once.

"I thought you'd be an excellent dancer! You're so graceful all the time." She chided me.

"Normally I am."

"Then why do you seem to have a hard time dancing with me? The dance moves are really simple compared to the ones I learned tonight." She pouted slightly. It was adorable.

"Distracted." I bit out.

"Oh? What is it?" She asked, curiosity and concern warring in her expression.

"You." I rasped.

Amelia blushed hard, the pink tinging the slight points of her ears and coloring her shoulders. We stopped dancing then and stood in one another's arms. Gazing into her eyes, I felt myself fall into them, like an endless warmth that filled in parts of me I didn't know were empty.

Partygoers loudly returning to their homes nearby laughed, and it snapped my attention back to our surroundings.

"Come, I should get you back." She said nothing in reply, but her arm seemed reluctant to leave my shoulder.

Her hand in mine, I led her back to my home tree. Hifasa snoozed in her shelter at the base of the trunk with Luther flopped half atop her. The sight tugged my mouth up into a small smile. I stopped at the base of the stairs and coughed. If I followed her up to my hammock, I'd never make it. I'd claim her mouth at the door when she bid me goodnight, pull her tight to me, and hope she drew me inside with her —

"Thank you for the dance, pearl. It was lovely." I cleared my throat again before continuing. "You should go up to bed. Rest your ankle. I'm here and I'll keep watch. You're safe."

"I know." She smiled and squeezed my hand briefly before letting go. I felt the loss of her as her fingers slipped from mine. And my hand hung there damnably in the air for a moment before I could recover and cross my arms over my chest. "Goodnight, Rhuger."

And gods, the way she said my name. Sweet and almost husky. Her uisge-beatha eyes twinkled in the sunstone lanterns. I'd never felt more lost in my life.

"Goodnight, Amelia," I whispered to her receding footsteps as she climbed the stairs. She looked over the railing and gave me a small wave and a smile before going inside my house and closing the door behind her.

The door closing might as well have been a slap to the face. The sudden loss of her hit me like a nocrys. Realization hit me then, tight on its heels.

I'd well and truly fallen in love with her.

CHAPTER 28

RHUGER

One of the young orclings came running up to my home tree just as the suns were rising over the edge of the world. Hifasa and Luther yowled an alert from where they were. I got to my feet and met the out-of-breath lad at the base of the tree. Runners, usually young orclings, scurried all over the Oc'Dellor, delivering messages and small parcels.

They rarely came to my home tree. And only when something was wrong and Rìgh Thorn needed me.

"What's happened?" I asked him without preamble.

"Rìgh Orok has arrived on an unannounced visit. Rìgh Thorn wished me to tell you and to request Lady Amelia come after breakfast." He panted, and I handed him two clips. The lad grinned and bolted off somewhere else. The clips were a form of currency for the runners. It showed the amount of work done for the day and helped develop them into trustworthy messengers.

Though the orcling had been smiling, the news he'd delivered couldn't have been grimmer. I bared my teeth in irritation before taking the stairs two at a time. I pulled a tunic out of my bag and threw it on over my head before bending down to put my boots on.

Of *course,* Rìgh Orok had arrived unannounced. That didn't surprise me. But what had set my teeth on edge was the *why* of him being here. Rìgh Orok was the leader of the Oc'Turin clan. And my nemesis.

There was only one reason I could think of that would bring him here. The giant orc who'd followed Amelia's scent when she'd first arrived had told Rìgh Orok. Possibly recognized my scent. Deduced where I might have taken Amelia. I'd already lost a female to Rìgh Orok's cruelty. I wasn't about to let Amelia face him without having her back.

I finished lacing my boots and tucking in my tunic. A quick knock on the door had me pacing as I waited for Amelia to rise.

"Coming..." I heard her call, sleep coloring her voice into something husky that pulled at my heart and my loins. She opened the door and rubbed her eyes. "What's wrong?"

"Rìgh Thorn has summoned you. You need to dress, and we'll go get breakfast on our way."

"Wait, why are you wearing a shirt?" She asked me and then blushed, looking away. Adorable.

"Rìgh Orok is visiting." Was all I said as I tried to keep my gaze from wandering her sleep-mussed form. She was wearing one of the nightdresses I'd picked out for her and it clung to her lush body in a way that made my mouth water. I was grateful she couldn't scent my emotions like a full-blooded orckin, or I'd have hell to pay.

"Is that why I'm being summoned?" Amelia's frown was wary.

"Likely it is," I told her as I strapped on all of my weapons. Bow, quiver, and long sword included. A visual reminder for Rìgh Orok that I was an expert in all forms of battle.

"Who is Rìgh Orok, again?" She asked as she ran her fingers through her hair and rubbed her face in an attempt to wake herself.

"He's Rìgh of the Oc'Turin," I murmured, and her head snapped to look at me. My gaze met hers and I watched as her mind raced. As it registered what that meant from what I'd told her in a matter of seconds.

"Well, isn't that nice?" She said sarcastically. "I get to meet the shitiest shit-pile to ever shit."

"What?" I asked, a chuckle escaping me.

"Don't mind me, brain is having trouble braining right now. Ugh, what I wouldn't do for some damned coffee," she groaned as she went back into her home tree. "I'll get changed, but I'm not wearing a dress!"

"That's preferable," I replied, and I meant it. I'd rather she wear her daily wear that was made for fighting rather than a dress that brought attention to the plush softness of her body. Not that *I* minded one bit. I found I quite enjoyed seeing her in dresses.

Last night, when she'd come and danced before me as I played on the lute. I could smell her joy, her arousal, and some primal edge to her that set my blood on fire and stiffened my cock so fast I'd fumbled a few notes. My instincts roared to go to her as she writhed like a serpent, her arms stretched towards the sky, to grasp her to me. To feel myself sink into all that softness as I finally learned what that tiny pink tongue of hers tasted like.

But I'd held myself back. Barely.

Memories from the night before cascaded through my mind as I waited for Amelia to come out. How she'd folded her fingers with mine, how she'd rested her head against my shoulder as if it were the most natural thing in the world as we sat with our friends in the little garden.

What she'd looked like standing in the tall grasses surrounded by sparkflies. Her body flush with mine as she taught me a human dance I failed miserably at. Her smile as she bid me goodnight. And how my heart had longed to burst from my chest and follow her up the stairs.

The door to Amelia's tree home opened, and I knew my face was flushed when I turned to look at her. She was dressed in her leather pants and tunic, the hood up over her hair to keep back the morning chill. Gods, she could have been wearing a sack and still be gorgeous.

"Are you ready?" She asked, tilting her head to the side. Studying me as if she could somehow unravel what must lay in my eyes.

"Yes." was all I could manage around the lump in my throat, my stomach fluttering as if filled with the sparkflies she'd danced amongst the night before.

AMELIA

Rhuger seemed out of sorts that morning. He kept walking awkwardly and stealing glances my way when he thought I wasn't aware. Did I have something on my face? Or in my hair? I surreptitiously brushed at my face and hair to hopefully dislodge whatever he was being too polite to point out.

As we approached the roll-up doors at breakfast, Sharn and Sigg popped up on either side of us. "Sweet cheese on a cracker! Sharn, what the hell?"

"What? You look more awake now." She grinned, her sharp teeth and lovely face so at odds.

"Do I have anything on my face?" I whispered to Sharn as Sigg was talking to Rhuger.

"No?" she replied, cocking an eyebrow and snagging a bowl of porridge and a sweet roll.

"Good." I sighed and snagged my own food.

"So, what are you guys up to today?" Sigg asked as we all moved towards one of the tables.

"Rìgh Orok is here." Rhuger nearly growled. The others paused mid-motion to sit, openly gawking. "Rìgh Thorn wishes for Amelia to meet him."

"Uh, what? No. No, absolutely not." Sigg spat as he sat down next to Rhuger.

"It's not my choice." Rhuger bit out between his teeth.

"That's really not a good idea," Sharn murmured as I sat down next to her. "He's..."

"A cruel bastard?" I asked, and everyone turned to look at me. "I gleaned that. He won't be the first cruel male I've met and he won't be the last." I dug into my food. All the dancing from the night before had burned more calories than I'd thought, and I was starving. It took me a moment to realize they were all staring at me. "What?"

"Pearl, he's not your average kind of cruel," Rhuger said, brows furrowed in concern.

"Well, what is he going to do with you and my grandfather there? Spit at me?" I retorted. Everyone paused again, exchanging a look. "I know I seem all sweet and harmless, but I've got a vicious streak, I promise."

They didn't look convinced. I shrugged and dug back into my food. We ate in companionable silence for a few minutes before Sigg shared a mischievous look with Sharn and elbowed Rhuger in the side.

"So, I heard a rumor that a certain bodyguard and his charge were spotted dancing in a field amongst the sparkflies." He took a drink from his cup, waggling his eyebrows at us.

"How romantic." Sharn crooned, propping her elbows on the table and cradling her face with her hands, batting her eyelashes.

I felt my face explode in heat, shoulders up to my ears, completely unable to deny it. Sneaking a glance at Rhuger, I saw his hand over his mouth, elbow propped on the table, ears, and cheeks neon green.

"Does the whole clan know?" Rhuger grumbled from between his fingers.

"Och, that they do. You two were spotted, and it's been the hot topic of gossip all morning." Sigg chuckled as he tossed me a wink.

"Don't worry, Amelia, some other rumor will start about someone else soon enough," Sharn said, attempting to console me.

"I know how rumor mills work, Sharn, thank you," I replied with a little bit of a bite as I tucked back into my breakfast, now unable to taste it.

"You don't have to worry. I treated Amelia properly and held to my oath." Rhuger stated. Sharn and Sigg stifled their laughter and got back to eating.

Feeling eyes on me, I flicked my gaze up and caught Rhuger looking at me from the corner of his eyes. He quickly looked away and got back to eating. Pretending as if the last few minutes hadn't happened.

Did he regret it? Our dance? I... really shouldn't have insisted on it then. I didn't like the idea that perhaps he'd felt trapped by duty. Only danced with me because he felt he had to. It didn't sit right.

The walk to Daingneach was quiet. But an awkward quiet.

As we neared the keep, Rhuger's expression blanked. After days of watching his face alight with emotion and thought, it was unnerving to see. And that wasn't the only thing that changed. He wasn't walking with the relaxed ease or stalking grace he normally did. He stood to his full height, head high and chest out, with a regal bearing that bordered the military elite.

It was almost like watching someone don armor before a battle. It made unease bloom in my stomach.

"I should warn you..." Rhuger murmured as we passed the guards at the door to the keep. They nodded respectfully as we strode through the open doors. "Rìgh Orok is not just cruel. Vicious would be the best term for him. He doesn't treat females with the respect they deserve, either."

"Well, fun." I sighed. Rhuger's gaze flicked down to meet mine as we strode into the hall.

"I will be there as well as your grandfather, Rìgh Thorn, and his guards. No harm shall befall you, this I swear." A hardness had entered his tone and his gaze sharpened as he spoke. As if steeling himself for the absolute worst.

"Somehow, I'm not all that comforted," I murmured as we approached the large wooden doors that led to the throne room. Guards on either side opened them for us. Rhuger strode ahead, his hand snaking out to tug on my pinky before leading the way to whatever crazy meeting this was with a neighboring Rìgh.

That small, teasing touch did more to buoy my spirits than anything else.

We strode into the main hall and where the tables and benches, the decorations and flowers had been the night before, was now all empty. A great echoing space only softened by high windows and the usual banners and tapestries.

Our steps echoed in the cavernous space and drew the attention of the two powerful orckin males whose presence seemed to engulf the entire room in a clash for dominance. My Grandpa Thorn, Rìgh Thorn, and the neighboring Rìgh Orok. Their gazes snapped to us. My grandfather's shuttered and Rìgh Orok's was... wandering.

I didn't miss the two contingencies of guards on either side. Eyes alert and weapons within reach. I straightened my spine and held my head high as we approached. I sure as hell hoped this went smoothly, and I didn't say or do something stupid to incite a bloodbath.

"Granddaughter." Grandpa Thorn called and held out his arm. I came and took it, standing at his side, facing Rìgh Orok as Rhuger took his place at my back. "I'd like you to meet Rìgh Orok of the Oc'Turin, our neighbors to the south. Rìgh Orok, this is my granddaughter, Amelia Oc'Dellor."

I didn't let my surprise show at my grandfather using the clan name as my last name instead of what it actually was, Chance. Instead, I looked up into a pair of sickly yellow eyes set into black inky pits. He stood a few inches shorter than Rhuger. His skin was a muted grey-green. Scars crisscrossed his chest and his tattoos curled up his shoulders to his neck in thick, harsh, unforgiving lines.

He wore a broad belt that protected his abdomen, which was bristling with knives. A leather kilt hung down past his knees and high boots reinforced with metal plates guarded his shins. A sword and axe hung at his belt. His broad shoulders were thick with muscle and were protected by leather pauldrons that were also reinforced. Rìgh Orok was dressed as if he were about to go slaughter people on the battlefield, not have a nice little meeting with a neighboring clan.

His banana slug gaze raked over me a few times as I took in his face. He had high cheekbones, a strong jaw, and a firm chin. Four long scars ran from his forehead down his cheeks on either side, framing his proud nose. Almost as if someone had attempted to claw his eyes out.

Rìgh Orok could have been handsome if it weren't for how his sneer twisted it into something almost sinister.

"The pleasure is all mine, pretty Neamhnaid." Rìgh Orok crooned in a voice that was a few octaves higher than I'd expected to come out of his thick throat.

"I'm sure," I replied dryly, gaze still locked on his as he purposefully allowed his gaze to continue to wander my body. Grandpa Thorn stiffened beside me. I could practically hear Rhuger's teeth grinding behind me.

They thought that this skidmark could really do anything to me by ogling me like a perv? It was cute how they thought that this moment mattered. My honor was made of stronger stuff than this.

"It's rude to look at someone like they're a broodmare you know," I said casually and Rìgh Orok's gaze snapped to mine.

"I'm unaware of what a broodmare is, Neamhnaid." His gaze was a little too interested as he focused on my words and this time, I *could* hear teeth grinding.

"A female used to pump out offspring."

"Och, but isn't that what you are? A pretty Neamhnaid so ripe for bearing orclings?" His slimy smile made my lip curl. I felt, more than saw my grandfather move to say something, but I beat him to it.

"If you think that, then you're sorely mistaken," I replied. "Rìgh Orok." I let the insult of the pause and the tone I used for his name to speak for me. His smile turned into an ugly frown, the scars pulling in a way that twisted his face into something awful.

"Why, Rìgh Thorn, you let your granddaughter speak so freely?" Rìgh Orok said as his gaze blanked, pretending I no longer existed to my face.

"She can speak for herself, Rìgh Orok." He replied, voice

resonant and forbidding. The two Rìghs stared one another down. I dared a glance over my shoulder, to check on how Rhuger was faring with all of this posturing.

Rhuger stood between two columns of the great hall behind me, arms crossed and looking forbidding. His scowl was furious, and it didn't take a genius to recognize that he knew this Orok personally. And hated his guts.

When I turned back, Rìgh Orok's gaze flicked between Rhuger and me in avid curiosity. I didn't like it in the slightest. Rìgh Orok's grin then was absolutely vulpine, and he returned to ogling me openly like a creep.

"Rìgh Orok." My grandfather began, and our odious guest cocked an eyebrow at my grandfather. "You've yet to see my little Amelia's talents."

A slow, lascivious grin split Orok's face and I wanted to gag.

"Talents, och?" He chuckled darkly. The curl of my grandfather's lip screamed that Orok should watch his tongue. Or lose it.

"It's been some time, but surely you still remember the tricks I taught you when you were a child, my little chestnut?" My grandfather asked, his bushy eyebrow cocked at me and a devious half-smile curving his beard.

Oh, I remembered alright.

"I might be a bit rusty," I said. "But I should be able to manage it."

Grandpa Thorn's face split into a massive grin as he clapped Rìgh Orok on the back. Making the other Rìgh scowl.

"Excellent! To the training yards!" He crowed, Rìgh Orok looking confused as hell as my grandfather passed him. Grandpa Thorn led the way to the training yards through a side door in the great hall. Rìgh Orok glanced at me and I let slip a smug smile before Rhuger stepped between us, blocking me from Rìgh Orok's view.

"Right this way, Amelia." He said with a courtly air I wasn't expecting. Rhuger's hand was gentle as he placed it at the small of my back and guided me after my grandfather, following behind me.

Making sure he was between Rìgh Orok and me.

I could have kissed Rhuger for his thoughtfulness.

The training yards, which I hadn't had the opportunity to visit yet, were packed with male orcs. All of them were running drills of some kind, sparring, shooting arrows into targets, and tossing spears and axes with deadly accuracy.

"Amelia, chestnut." Grandpa Thorn caught my attention and waved me forward toward Uther, the Master at Arms. I smiled and nodded at him as I approached. He stood in quilted leather armor, a strange harness over his shoulders and chest, almost like a backpack. "I'd like to personally introduce you to our Master at Arms, Uther. Uther, this is my granddaughter, Amelia."

"We've met, Rìgh Thorn." Uther bowed gracefully and my grandfather looked surprised. I'd been introduced to Uther briefly at the party, but we hadn't officially chatted under my grandfather's watchful eye. "Your granddaughter helped calm my son when he wouldn't take the bottle. She is very good with orclings. She does you proud."

My grandfather preened under the praise, and his chest swelled with pride for me.

"How is little Nashton?" I asked.

"See for yourself." Uther smiled and turned around. It turned out the harness was a type of baby carrier! Little Nashton was bundled up, his wide eyes drinking in the sights and sounds of the training yard.

"Nashton!" I crooned and approached the little one. Uther watched us from over his shoulder and I could feel Rìgh Orok's gaze worming up and down my spine. But I ignored it.

Little Nashton broke out in a toothless smile when he saw me. He began gurgling and laughing as I booped his nose.

"You been a good boy for your father, huh? No more crying fits?" I asked him softly.

Nashton just gurgled happily.

"You know, Uther, I wouldn't mind babysitting for you if you need it. Nashton is such a sweet boy."

"It would be an honor, Lady." Uther turned back around and ducked his head.

"The noises of the training yard don't bother him?" I asked, concerned.

"Nah, he loves the sights and sounds. He'll replace me one day yet, I'll bet." Uther's scarred face broke out into a proud grin.

"I'm sure he will!"

My grandfather clapped Uther on the shoulder and led the way to some targets for knife throwing. Shooing away the orcs who were practicing there. Rìgh Orok stood with his feet wide apart, his arms crossed over his barrel chest. Rhuger stood between him and me at all times. When I moved, so did he. Grandpa Thorn waved me over to the starting line before one of the targets, and I went to stand where he indicated. I took a moment to stretch as everyone moved around.

"Oc'Turin." My grandfather called and Rhuger looked up, bowing his head in acknowledgment. "Lend my granddaughter your knives."

With fluid grace, Rhuger removed the three knives from his bandolier and handed them to me hilt first. His gaze was full of curiosity and worry. I just beamed up at him and took the knives from his scarred hands gently.

"Everyone move!" My grandfather hollered, waving his arms, and everyone cleared in a hurry. There was a healthy distance between the gathering orckin and myself. All of them stood well behind me, including my grandfather. As if I were dangerous and unskilled. I huffed a laugh.

Focusing on what I had to work with, I tested the weight of each knife. They were all beautifully balanced. I expected nothing less of Rhuger's weapons.

"At your leisure, chestnut." Grandpa Thorn grinned at me when I glanced at him.

Nodding, heart in my throat, I turned and took in the crowd that had gathered to watch. There were... a lot of curious faces. My anxiety rose to choke me but I shoved it down hard.

I'd show them what I could do. At least a little of it.

So I faced the target and took a deep, slow breath. I let my limbs relax on my exhale, finding my center. I'd done this trick thousands of times since my grandfather had left. It'd been the last thing he'd taught me and I'd practiced it until I could do it in my sleep. All so I could feel closer to him.

I wasn't nervous about performing the trick—my grandfather would be proud I still remembered. Hopefully, Rìgh Orok would decide I wasn't ladylike enough for him and stop ogling me like a lecher. And maybe the other orcs would have more reason not to step beyond what was proper with me. But I was nervous about what Rhuger would think.

Stealing a glance, I noticed his piqued interest, his powerful arms crossed in front of him as he waited to see what I'd be doing with his knives. I glanced back down at them before slipping into a fighting stance. I'd show them all how good I was at this.

With one last look at the target to gauge myself, I ripped free the lovely kerchief I had around my neck, rolled it into a band, and tied it over my eyes. I could hear the murmurs of surprise—especially from my grandfather—but I ignored them and tuned into the wind instead. I held the knives at the ready, one in my left hand, two in my right. When the wind paused, I flew into motion.

My left arm lashed out, snapping the knife out to fly. Without waiting to hear it land, I twirled and let one knife in my right hand flick toward the target underhand. In the same motion, I tossed the third knife into the air, spun forward, and executed a 360 kick, hitting the hilt of the knife with my booted foot and sending it flying.

I could hear the three knives hit home as I landed on the balls of my feet. This version of the trick Grandpa Thorn had taught me was a lot more advanced as I'd added the blindfold and upped the type of kick from an axe kick to a 360. Also, how the knives landed had changed over the years. The added challenges kept me from getting bored and allowed me to keep honoring his memory.

I reached up and tugged off the blindfold, looking down the field to where all three knives had landed—tips embedded into the handle of the knife before it, the first one hilt deep into the dead center of the target.

The grin of triumph on my face was impossible to hide. I still had it. The quiet of the training field was enough to tear my gaze away from the target to see a bunch of shocked male orcs. The hushed silence was broken by Grandpa Thorn.

"That's my girl!" He hollered, throwing his hands out at the target, face lit with glee as he looked around the gathered orcs. "Would you look at that?"

My grandfather was whooping and crowing with pride, practically beating his chest. Rìgh Orok was unsettled and had a sneer on his face. As if what I'd done was distasteful. The rest of the orcs were either clapping or reappraising me. But it was Rhuger I looked to.

His black and silver gaze was flickering between surprise, respect, and... what seriously looked like lust. I couldn't stop the color from rising to my cheeks. He'd *liked* watching me be deadly?

That was a first.

My ex-husband never said anything about my proficiency with martial arts or weapons, but he still somehow made me feel like I was shameful and unlovable for it. So I'd only practiced in the backyard when he wasn't home.

Rhuger looked like... well, like I was his Xena Warrior Princess. Or I was Brienne of Tarth and he was a very tall Tormund Grey Mane. Like he wanted to eat me alive.

What the fuck?

Rìgh Orok saw the looks that passed between us and got a dark expression on his face. I didn't like that, so I looked away from Rhuger and turned around, but before I could even gather the knives, I was swept up into my Grandpa Thorn's bone-crushing embrace.

"You didn't forget a thing, did you, chestnut?" He laughed, eyes sparkling as he set me down. "Och, had to go and make it fancy, did you?"

"Of course, I got bored." I smiled up at him and my grandfather's eyes were teary with pride, his chest puffed up. I glanced up at the target, eager to get the knives and apologize to Rhuger for the damage done to the hilts, but he was already plucking the knives out of the target. He looked at me then and his expression was unreadable.

CHAPTER 29

RHUGER

She wasn't just a fair, pretty neamhnaid. She was just as vicious as the moileasgan they came from. I didn't think my desire for her could burn brighter, but I was wrong. It was like a raging bonfire had been lit within me and no amount of water would ever douse it.

Even so plump and soft, she had executed the knife trick with vicious efficiency. Two of my knives now held small holes in the ends of the grips where the other blades had sunk into them. Normally, I would be furious if someone mistreated my blades. But Amelia doing it? I'd never fix them and think of her prowess each time I used them.

Rìgh Thorn had been over the moons with excitement at how well she'd done. She'd have made a fierce Iolaire'lasair if they still existed. The Iolaire'lasair were the once exalted female warriors within each clan. They were named for the fire eagles that fiercely protected their territories in the wilds. Delicate, vicious, keen, and powerful, the fire eagles were nature's equivalent of the female orcs of the same name. Known to raze forests to the ground as their counterparts razed enemies in the field.

Amelia would have found a welcome home amongst their ranks.

Her approach to performing the trick before dozens of orcs had tipped me off that she probably knew far more fighting techniques than she'd otherwise let on. I would have to learn the breadth of her capabilities. And ask why she'd frozen when that damned Tintain had entered her bed in the dark of night.

That night still troubled me. Even more so now that I knew she was deft with a knife. She'd mentioned her ex-husband had forced himself on her. Rage burned my blood to smoke in my veins, even as her haunted expression waited for me behind my eyelids each time I blinked. I hadn't asked her about it, hoping she'd trust me enough to tell me one day.

My gaze moved from where Rìgh Thorn was waxing poetic over his granddaughter to where Rìgh Orok stood. He looked on with an expression of disgust. Even after all these years, my brother was still ugly as sin. The darkness in his heart leaked outwards to twist his possibly handsome features into something vile.

I hadn't seen the bastard in years. I'd hoped it would be years still until I'd see him again. But that giant orc who had come hunting for Amelia when she arrived on Talam had been one of Orok's minions. Ergit. He must have told Orok about the strange-smelling female he'd found near the Craobh na Beatha. There'd be no other reason my brother would deign to show his face to another clan.

Thinking of the wretch seemed to summon him. He sauntered over to me and sneered.

"Fògradh." His voice was still grating with a faint whine that reminded me of biting insects. I just lifted my lip in a snarl in reply. "Wormed your way into Rìgh Thorn's good graces, have you? If you'd been loyal to me, brother, I would have conspired with you to overthrow this clan. So you could lead it yourself. But you're loyal to no one. Not even kin."

"That's not true, and you know it," I replied and looked away in dismissal. "I am loyal to the Oc'Dellor. Was once loyal to the Oc'Turin, to our father. Plus, I have no rightful claim to lead the Oc'Dellor. It is not my place."

"The only claim there is, is power." Orok hissed, puffing his chest out. As if he was the one here with the most power.

Even after all these years, he still attempted to compete with me.

"Says the orc who used guile to take the Throne of Fangs from me," I said drolly, gaze sliding indolently to him. Orok growled and looked to say something else, but Rìgh Thorn caught his attention.

"Come, Rìgh Orok. Join us for dinner in the great hall." Rìgh Thorn's tact was appreciated. I didn't want to have to come to blows with the leader of my old clan and start a clan war.

"Alas, I must return to my people, Rìgh Thorn." His smile turned slimy as his gaze raked Amelia. I saw red and had to restrain myself from plucking his eyes from his skull with my bare fingers for the affront against the female I loved.

Amelia, the blessedly brave female, made an expression of disgust before crossing her arms over her chest.

"Aww, too bad. I had a few more tricks up my sleeve." Her grin was half mad and my vile brother drew back slightly at the sight. He'd never cared for strong females. He loved being in charge too much and wasn't strong enough at heart to win the love of one, anyway.

He had little knowledge of how to handle such a brave and strong-willed female as Amelia. His automatic response was one of revulsion and distaste. Idiot.

He also had a male lover who he refused to claim as a full mate. The poor male was relegated to a pleasure mate. He deserved more than what pain my brother gave him and called it love.

But it was obvious he wanted something from Amelia. Be it power over her or her knowledge of what lay beyond the Geata. I wanted to rip out his throat for his insolence.

"Another time, perhaps, Neamhnaid." Orok crooned. Rìgh Thorn's gaze was flat and intent on my brother. If Orok hadn't been the Rìgh of another clan, Rìgh Thorn would have killed him for breathing in his granddaughter's direction.

As it was, Rìgh Thorn's gaze flicked to mine, then to Amelia, before flicking to the keep. He didn't need to tell me twice. I stalked forward, past my brother, and stood between him and Amelia, blocking his view of her again.

"Come, Lady Amelia. It's time to visit the nocrys." I held a hand to her elbow, ready to steer her away. However, she leaned around me and squinted her uisge-beatha eyes at Rìgh Orok before bringing her hand up to her face. She fisted her hand, index and middle fingers extended, and pointed them at her eyes, then at him. And again.

It must have been a human gesture to indicate she'd be watching him. I had a hard time hiding my bemusement. She let me steer her away then, toward the exit of the training yards. She was practically stomping in front of me, fists clenched at her sides. When we were past the gates, she looked at me over her shoulder.

"I hate that orc!"

"You're not the first, nor the last." My lips twitched.

"What is his deal, anyway? Why is he so gross and slimy?"

"He's a Rìgh and leader of the Oc'Turin. He doesn't exactly have much tact or respect for females." I replied.

"Ugh, he's a creep!" She snorted.

"Creep?" I asked, not sure of this word.

"He's creepy—so he's a creep." She explained, gesturing with her hand.

"Ah."

"He couldn't decide if he was disgusted with me or wanted to be a lecher." Amelia's face scrunched up in distaste.

"You're far more capable and brave than the females of the Oc'Turin," I murmured, both saddened by the state of the females of my birth clan, and awed by Amelia's capability.

"Thank you." She replied shyly. "So where to now?"

"I think Rìgh Thorn's study would be the best place for now. I'm sure he'd like to speak with you after all this." Reaching the great hall, we passed through the echoing chamber to the other side. Then up the stairs to the doors of Rìgh Thorn's study. I opened them for Amelia and she stepped through as I followed.

Once inside, she paced in front of the fireplace, not unlike her grandfather. A small smile twitched at my mouth as I watched her pacing, deep in thought. I leaned against a bookshelf and allowed my thoughts to wander as well.

Orok wanted something, that I was certain of. I needed to protect Amelia from him. But I wasn't even sure where to begin. He was a Rìgh, and I was an exile with a tenuous acceptance into a rival clan. I was her bodyguard, but it wasn't like I had any power beyond that.

The Oc'Turin prized power above all else. I'd always shirked the need for it outside of my personal betterment. Never before had I longed for power more than I did at this moment.

I took a deep breath then, scenting Amelia's agitation, and forced aside my tumultuous feelings. They wouldn't help me right now.

All I could do was wait for Rìgh Thorn's return and watch for an opportunity to better protect Amelia.

"What is a chestnut?" I asked, trying to break us both from our helpless mental spiraling. Amelia paused in her pacing and looked at me in surprise.

"It's a type of nut where I'm from. They're very tasty when roasted. Grandpa Thorn loves them and has always said my hair looks like the color of chestnuts. And my eyes. So it's his nickname for me."

"I see."

"I don't know about you, but I'm hungry." She declared, her stomach rumbling in agreement.

"I can run and get you something. Rìgh Orok is going to be leaving, so you will be safe. Wait here." I murmured, hoping she didn't go charging about and get herself into trouble.

"Thank you!" She called after me as I closed the door behind me.

CHAPTER 30*

AMELIA

I watched from a casement window in Grandpa Thorn's study as Rìgh Orok and his small guard leaped upon their nocrys within the bailey and galloped away. My grandfather's shoulders sagged once Rìgh Orok was out of sight of the keep. It seemed Rìgh Orok's presence had been a strain on everyone.

Grandpa Thorn turned and spotted me in the window. He beckoned me out to him, and so I went. Leaving the study behind me and retracing my steps to the front of the keep as if I'd lived there my whole life. Rhuger still hadn't returned from the kitchens, but I knew he would find me. He always did, after all.

I took the steps down to the courtyard and stopped before my grandfather. He looked tired—as if he'd aged years since Rìgh Orok had arrived.

"What's going on, Grandpa?" I asked, concerned.

"Walk with me, chestnut." He turned, and I linked arms with him, offering the support of my much smaller frame.

We wandered for a while in silence and ended up in the

gardens. An orc I saw sitting next to Sharn at the feast was bent over some roses, trimming them back. He was huge, built like a powerlifter, with beefy muscles and a solid stomach. Peak stronk dad bod vibes. Seeing such a giant orc bent over such small blooms was so incongruous.

"What's on your mind?" I asked as we passed the flower gardens and entered a walled garden for herbs. Grandpa Thorn released my arm and sat down on a bench carved from a large root system of some long-fallen tree. Some kind of mint crossed with ivy crawled up the stone wall behind the bench, perfuming the air with a fresh, minty scent.

Grandpa Thorn just looked up at me wearily. He took a bracing breath and set his hands on his knees like the Rìgh he was.

"I've been approached for your hand." The words dropped at our feet like stones.

I swallowed, skin rankling and unease curling in my gut.

"It was Rìgh Orok, wasn't it?" I asked, voice gone hoarse.

"Och. He wants to bring peace between our clans. And sees taking you as his mate as a means of achieving that."

"And you believe him?" I cocked an eyebrow. Rìgh Orok was repelled by me, so it was something else he was after. Power.

"Not that scheming rat." Grandpa spat.

"You know, he's got to be curious about where I came from." I cocked my hip and gazed down at my grandfather.

"Och. I ken he'd wish to use the Geata to bring more females to our world if he could. If he knew that was where you were from. He suspects, but there's no proof." He spread his hands wide as if to illustrate.

"What did you tell him, then?" I asked, crossing my arms over my chest as he ran his hand over his face.

"That you were long away. Raised by a loyal retainer far from the scheming of the clans." He sighed.

"And he bought that? No offense, grandpa, but that lie's got so many holes in it, it'd sink if it were a ship." I spat. Rìgh Orok might be slimy, but he wasn't stupid. Unfortunately.

"No, he didn't. He'll be back, I'm sure." Grandpa Thorn sighed. "He's dead set on the match enough that he's claimed he'd set aside his current mate. Something he can easily do as she hasn't given him an heir."

"So, what now?" I pinched the bridge of my nose, feeling a headache settling in.

"Now you and I must discuss either sending you back or finding you a mate." As he looked up at me from under his craggy brows, his gaze was hollow and sharp all at once.

"Excuse me?" I hissed, furious.

"You heard me, chestnut." He leaned forward, elbows on his knees, and tapped his fingertips together.

"You can't be serious." The silence stretched out. "You're serious..."

"I am. As much as I love you here, chestnut, it is not safe. Earth would be safer for you."

"Earth wasn't safe for me, you should know that."

"It's safer for you than Talam." He amended.

"But there is no way back, is there?" I hedged. Ruksala had said they couldn't determine what caused the gate to occasionally open and close.

"Not that I know of. I will send messages to the Oc'Veltas, begging for their aid in this, their knowledge."

"They're the ones who live in the Citadel, right?"

"Och."

"And if they can't help us?"

"Then we need to find you a mate. And hope you become pregnant quickly."

I froze and stared at him like he'd grown two heads. With a snort, I laughed. I couldn't help it. Before long, tears were streaming down my cheeks, and I couldn't tell if they were from mirth or despair.

"So wait." I wheezed, slapping my thigh. "So not only do I need to find a mate... but I have to get knocked up, too?"

"It would help." Grandpa looked defeated. "If you were mated and married, Rìgh Orok could not declare war over you. As it is, he's demanding an answer within the next fortnight."

"So this bastard will wage war if I don't become his mate?" Grandpa's silence was all the answer I needed. "I get no say in this, do I?"

"I will give you what choices I can. I will procure you a list of orcs I deem worthy to be your mate. You can choose from them. And if I can convince the Oc'Veltas to aid us, it will be your choice to stay or to return to Earth." He hung his head then. "It's this or we go to war and many die. Our kind will die out if warring continues like this."

Silence stretched out between us, and I fumed. I had no real say. I couldn't say no and I'd rather die than end up in Rìgh Orok's filthy clutches. The orc was a walking porcupine of red flags.

I had two weeks to find a mate and get knocked up. As if my biology would even allow that, given I wasn't set for my period for another week. And who the hell was I going to take to my bed?

Rhuger's face flooded my mind and my heartbeat skittered. If I had my choice and he agreed, I'd hands down go for Rhuger. He was the kindest male I'd ever encountered, here and on Earth. But somehow, I knew without asking that Rhuger wouldn't make my grandfather's list.

"Rìgh Orok already has a mate, but no orclings. I believe he's becoming desperate. And he possibly wishes for his line to have control over not just one, but two clans."

"What do you mean?"

"I've never taken another female after I fell back through the gate. Your grandmother is my only mate and always will be. Your children will inherit the Oc'Dellor clan."

I felt my heart break then, for my grandparents. Separated by light-years and yet so close with a malfunctioning gate. It must be absolute torture.

"Grandma dated no one after you left. She still thinks you're alive." I whispered, and tears slipped down his face. "Looks like I'm going to need to find a mate," I murmured.

"Good thing the tournament starts in a few days." He replied, wiping his tears away.

"The what?"

"The mating tournament. It's a yearly event for the males to show their prowess and it's followed by a party where females and males can... test the waters, so to speak." Then my grandfather's gaze turned sharp and serious. "You will need to be at the tournament by my side. The party you may not attend."

"Why not?"

"It's not something you'd like." He hedged, and I rolled my eyes. Of course, he wouldn't explain... but hopefully, Rhuger and Sharn could help fill in the blanks.

"Then let's hope I find a mate sooner than later," I muttered, dryly.

"Do me a favor?" He asked, and I looked at him with a cocked eyebrow. "Have Rhuger take you to the smithy. Have them craft a set of knives for you. I want you armed from now on."

"Okay," I replied, rather surprised. But grateful too. "Thank you, Grandpa."

"The Oc'Turin is a fine warrior and a good bodyguard, but I still want you armed as a precaution." I was stunned. That was some high praise coming from my grandfather.

"I'll make sure I'm armed, then."

RHUGER

I found Amelia missing from Rìgh Thorn's study, but hunted her down in the gardens. I saw her leave the walled herb garden, she looked withdrawn and upset.

"What's troubling you?" I asked her as I caught up to her, a wrapped bundle in my hands.

"Oh!" She flinched in surprise and her cheeks pinkened before she looked away. "Nothing, don't worry about it. Just discussing a few things with my grandpa."

"Ah." So much lingered in that one syllable, and she sighed.

"I'm not sure if I can talk about it yet. There's a lot to... process." She admitted, tucking a tendril of hair behind one delicately pointed ear. "But my grandpa did want you to take me to the smithy. To have them craft me a set of knives, so I'm armed from now on."

I froze. Did Rìgh Thorn not think me protection enough for Amelia? But then, I thought of what I'd do in his stead. And arming Amelia was just the beginning of what I'd do to keep her safe.

"Alright, then," I said and proffered her the wrapped bundle. "Are you hungry still?"

"Ah, actually, maybe in a bit?" She wavered. Whatever Rìgh Thorn and she had discussed had stolen her appetite. "I'll hold on to it, though. Thank you."

"If you're sure?" I asked as she took the bundle from me.

"Yes, you need your hands free, don't you?" She asked with a smile as we strode to the gate and Baile Coille beyond. I didn't bother to respond.

We made it to the smithy in that companionable quiet that we shared. It was easy being with Amelia. And despite her different needs, being around her wasn't taxing at all. Instead, it was refreshing.

Something within me warned that this wouldn't last long. That our bond of bodyguard and charge wouldn't last. And I feared what would happen next. Because I was beginning to understand that I couldn't live without her.

AMELIA

We approached the smithy and the sound of clanging metal and the scent of hot ore greeted us before we even entered the workroom. I looked around in awe at how meticulously clean the space was. How everything seemed to have a place, an order to it.

Within, hammering a piece of hot steel next to a massive pit of sunstones, was a wiry male with powerful arms and shoulders. He was older than me, maybe nearing his forties. His skin was a strange blue-grey and his arms were flecked with scars and burns. Alongside the male were two younger males, assisting him with whatever he needed. Changing out hammers or using bellows to spark more heat from the glowing sunstones as the smith sunk the metal back within them. Clearly apprentices or assistants.

"What do ye want?" Called the smith without looking up at us. His accent was thick as it rolled from his tongue. "Ay've got plenty ta do today, so get me yer order and get gone."

"Hello, Conn. I've got a special order from Rìgh Thorn." Rhuger called as we stepped into the workroom.

"A special order from the Rìgh, och?" He sighed and looked at us, pulling off his leather gloves. He paused for a moment at the sight of me. "Well, if it ain't the Neamhnaid."

"Hello," I replied with a small wave.

"Conn, this is Amelia. Amelia, this is Conn Oc'Ain. He's from one of the smaller clans under the Oc'Turin clan." Rhuger said, motioning between us. I caught the grimace on Conn's face and frowned. "He's the best master smith I've ever encountered and will make you some fine knives." Again that grimace.

"It's lovely to meet you, Conn," I said and then paused. "I have a personal question?"

"Och? What do you want to know?" He hedged, looking at me directly.

"You don't like being called 'he', do you?" I asked.

It was as if I had snuffed the life out of the entire smithy. The apprentices exchanged wide-eyed looks and quickly left. Rhuger looked between the two of us in confusion. Conn's mouth flattened into a thin line.

"And what if Aye don't?" He nearly spat.

"Would you prefer I call you 'she' or 'they'? I want to make sure I use the pronouns that make you the most comfortable." I replied honestly.

Conn looked as if I'd slapped him. He blinked a few times, his brow furrowing as he shook his head in confusion. The two apprentices peeked out from the doorway. Conn made to say something, then closed his mouth.

"On Earth, we try to honor a person's pronouns. Gender is a spectrum and some people are non-binary, meaning they don't identify as either male or female. Some people identify as both. And others change their gender from day to day." I tried explaining. "There are also more genders than just male, female and nonbinary, but I'm not an expert on what those are. It's not a perfect system by any means, and some people don't honor them at all. But I don't want to be rude by not using your preferred pronouns. My momma and grandma raised me better."

I wasn't sure if I was getting my point across at first. Until Conn's eyes lit up with understanding. It was almost as if ten years had dropped from his narrow, scowling face as his expression softened. He stared at me, unblinking as I fidgeted, waiting for his answer.

"Aye would appreciate it if ye called me 'they' if ye'd be so kind." They murmured into the quiet. "Do ye have a preference, yerself?"

"Oh, I don't have one. Most people use 'she/her' as I look female, and that's absolutely fine." I replied. Glancing up at Rhuger, he looked startled by the conversation even as a smile of understanding played on his sinful mouth. I couldn't blame him. It seemed the orckin were very focused on the male/female binary for their survival. Anything outside of it must seem strange.

"Yer the first person ta ask me that. Thank ye." They said.

"No problem, Conn," I replied with a smile.

"So, what is it ye need, then?" They asked as they came forward.

"Uh, Rìgh Thorn wanted to know if you could forge Amelia a set of knives for defense," Rhuger explained. "Amelia, h-they made my knives that you used earlier."

Rhuger stumbled over the change in Conn's pronouns, but Conn shot him a look of thanks all the same.

"Aye, how do ye want yer knives to look? Let me see yer little Neamhnaid hands." Conn asked as they came closer, taking my much smaller hands into their broad ones, their palms thick with callouses from years spent hammering and molding metal into lovely and wicked things.

"I'm not entirely sure. Rhuger's knives are exquisite. I've used all kinds of knives, so I'm open to whatever you think would be best." I explained.

"Och, Aye heard about yer fancy knife trick." Conn cracked a smile as they turned my hands this way and that, gauging the length of my fingers and palms. Rhuger scowled as he watched Conn with my hands in theirs. If I didn't know any better, I'd say he was jealous.

"You did?" I asked. "That sure was fast."

"Just like your knife trick, pearl," Rhuger murmured and Conn barked a laugh.

"If ye keep this up, Neamhnaid, ye'll be bringing back the Iolaire'lasaire before long." Conn chuckled as they released my hands. "Aye've got an idea in mind for yer knives."

They called me over to a worktable in the corner, and we followed. We spent a great deal of time hammering out the details of my knives. Conn wanted flair, Rhuger wanted utility, and I just wanted to be able to count on them when I needed them.

The suns had set beyond the spires of the Fàinne Sleagh by the time Conn and their assistants waved us goodbye. We made our way towards the kitchens for dinner. I had left the bundle of snacks Rhuger had pilfered for me for the assistants as they'd missed lunch to help us.

I'd just sat down at a dining bench as I waited for Rhuger to get our dinner. I'd normally go with him, but after today my mind was too full. Too much to process.

There was a couple at the dining bench near ours. One was a large brown-skinned male orc who looked like a warrior who held a smaller, delicate-looking male orc with pale silver skin in his lap. They were being super cute, nuzzling one another, and just ignoring their dinner.

It was adorable and brought a smile to my face. I hoped whoever I ended up with at the end of the next two weeks was sweet like that with me. With a light growl, the larger orc pulled back from their make-out session and looked down at his mate.

"Och, Rist, you're looking... very submissive and... breedable..." the larger orc breathed into the smaller orc's ear.

UM... WHAT...

The larger orc ran his tongue along the smaller orc's neck to his ear, leaving the smaller orc flushed and trembling. The scene looked a breath away from turning into a fuck-fest right there on the dining bench. I knew I was staring, my brain still trying to process the whole 'breedable' bit.

Rhuger arrived and sat down next to me. Something must have shown on my face because he elbowed me. I sputtered and turned to him, eyes wide and face beet red.

"What?" He asked. "I would have thought you'd seen two males together already?"

"It's not that... and I have, though not so casually, at dinner." I mean, I grew up in a very liberal and pro-LGBTIA+ state. It's common to see two men together and not a problem. Plus porn and the internet made just about every inkling accessible. Not to mention the fact that I'd seen a lot of orckin couples go at it in public in the few days I'd been in Baile Coille. Rhuger hadn't lied when he'd said orckin weren't a shy people when it came to pleasure seeking. None of it bothered me and I just opted to mind my own business.

"Then what, pearl?" He cocked an eyebrow at me and shoved a bowl of some sort of stew at me.

"Um." I shook my head and picked up a spoon, but didn't touch my food. "I heard the larger orc tell the smaller one that he looked... breedable?"

"Ah." Rhuger's faint censure turned amused. "Orckin have always... enjoyed the concept of breeding. And with the demise of our species and the reduced number of females, breeding is a very titillating idea for most orcs. Even to the males who have chosen male mates. And some males wish they could be bred by their male mates like a female."

"Oh." I tilted my head and digested that. "So it's a kink then? A species kink?"

"Och, you could say that. Do humans not feel this way?" He shoved a spoonful of stew into his mouth and kept his eyes on me. The couple at the other dining bench had already escalated to heavy petting and moaning.

"Having kids is something we're expected to do. But not everyone has that kink." Quiet descended, and we began eating. Rhuger took a sip of his drink. "Do you have the breeding kink, too?"

Rhuger spewed his drink everywhere. He whipped his head to look at me, face gone so bright green as to reach yellow. He absentmindedly wiped at his mouth, his eyes enormous.

"I-I'm sorry that was a totally inappropriate question..." I laughed nervously, my face exploding with heat before I turned my attention back to my stew and tried not to shove my face into it in an attempt to escape my own embarrassment.

WHYYYYYYYYYY?!

"For the right female... yes," Rhuger mumbled, and I glanced at him. He had his elbow on the table, his face resting on the heel of his hand, and his fingers wrapped around his mouth. As if he were trying to hide his embarrassment. His eyes flicked up and met mine for a moment and the heat there set a fire low in my belly. My mouth went dry.

RHUGER

Breeding kink? It never hit me like it had the others. Not until I'd met Amelia.

Her asking me if I had the breeding kink conjured up a flood of images. None more prevalent than one of me sinking my cock into her to the hilt, releasing my seed deep inside her womb. What she'd look like, swollen and ripe with my child.

My dick hardened so fast at the mental images I'd nearly choked on my mead. Instead, I sputtered and then stared at her, my face feeling like it would implode with heat. My groin throbbed painfully as it sought to do what my wretchedly dirty mind had conjured.

Why did she want to know if *I* had the breeding kink? Did she, perhaps, feel even a little for what I felt for her? Gods, I hoped so.

I'd wiped away the mead absently as she stammered an apology and something about it being an inappropriate question. From her, it was a totally appropriate question. She was so adorable, her shoulders hunched up to her delicately pointed ears, that pink flush nearly making her neamhnaid skin glow in the dark.

I rubbed my face and rested my elbow on the table, covering my mouth with my hand in a sorry attempt to hide how desperately I wanted to breed. With *her*.

"For the right female... yes," I mumbled. *For her.*

I felt her gaze on my heated skin and so I looked at her then. Something must have shown in my eyes because she swallowed thickly, her heartbeat fluttering in the hollow of her throat. And with my next breath, I caught her scent. Her ripe arousal.

It took every ounce of pride and will to not roll my eyes and groan aloud. To get on my knees to beg her to let me worship her with my body.

I got a stranglehold on my desire and ripped it back, shoving it down deep. Instead, I turned and dug into my meal, wolfing it down quickly. I could have been eating ashes for all that I tasted of it.

Amelia followed suit, and in a matter of moments, we polished off our food. We quietly beat a retreat for the kitchens to deposit our bowls as the couple near us had begun to strip, orcs nearby watching on in interest. I didn't want to be near them when they fucked. My control was already slipping as it was.

My erection strained against the leather of my kilt, and I cursed under my breath. I was going to need to strap the damn thing to my thigh at this rate. As it was, I was walking funny.

"Are you okay?" Amelia called behind me and I swallowed my

pathetic laughter. Was I okay? No.

"Just tired." I lied.

"Did you hurt yourself? You're walking weird." Curse her for being so sharp.

"Uh, yeah, old injury." It wasn't a complete lie—I had an old injury that bothered me occasionally. Just not right this second.

"Oh, I'm so sorry! Do you need a massage? I learned some tricks from a friend who was a massage therapist that could ease the pain." She offered so naively.

Fuck. I'd love to let her do with me as she pleased. Do whatever she wanted to me with those little neamhnaid hands of hers. Slick wetted the leather of my kilt and I tried not to hiss. One day, if the gods were kind, I'd let her. But today was not that day.

"Thank you for the offer, but it's not right," I explained over my shoulder.

"Why?" she asked, confused.

"Pearl..." I began and sighed as we reached the window and placed our used bowls and utensils into a basket. I looked at her with all the sincerity I could muster. "You're offering to lay your hands on an unmated male. That's an invitation."

Her face exploded in a pink wave.

"I'm your bodyguard, pearl. You shouldn't say things like that to me." I internally kicked myself. Self-sabotaging moron! But I couldn't, in good conscience, let her continue with this sort of thing in ignorance. Because if she continued, I feared there would come a day when I wouldn't be able to hold back anymore.

I couldn't risk her well-being, her trust, and friendship, or Rìgh Thorn's approval.

"I'm sorry." She mumbled and tucked her hair behind her ear, looking away. "I didn't mean it that way."

"I know, pearl. You only intended the offer to help me. I need you to keep in mind the situation, okay? I don't want to risk you needing to be put under another's watch." I explained. And it was true. I didn't want anyone else protecting her. Because if they parted me from her, it would be a death I wouldn't recover from.

"Because they can't be trusted like you can." Her eyes were so open and honest and trusting and I groaned inwardly. She shouldn't trust me, either.

"They wouldn't be able to resist the temptation," I whispered. She went a little ashen, and then her expression turned sad.

"Oh. Okay." It was like what I said had dimmed something inside of her. It hurt. I couldn't see any way to ease whatever pain I'd inflicted, though.

"Amelia! Rhuger!" A familiar voice called, and I looked up to see Sharn and Sigg walking up to us. I nodded respectfully and Amelia seemed to perk up.

"So how is our little neamhnaid today?" Sigg asked with a crooked grin. I wanted to punch the grin from his face.

"I've... been better." She admitted and sighed.

"We heard Rìgh Orok had visited." Sharn prompted.

"And that you showed off an amazing knife trick!" Sigg laughed. "I heard it from some warriors. You've really impressed them. They didn't think females were capable of moves like that—accuracy like that."

Sharn looked drolly at him and Amelia shrugged.

"We've always been capable of far more than males or men give us credit for." Amelia winked at Sharn, who grinned.

"Och, don't I know it?" Sigg's grin was infectious. "I also heard Rìgh Orok wasn't pleased. Rìgh Thorn was over the moons, and this one here was impressed."

Now I *really* wanted to punch the grin off of my friend's face.

"You were impressed?" Amelia asked, looking shyly up at me.

"Och, very impressed," I said softly, swallowing hard. Such a soft, pretty, deadly little thing my pearl was. I froze.

My pearl. When had I truly started thinking of her as mine? Somewhere between that day at the market when I'd first thought it and now, I'd slipped into thinking she really was mine, despite my conflicting thoughts and feelings. It was as natural as breathing to call her mine, yet I had no claim on her. She'd somehow slipped through my defenses and curled up with my wretched, shredded heart.

Sharn's eyebrow shot to her hairline as she looked at me. She saw through me. She knew. Was I so damned transparent?

"So, will you be coming to the Mating Tournament, Amelia?" Sigg asked, leaning up against the kitchen wall.

"I... well, I'm expected to go." Amelia's tone turned somber again. "I'll be there."

"Has anyone told you about it yet?" Sharn asked her, linking arms with Amelia.

"Not really? Just that it's a yearly event where males can show off to the females. At least that's what my grandfather said."

Grandfather. Not Grandpa. So something had come between them when they'd spoken in the herb garden.

"Well, it's one of the largest events of the year for us," Sharn explained, patting Amelia's arm. "All the males can show off their prowess with arms and there's feasting and an after-party."

"I'm evidently not allowed to go to the after-party," Amelia said dryly.

"Why not?" Sigg asked. "You're orckin?"

"Rìgh Thorn doesn't want her mating with some random orc when she could help the clan by mating with someone of import." Sharn knocked Sigg upside his head. "Idiot!"

"Oh, that makes sense," Sigg said, trying to avoid another smack by Sharn.

"My grandfather wants me to find a mate or he'll choose for me," Amelia whispered so softly I barely caught it. The others didn't hear it and were laughing at each other.

I looked at Amelia then, and she looked drawn and pale. So that's what she and Rìgh Thorn had discussed. My gut twisted as I realized why Rìgh Thorn wanted her to find a mate. Rìgh Orok was likely making a play for her hand. No wonder she wasn't excited about the Mating Tournament. But if that was the case, why not let her participate in the after-party?

But then I thought about the debauchery that ensued at the after-party and nearly shattered my fangs from gritting my teeth so hard. It was common for females to be shared amongst the males, put in a state of frenzy by voluntarily drinking the luibh gaoil.

The thought of her drinking it, while tantalizing, was immediately soured by the knowledge that she'd end up bedding multiple males. Likely, none of them me. Understanding that I'd have to watch over her, watch as she was intimate with other males, made me want to vomit and made something tear in my chest.

The Source bless Rìgh Thorn for refusing Amelia to attend the after-party to find a mate. It was a relief. Even though I knew he wouldn't approve of me courting his granddaughter. That I wasn't worthy of a princess. There was still a small spark of hope that danced in my chest like a lone sparkfly.

"There is a whole festival with lots of food and drink and games after the tournament itself and before the after-party. I think you might enjoy that part." I attempted to console her and shift my mind away from the heavy burden we both carried. She brightened a little at that.

"It's been years since I've had the opportunity to go to a festival. That should be fun." Her smile was like rays of sunlight parting the clouds on a dreary day and I smiled back.

"I promise you'll enjoy it," I murmured, and I saw Sharn and Sigg share a look in my peripheral vision.

"Okay. If I get to spend it with you guys, then I know I'll enjoy myself." She turned her smile to include Sharn and Sigg, who grinned back at her. And I felt a pang of jealousy that didn't sit right. Why should I be jealous of her spending time with our friends?

Then it hit me.

Because she wasn't mine. And both Sharn and Sigg were unmated and unlikely to find mates, even at the festival. Not because they weren't a good catch. But because neither wanted casual pleasure-mates. They wanted their cridhes. Just like me.

"If you'd like, Luther has been down since you've left. I know he'd love to see you and I'd be happy to begin your nocrys training." Sigg offered.

"I'd love that! I already miss Luther. Is he listening to you like I told him?" Amelia's smile was genuine and that eased something in my chest. Her happiness brought me such contentment.

"Och, still a willful, vain little nocrys, but he's listening well enough." Sigg laughed. "Come by tomorrow morning and we can start your training."

"Sounds great, thank you!" Amelia clapped her hands and bounced in excitement.

Sigg's gaze became a little *too* interested, so I cleared my throat. Everyone turned to look at me.

"Sigg will want to begin your training early. It'd be best if you got some rest."

"Oh, right," Amelia turned back to our friends and smiled. "It was good seeing you both! I'll see you guys tomorrow, right?"

"Och, I've got breakfast duty, so I'll see you first thing." Sharn smiled and threw her arm around Sigg's shoulders. "Goodnight, Amelia!"

"Goodnight, Neamhnaid!" Sigg called as Sharn dragged him away.

"Goodnight!" Amelia chirped, waving a hand in farewell.

I couldn't muster the energy to wave them off. We watched them as they walked off, laughing and shoving one another. If either of them had an inkling for the other, they'd make a good pair. As it was, Sharn preferred females and Sigg wasn't interested in anyone that wasn't interested in him. It didn't stop him from feeling out Amelia, though.

As much as I liked Sigg, I'd fight him if he did more than flirt with her, without a moment's hesitation.

Amelia and I walked back to my home tree, and she headed up the stairs. I stayed frozen at the base of the tree. At some point, she registered I wasn't following her and turned to look at me.

"What's wrong? You've been off all day." She asked softly. I wanted to answer her—be truthful. But the truth was something that would burden her. So I'd tell her the truth, just not the one that was burning a hole in my chest. Not yet. Maybe never.

"Just a lot to think about, pearl. Not to worry. I know you've had a lot on your plate." I began shrugging my shoulders. "You're still adjusting to life here. Learning our ways. I just hope you know how special you are. Do me a favor and don't get drawn in by Rìgh Orok. He's not a good orc. Trust me on this."

And it was a truth that was weighing on me. If Rìgh Thorn was making Amelia watch the tournament, it meant he wanted her to think of finding a mate. The worst option would be my brother. He'd break her.

"Don't worry, Rhuger." Amelia's shoulders eased, and she smiled. "The last orc I'd want to spend any time with is Rìgh Orok. The guy is..." She shuddered and a look of serious distaste flitted across her features. "I'd rather lick a cheese grater."

"A what?" I asked, trying not to laugh.

"It's a-a tool made of metal used to shave cheese from a block."

"What's cheese?" I asked, confused.

"It's tasty. It's made from milk from cows and goats and sheep. I'm not sure of the process, but it gets treated, and the milk turns into a hardened block. There are all kinds of cheese and they're all delicious." She shrugged. "Sorry, my knowledge is pretty limited on a lot of human stuff."

"It's okay," I replied. "I think we have something similar. There's a type of tree that produces a sap we use in our porridge that we can also set in the sun. It hardens, and we cut it and add it to some of our dishes."

"Ah! So it's... tree cheese?" She laughed at the mental image and I smiled with her.

"I guess?" I chuckled. "We call it càise."

"Good to know!" Her expression turned pensive. "Hey, do you think I could find someone to teach me Black Tongue?"

"Of course. It's something you should learn, as some clans speak Black Tongue more than they do Common." I scratched my chin as I thought. "I'll ask around and see who would be a good tutor for you."

"Oh, that would be wonderful, thank you!" She grinned at me and something fluttered in my belly at the sight. "I really don't like being ignorant. And it's uncomfortable when others speak in Black Tongue and I don't understand what they're saying. I feel self-conscious..."

"Not to worry. I'll help you. Now, go get some rest. You've got an early day tomorrow." I nodded up to the door. "I'll keep watch and wake you when it's time to go."

"Thank you, Rhuger." The way she said my name rippled along my skin and I felt myself melt a little. "You're always so good to me. I want you to know how much I appreciate you, your help, and your friendship."

My throat tightened, and I just nodded, unable to speak. She offered me a kind smile before she headed up to the home tree. With a little wave of goodnight, she closed the door behind her and I was left standing in the mosses at the tree's base.

I looked over at Hifasa, who sat there judging me.

"Don't you dare judge me, Hifasa," I muttered. "I know what I'm doing."

At least I hoped I did.

CHAPTER 31

AMELIA

The following day, Rhuger woke me up with a knock at my door just before dawn. I groggily got to my feet and dressed before following him down to breakfast. Sharn was there, just as she'd said, and offered me some porridge, a roll, and some sort of spiced drink that had a kick like coffee they called cofaidh. She ruffled my hair before slapping Rhuger on the back and returning to the kitchens.

She was a good person and a good friend.

Rhuger and I ate in silence. I knew he had a lot on his mind. And I did too.

It'd taken me hours to process enough to fall asleep. I'd heard Rhuger's voice as he'd taken care of Hifasa and his footsteps as he quietly climbed the stairs to sleep in his hammock. I couldn't help the restlessness that stirred in my body and kept me awake.

It took me a while to realize it was because I was just plain horny. So I'd clamped a hand over my mouth and slipped my hand down under my nightdress. I didn't want Rhuger to hear me. Even though the thought of him hearing me touch myself lit my blood on fire.

I couldn't get the look in Rhuger's eyes after he'd told me he'd have the breeding kink for the right female out of my mind. The heat in his gaze had hinted at something I couldn't bear to hope for. I felt wretched as I flicked my fingers around my clit and my hips bucked. Thinking of Rhuger being the one to touch me like this drove me to the edge in record time. I grabbed a pillow and shoved my face into it, biting the fabric between my teeth as my release shuddered through me.

As I came back down into my body, I finally felt sleep tug at the edges of my mind. But it hadn't been enough. I needed far more than just my fingers to sate the lust that was roaring in my blood. Unable to be sated the way I wanted, I settled for the gentle throbbing between my thighs and slowly slid into the oblivion of sleep as my fingers slid out from under the waistband of my panties.

I'd awoken irritated and horny.

When I'd opened the door, the look on Rhuger's face was like I'd slapped him. Then it turned heated. It was like he could smell what I'd done last night in a desperate attempt to find sleep. I liked the idea far more than I'd ever care to admit out loud.

The early morning air was bracing as we walked towards the nocrys paddocks. Crisp and clean and smelling like cut grasses. I breathed it in deep, hoping it could clear the cloud of lust that wracked my brain.

It didn't.

I mean, being around the very yummy-smelling, graceful, gorgeous, and thoughtful Rhuger was killing me slowly. And being proper around him like he requested of me was proving to be far more difficult than it was with anyone else. Bit by bit, I was falling for him. I knew it and no matter how hard I tried, I couldn't help it. It was physically painful to know Rhuger wouldn't be on my grandfather's list of potential mates.

If he even wanted me.

The thought of mating with anyone other than Rhuger made me supremely uncomfortable. Even flirty and handsome Sigg made me rankle when I thought of being intimate with him. This whole 'find a mate in two weeks' thing was quickly turning into something impossible.

Sigg hailed us from where he stood by the barn just then. We walked toward him and he grinned. Luther was a shaking mess at Sigg's side, yowling and eager to see me. I laughed and Luther flopped onto his back.

"Good morning, you two." Sigg grinned. "Someone's been missing you, Neamhnaid."

"I can see that!" I laughed and got to my knees to rub Luther's belly with both hands. Luther went limp and drooled.

"Sigg." Rhuger's rough voice caught my attention, and I looked up. "I'm going to leave Amelia in your care. I need to find her a tutor."

"A tutor?" Sigg asked, intrigued as he looked between us.

"Och, for Black Tongue. She should learn it, being a Rìgh's granddaughter." Rhuger crossed his arms and cocked his hip and I had to stop from letting my jaw drop. His muscles bulged and flexed and his stance was loose and poised with power all at once. It was enough to set my mouth watering, and I had to pointedly look away.

"Huh." Sigg scratched his chin where his short blond beard clung to his firm jaw. "I'd expect Hisouk to be an excellent teacher. He's patient and very knowledgeable. I wouldn't ask one of the councilors, they'd bore her to tears."

"You think? I was considering asking a female who cares for

the children." Rhuger pondered.

"Och, they've got enough on their hands with the orclings." Sigg waved a hand. "I doubt you'd find a willing female to tutor her outside of Manira or Sharn, and both are busy."

"Why's that?" I asked. Seemed like an odd reason not to tutor someone.

Sigg just looked askance at Rhuger. Rhuger turned bright green again. I had to admit that he was lovely when he blushed. When Rhuger refused to answer, Sigg shrugged.

"It's because many of the females are jealous of the time Rhuger spends with you," Sigg explained.

"Why?"

"Well, he's got several females who would mate with him if he were interested." Sigg's mouth quirked up in a smirk. "They wouldn't want to help the competition, even if it meant spending more time around Rhuger."

"I don't want anyone but my mate, whoever she may be," Rhuger growled and something warmed in my chest.

"I'm competition?" I asked, huffing a laugh. Then I remembered the peach-clad female who'd called me 'wide'. Who said I looked like a pile of nocrys shit next to Rhuger. The laugh died in my throat.

"Och, you take up most of his time, don't you? It's enough for the females to look at you as competition for him." Sigg chuckled.

"Well, that's dumb." The words fell from my mouth. "If he's not interested in them, then he's not interested and they should look for someone else."

"It's not that simple." Rhuger sighed.

"It should be." I snarked on his behalf. I couldn't tell if this was indignation or jealousy that bubbled up from inside me. "It's not respectful to you. If they keep hounding you, let me know. I'll put a stop to it."

Sigg's eyebrows shot up into his hair and he slapped a hand over his mouth attempting not to laugh. Well, Sigg hadn't seen me stand up to Peaches.

"Och, now you're going to be protecting me?" Rhuger's sinful mouth quirked up into a devastating half-smile.

"From unwanted attention? Of course." I looked away, back down to Luther, so nothing showed in my eyes.

A strange silence fell, and I looked at the two orcs. Sigg was hiding a smile and Rhuger shifted—his expression both bemused and something else I couldn't place.

"Try asking Hisouk," Sigg told Rhuger, breaking the silence. "He's usually got a full day, but he's also got a lot of orcs under him so he can leave a bulk of the work to them. He's trustworthy and would be respectful towards Amelia. That I can guarantee."

"Och, that's true," Rhuger grumbled and ran a hand over his braid.

"Who is Hisouk?" I asked, rather belatedly given the conversation.

"He's the head gardener and Manira's brother. Very kind and gentle for such a big orc." Rhuger explained. Then he flicked his hand between Sigg and himself. "He's like us—he only wants his mate, not a pleasure mate—so he'll be respectful of you."

"Ah," I replied as Luther purred and head-butted my thigh for more attention. I scratched his cheek and got my hand covered with drool for my efforts. "As long as I don't have to worry about fighting someone off and they'd be patient with me, I'm open to whoever you guys think is best to tutor me."

Both Sigg and Rhuger nodded.

"It's decided then. If you'll begin Amelia's training, I'll head out to ask Hisouk if he'd be willing to tutor her." Rhuger looked to Sigg, who leaned against the side of the barn, all boneless and languid yet still predatory. "I'll be back in a few hours. I need to meet with Rìgh Thorn as well."

"My grandpa?" I asked, perking up.

"Och, I need to update him on various things he's tasked me with monitoring. Including you."

"How much do you tell him?" I asked, suddenly nervous.

"Nothing as personal as you're imagining, pearl. I promise." Rhuger soothed. "Mostly just how you are faring and anything you might need to help you adjust. Nothing more than that. Rìgh Thorn wishes for your happiness and comfort."

"As do we all." Sigg smiled warmly and his rough-hewn face turned soft in a lovely way that would have intrigued me if Rhuger didn't exist. But he did, and he was quickly becoming the only male I saw.

"Thank you. You both have been so kind and such a great help."

"It's difficult adjusting to a new world, a new way of being." Sigg gave me a half-shrug before jerking a thumb in Rhuger's direction. "It took a while for this one to get used to life here in Oc'Dellor after all those years in Oc'Turin."

"I can imagine from what you've told me Rhuger," I murmured with a gentle smile. From what it sounded like, living amongst the Oc'Turin was a nightmare. One I now desperately needed to avoid by finding someone to mate that my grandfather would approve of. "I'm glad you're here now."

Rhuger coughed, fist up near his face as he said a thank you. Sigg was just grinning at his friend's discomfort. To give Rhuger a break, I looked back down to Luther, who was nearly asleep with his head in my lap.

Again, and again, and again Luther bucked me off, and I ended up landing hard on my ass. I rolled over onto my stomach and pushed myself up onto my hands and knees, panting and covered in dust. Groaning, I staggered to my feet and rubbed my tailbone and low back. I'd be surprised if I didn't have a big ole bruise on my backside come the next day.

"Again," Sigg said, a twinkle in his eye.

"What am I not getting?" I asked in a whine.

"You're trying too hard," Sigg explained. "You're thinking too much."

"You're supposed to teach me, not goose-fraba me." I grumped, and he cocked a blond eyebrow at me.

"You're supposed to be good with felines." Came his dry reply and I sighed, tilting my head to the sky and rubbing my low back.

"Touche."

"Too-what?" Sigg asked.

"A word in a human language called French that essentially means 'good counterpoint'." I rattled off the explanation like a walking dictionary. It was a habit I normally suppressed because it was 'weird'. But I didn't have the energy to care.

"With a mind like that, you'll master Teanga Dhubh in no time." Sigg grinned and motioned for me to get back up onto Luther, who sat nearby licking his paw like a prim little snob.

"I doubt it," I muttered. "Are you sure I'm not too heavy for him?"

"I weigh more than you, Neamhnaid, and I can ride him just fine." Sigg patiently told me for the fifth time.

With a grimace, I walked back up to Luther, patted his rump so he'd stand on all fours, and put my foot in the stirrup. Hauling myself up into the saddle, a contraption that braced your entire shins to help keep you in the saddle easier, I struggled to keep Luther still as I got my other leg into the harness. Nocrys might be the size of a destrier, but their anatomy and movement were different. Thus, they needed a different type of saddle.

One that was a fucking nightmare to get into. I didn't know how the orcs did it so easily.

Finally, slipping my other leg into the harness, I grasped the reigns and was about to use the call Sigg had taught me to get him to walk forward when Luther decided to yeet me. He bucked and hunched, shaking back and forth to dislodge me.

Despite my best efforts to grit my teeth and last like this was a rodeo bull, I was tossed from the saddle like a sack of potatoes. This time, I landed on my side. I rolled over onto my back and looked up at the midday sky as clouds scuttled across the suns.

Frustration, rage, and resentment bubbled up inside of me. Tears burned like acid in my gritty eyes as I sat up. Sigg came to stand next to me.

"You alright?" He asked in an even tone.

"No!" The word bit as it barked from my mouth. I was

shuddering and shaking. And Luther was looking at me like he was supremely annoyed with me. Like I wasn't enough to be his rider.

The old mantra that plagued me like a ghost echoed in my head. *Too much, not enough. Too much, not enough...* It felt like nails on a chalkboard on the inside of my skin, setting my teeth on edge. Panic hissed through my body as my breathing came quick and shallow.

"What's wrong?"

"He'd be better off with someone else! Someone who understands him better! Someone who's better than me!" I cried. And on the heels of those words came the understanding that it wasn't just Luther I was talking about.

"Well, first of all, the last thing we're going to do right now is what?" Sigg asked me, dropping down into a crouch next to me.

"Cry?" I nearly sobbed.

"No, you can cry all you want." He *tsk*ed me and gestured for me to continue. When I didn't immediately respond, he cupped a hand to his pointed ear.

"Give up?" I asked, voice tremulous.

"Yes!" He said and looked me dead in the eye. "It's hard right now, but it's not impossible. You will get through this. You'll come to understand it and it'll get easier. Just like with your knife trick."

I nodded. The knowing look in Sigg's eyes said he was talking about more than just my nocrys riding. The panic eased back and my breathing evened out.

"Now that that's out of the way..." Sigg got up in my face and looked at me hard. "Whoever said he'd be better off with someone else? *You?*"

I tucked my lips between my teeth and wiped at my eyes. Sigg batted my hand away, staring hard into my soul. He waited. Large, imposing, getting all up in my business—and calling me out on my bullshit. I hated it.

"Yes!" I nearly growled. Sigg's eyebrows popped up towards his hairline and he looked supremely unimpressed.

"I hate to break it to you, Neamhnaid, but you don't get to choose that for someone else." I nearly did a double-take as that whammy hit me over the head like a loaded flower pot. "You know who gets to decide if you're good enough? Strong enough? Loving enough? Understanding enough for him?"

I faintly shook my head.

"*He does.*" My eyes felt huge in my face as I stared at Sigg without blinking. "And by questioning his *choice* in caring for you—you might as well just spit in his face. Because you are questioning his sincerity, his loyalty, his honor, his wisdom, and his intelligence. Because despite the bonds that can bind us to others, loving someone is a *choice.*"

I swallowed and tried not to sob. Sigg was giving me the double-barrel shotgun truth and that fucker hurt. Because my ex-husband had made the choice not to love me. And here I was, looking at a gift horse in the mouth just because I questioned the choice to love me. Questioned my own worth.

"It's okay to question your worthiness and strive to be better." Sigg continued, softer as if he'd heard my thoughts. "It's not okay to make that assumption for someone else when they've made an informed decision about you. Because it shows your lack of trust, lack of faith, in him."

Silence stretched out between the two of us for a bit. I hiccupped. Sigg fished into a pocket a procured a clean square of cloth, handing it to me. I used it to rub my eyes and blow my nose.

"Do you trust him?" Sigg asked softly.

I looked him in the eye again as the truth that Sigg spoke settled into my being. Did I question my own capabilities and worthiness because I was now on a completely different planet, learning the ways of different people, and still working through all the baggage I'd accumulated by surviving my ex-husband?

Absolutely.

Did I trust Rhuger? Trust Luther? Did I do everything I could to honor their choices and their personhood?

Without a doubt.

What was left between the two was a leap of faith. To trust in Rhuger and Luther. To honor their decision to care for me by doing the best I could, instead of whining about not being good enough. Sigg was right. It was their choice. Just like it was mine to care for them, love them.

Because I did.

And I couldn't let my fear get in the way. Wouldn't let the ex-bastard-husband win.

"Implicitly." I croaked. Sigg's answering grin was blinding.

"Then let's try again, och?" He stood up and held down a hand. I hesitated a moment before I grasped it and he helped haul me to my feet.

I gave Sigg a brusque nod, and he grinned, smacking my back. I stepped past him to where Luther lay like a giant kitty loaf on the ground, watching me with slitted eyes. Pausing, I rethought my approach.

Wasn't I treating this situation like I'd treat a horse? A horse that was already broken to the bit and saddle? It was clear that Luther was *not* a horse. He was a feline. Sigg's words floated back to me as I strode forward with my hand loose in front of me.

"Hey there, Luther baby." I crooned low. "I'm sorry I've been a pain in the ass."

He tipped his head out towards me, sniffing. Taking that as encouragement, I eased up to him until his nose was inches away. Luther bumped my fist until I placed it on his lightly armored nose. I took my time, gently petting him and rubbing between the scales on his nose and head. His rumbling purr and cant of his ears with their little tufts let me know he was okay.

Using both of my hands, I cupped his cheeks and scratched behind his whiskers. His eyes opened and we spent a few minutes just slowly blinking at one another. Eventually, he leaned forward and head-butted me gently. I smiled and kissed his head.

"Shall we try again, Luther?" I murmured and he rubbed his head against my body in answer.

So I calmly walked around to his side, petting him as I went so he'd know where I was. I had a bit of a limp, and my ass was killing me, but it wasn't enough to startle him. When I got to where the saddle draped over his armored back, where he lay like the biggest of kitty loaves, I patted the saddle to let him know my intentions.

Luther chirruped at me, sounding more like a sputtering motorcycle than a chirrup. Taking that as assent, I put one leg into the shin cradle on the saddle and swung my leg over to the other side. Luther startled a little bit, so I sat still and calm until he acclimated to my weight. When he'd settled and huffed out a breath, I maneuvered my other leg into the shin cradle.

"That's a good boy, Luther," I murmured, reaching forward to pet his neck and shoulders.

I realized they built the saddle more like a harness as it arched over his shoulders and down his chest to his belly. The reins attached to the arms of the harness over his shoulders. Acting more as a guide than a forceful bit used for horses. Which was good because no cat would put up with that.

"Don't forget to guide with your knees, not just the reins," Sigg called. "That's part of the purpose of the cradles."

"Okay!" I called before patting Luther in the rhythm Sigg had taught me to let him know I was ready to go.

Luther stood, stretching a bit and I had to hold on to the pommel to keep from falling face-first into the spikes at the top of his head. He evened out and waited, alert, with his ears swiveling. I nudged him with my right knee as I pulled on the left rein. With a chuff, he turned to the left, and I gently tapped my heels against his sides, and he loped forward in a canter.

"It's working!" I laughed as the wind lifted my sweaty hair off of my neck.

"Bank right!" Sigg called from behind me and I did. Luther turned with me and Sigg called out maneuvers. And for the first time since I got to Talam? I felt like I had this. Just Luther and me weaving through our paces to Sigg's calls. Our trust built with each nudge. Our understanding of one another grew with each executed move.

"You know, Rhuger built your home tree himself?" Sigg asked as I slid from Luther's back hours later.

"He did?" I queried, at a loss as I attempted to straighten my aching legs and backside. I was waddling bow-legged as I shuffled to Sigg's side.

"Och. Males build homes for their mates, so there are many

skills required to build one that tests a male's abilities. Rhuger's one of the most competent orcs I know. I was surprised he could build such a lovely structure. To be honest, I helped him in the beginning—hoisting the wood necessary for the base beams can be challenging. Especially when trying to gauge the tree's potential growth. So I helped him with that. But everything else? All him." Sigg explained, cocking an eyebrow at me as he showed me how to remove the saddle from Luther's back.

"Even the little carvings?"

"Even those." Sigg's smile was warm. "Not something you'd think a warrior like him capable of, och? Carving all those pretty flowers."

"Does he like flowers?"

"Not that I'm aware. Not like Hisouk or some others gifted with plants. He never said outright, but I think he'd hoped to find a mate all this time. And that he built it for her. Whoever she may be." Sigg winked at me and I... didn't know what to do with that information.

He'd built that house for a potential mate. Had been waiting for years to find one. Poured all his time and love and hope into building that house to keep the loneliness at bay. And now, he was letting me live in his house. THAT house.

Did this... mean he felt something for me? That maybe he hoped to make me his mate if I wished? My heart ached. If I knew one thing, I knew my grandfather wouldn't approve.

"Why didn't he tell me?" I asked, baffled. "Why did he hide it from me, that he was letting me stay in a house that he'd built himself? For a future mate?"

"I believe he didn't want to scare you off. If you had known he'd made it himself and understood how much time and love he'd put into building that house. Would you really have accepted it? Or would you have run?" Sigg asked me quietly as he pulled off Luther's harness saddle and held it. Held my gaze too.

"I don't know," I whispered. Sigg gave me a wry half-smile and set down the saddle on a rail before turning back to me.

"Then it's a good thing he didn't, och?" He asked. "Gave you the time and space to acclimate, to heal, to learn about our ways. And him. Before outright dismissing the offer because you..." He tapped my nose and I was startled out of the fog of thought I'd been in. "... didn't think yourself worthy."

Sigg clapped me on the shoulder.

"Be kind to him, och?" That caught my attention. "He's been through too much. If you cannot give him what his heart wants, don't lead him on."

My face went pale. My grandfather's demand that I take a mate roared to life in my head. Grandpa Thorn hadn't explicitly stated who was on his list yet. But he didn't seem to like Rhuger very much, and his proximity to me even less.

The last thing I wanted was to lead Rhuger on. I couldn't bear to hurt him. I also knew already that no other orc held a candle to him in my mind. Crazy as it sounded after so short a time together. But I wasn't sure how I could choose someone else when Rhuger existed.

CHAPTER 32

RHUGER

Finding Hisouk was easy. No matter the time of year or weather, he enjoyed spending his mornings in the large potting shed within the bailey.

It was more like a stone hut than a shed, taking its building techniques from the stone and moss houses of the Oc'Turin. Moss and ferns lay like a cape over the long structure. Grasses and wildflowers crowned its sod roof in a feathery crown that bent with the breeze. An outdoor work area, screened by dwarf fruit trees, helped hide it from view.

I trod the flagstone path that led to its door, scuffing my boots to alert Hisouk of my presence. He was a gentle soul who startled easily, so I'd made it a habit to be noisy when I came to visit. Light spilled from the open doorway in the early morning shadows. And a deep, sonorous voice called out from the potting shed.

"Come on in, Rhuger."

"Good morning, Hisouk," I called as I stepped within. "How'd you know it's me? I could have been any foul-tempered lout."

"The only foul-tempered lout I know who comes to visit me first thing in the morning is you, Rhuger." Humor lit his voice as he looked up at me from over the rim of his earthenware mug. A small smile curled his mouth before he took another sip of his morning tea. I chuckled as I leaned against the door frame.

The inside of the potting shed was surprisingly spacious. One long table ran across one side, with shelves above and drawers below. Stacks of pots and jars of seeds filled the shelves while, on the opposite wall, tools and herbs were hung with meticulous care. A small brazier with a kettle over it sat in the back of the room, next to a table and chairs. Hisouk was seated at the table, a small pen in his massive fist as he worked on his records.

He was so large in this snug space that he should look out of place, yet he looked like he belonged. Dressed in a grey tunic and brown pants tucked into his boots, his belt held pouches, shears, and other gardening tools. A bold contrast to the weapons that littered my belt. His coppery skin tone and short wavy hair complimented his powerful physique and the balance between the harshness and softness of his facial features that he shared with his sister. He was a handsome male and a kind one at that.

"So, what brings you to my humble haunt?" Hisouk asked as he waved to the other chair.

"I have a proposition for you." I began pushing off of the door frame and taking a seat across from him.

"Oh?" Hisouk prompted, one eyebrow raised as he poured me a mug of tea from the kettle. "Does it have to do with your charge?"

Hisouk was always so shrewd and perceptive. I'd always been able to shutter my reactions and emotions. I had to learn it to survive within the power-hungry halls of the Oc'Turin. But from what it seemed like, I was being blatant in my regard for Amelia. I shifted in my seat as I took the proffered mug of tea and tried not to let my discomfort show.

"Och, she needs a tutor to learn Teanga Dhubh. I was hoping you'd be able to help with that." I took a sip of the steaming tea and it was bracing. Herbaceous yet floral with a hint of honey.

"And you think I'd be the best orc for the job instead of a teacher or scholar from the academy?" He asked me with a frown.

The academy was where orclings got a basic education and more scholarly-minded orckin could pursue their intellectual interests. It had taken some work to create and was one of Rìgh Thorn's greatest achievements for the Oc'Dellor. Few clans outside of the Oc'Veltas had such an available education. The only reason I'd been educated amongst the Oc'Turin was that my mother was the Banrigh.

"I do. Most of the teachers at the academy are females who might not agree."

"Because a number of the teachers are willing mates, you refuse to entertain." Hisouk's sardonic smile made me cringe. "And you believe that they wouldn't help Amelia or would lead her astray?"

"Yes." I bit out, uncomfortable.

Hisouk just stared at me, as if he could peel back all the layers of what made me who I was, and see the true reasoning behind my request. It was something he had a knack for. Knowing things and seeing through facades to the core of things. Often I wondered if he had seers blood. Not as strong as that of a Fear a Chì, but a genetic remnant of magic like my healing ability.

But I'd never asked. And he'd never offered the information.

"I'll do it," Hisouk said, looking back down at his journal and flipping through its pages. "The afternoons would be the best time for me. I can begin today if she's willing."

"Thank you, Hisouk," I said. "You are a staunch friend and an honorable orc."

"Get yourself gone, Oc'Turin." Hisouk chuckled and shook his head as he returned to his journal.

Stalking from the potting shed, I mentally ticked that task off my list. The next wouldn't be so amenable. With a heavy sigh, I went through the bailey to the keep and Rìgh Thorn's study. As I arrived, I heard talk in his study and waited outside. In the hallway's quiet, I suddenly recognized the voice within as Asterun's.

What could he want with the Rìgh?

I quietly crouched down at the keyhole in the carved doors and placed my ear near it. The voices were quiet, hushed even, but I could hear them all the same. What I heard made my blood run cold.

"I'll think about your request, Asterun." Rìgh Thorn said, his voice clipped.

"Thank you, my Rìgh. I assure you, I'd make a good match for your granddaughter." Asterun replied. I gritted my teeth. Teeth I wanted to use to rip out his rutting throat.

"That remains to be seen." Rìgh Thorn said. "Let's see how you do at the mating tournament and I'll consider it. You're dismissed."

"As you wish, my Rìgh. I'll win that tournament in her honor." Asterun declared, voice strong and sure.

His footsteps drew close to the doors, and I smoothly stood and moved back, acting like I was just approaching the double doors. They flung wide and Asterun stalked from them like the study was his. Did his arrogance know no bounds? Asterun's black and purple gaze landed on me and he curled his lip in disgust.

"Oc'Turin Fògradh." He spat as we stepped forward, meeting mere inches from one another. Asterun had to look up at me. "What is someone like you doing here?"

"I was summoned by the Rìgh," I replied, my smile more a baring of teeth than a grin. "Were you summoned or did you just assume you could interrupt Rìgh Thorn's day?"

Asterun's eye twitched, and I got my answer.

"At least I'm a part of the clan. Not a dog entitled to nothing more than scraps." Asterun's grin turned wicked.

As if he could hurt me with that. I'd known it since the day I'd approached Rìgh Thorn to allow me to live amongst the Oc'Dellor. I hadn't been afforded much, essentially being a refugee from my clan of origin. But it had been a start.

"At least I've earned what I have," I replied drolly, bored. And it was true. "And I don't spit out promises to females and then renege on them."

Asterun snarled at me and slammed his shoulder into mine as he passed me on his way to wherever the hell he thought he deserved to be. It wasn't at Amelia's side, that was for damned sure. I'd have to petition the Rìgh to not allow that to happen. Asterun wouldn't understand her, and wouldn't have her best interests at heart.

And it was true. He'd offered promises to willing females, then backed out of them. Promises of becoming mates, promises of futures together, even promises of orclings. But each time he mated with a female, he'd backed out, spent himself on their bodies instead of inside them. It was unfair to the females who truly wished for the future he painted for them. He had this terrible reputation, yet they still threw themselves at him. Hoping they'd be the ones to win him.

Many males hated him for this. I was one of them. And he'd have to pry Amelia's hand from my cold, dead body.

"Oc'Turin!" Rìgh Thorn's voice thundered from his study. "Stop standing there and get in here."

Shaking my head to clear it of the haze of rage and the need to shred Asterun to ribbons, I entered the study and quietly closed the door behind me. Rìgh Thorn sat behind his desk, a stack of papers before him. He braced one elbow on his desk and propped the side of his face up with his fingers. Copper and onyx eyes bored into mine as I stood before him. His expression was blank.

"I've heard some interesting reports, Oc'Turin." He said dryly, and I stood ready to receive whatever punishment he deemed fit for my insolence. For being unable to wrangle my draw to Amelia. "As much as I'd like to string you up for ogling my granddaughter, it seems I need to thank you."

"What?" I asked, taken aback.

"Since Amelia has been here, you have been understanding and accommodating to her limitations. You've treated her as a person, no different from any other within the clan." He took a deep breath and let it out slowly. "It's been many years since I've seen her. I'd forgotten, and you recognized and helped her where I did not. For that, you have my thanks."

"Anyone else would have done the same," I muttered, suddenly uncomfortable with his praise.

"No. They wouldn't." Rìgh Thorn replied bluntly. "I've also been remiss in making sure she settled in well. Meanwhile, you've already sought to have her trained to ride a nocrys and I hear, you even got her a tutor for Teanga Dhubh. Both teachers that would treat her well."

"I didn't want her to feel left out. Her tutors are also her new friends. I thought they'd understand her needs the best." How did he learn of me finding her a tutor so quickly?

"You've done well as her bodyguard. You will be rewarded for it." Rìgh Thorn looked down at his papers and shuffled a few around aimlessly.

"Thank you, my Rìgh," I murmured. Pausing, I opened my mouth to speak, then closed it. Unsure of how to ask him what I desperately needed to know.

"Spit it out, Oc'Turin." Rìgh Thorn commanded, almost bored.

"I overheard your discussion with Asterun." I began clearing my throat as his gaze flicked to mine in cutting distaste. "Amelia has told me about your decree that she be at the Mating Tournament. I beg you, Rìgh Thorn. Do not allow Asterun to win her hand. I can tell you right now that he does not have her best interests at heart."

"Your constant bickering and posturing with the Master at Arms's apprentice has nothing to do with this?" He asked.

"I don't care about that," I explained with frank honesty, earnest that he listened to me. "I only care about Amelia's well-being. And Asterun would not care for her as he should."

"And you think you have the right to decide who I match her with?" Rìgh Thorn's tone was forbidding. "Do you presume to have a claim on her hand as well?"

"No, my Rìgh. I don't assume to have any such rights or claims. I know I'm not worthy of her. My only hope is that you'll heed my warning. For her sake." I told him, holding out my hands in supplication.

"I'll think about it." Rìgh Thorn said, returning his gaze to his papers and waving his hand in dismissal. "Does Amelia need anything else?"

"I'd suggest providing her with more clothes. And since she'll be at the Mating Tournament, something nice to wear, as she will be at your side." I murmured.

"Mmh." He said and began writing. "If that's all, then you're dismissed."

"As you will, my Rìgh." I bowed and left, closing the doors softly behind me.

My heart beat wildly in my chest as I walked away. More confused about where I stood with Rìgh Thorn than ever before. He'd rarely offered me praise. Or rewards. Yet he was acutely aware of my attraction to his granddaughter.

I walked a fine line. But it was one I was more than willing to walk to ensure Amelia's wellbeing. In all ways.

AMELIA

Rhuger found me sometime later napping in the hay. He nudged my boot until I snorted awake and glared up at him blearily. Trying to discern his face in the shadows cast on his features by the afternoon suns overhead.

"Wake up, sleepyhead." His warm rumble soothed the pissy edges of my psyche. Kind of hard to be mad at a guy waking you up with a voice like that.

"Unff," I grunted and pushed myself up in the pile, groaning at how my muscles ached. I sat in a slump and rubbed at my face, attempting to wake up. I stretched and a bunch of things popped in my shoulders and back.

"I didn't know you snored." Rhuger's voice rumbled again, that warm tone edged in amusement. Okay, pissy edges were back.

"I do when I'm exhausted." I scowled up at him. His grin was as bright as the suns and I squinted. It wasn't fair he looked so good all the time. He could get run over by a cart full of shit and still manage to look like he'd walked off a runway.

Rhuger offered me a hand, and I took it reluctantly. He helped me to my feet and then started pulling the straw out of my hair as I brushed nocrys fur and hay off of me. His fingers were gentle as he did so. But when his fingers accidentally brushed the shell of my ear and my neck, I nearly moaned. Instead, a shudder wracked me and I stepped away, blushing. He pulled his hand back.

"So, what brings you here?" I asked. Then realized it was a stupid question. He came here for *me,* duh. I was his charge, his *job.* I winced.

"I've come to take you to your first lesson in Teanga Dhubh." He replied, voice neutral as I shook out my hair to hide my embarrassment.

Sigg had heavily hinted that Rhuger felt some sort of way about me. But Rhuger'd *also* made it clear I was his duty. I didn't know where that left me in between the two. And it frustrated the shit out of me. Made me crabby. I never liked not knowing where I stood.

I knew how I felt about him. Acknowledging that I loved him wasn't the big revelation romance books talked about. That understanding had settled into my being easily as if I always had. It was as effortless as breathing, the transition of emotion seamless and true.

"Who's going to be my teacher?" I asked, trying to get my brain off of the orc I'd fallen for as he stood before me.

"Hisouk agreed to teach you." He replied as he gestured for me to follow him. I did, walking stiffly as my body remembered what to do with my legs after riding all day. "Sigg put you through your paces, huh?"

"You can say that again," I grunted, popping my back as we left the stables and headed back towards Daingneach. "So, what's Hisouk like? I mean, you kinda told me, but is there anything I should know in particular?"

"He's the head gardener for Baile Coille. Big, strong, likes roses, and is pretty quiet." Rhuger said calmly. "He's of Oc'Blyre ancestry, which is why he's so big. And he's a good friend. Perceptive too."

"And you trust him?"

"Och, pearl, I trust him." Rhuger chuckled. "He's a good male. Only wants his cridhe, so you don't have to worry about him making advances."

I paused as we approached Daingneach. There was that word again. Cridhe. Rhuger had said, the other night during the party that when he looked into my eyes, he saw his own cridhe looking back at him. What did it mean?

Perhaps I'd need to ask this Hisouk to translate. To help me understand. Because I had an inkling that Rhuger would avoid explaining.

He led me into the bailey and over to a stone hut against one of the curtain walls. Small trees and shade plants surrounded it as if trying to hide the hut from the rest of the world. It was charming and cool after being in the sun all morning. Rhuger stopped at the doorway and knocked on the open door.

"Hisouk, Amelia is here." He called.

"Have her come in." A deep voice called. It was calm, and clear instead of gravelly like Rhuger's.

Rhuger cocked an eyebrow and tipped his head towards the interior of the hut, beckoning me forward. I drew in a breath and let it out before walking inside. Whatever I'd imagined the interior would look like, I'd been wrong. It was clean and meticulously kept. Everything from tools to pots to jars, even drying plants, all had a place.

Looking around in wonder, I drew in the tiny details. How the jars were carefully labeled in a clear hand. How all the little drawers, almost like an apothecary's, were labeled as well in the same hand. Bundles of plants were hung with colored twine and a shelf held a neat row of books.

Then there was the orc in the back. He was huge, and I recognized him from the time I'd met my Grandpa Thorn in the garden, and from the feast. I could see the family resemblance to Manira immediately. They both shared the same coppery skin tone, full mouth, and strong facial features, Hisouk's more chiseled than his sister's. He kept his dark hair short, and he wore simple trousers and a tunic with a belt of gardening tools around his waist. Hisouk sat at a table near a brazier, and I could smell some sort of tea being brewed.

"Hello," I called and offered a small wave.

"Welcome, Amelia. It's lovely to officially meet you. I'm Hisouk. I heard you're friends with my sister, Manira." Came his deep, calming voice.

"Yes! Your sister is incredibly sweet and kind. She's helped me out so much since I got here and I really appreciate her friendship. And it's nice to meet you too." I replied earnestly.

"I'll leave you to it," Rhuger murmured from behind me. I whirled to see him halfway out the door.

"You're not staying?" I asked, slightly adrift.

"No, pearl. I'd be nothing more than a distraction from your studies. But don't worry. I'll be nearby if you need me, och?" He said with a smile.

"Oh, okay. Thank you." I replied, relaxing a bit. It helped to know he wouldn't be too far.

"I'll return for her at suppertime," Rhuger called to Hisouk, who just waved him off good-naturedly. Rhuger slipped quietly from the stone hut I now recognized as a potting shed.

Not the most common place to have language lessons, but better than being in a traditional classroom. I'd always excelled in school but had done anything and everything to shut out the stimuli of the classroom setting. Even going so far as to hide the earbuds I was using to listen to music in my hoodie's hood or my hair.

"So," Hisouk said, and I turned to look at him. "Why don't you have a seat and we can have a chat? I've got tea on the kettle if you'd like some?"

"I'd love some, thank you," I murmured and took a seat in the chair opposite Hisouk.

I watched as he poured me a cup of tea in an earthenware mug, with the same studious and meditative approach I'd witnessed in Japanese tea ceremonies. He filled the cup, set the kettle back on its brazier, and set it before me, turning the cup so the handle was in easy reach.

Carefully taking the cup in hand, I blew on the hot liquid and took a small sip. It was lovely, bright, and floral with something akin to citrus in it.

"It's really tasty." I offered, and Hisouk smiled.

"So, what are you hoping to learn?" He asked me.

"I'd like to learn Black Tongue so I can understand. So I'm not ignorant or left in the dark. If I'm going to be living here on Talam from now on, I need and want to learn more about its culture and language is a good place to start."

"Very astute." Hisouk sounded surprised as he sipped at his cup. "How did you learn your own language?"

And so began a long, interesting discussion with Hisouk. We

talked about my education on Earth, how language was normally learned, and in what steps. And he explained Common, Teanga Dhubh, and a small number of dialects some of the other clans used.

After a time, my cup emptied and Hisouk picked up my cup and inspected the remnants of my tea. His brow furrowed as he turned it this way and that, before setting it aside.

"I think you're going to initially need to learn how to speak Teanga Dhubh conversationally. Then, we can start teaching you our written language. How does that sound?" He asked.

"Sounds good to me."

"Do you have any questions?"

"I do," I murmured, hedging a bit. Drumming up the courage, I looked Hisouk in the eye. "What does 'cridhe' mean?"

I was *not* prepared for Hisouk's face to change colors. It went from coppery to pale to rust red in the span of a few moments, as his expression told me he was internally screaming. I waited, still staring him dead in the eye.

"Where did you hear that?" He finally said as he cleared his throat.

"Rhuger's said it a few times now," I said, shrugging. "I wasn't sure what it meant."

"Hoo..." Hisouk sighed and rubbed the bridge of his nose. "That male has himself all sorts of twisted up."

"What does it mean?" I asked. Hisouk looked skyward as if he were beseeching his deities, before looking back at me with his black and green gaze.

"I assume you've heard talk about mates, correct?" He asked.

"Yes, of course," I replied.

"Well, 'cridhe' translates to 'heart' but it is much more than that. To us orckin, a cridhe mate is our one true soulmate in the universe. When a cridhe pair find one another, mating marks appear on their chests." Hisouk placed his hand reverently over his. "We don't know why, but cridhe pairs have ceased to happen. Ruksala and your great-grandfather Tyras were the last cridhe pair on Talam."

"So when he said you only wanted your cridhe, that means your soulmate," I said.

"Yes. It's the same for a lot of males. Some seek pleasure mates to pass the time, so to speak. Others commit themselves to one another. The females have little choice, as there are so few of them." He explained, and my brow furrowed as I processed. "How else did Rhuger use the word cridhe?"

"Well..." I looked at Hisouk and figured he was trustworthy enough to tell. "When there was dancing in the city center after the feast, he told me that when he looks in my eyes, he sees his own cridhe staring back at him."

The silence that followed my statement was *deafening*. Hisouk blinked at me a few times, closed his eyes, and held his hands together in front of his face as if in prayer. If I'd thought he looked like he was internally screaming before, he was outright howling inside right now.

"Does cridhe have a second meaning?" I asked. Not daring to hope it only had one meaning. That perhaps Rhuger truly felt something for me, too. Something from his own mouth and not Sigg's observations.

"There is only one meaning." He said flatly, hands still in front of his mouth as he stared at the table, unblinking. "That male is going to dig himself an early grave."

"What?" I asked, confused.

"Nothing," Hisouk replied, placing his hands, palms down, on the table. He looked me in the eye as he leaned forward. "If you care about him at all, if you want him to continue being your bodyguard, for the love of the Source, do not tell anyone else."

"I haven't. I won't." The words tumbled out of me quickly. "Is it bad that he said that? I'm not sure I'm following the context here."

"The context, Amelia, is that you are Rìgh Thorn's only granddaughter. You are destined for a prestigious match. One of political importance. Rhuger is being a thrice-cursed *fool* and will probably get himself strung up at this rate." Hisouk muttered.

"What did you see?" I asked. "In the tea leaves."

Hisouk's brows shot up into his hairline. I got a distinct impression that Hisouk wasn't used to others being perceptive of him in kind. He sighed heavily before grasping the cup again in his large hand. So large that if I were to hold hands with him, it would look like he was holding a small child's hand. Emerald and black eyes flicked to mine and his mouth drew flat.

"How did you know I can see things in the leaves?"

"Well, reading tea leaves is a really old divination tool back on Earth. I didn't think it would be used here." I explained. Hisouk's eyebrows flicked up in surprise. "My Grandma Ruth is pagan and is into that sort of thing."

"It seems there are fewer differences between humans and orckin than I thought." He murmured before holding the cup so I could see the tea leaves inside. He pointed at one area. "See this? It shows a power shift. This bit here tells me there will be a harsh conflict. And this part..." Hisouk paused, that rust color riding high on his strong features. "Well, it means mating. And with the size and position... It means a *lot* of mating."

"Great. Just what I need. More conflict." I sighed and rubbed my face before asking the next obvious question. "Can you tell *who* I'm supposed to be having all this sex with?"

"No." Hisouk shook his head. "But you need to be careful. There are multiple plots aimed at you. You are at the center of what's going to happen. The star is here, though, so there's hope."

"I guess it's all good for the plot line," I muttered.

CHAPTER 33

The next few days fell into a rhythm. I'd get up at the ass crack of dawn, go learn how to herd my particularly particular nocrys, and then sequester with Hisouk in the potting shed to learn how to speak Teanga Dhubh. Then Rhuger would come to get me, we'd eat dinner, or more accurately I'd do my best to not fall asleep in my bowl, and then I'd go home and fall face-first into bed.

Somewhere in there, Sharn had whisked me away to the baths, thank goodness. There was only so much I could take of smelling and feeling gross. I got more clothing too, so I could change more often, which was a blessing. But as the days passed, my mind kept wandering back to that first night when Hisouk had read my tea leaves.

When Rhuger got me, I'd been a mess. Exhausted in body and mind. And heart. My thoughts kept tumbling around in my head like rocks in a dryer. I kept trying to push away the knowledge of what cridhe meant. To push away the knowledge that I'd evidently get banged like a screen door in a hurricane pretty soon. Because there was no way to know if it was with someone I wanted or not.

Rhuger had snagged us bowls of stew and some rolls before

ushering me through Baile Coille to his home tree... My home tree... *Our* home tree? All I know is that Rhuger had bid me goodnight, and the way he'd called me 'pearl'? It had slid down my spine like a caress.

I knew that Grandpa Thorn wouldn't approve of Rhuger. I'd learned from Rhuger's friends that he evidently felt some sort of way about me. One he was adamant I didn't know about. Time was running out for me to find a mate and get knocked up, or else I'd get hitched to Rìgh Orok the Slimy. If I said no to being his mate, I'd risk a clan war the orckin could not afford as a species.

In the quiet dark of my home tree, Hisouk's words came back to haunt me. I knew it wasn't a coincidence that he became my tutor. That he'd read my leaves. A pattern lay here somewhere, too large for me to see yet. One that Hisouk had hinted at.

I could feel something coming. It was there in the air, a thrumming and a primal knowing. Like when a big storm is about to break over the world. With each breath, I drew closer to the cusp of whatever was about to happen. So I made a choice.

I would not let the scheming of others dictate my life. It was mine. So no matter what, I would choose myself. Even if it meant I ran away to live alone in the forest. Or find some way back to the gate, back home. Or somehow, beyond hope, find my purpose and my happily ever after.

One morning, I woke up and sat on the edge of my bed. Yawning and groaning as I stretched in the pre-dawn light. A soft knock sounded at my door, a knock I knew well.

"Coming!" I called and shuffled over to the door, scratching my side as I went. When I opened it, Rhuger stood there. He swung his head to say something to me and froze with his mouth open. "What is it?" I mumbled, rubbing the sleep from my eyes.

"Uh," He started and coughed, looking away. That bright green high on his cheeks. "I wanted to let you know that there are no lessons today."

"No?" I asked, confused.

Glancing down at myself to figure out why he got all bashful all of a sudden, I saw that my proverbial headlights were on. Really? My nipples puckered against the pre-dawn chill were enough to make this warrior a blushing flower with delicate sensibilities? I wasn't sure if I should be irritated or think it was cute. I settled on both.

"Today is preparation day for the tournament." He said, glancing at me out of the corner of his eye. "We're all to pitch in to help set up for it. So instead of lessons, we'll help where needed."

"Oh. Okay." I mumbled, and he made to move away. "So this is the Mating Tournament, right?"

He froze, ears practically glowing neon green in the soft gray light.

"Yes." Came his rather strangled reply.

"Can you tell me about it?" I asked, leaning against the door frame, head propped against the wood and arms crossed over my chest.

"How about you get dressed and I'll tell you on the way to breakfast?" He replied.

"Okay." I shrugged and turned to go inside, but not before I saw him stare after me.

A few minutes later, I was dressed, and we were on our way into Baile Coille proper. Even for it being so early, with a pre-dawn mist rising from the ground in the cold light, people were hurriedly rushing about with tools and armfuls of banners, carts of barrels, and more.

Orclings were running around underfoot, carrying messages and small parcels. And everywhere there was laughing and excited chatter.

"When our three moons align, once a year, we offer praise to the gods and celebrate," Rhuger explained as we passed people decorating the large sunstone lanterns that led the way along the cobbled avenues. "It's a big day, as the tournament is for males to test their mettle against one another for glory, for recognition, and possibly to win the heart of a female."

"Females can't compete?" I asked, cocking an eyebrow up at him. Sounded rather sexist to me.

"Och, no. Females are too precious to allow them to compete. There are so few left we can't risk it. No matter that it would do our people good to have females who could fight again." He shrugged, ducking under a low-hanging banner.

"Again?" I asked. That caught my attention.

"The Iolaire'lasaire. They were a fighting force comprising female warriors within each clan. Named after our fire eagles who soar over the wilds." The smile on his face was wistful. "My mother used to tell me stories about them when I was small."

That brought a smile to my face. Imagining Rhuger as a small orcling, sitting on his mother's knee. A wistful pang cut deep into my heart that he didn't have a mother or a father. No one to love him. To be proud of him or encourage him.

I desperately wished then that the gate was fixed. So he could meet *my* mother and grandmother. I knew they would love him and accept him almost immediately. Imagining my Grandma Ruth shooing him into her kitchen to eat cookies or my mother giving him a big bear hug warmed my heart. He deserved a family who loved him.

Wait... I wanted him to not just meet my family, but to become part of my family. *Shit.* I was in far deeper than I'd thought. I flicked my gaze up to look at his face as he surveyed the bustling avenues. It was going to be agony to let him go. To say goodbye.

We reached the city center and all hope of asking Rhuger more about the Mating Tournament and the fire eagle warriors went out the window. It was so damned *loud* as orckin were rolling in barrels full of uisge-beatha and the floral wine they called fion-math. Tables were brought in and a stage was being built for musicians. And then there was the market. Carts and barrows were being rolled down the broad market avenue from the square with musicians playing to keep spirits high.

More than once, Rhuger gently guided me through the throng. He kept me from bumping into people and caught me when I tripped over a streamer that lay on the ground. I wasn't very graceful this morning, but with everything going on, it was hard for me to mentally filter through all the sensory information I was absorbing. Luckily, we exited the city center and ended up at the kitchens before I went into sensory overload.

"Amelia, Rhuger, over here!"

"Sharn!" I cried, embracing the tall female. Sharn was all smiles, and she wrapped her arm around my shoulders as we let go from our hug.

"You've got tourney duty with Sigg today, Rhuger." Sharn grinned and Rhuger groaned.

"How am I supposed to protect Amelia and help build the tourney at the same time?" He asked, irritated.

"You don't." Sharn laughed. "Amelia will be with me today. We're going out to pick flowers before the suns rise."

"You'll stay within Fàinne Sleagh?" Rhuger's face and tone were forbidding.

"Of course, you dunce. I'm not dumb enough to take her out into Noc'tal Forest without a guard, least of all without you. You'd put me in an early grave if I tried."

"I'm glad you know it." Rhuger bit out.

"You really ought to curb that territorial bent you have, friend," Sigg said as he joined us, elbowing Rhuger in his side.

"I'm not territorial." Rhuger snapped.

"And I'm not blond," Sigg replied dryly. Sharn sniggered, and I just looked at all three of them like they were children.

"Rhuger," I began, and his gaze snapped to mine. "I promise I won't leave the stone ring, okay? I promise I'll stay with Sharn and the others who are flower-picking."

The way the stress seemed to melt from him was palpable.

"Good lass." He murmured and the way he said it brought a flush to my cheeks.

"Oh, for the love of the Source, would you cut it out?" Sharn asked, smacking Rhuger's arm. His gaze broke from mine.

"What?" He asked, affronted.

"You're ridiculous and you're getting more annoying than you're worth." Sharn's lip was curled and Rhuger bared his teeth at her briefly.

"Let's go, Rhuger. Amelia has promised you she'll be a *good lass* for you. So let's get to work. I already grabbed us some hand pies so you can curb your *hunger*." Sigg said, grabbing the collar of Rhuger's shirt and hauling him bodily behind him. Rhuger protested, but Sigg was powerfully built and was used to far feistier beasts.

"Bye!" I called and waved.

"That male is an idiot." Sharn sighed.

"What do you mean?" I asked. Sharn's sapphire and obsidian gaze slid to mine and softened. She reached up and ruffled my hair, and I had to bat her hand away.

"You're sweet and precious, and he's an ornery fool." She smiled gently at me. "Now let's get some food and get to work, shall we?"

Sharn had led the way to a small group gathered on the outskirts of the fields near the stables. We'd eaten our breakfast on the way, delicious fruit hand pies with that coconut-like syrup. As we approached, I immediately recognized two of the orckin gathered there as they towered over the rest.

"Hisouk! Manira!" I called and waved wildly. Sharn held up her hand in greeting as we walked through the tall grasses.

"Amelia, Sharn, good morning!" Manira called, waving politely back.

"Good morning, you two." Hisouk's clear, deep voice cut through the chatter of the rest of the group. "Well, now that we're all here, we can begin."

"Pft. Finally, decided to show, huh?" A voice called, and I rolled my eyes heavenward for patience.

"Good morning, peaches," I said, looking over at the pretty female and her gaggle of cronies.

"Took-" she began, looking me up and down with a sneer on her face.

"NOPE!" I interrupted as I held up a hand at her. "We are *not* going to do this today."

She looked constipated as she swallowed the rest of what she'd planned to say. Everyone openly stared at the both of us as I kept my hand raised and side-eyed her. Hisouk coughed pointedly, and we all looked at him.

"As head gardener, I'm going to lead our tasks for the day. I've got lists of the flowers we need. You'll be in groups of two or three. Please grab gathering baskets." Sharn and Manira waved to me and I gave them both thumbs up before grabbing our baskets. Peaches put her hand on the first one I grabbed, so I just dropped it and grabbed the next one. No need to play into any drama she might want to create over choosing *baskets* for crying out loud. She made a frustrated sound as I turned back to my group, a stack of baskets in my arms. "Good. Now, we'll be gathering flowers in the uninhabited portions of Baile Coille and the slopes leading up to Fàinne Sleagh. I need to warn you *not* to go into Noc'tal Forest. There have been dorcha'aon sightings and your safety is paramount. Therefore, we have an armed escort from the guard. There is little to be worried about, as it's daylight, but we need to be extra cautious."

We looked from Hisouk to the small contingent of guards off to one side. A pair of black and amethyst eyes locked on me as I stood with my friends. It was Asterun. Luckily, Ophir was next to him, his calm, calculated gaze sweeping over us, assessing. At least there was someone with some sense amongst the guard.

Our ragtag group of flower pickers consisted mostly of females, the elderly, and orclings. That we needed a guard meant the threat of the dorcha'aon was serious. And here I was... without my territorial bodyguard.

"Rhuger is going to be *pissed*," I whispered to Sharn, who was frowning. "Is a guard normal?"

"No. This is new." Sharn murmured low.

"We never needed a guard before," Manira whispered. "Where's Rhuger?"

"Off with Sigg building the tourney," Sharn muttered dryly. "If I would have known the plan, I would have told him to come with us."

"Okay." I sighed. "Time to *really* stick to the rules or he's going to flip."

"He's going to flip, anyway." Manira huffed a laugh.

"Should I go get him?" I asked.

"No time." Sharn sighed before looking down at me. "You are going to have to stick close to me, okay?"

I nodded as we all began pulling the harnesses for the baskets over our shoulders. The baskets themselves were cylindrical and hung from hip to knee. The harness went over the body crosswise, and a second strap secured it to the waist. Smaller baskets were worn like backpacks by the orclings and elderly.

"As with each year, the person who collects the most flowers will receive a bead," Hisouk called as groups took the lists of flowers from him and headed out into the slopes and forest of Baile Coille.

A guard peeled off and followed each group. I kept Asterun in my peripheral vision and saw him hang back until we had gotten the list from Hisouk. Then he'd slipped in front of the guard who was meant to go with us, a young green-eyed orc who couldn't keep his eyes off Manira. He was a whole head shorter than she was and I was instantly rooting for the short king. I was *not* rooting for Asterun.

"Good morning Neamhnaid, Sharn, Manira." Asterun said with a flourishing bow, nearly knocking the young guard over with his ass.

I stood staring down at the back of Asterun's arrogant head. He glanced up, and I lazily looked away from him. Asterun frowned and Sharn was trying not to laugh behind me. I looked up to the young guard, who was scowling something fierce at Asterun's back.

"Hey, what's your name?" I asked. Startled, he looked up at me, his expression softening.

"I'm Rorich, Neamhnaid." He said with a small bow.

"Amelia is fine, please," I said, waving the platitude away. I hoped one day everyone would get the picture and stop calling me Neamhnaid. "You're with us, okay?"

"Uh, yes! Yes, ma'am." He said and stood taller, matching me in height. His gaze flicked to Manira and his storm-grey skin turned silver high on his cheeks. Cute.

"Now, wait a minute—" Asterun began, but I let my basket whack him in the head as I passed him by.

Sharn barked a laugh as Manira giggled behind her hand. Rorich was entranced by his giantess's giggles. And poor Hisouk was trying to help Asterun up from where he'd landed on his ass.

"Bye, Hisouk!" I called, waving without looking back.

"I'm not sure you should have done that. Asterun can be quite..." Manira began as we strode into the forest.

"An audacity-filled asshole?" I asked. Rorich sputtered and tried to hide his mirth behind a fist.

"I was going to say troublesome." Manira cocked an eyebrow at me. "He's not one to embarrass lightly."

"Well, tough shit." I bit out. "I'm tired of people trying to manipulate me into doing what they want."

"Still, he's one of Oc'Dellor's finest warriors," Sharn murmured. "If Rhuger isn't here, he'd be a close second. No offense, Rorich."

"None taken." Rorich shrugged. "I'm still new to the guard. Asterun is an excellent fighter."

"Still wouldn't want him within slapping distance," I muttered in reply.

"Here, this way," Sharn said and veered off the path the others were taking. "There's a glade I hit every year that few people know about."

We followed her through the multi-colored ferns and bushes beneath the gnarled branches of the towering trees that would one day become homes. Tiny critters that looked like a chipmunk, a lizard, and a piglet had a deranged love child clambered over the roots of the trees out of our path. Butterflies with ridiculously long tails flittered above us in the buttery shafts of sunlight that filtered through the canopy.

We picked flowers we found along the way, attempting not to strip the forest as we did so. Some were lovely, with ringlet petals like curled ribbons that trailed to the ground. There were others that were in tiny vibrant clusters that smelled like lilacs and apple blossoms. Then there were the seven-petaled crimson flowers of the dearc ruadh.

Rorich, unsurprisingly, fell back to talk with Manira. She was telling him about the plants we were picking. She could have been reciting the tax laws from the year I was born and he wouldn't have cared. It was adorable, and I hoped they found sweetness together. Which reminded me.

"How does everything work? Finding mates and all?" I asked Sharn as we followed the trail.

"Why do you want to know?"

"To understand the heritage of my people?" I asked, confused and also unwilling to admit I had only two weeks to find a mate. Or end up Rìgh Orok's.

"Don't you mean because there's a certain orc you can't stop staring at?" She asked as she leaned down and winked at me.

"I-I mean..." I stuttered, bright red. She laughed warmly and clapped my shoulder.

"Rhuger's a wonderful male if you choose him. Females aren't allowed to train since we're so prized. But he trains me sometimes. It helps me stay grounded." Sharn told me, suddenly sobering. "I'm... not really looking forward to the Mating Tournament."

"Can you tell me more about it?" I asked, cocking my head.

"It's a yearly event for the unmated. Males compete to prove themselves worthy of the unmated females in the games. There are fewer of us this year as three of the females from last year are now mated and no young females are yet of age to join..." Sharn sounded so weary of the whole thing. "We're encouraged to sleep with many males once the games are over during the party—any that catch our interest really—to increase the chances of becoming pregnant. We get the choice of who, thankfully. But when you're like me, and males are unappealing to begin with..."

"Oh, Sharn... I'm so sorry." I told her, taking her hand in mine and giving it a good squeeze. She just smiled wanly at me.

Then a thought scratched at the back of my mind and panic set in.

"Will I...?" I gulped, not even able to finish my question. My grandfather had forbidden me from going to the party. But that didn't mean there might be expectations of me to participate in some way. She must have seen my fear, for her smile was real then.

"No. You won't be encouraged to mate like the rest of us will. Or allowed at the party. You're new to us and are still adjusting to our ways. Also, you're the Rìgh's granddaughter and you'll be expected to make a prestigious match." She said, reinforcing what she'd said a few days prior.

"Oh." I deflated. My mouth suddenly went dry with the realization that like the orckin females, I likely wouldn't have much of a choice.

"Rìgh Thorn will listen to you and your wishes. He loves you dearly. He'll give you a say." Sharn attempted to console me. It was something, I guess, that my grandfather would bother to listen to me. Still felt wrong to be wed off after growing up a feminist.

"He's given me two weeks." I finally confided.

"For what?" She asked.

"To find a mate. Or I'm to be mated to Rìgh Orok when he returns. If I don't? It'll start a clan war." I sighed.

"What?" Sharn asked, coming to a full stop. I turned to look at her and gave her a defeated shrug. "You can't be serious? Source be damned, you're serious."

"Grandpa Thorn was supposed to give me a list of 'approved males' to choose from, but he hasn't. And I've only got a few days left." I picked one of the ribbon flowers to distract myself, swallowing hard against my fear.

"Who would you choose? Of everyone?" She asked, the only person to bother.

"I think you know the answer to that already." I smiled sadly at her. "But... He only sees me as a job. As his duty. He said as much himself. I refuse to force anyone into this. I wouldn't be able to live with myself."

"Oh, Amelia..." Sharn looked devastated. Then furious, her brows drawing together and her blue eyes darkening to the color of an angry midnight sea. "I'm going to have to knock some sense into that blasted idiot. If Sigg doesn't do it for me."

"Please, don't." I pleaded, placing a hand on her arm. "I don't want to cause any problems, okay?"

"So what, you're just okay with being Rìgh Orok's plaything? Okay, with him seeking to break you?" Her voice rose and Manira and Rorich slowed down, staring between us.

"No. I'm not." I shrugged. "It won't come to that."

"Then what are you going to do?"

"Either I'll find someone willing who I can tolerate touching me." I drew in a shaky breath and let it out. "Or, I kill Orok."

No one breathed. Not even the breeze dared shift the leaves in the canopy overhead. Rorich's eyes were nearly bulging out of his cute head. Manira was scandalized and placed a hand over her heart. And Sharn? Sharn looked mournful.

"You'll start a clan war." She murmured.

"If Rhuger's taught me anything about the Oc'Turin, it's that they value power. What's more powerful than murdering their Rìgh?"

"You mean it."

"Yes," I whispered.

Sharn stared at me for a heartbeat before shaking her head and looking over at Manira and Rorich. "We tell no one what we've heard. Got it?" They both nodded vigorously. "We need to deny we heard any talk about murdering a Rìgh."

"Doing what to what Rìgh?" Rorich asked, shrugging and playing dumb.

"Exactly," Sharn murmured. She looked back at me and shook her head. "I'm going to really have to beat some sense into that bodyguard of yours. I swear to you it won't come to that. Too many people care about you to let you end up in Rìgh Orok's clutches. Do you understand?"

"I'd like to think that." I gave her a soft smile.

"You need to value yourself more," Manira murmured, and I looked at her. "You've had more of an impact than you think."

My smile turned watery as I fought back tears. "How close are we to the glade, Sharn?" I asked, and turned back to lead the way along the trail. Deafening quiet followed me into the wild tangle of the forest.

CHAPTER 34

RHUGER

Sigg and I were tasked with building the railing that would encircle the arenas for the tournament. The posts had already been set into the earth, and we were hefting the railing beams into place on top of them. After years of doing all sorts of manual labor in Baile Coille, two weeks of monitoring my charge had left me soft. I was surprised to find my muscles burning a little when they wouldn't have before. I resolved to return to the training yards while she had her lessons.

"So, how long are you going to wait to tell her?" Sigg asked me as we hefted a beam and carried it to the posts for the railing.

"Tell who what?" I asked, focused on the task at hand. We placed the beam on top of the posts and began fitting them into the holes cut into the beam. There'd been some slight warping of the beam, so I had to hammer it into place.

"Tell Amelia how you feel about her."

I was mid-swing with the wooden hammer when his words registered. Instead of hitting the top of the beam, I hit my thumb where it gripped it. Roaring behind clenched teeth, I dropped the hammer and grasped my thumb in my hand. Applying pressure to help ease the explosion of pain that lanced up my hand and arm.

Sigg laughed. I looked at him, bent over, and snarled. My expression and anger didn't faze him. He leaned against his side of the beam where it'd fit perfectly onto the posts.

"Word's gotten around that Rìgh Thorn has given her two weeks to find a mate. Or be married off to Rìgh Orok. He demanded her hand when he was here, you know." Sigg's smile faded.

"I *know*." I snapped, still trying to ride out the pain without lashing out at my friend. I'd overheard the gossip on the way to the tourney field, the details Amelia had left out the other night when she'd whispered it so softly I barely caught what she'd said. How it rankled and left me nearly vibrating with rage.

"Time's ticking. She hasn't chosen anyone yet, and the tournament will likely decide who she mates. Rìgh Thorn's a doting grandfather, but he won't let her fall into Rìgh Orok's clutches. She *will* have to mate with someone before Orok returns for her. Asterun has already begun boasting that she'll be his."

"Don't you think I know all of this?" I raged, releasing my thumb to throw my arms wide. The throbbing of my thumb matched the aching throb in my heart.

"Then what the hell are you doing? It's obvious how you feel about her. Tell her and get this over with. Spare her from your brother." Sigg snapped, leaning forward. I paused. I'd never seen him lose his temper before.

"Don't you get it? I'm not *worthy* of her! I am an *exile from clan Oc'Turin.* Do you really think, after all these years of me trying to be accepted here, that Rìgh Thorn will just magically accept me as his granddaughter's mate?" I yelled, teeth bared.

Sigg stared at me as my chest heaved with my ragged breaths.

His expression was stony, disappointed, and angry. Fury thinned his mouth into a white line.

"I'll tell you what I told Amelia." He said, voice quiet amongst the bustling of the builders. "*You* don't get to decide if you're worthy enough. *She* does."

I paused, taking that in. What he'd told Amelia?

"I really thought better of you, Rhuger," Sigg said, lip curling. "This isn't about *you*. It's about keeping *her* safe. She is my friend. She is smart, kind, and lovely. And if you think for one *moment* that I'd allow her to go to Rìgh Orok or Asterun, you're sorely mistaken. If *you* won't be her mate? Then *I will.*"

"*You wouldn't dare...*" I whispered, the words dropping from my mouth like molten slag. Shock slid over my skin in a cold, sick wave. What kind of betrayal was this? My friend declaring himself for the female I loved.

"I would. And I *will.*" He stared me down from under a lowered brow, expression thunderous. "I'll be far kinder to her than Orok or Asterun would."

"She's not your cridhe," I replied, still sick with shock.

"She doesn't *have* to be, you absolute dunce." He spat.

"Why?"

"Must you really ask me that?" Sigg was incredulous. "I have the ability and position to challenge Asterun and to be accepted as her mate within the Oc'Dellor. I will be her mate, care for her as she deserves, and protect her until either of us finds our cridhe. And if I don't, I know Hisouk would."

I felt the blood drain from my face.

Two of my closest friends in the clan were ready to pledge

themselves to Amelia. Despite only ever wanting their cridhe. Ready to use their positions and power to protect her from my deplorable brother. I was her bodyguard, yet here my friends were, ready to lay everything on the line.

Sigg was right. Her well-being and safety came before my discomfort. My feelings of unworthiness.

"If you don't like it?" Sigg asked. "Then do us *all* a damned favor, including Amelia, and *tell her* how you *feel*. She knows you, trusts you over anyone else besides her kin, cares for you, and she *makes you happy*. And if you weren't aware, *you* make *her* happy!"

"She deserves better," I muttered, still staring at Sigg. Because she did. She deserved the world and the stars above.

"Then *be* better! Coward!" He shouted, and I flinched. He let out a bark of a roar and strode towards me, slamming his shoulder into mine so hard I had to take a step back as he passed. Leaving me to finish hammering the beam into place on my own.

I stood there as the rest of the builders continued putting together the bleachers and dais. Like a boulder within a moving stream. Sigg's words rang in my head as I blinked down at my calloused and scarred hands. My thumb was now badly bruised.

He was right. I was a coward. But what was I afraid of? Her rejecting me? I somehow doubted that she would. She'd likely accept me as a mate, as she'd accepted everything else about me.

But maybe that was it. I'd never been accepted like this before. Cared for and considered before. Perhaps I wasn't scared because I feared rejection. I was scared that she would be my mate. Source, I was scared that she might even be my cridhe. Hadn't I told her I saw my cridhe when I looked into her eyes?

I was a coward because I was afraid of being loved, afraid of what that looked like and all the ways it could destroy me. It wasn't a question of *if* she was worth setting aside my fears for. That was an immediate yes. It was, *could* I?

AMELIA

We'd eventually made it to the glade, which was high on the slopes at the outer edges of the forest. The stone spires curved above us towards the center of Baile Coille, almost like curved claws, casting shadows that the twin suns above couldn't penetrate. The little glade itself was rife with all kinds of flowers that thrived in the cool shade cast by the stones overhead.

We spent at least an hour collecting flowers as the sun rose and mist curled along the dew-covered ground. I'd wandered out into the trees as there were more of the dearc ruadh flowers under the gnarled limbs of the canopy. I popped a few of the berries into my mouth, snacking as I moved, following a small trail of glowing mushrooms.

I wasn't an idiot. I kept the glade in sight between the tree trunks. The others were chatting and picking flowers nearby, too. But then I heard it, a rustling in the opposite direction of the glade. I could see the green swathes of the slopes between the trees. And there was Peaches, leaving the forest behind, looking over her shoulder suspiciously before starting the climb up to the base of the stone spires.

"Shit!" I bit out quietly.

She was acting too suspicious and if she was about to do what I thought she was, she needed to be stopped. But there wasn't enough time to hunt down the others to go get her. So I cursed myself a fool and left the forest behind me, following her up to a section where trailing vines filled in a deep crease in the stone. Ferns and moss spread out from it on the stone spires like a bruise.

"Peaches!" I snapped, panting as I watched her push aside the trailing vines. "The hell do you think you're doing?"

"I'm going to go get more flowers. What does it look like I'm doing?" She asked me, incredulous.

"We're not supposed to go out into Noc'tal Forest!" I hissed, recognizing that this path lead out past the Fàinne Sleagh.

"Well, if *someone* hadn't needed a feast, there would be enough flowers for the tournament," Peaches said, head high and regal as if she were a queen. A queen of idiocy, more like.

"Like I *asked* for the feast?" I laughed. "You *clearly* don't know the first thing about me."

"*Clearly*. I don't care. Now leave me be. I'm going to go get the flowers we need. The orckin who gathers the most gets a bead and I need one."

"What on Earth do you need a bead so damned badly for?" I asked, being a *total* idiot as I followed her through the curtain of vines that blocked the opening to Noc'tal Forest. Behind the vines, with their lovely smelling flowers under the leaves, was a narrow winding passage through the stone.

"Please. Are you always such a bore? Why don't you be a good little Neamhnaid and stay where Grandpa Rìgh Thorn can protect you." Her tone was dripping with condescension. And jealousy.

"The dorcha'aon threat is serious, Peaches! Rhuger saw one when he brought me to the Oc'Dellor!" I exclaimed, trying to get her to see reason. She pushed through some ferns and I followed her out into Noc'tal Forest.

"My *name* is not *Peaches!*" She yelled, startling a flock of birds to take flight. "My *name* is *Inassa!* I don't even know what a peach *is!*"

"Fine, please keep it down, Inassa!" I hissed. "And for your information, peaches are an Earth fruit the same color as your skin.

Quite tasty, actually."

She paused, looking down at me, her lovely face screwed up into an expression of confusion.

"I'm not sure if I should be offended or not." She muttered. "Calling me after a fruit."

"Well, y'all are calling me after a damned *pearl,* so..." I flapped my arms uselessly. She gave me a droll look and continued on her way, stopping to pick flowers each time she came near a cluster. "Look, I don't care if you need a bead. It's not safe and I'm not leaving you out here alone!"

"Why not? You owe me nothing. And I'm not one of your fawning followers." She sounded so bitter.

"Because you're a *person,* you idiot!" I hissed, and she jerked back as if I'd slapped her. "Look I don't particularly like you, and you obviously hate my guts, but you're a person and I can't in good conscience leave you out here *alone* when there are *monsters who can eat your face off* prowling the gotdamned forest!"

And, of course, as if I'd irrevocably tempted fate by slapping her in the face with a rotting salmon, a weird, skittering growl echoed around the little glade we found ourselves in. The sound slid up and down my spine as we both froze, flowers in hand. The sound of something parting the leaves nearby had us both turning our heads in the direction of the noise in abject terror.

"Oh, *fuck.*" I breathed as Inassa whimpered.

Because an enormous head peeked out at us from behind some bushes. It was vulpine in shape with large ears, a wicked scar across its face, and six glowing red eyes set into inky black flesh. Its head alone was the same size as Luther. In the next breath, it slowly stalked from the greenery onto the mossy ground. It made that weird skittery sound again, like rocks being slid against metal.

The terror I felt choked me and made my stomach churn, made my bowels and bladder go watery, and made me want to weep and run and fight and pass out all at once. Because this thing? It was fucking enormous. With six legs, six! All twisted and bent and lean like it hadn't eaten in a long, long time. Its fur was inky black and patchy, shiny black skin showing through the mangey bits.

Then I noticed its talons as it took a powerful step forward, cocking its head at us in the way predators do. Like we were its dinner, and it was deciding which one to eat first. It was huffing, scenting us. It cocked its head the other way and approached us boldly.

Inassa let out a keening noise, and I instinctively slid in front of her into a defensive stance. What I thought I could do with my tiny claws against this titan I didn't know. Looking in my peripheral vision, I couldn't spot anything on the ground I could use as a weapon. Not a rock, a fallen branch, hell, even a *stick*. But the forest provided nothing, and I doubted a fistful of flowers would make it flee.

It prowled closer, the gap between us growing smaller, darker, with each breath. Until it came to a stop with its head lowered, its eyes focused intently on me. It made that skittery sound again, eyes stacked in two columns of three over its cheeks and forehead set into its vulpine skull, flickering crimson, and bright red. Almost like sunstones.

And here I was. Admiring a monster's peepers. Breaking *all* the rules. Out in Noc'tal Forest, without a guard, outside the Fàinne Sleagh, nowhere *near* the groups. Face to face with a nightmare-made-flesh that must be a dorcha'aon. With nothing to defend Inassa and me with, but a basket of flowers.

Its withered lips peeled back from rows upon rows of serrated teeth, the length of my forearm, mere inches from my face. I could see my terrified reflection in its flickering crimson gaze as it snarled and gnashed its teeth. And I wondered precisely how much it would hurt to die.

CHAPTER 35*

AMELIA

I stood stock still as the dorcha'aon breathed against my face. Its huffs of foul air stank of charr and a sickly sweetness as it scented me from its wickedly curved nostrils, so narrowly slit that I hadn't noticed them at first. I didn't blink. I barely breathed. Just let time crawl by as this massive beast exhaled on me.

It lowered its head slightly and bumped my chest, nearly sending me sprawling backward on top of Inassa. I held my ground though, and it bumped my chest again, a little harder. It wanted something, but my bleating brain couldn't come up with a single idea of what it could want. I had nothing but flowers!

It let out a ragged, frustrated growl, and I took an involuntary step back. I could hear Inassa sobbing quietly behind me and I mentally begged her to shut the hell up. Vaguely, as if the memory couldn't quite rise through the fog of my horror, I remembered dorcha'aon were nocturnal. If so, what the hell was this one doing out in the damned sunshine?

"Amelia! Inassa! There you are!" a voice cried as Asterun broke through the foliage beside us. He pulled up short as we all turned to look at him in horror. Dread pooled in my gut as I realized I was going to die now. That we were *all* going to die out here.

Asterun's purple gaze snapped from Inassa on the ground behind me, to where I was facing down what orckin nightmares were made of. I saw him swallow hard, hand reaching instinctively for a weapon. His eyes wide with the realization he couldn't fight it, that he was facing death the same as us.

The dorcha'aon roared at Asterun. The sound was like a train breaking hard on railroad tracks and crushing stones in a quarry. I raised my hands to cover my ears. My eardrums fit to burst so close to the source of the shrieking noise.

Between one heartbeat and the next, it lunged at me and snapped closed its jaws. My breath caught as I saw my life flash before my eyes. I was dead. I was dead, dead, dead, *dead, DEAD!*

But then, I was yanked sideways as the dorcha'aon took off into the forest with me. I couldn't help the wail that escaped me as I realized it hadn't bitten down on *me*. It had bitten down on the *basket of flowers* and I was just conveniently dangling from it by the leather harness.

Desperate not to get brained against a tree or boulder, I balled up the best I could around the basket. Trying not to gag at the scent of its breath as it panted, I hung on for dear life. Almost as suddenly as our wild romp through Noc'tal Forest started, it stopped. The dorcha'aon's maw opened and the basket shredded to ribbons on its teeth, giving way. I squeaked as I tumbled to the ground and landed on my back.

Blinking wide up at the sky, still half in a ball of terror, I looked into its crimson gaze. Scrambling, I sat up and moved away. We stayed like that, frozen in time for a few fluttering heartbeats. Then it blinked slowly and began to *shift*.

I watched on as this absolutely *massive* creature shrank. Compressing down, folding in on itself. Bones and tendons creaked and cracked in obscene ways that made bile burn up my throat. In ways that weren't supposed to be made by any living thing. I swallowed it down hard. In moments, its far smaller form stood upright on two legs.

My mind was still reeling, trying to wrap around what I'd just seen and what stood before me now. All I could do was stare at it, aghast, as I tried to remember how to breathe and blink. It cocked its head at me in that predatory way again. Only this time, it looked more like puzzlement instead of hunger.

"What... are... you...?" It... *He* rasped around his jagged teeth. As if he had forgotten how to speak, how to form words.

What the FUCK.

"What?" I warbled, traumatized by witnessing a six-legged, six-eyed nightmare shift and compress itself down to an eight-foot-tall man with four arms, wolf-like ears, and a gods honest *tail*. Who then *spoke.*

"What are... you? Not orckin. What?" He asked again, pacing back and forth in front of me. His hands gripped so tightly, his forearms were corded and his veins pulsed. He cracked his neck and grit his teeth as if fighting against something.

"Human." I managed past my dry lips. "Well, mostly. Part orckin."

"Hew-mahn..." He said, pausing, suddenly calm and still. The top and bottom sets of eyes slid closed, so only the main middle pair were open.

He looked a lot more like a person now and less like a monster. He had skin so dark grey it was almost black, with an iridescent sheen to it like raven feathers. His face was angular, still with that vulpine cast to it. But it was more similar to an orckin's. Or a human's. His lips were cracked and his black hair was a wild tangle around his perked ears that were canted toward me. Brain still boggling, I tried to absorb the fact he had an entirely secondary set of arms halfway down his torso.

"Human," I repeated, exaggerating my mouth's movements so he could see how the word formed in my mouth. His crimson gaze locked onto my mouth, and he cocked his head to the side.

"Hu-man." He repeated, and I nodded. "Human."

"Yes," I whispered. "Are you going to kill me?"

All six of his eyes flashed open, and he stared at me. I was trembling at his feet, ready to piss myself in fear. Afraid I'd never see Rhuger again. I'd asked the million-dollar question, and I was afraid that he'd eat me now that he had his answer.

I hope he made it quick.

RHUGER

Sigg still wouldn't talk to me as we continued hammering the rail beams onto the posts. We were both drenched in sweat under the midday heat of the suns. The rails were almost complete when we heard a clamoring coming from the direction of the forest near the slopes. I frowned and set down my hammer as a voice broke over the crowd.

"Where's Rhuger?!" cried a voice I knew and loathed.

"Here!" I called, raising an arm. He broke through the cluster of orckin and sprinted for me.

I could smell his terror even before he reached us. He was dressed in his guard gear and coming from the slopes where the flower picking was traditionally done. Where Amelia and Sharn had gone. Horror dripped down my body in cold waves as something in my gut felt irrevocably wrong.

Amelia.

Asterun skidded to a halt and bent over, attempting to catch his breath. He'd run the entire way here. So whatever news he carried had to be urgent. He stood tall, gasping like a fish out of water.

"Amelia..." He gasped past his labored breathing, holding his ribs. "Noc'tal Forest. Dorcha'aon... took her."

"What do you mean, *took her*?" Sigg shouted, his hammer clenched in his fist until his knuckles were white. If I knew anything at that moment, it was that Sigg had spoken true. He cared for Amelia. But he'd never love her as I did.

Asterun turned his fearful gaze to mine. A solid certainty slammed home over me. I would find Amelia. I would save her. And then I'd make sure she never left my sight again.

"Show me." I snarled. Voice quiet, deep, but full of the promise of death to all who would get in my way.

Asterun nodded and turned around, breaking back out into a run. I was a heartbeat behind him and I heard Sigg drop his hammer, his loping gait pounding in my ears. We passed the armorer who was bringing in the weapons and armor to be used for the tournament. I only paused long enough to grab a bow and two quivers of arrows. Sigg snagged himself a weapon as well. I didn't bother to look at what he grabbed. I knew him too well.

I'd left my bandolier of knives with my shirt when I'd removed them to work on the railings. All I had on me besides the bow was my axe at my waist. I wore no armor. I held no shield. And yet, no army could have stood between me and my cridhe.

We reached the slopes in record time. I saw the rest of the guard around a small huddle of females, elderly, and orclings, herding them down the slopes to safety. Hisouk saw us coming and pointed up the slope at the only opening in the Fàinne Sleagh on this side of Baile Coille. An old one, oft forgotten except by the guards and the warriors.

Asterun was lagging, his feet and lungs failing him after running so fast for so long. I left him behind. I left Sigg behind too, not caring if he could keep up with me as I sprinted up the steepest part of the slope toward the path and the opening. All I knew was that Amelia needed me, and I needed to get to her NOW.

As I burst through the hanging vines that draped over the entrance, I pulled free my bow and took off through the brush. My feet pounded against the moss and detritus of the forest floor as my heart beat a reverberating tattoo in my chest. My breaths came easily into my lungs despite the distance I'd run. It was as if my entire being was narrowed to this one purpose.

To reach Amelia in time. The only person who had ever seen me, cared for me, understood me. And as if my own soul called to hers, I could have sworn I saw a red strand lead me forward, stretching out from me to my target. Never erring in its path to her, never wavering.

I crashed through some bushes into a clearing and came to a skidding halt. Even as I ripped an arrow from its quiver, notched it, and drew. Because before me was Amelia, prone on the ground, the flower basket nothing but shreds at her side. Terror, confusion, and sorrow rolled off of her in waves, so thick I could have sunk my teeth into her scent. And above her? Above her stood something I'd never seen before.

Both of them looked at me. Amelia's round, uisge-beatha eyes met mine. The other creature snarled at me and I froze. It had six limbs, stood like an orckin, had rows of serrated teeth it flashed at me in the warm sunlight, and had six red eyes and a wicked scar across its face. It... was a dorcha'aon... But not like any I'd ever seen before.

"Rhuger..." Amelia whispered, and the dorcha'aon looked back at her. His attention was solely on her, dismissing me as if I weren't worth his time. A part of me wanted to fire an arrow straight into his throat for that. But I wouldn't risk Amelia for anything, not even my pride.

"Let Amelia go!" I hollered, and he turned, baring his teeth again at me in a snarl.

Then he paused, cocking his head to the side. His six-eyed gaze narrowed as he looked first at my chest, then across to Amelia's. Then back again. His eyes shot wide, and he backed up a few paces, as if stunned. I blinked and the giant monstrous male shifted, his bones cracking and elongating as he reformed as the dorcha'aon I'd witnessed outside of the gàrradh.

With a screeching yowl, he disappeared into the forest. A few tense heartbeats later, when I realized he wasn't coming back, that I had indeed watched the dorcha'aon shift forms, I dropped my bow and ran to Amelia.

"Rhuger!" she cried, tears sliding down her lovely, round cheeks. My name on her lips was like a balm to my ragged soul.

I skid to her on my knees and gathered her up in my arms, crushing her to me as if I could crush her heart to mine, where they could fuse as the one they should be. She flung her arms around my shoulders and buried her face in my neck as I tangled my fingers amongst her riotous waves.

"You are never leaving my sight again. Do you understand?" I growled into her hair and she nodded vigorously against my neck. I couldn't hold back the territorial bent that eclipsed me then. "You are *mine* and I will protect you."

She just hugged me closer, and I reached down, scooping her

up into my arms, and hurried back the way we'd come. I didn't know what had shaken something as powerful as the dorcha'aon enough to make him flee. But I wasn't about to wait to see if he returned. Halfway back, we met with Sigg, who had been following my trail, a spear in one hand and a sword in the other.

The relief on his face when he saw us was enough to set my teeth on edge. It didn't matter that he was my friend. That he'd run here to help save Amelia, too. This encompassing need to hide Amelia away from the rest of the world, to protect her, to kill all who came near, was blistering in my veins.

"What happened? Did you kill it?" He asked as I stalked past him, my only goal was to get Amelia to safety.

"No," I growled. I hadn't killed it. Hadn't even shot a single arrow. And I couldn't shake that it'd seen something we couldn't. And that's why it had run.

"Is she harmed?" Sigg asked, following behind. "Do I need to fetch a healer?"

"No." I bit out again, hands grasping Amelia to me a little tighter. Ensuring she was here, she was safe. We made it to the opening in the Fàinne Sleagh and I strode forward through the vines that whispered over us as we passed. Blissfully, Sigg didn't ask any more questions until we were through to the other side, the sweeping slopes and forest before us.

"Rhuger, tell me what happened." He demanded. "How is she unscathed?"

"This isn't something to talk about now. Get Asterun and anyone else who saw what happened, and bring them to Rìgh Thorn's study as quickly as possible. And Ruksala." I ground out. "We'll speak of it behind closed doors to the Rìgh first."

"Alright," Sigg replied, then his gaze slid to the mussed top of my charge's head. "I'm glad you're safe, Amelia."

Amelia just shuddered and wrapped her arms tighter around my neck. I leaned my head against hers and flicked my gaze from Sigg to the group of flower pickers we could spot down below. He nodded and headed down to them, to do as I'd instructed.

Whatever had happened with the dorcha'aon was completely and utterly unprecedented. Because that was the same dorcha'aon that had stopped outside of the gàrradh that first night Amelia had been on Talam. It had stalked her in the daylight. And had shifted forms.

Pushing those worries out for the moment I sat on a rock with Amelia in my lap. I slipped my arm from under her knees and pulled back, brushing her hair from her face so I could see her. She was so pale, her eyes wider than I'd ever seen them as she blinked slowly and started to shake.

"Och, there, there, pearl. I'm here. You're safe." I told her, slipping into Teanga Dhubh then. Murmuring to her soothing platitudes in my mother's tongue. Petting her head and her arms as she stared sightlessly into mine until that distance faded and she was back in the present.

"Rhuger..." she croaked, voice strangled. "What the fuck was that?"

"I don't know, pearl," I said honestly. "But we'll figure it out. We'll talk to Rìgh Thorn and Ruksala. Make sure this is kept quiet for now so we don't start a panic within Baile Coille, alright?"

"Alright." She nodded. "That's a good plan."

"Thank you, pearl." I huffed a humorless laugh. Unused to being complimented. Let alone after facing the sort of dreadful experience we had. "Can you walk? I can carry you if you want."

"I can walk," Amelia said firmly, standing up from my lap.

Immediately, I felt the loss of her body against mine like a visceral ache. She was still shaking a bit, but she stood tall before me. A brave goddess I would happily kneel before and worship. To hide the sudden jolt of lust I had for her, I stood and bent down to whisper into her ear.

"Good lass. So brave for me." She gasped and the scent of her arousal came hard and fast, wiping out the scent of fear like a tidal wave. I nearly lost my mind, nearly turned my head to capture that lovely pink mouth with mine, and not let go until I was satisfied. Until *she* was thoroughly satisfied.

And it would take lifetimes to be satisfied, sated, and spent.

I knew, right then, that the fleeting thought I'd had as I'd raced to Amelia's side had been true. That, mating marks or no, she was my cridhe. I didn't care who tried. No one else would ever have a claim on her. She was *mine*.

All I needed to do now was figure out how to make sure I could secure that future with her.

CHAPTER 36

RHUGER

Sigg had done as I'd requested, even hunted down Rìgh Thorn himself. So when I walked through the double doors of Rìgh Thorn's study behind Amelia, Sigg was leaning against the fireplace and Rìgh Thorn was pacing and cracking his knuckles before the fire. The moment the sound of the door opening registered, Rìgh Thorn was a blur of movement, sweeping his plump granddaughter up into his burly arms.

"Put me down, Grandpa!" She groused, kicking ineffectively against his knees. He wailed into her hair and warbled in Teanga Dhubh. I couldn't make much of it out, but his relief was enough to clue me in.

When Rìgh Thorn was finally persuaded to set Amelia down, he ushered her into the room, stepping between us. His hulking frame blocked her from my sight. I had to throttle my territorial bent, which was becoming increasingly inconvenient. Had it been like this for the late Rìgh Tyras for Ruksala?

Because the more time that passed from that first self-admonition of her being my cridhe? The more its certainty settled into the remnants of my soul. I didn't know if her human heritage would keep the mating marks from rising. But it didn't matter.

"What are you waiting for, Fògradh?" Asterun bit out and I glared at him over my shoulder. I owed the male his swift feet, but I wasn't above freeing him from them. I bared my teeth in warning before prowling into the study. The others quickly followed behind.

Rìgh Thorn had Amelia ensconced in one of his leather chairs, bundled in the thickest blanket I'd ever seen. She looked like a tiny Iolaire'lasair chick peeking out from its nest of feathers and ash. I made to go stand next to her chair, but Rìgh Thorn shot me a forbidding look. So instead, I went to stand in the corner, where Amelia could still see me. And where I could watch the others and the door.

Inassa was similarly bundled up and placed in the other leather chair. Ophir had carried her here and had left again. Hisouk was here also, as it was his excursion that this had happened on.

And Sharn. Mainly because keeping her out of it would have been more trouble than it was worth. As I'd trained her, she found another corner to lurk in and kept sharp, moving eyes on everyone within the study.

"Hey, are you okay?" Amelia whispered, leaning over to catch Inassa's gaze. But the female was staring at nothing. Sweet Amelia still reached out and held her hand.

"So..." Rìgh Thorn began, standing tall and placing a meaty hand over his granddaughter's rounded shoulder. "Sigg has informed me that not one, but *two* females, one of which was *my own granddaughter,* found their way out of the Fàinne Sleagh. *Into the clutches of a dorcha'aon.* Without a guard."

His gaze riveted on me then. Rage a burning bonfire in his copper eyes. I'd broken his trust. Trust I'd have to work hard to earn again.

"I need you all to debrief me on how this happened." Rìgh Thorn's tone was thunderous, his anger a writhing, living thing.

"I guess I shall start." Hisouk coughed quietly and sat straighter in his chair, getting settled. "The Steward gave me instructions and a list of people to organize the flower-picking party. Amelia and Inassa were on the list. Rhuger was not."

"Likewise, the organizer for the tourney build was given instructions by the Steward. I checked with the organizer and Rhuger was explicitly on the list. Because of his size and strength, evidently." Sigg chimed in. "We'd found it odd, but seeing that Amelia would be with Hisouk and Sharn and would stay within the Fàinne Sleagh, we didn't raise a fuss."

"He is her *bodyguard*. What use is he then if he isn't *with* her?" Rìgh Thorn growled.

"She has been in our care, one on one, for her lessons. One of us has always been with her to ensure she was safe, as there are times Rhuger's other duties call." Hisouk explained.

"So I need to speak with my Steward." Rìgh Thorn bit out. "Well, what happened next?"

"I went with Sharn, Manira, and the guard Rorich to a glade to pick flowers," Amelia said. "I was on the edge of the glade when I saw Inassa heading towards the exit in the cliffs. We argued as I caught up with her. I didn't feel right letting her go into Noc'tal Forest alone, so I followed her through the passage."

"Where is this Rorich?" Sigg asked.

"He and Manira are waiting in the hall in case we need to bring them in," Asterun replied. "I wasn't sure if they needed to know what we do, so I asked them to wait."

"The fewer who know, the better," I said. "Rìgh Thorn, you've fought the dorcha'aon. Aren't they supposed to be nocturnal?"

"Yes!" Rìgh Thorn snapped. Amelia flinched, and I had to clench my fists, claws biting into the palms of my hands to keep from going to her.

"What now, Rìgh Thorn?" Asterun asked, purple gaze flicking between us all as the quiet grew.

"Now?" He bit out. He'd begun pacing again and was growing more agitated with each step. "Now. You want to know what to do *now*."

"Grandpa, please," Amelia murmured.

"Don't get me started on you! Or you, Inassa! *None* of this would have transpired had you both *stayed with the group!*" Rìgh Thorn bellowed as he pointed at the females, and Amelia cowered away from him, tucking her shoulders up to her ears. The scent of her fear cut through all the other tumultuous emotions in the room and drew me to her.

I wove through the others like water through unforgiving earth. I knelt before Amelia and tucked the blanket up around her. Brushed her free hand with mine, seeking to ground her and reassure her with this small touch. To remind her she wasn't alone. Would never be alone again.

"Don't you touch her, Oc'Turin!" Rìgh Thorn snarled, snapping his teeth at me. "Where were *you* when she was in danger?"

"I understand you're... concerned over Amelia and Inassa's welfare," I said, gaze flicking up at him, head tilted in just enough respect to not be beheaded on the spot. But also refusing to let her hand go. "All the things that fell into place to make this happen should and will be addressed. However..."

That one word fell into the utter silence that fell. Rìgh Thorn wasn't exhibiting *concern* but unadulterated fear and rage. Everyone here was unsettled, afraid, and confused. Now wasn't the time for their Rìgh to waver.

"It's my fault." Inassa's voice cut through the quiet like a knife and we all turned to look at her. She was still pale and wan, eyes far too large in her head, but she stared at Rìgh Thorn all the same. "Amelia only tried to stop me. If it wasn't for her I..." She looked at Amelia then, who was still holding her hand. They shared an understanding look. One only built from shared experience. "I'd be dead if it wasn't for her."

Before anyone could say anything more, Ophir strode in with a bundle in his arms. A bundle that was a snarky Ruksala, waving her staff in irritation. He gently set her on her feet as she fussed and scowled at us all. Then he got her a chair and a cushion to sit next to Amelia and she calmed, mollified. Once she was comfortable, she shot us a collective frown.

"Don't bother trying to catch this old biddy up on things. I'm already aware." She groused, her pointed glare cutting over to Amelia and me. "And you!" She shook her walking staff at Rìgh Thorn, who looked affronted. Ruksala then pointed at Ophir, who stood at her shoulder. "You ought to make this one the Captain of the Guard. You need a new one, yes? Perfect. It's settled then."

Rìgh Thorn blustered, the wind taken out of his proverbial sails. Ophir's eyes nearly boggled out of his head as he looked between his Fear a Chì and his Rìgh. Captaincy was a tremendous step up for someone within the clan. It was almost guaranteed that he'd be granted the right to build a home tree.

"There are some things you ought to know about the dorcha'aon we faced." I began, capturing everyone's attention. "Amelia, could you please tell us what happened, pearl? From your perspective."

"Oh, of course." She replied, sitting tall in her chair, hand still clasped with Inassa's.

And so she began her tale. None of which I'd heard yet. About how she'd followed Inassa through the folach vines. How they'd argued just past the Fàinne Sleagh. And how the dorcha'aon had approached them in broad daylight.

Amelia described it in such detail that it confirmed what I'd suspected, that it must be the same one that had shown up outside of the gàrradh. The one who'd twice now had fled instead of fought. She faltered in her tale when she got to the part where the beast had snatched her up. Her eyes went blank as she remembered it. I rubbed her knuckles to bring her back, still on my knees before her.

The only person I'd *ever* kneel to.

Her eyes snapped to mine and cleared. A twitch of her lips and a gentle squeeze of my hand were my rewards. Amelia explained how the dorcha'aon had snatched her flower basket instead of her, carrying her off, still attached to it by the harness. How it had dropped her and then transformed.

"The way it... shifted. Reminded me of those werewolf TV shows." She murmured before looking up at Rìgh Thorn.

"What do you mean, it *shifted*?" Rìgh Thorn demanded.

"*Werewolf? Tee-bee?*" Sharn asked. "What are these things?"

"Oh, a werewolf is a supposedly mythical creature from Earth. It can change forms from human to wolf. An animal that isn't as big as a nocrys but similar. And it's a canine instead of a feline. The moon dictates their shifting. And TV is... well, it's a form of entertainment?" She looked back up at Rìgh Thorn. "It shifted, it changed forms."

"What did the shifted dorcha'aon look like?" Asterun asked.

"Well..." Amelia began, but then looked at me, seemingly at a loss.

"It stood as tall as Hisouk. Body similar to an orckin's. Except it had four arms, two on each side. It also had the same teeth and eyes as its larger form. But its face was orckin too. And it had ears and a tail like a nocrys." I explained.

"It's no coincidence that this is happening now." Ruksala said sagely, raising her chin.

"Because of Amelia's arrival?" Sigg asked.

"No, you dolt." Ruksala scowled at him, frustrated she couldn't give him a whack with her staff from so far away. "The moons! They align tomorrow."

"When have the dorcha'aon shown up?" My lovely pearl asked, her brow furrowed in thought.

"Every few decades. Sometimes more often." Rìgh Thorn said, stroking his beard as he paced before the fire once again.

"No, I mean, what time of year?" Amelia asked. A silence descended on the study as we all looked at one another.

"When the moons are aligned," Hisouk said.

"Or when they are farthest apart," Ruksala added.

"But that doesn't explain how infrequent it is in terms of years, then." It was Inassa who spoke, and we all looked at her.

"Maybe other celestial bodies are involved. Like the suns?" Amelia asked.

"That could be it. The Oc'Veltas would know for certain. They've flown to the stars." I replied. "They normally refuse our messengers, but we have some information they don't. Perhaps they'll trade."

Rìgh Thorn grunted in acknowledgment. We all sat quietly for a time, overwhelmed by the enormity of it all. For there to be a pattern to the rising of the dorcha'aon could mean we could trace the past and predict their future surges. Maybe even figure out the mystery associated with them, the an'sgudal plague.

"It spoke to me," Amelia murmured, the sound of shifting sunstones the only backdrop to the deafening silence that engulfed the room.

"It *what*?" Rìgh Thorn demanded of his granddaughter. His expression was one of anger and incredulity.

I couldn't say I blamed him. To know that the dorcha'aon could not only transform into beings that looked not too far removed from orckin but that they were sentient too? It broke all known rules and lore about them.

"I should say he, as he appeared male. But yes, he spoke."

"What did he want?" Ruksala asked and Amelia looked at where my thumb still gently rubbed her knuckles.

"He wanted to know what I am. Before he'd snatched me, he'd smelled me. Bumped his nose against my chest a few times before Asterun arrived. Like when a dog or a cat is trying to smell something new. Trying to figure it out." She explained. "When he'd shifted, he had looked like he was fighting something. Trying to remain... focused. In the present. Then I asked him if he was going to kill me. That's when Rhuger showed up."

Her gaze rose to meet mine, and I wanted to drown in them. Her uisge-beatha eyes were more intoxicating than the spirit itself. But like the dorcha'aon, I needed to stay focused.

"When I arrived, I drew on the changed dorcha'aon. Demanded he release Amelia. He seemed... startled. And fled, shifting back into the form we know it as." I replied. Unwilling to say my true thoughts on his reaction just yet.

"Did you hear it speak?" Hisouk asked.

"No, I didn't." I shook my head.

Asterun then looked down at my cridhe and asked, "Neamhnaid, are you *sure* you heard it speak? Are you sure you didn't imagine it? Facing a beast such as that can bend the mind, let alone being taken by one."

Amelia turned and frowned up at him as if he'd slapped her. Her bowed mouth thinned into a white line of fury. As one, most of us in the room made to defend her when she grabbed Ruksala's staff from her and rammed the end into Asterun's gut. It knocked the wind out of him and his eyes were wide with shock. He held his belly and stepped out of the way of Amelia's next attack.

"Don't you *dare* gaslight me, you arrogant prick!" Amelia bit out. "Just because it was scary, does *not* mean that I lost my mind! I'm not that fragile!"

Silence followed her words, and Asterun had the grace to look properly chastised. When he looked at Rìgh Thorn, it was to see his furious glare stripping him down. He had no friends in this room to back up his claim.

"Her word is enough," I said. "More than enough."

Amelia released a breath and handed the staff back to Ruksala. Ruksala took the staff back, amused. The anger on my cridhe's face faded as she looked at me. My heart pounded against my ribcage like a nocrys attempting to escape a cage. That feisty streak she had was enough to set my mind to imagine what passion she'd have if I rutted her until she came undone. If she'd rake those little claws down my back. I shivered.

"Should we proceed with the tournament tomorrow?" Ophir asked, his measured emerald and black gaze belying the edge of stress in his tone. It was enough to allow me to shake free my dastardly thoughts before the scent of my arousal got me into more trouble.

"See? This one has a good head on his shoulders." Ruksala nodded in approval, making Ophir nervous. But unless you knew his tells, you'd never know it by looking at him.

"Och. It's too late to cancel it and it would cause panic if the clan knew what we do." Rìgh Thorn grumbled. "We'll have to double the guard. Work in shifts so everyone takes part in the... party."

Rìgh Thorn looked down at the back of his granddaughter's head and grimaced. Amelia rolled her eyes at his attempt to shield her from vulgarities like a clan-sanctioned orgy. He needn't worry because she didn't need to look any farther for her cridhe than where I knelt before her.

"As you will, my Rìgh." Ophir acknowledged, fist over his heart as he gave a small bow.

"I also want an additional guard placed on Amelia." Rìgh Thorn said, standing tall and proud once more. Ruksala made a *tsk*-ing sound as Amelia turned in her chair to stare down her grandfather, who pointedly refused to look at her. As furious as I was about that, I was also relieved. It meant when I wasn't present, another trusted guard could watch over her.

It meant courting Amelia would be that much harder. But who would he trust with this? If Ophir was now Captain of the Guard, he'd be unable to. Sigg and Hisouk were out as they had other duties. Which left... My gaze slid to Asterun, and I curled my lip.

"I'd suggest Rorich." Sharn piped up from the corner.

"Rorich? He's a green guard." Asterun said, shaking his head.

"Well, he didn't panic like some people when Amelia and Inassa turned up missing. He did well, getting everyone to work together and got us safely back to our starting point." Sharn said. "He's green, but he's level-headed. Plus, he has no designs on Amelia, unlike *someone*."

I could have laughed as everyone seemed to look at one another and then at me. But Sharn was staring hard at Asterun. Eventually, we all caught on to her meaning.

"Like I'm the only one." Asterun spat.

"I wouldn't touch you with a ten-foot cattle prod." Amelia snapped. Rìgh Thorn snorted and had to cover his mouth with his hand.

"What's a *cat-al prod*?" Hisouk asked, frowning.

"It's an electrified pole used to get large beasts to move. Nowhere near as powerful as lightning, just gives them a jolt." Rìgh Thorn explained, his expression controlled once more.

"Are you calling me a beast?" Asterun asked, scowling down at my cridhe.

"I'm telling you, I'm not willing to touch you." She curled her lip as she looked up at him from under lowered brows. I couldn't stop the grin that split my face.

"Och, you will be. Just give it time, Neamhnaid." Asterun's self-assured grin had Amelia flushing in anger. Anger that he'd misinterpreted as denied arousal. He opened his damned mouth again to speak, to say something lewd to her again.

But I'd already stood and snatched Asterun's jaw in my hand, claws sinking in ever so slightly to get his attention. I jerked his head, so he was forced to look at me. I pulled him in close, close enough to share breath.

"Touch her and you'll never hold a sword again. For I'll free you of your erroneously entitled hands." I whispered, gaze boring into his. His purple eyes dilated and a flush stained his cheeks as he bared his teeth at me.

"You don't own her, Fògradh." Asterun spat.

"Neither do you. So you will show her the respect she is due. It is *her* choice. Not yours." I shoved him away, releasing his jaw. He stumbled slightly and snarled.

"That's enough, you two." Ruksala bit out and we looked at her. "Us females are exhausted, and it's growing late. The tournament will continue tomorrow as planned. We'll worry about the recent developments with the dorcha'aon afterward."

"Och. No one is to speak of this meeting or anything we've learned until I say. If Ophir thinks Rorich is a good secondary guard, then I'll approve it." Rìgh Thorn proclaimed, crossing his arms over his chest. His bearing was back to normal now that there was a plan in place. Now that he had a semblance of control.

"Very well, my Rìgh. I'll inform Rorich of his additional duties." Ophir executed a swift bow and exited the study with Inassa.

After that, we all left the study. Rìgh Thorn had his arm around Amelia and was ushering her out of the door. He gave her a swift kiss on the head and left. Asterun stomped away to nurse his ego. Hisouk escorted his sister away and Sigg bid us goodnight before leaving for his home. Then it was just Amelia, Ruksala, Sharn, Rorich, and me.

"I'm ready," Rorich said to me, standing tall. We made our way out of the keep and down the steps to the bailey. I stood to one side and waited while everyone said their goodbyes. Ruksala tottered over to stand beside me.

"So, what aren't you saying, Rhuger?" Ruksala asked me, pursing her wrinkled lips and holding her staff before her. Watching the others leave the keep with keen eyes. Eyes that saw too much. And that's when I remembered a detail more concerning to me than it would be to the others.

"It... he looked between Amelia and me. Looked stunned, afraid, and transformed before retreating." I breathed, my breath pluming in the chill evening air.

"Where did it look?" Ruksala asked shrewdly, voice solemn.

"Our chests." I nearly choked on the words as I swallowed. We shared a glance. One that told me she knew. Knew that Amelia was my cridhe. That the transformed dorcha'aon had somehow *seen* and *known*.

"Hm," she muttered before looking away from me. Her gaze locked on her great-granddaughter who was a few paces away, consoling a stressed-out Sharn. "Sharn! Come help an old female to her bed, would you?"

"As you wish, Fear a Chì," Sharn replied, looking startled before she clapped Amelia on the shoulder and came to take Ruksala's arm.

With goodnight wishes, it was now just me, Amelia, and an awkward Rorich who stood some ways away. Amelia yawned, her little pink mouth opening wide and showing those white, blunted teeth. She slumped, eyes fighting to stay open.

"We should get you home, Amelia," Rorich said, going to stand next to her, looking at me for direction. The young orc was green, for sure. But he, at least, openly cared about her well-being.

"I'm honestly surprised Grandpa didn't insist that I stay in the keep from now on." She mumbled, rubbing her eyes with her lovely little neamhnaid fists.

"Would you prefer to stay here?" Rorich asked.

"No. I wanna go home." She pouted.

"Let's get you home then, pearl." The words smoothed the frown from her brow even as I strode forward and scooped her up into my arms.

She didn't fight, didn't even put up a protest. Just wrapped her arms around my neck and laid her head against my shoulder. Her cheek pillowed, so her breath tickled the shell of my ear. She'd had a long, rough day and had fallen asleep by the time I'd turned to cock an eyebrow at Rorich, who stood there blushing. I nodded in the direction we were headed and set out, his footsteps falling in step behind me.

"Do all females like that?" Rorich murmured as we left the gate of Daingneach.

"Like what?"

"Being carried."

"I'm honestly not sure," I said, looking down at him. "Amelia is the first female I've been close to."

I didn't count Sagra. She'd been my friend and my mother's personal servant. But I'd never felt for her anything close to what Amelia inspired in me.

"The first?" He asked, almost too loud, shocked at my admonition. "But you're so... so..."

"So?" I prompted.

"So, well, male. All the females fancy you. Even some of the mated ones. My baby cousin swears she'll be your wife one day." He chuckled.

"How old is your baby cousin?" I asked, my eyebrow cocked as I dreaded the answer.

"Five." Rorich grinned when I groaned and rolled my eyes. Amelia shifted and hugged me tighter, her lips now against my neck. I hid my shiver from Rorich.

"I've no interest in females." I shook my head.

"You've got an interest in her." Rorich nodded at the bundle of curves in my arms as we strode across the city center. The soft burbling of the streams was a piece of faint music for the last of the sparkflies to dance to.

"You're rather perceptive," I replied dryly.

"Don't worry, I'm not like the others." He bumped my elbow gently so as not to jostle Amelia.

"Others?"

"The other males who were in the study." He said. "They all fancy her. Some more than others."

"You like males then?" I asked. The moons danced overhead, almost a perfect line across the clouds of stars.

"Oh, no! I like females." Rorich blushed hard.

"So then, you're soft on a particular female. Who isn't Amelia? Let me guess... Manira?" I teased quietly. Rorich's ears nearly glowed white with how hard he was blushing. "I won't tell."

"I appreciate that." He mumbled. "We'll come of age next year, and I'll ask Hisouk for his blessing."

"You're a kind male. I'm sure he'll grant it if she's willing," I replied. "Makes sense why you were asking me if all females liked to be carried. She is tall and powerful."

"And elegant and beautiful. And I'm small." He groused.

"You ever think maybe *she* might be the one wanting to carry *you*?" I grinned in the low light of the sunstone lanterns that hung over the avenue leading to our home tree.

Rorich made a strangled sort of sound and I chuckled low. When we arrived at our home tree, Hifasa gave a cursory twitch of her nose in Rorich's direction before sticking her nose under her tail once more. I told Rorich where he could find a spare hammock in the shed out back and carried Amelia upstairs. Changing my hold on her so I could open the door, I carried her inside and gently laid her on the bed.

"Mmmh. Rhuger..." She mumbled a mere breath from my ear. Hearing my name on her lips was sweet torture.

I pulled back, sliding my arm out from under her legs as I gazed down at her. The moonlight was bright as it sliced in through the doorway to bathe her in its ethereal veil, setting her pearl skin to glowing. She was a tiny moon in my arms, with freckles like dark stars and eclipses for lashes. A moon goddess who didn't seem to mind or flinch from my darkness, but danced in it and set it afire with countless twinkling stars.

Gods how I wanted to kiss her then. But I'd rather cut off my arm than disturb her sleep. Gently, I cradled the back of her head, so tiny in my broad hand, and laid it down amongst the pillows. She rolled over onto her side, facing me, and I pulled up the blankets, tucking her in.

"Goodnight, my pearl," I murmured, voice gone a little hoarse. "My cridhe."

CHAPTER 37*

AMELIA

The morning of the games dawned bright. A light breeze rustled the leaves of my home tree and birdsong greeted me as I hurried to get dressed. I was still shaken from my experience from the day before, but I didn't have the culturally instilled fear the orckin had.

My mind wanted to melt and my stomach rioted whenever I thought about the dorcha'aon shifting forms. Hell, I'd had nightmares about it. Probably would for a long time.

But I had to confess that I was more curious than was probably healthy. How could I not be when not only had my arrival coincided with the return of the dorcha'aon, but one that walked in sunlight and could change forms? It posed a far too enticing a puzzle for my mind to fiddle with.

A knock on my door froze me in place.

"Who is it?" I called.

"It's me. Are you ready?" Called Rhuger. I shivered. Something fundamental between us had changed when he'd come charging into that clearing like green-skinned, black-haired Legolas. Drawing his bow and demanding the four-armed demon wolf-man let me go.

I mean, it'd been hot as all get out, just like everything he did. But the way he'd said I was *his* and he would *protect me*. That sentence had me clutching my proverbial pearls even as I clung to his neck. And every interaction after held this certainty, this unspoken promise that hadn't been there before.

"Almost. Give me a moment." I hurried over to the full-length metal mirror and fluffed my hair. I'd managed a sponge bath when I woke, so I was clean, at least. An attendant from Daingneach had brought me a new dress to wear for the games. And I was feeling very self-conscious about it.

The dress was a lovely lilac color in a shimmery lightweight fabric. It rode off my shoulders, baring my throat and upper chest, the tight upper sleeves helping to keep the dress from falling right off. Slits in the long, flowing sleeves cut up to my elbow, so I had freedom of movement with my hands.

A dark purple leather corset belt cinched my waist and lifted my breasts slightly. High slits on either side of the dress exposed much of my thighs and rounded hips. The skirt ended at my ankles and dark purple leather slippers graced my feet. It had taken forever for me to figure out the delicate golden chain harness that crossed over my breasts and stomach before dropping to wrap around each thigh.

Oh yeah, and with how the dress was made, I couldn't wear my bra or panties. So I was terrified a stiff breeze would grant the clans more than an eyeful. Luckily, the chain harness seemed to cage in the front panel of the dress, a flimsy guard of my virtue.

I felt pretty but also very exposed and I wasn't sure how I looked other than like an over-ripe plum. Snagging a few white flowers from the bundle in a vase on my table, I shoved them into my hair. I also dabbed a little of the perfume I liked on my throat and wrists. The perfume I had an inkling Rhuger had bought for me. With a huff at my reflection, I swallowed my courage before striding purposefully to the door and opening it.

Rhuger turned and froze when he saw me. His heated black and silver gaze raked over me once. Twice. And a third time. A high, bright green flush stained his cheeks, and that alone was worth wearing the showy dress. He opened his mouth to speak, had to stop to clear his throat, then closed his mouth, letting out a strangled sound close to a whine.

"Do I look okay?" I asked, trying not to smile and failing miserably.

"Exquisite." He croaked and cleared his throat again before holding out a hand for me, his gaze steady and sure.

"Thank you, you look nice too." I placed my hand in his and he escorted me towards the stairs.

And he did. He was dressed in a different kilt, similar to his daily one, but with some added flair. The skirt of it was elegantly tooled leather and was overlapped with additional leather pteruges, almost like a Roman skirt. His boots were different too, with buckles instead of laces, and the tufted tails of some poor dead critter dangled from the upper outer edges. He was without his vest. Instead, he wore a simple black shirt tucked into his kilt, the laces at the front left loose, his tattoos and gold torc peeking up out of the collar along his neck. He'd rolled the sleeves up to his elbows, his powerful hands and forearms on display.

Rhuger's hair had been freshly shaved on the sides. The long mop of hair he'd kept back either in a rough braid or with a leather tie had been immaculately combed and braided elaborately. Silver trinkets and beads winked in the dappled sunlight as we passed Hifasa at the base of the tree. One really long, oddly shaped feather fell alongside his braid. It was a riot of colors that shifted in the light.

Rhuger looked, well, courtly.

Okay, yes, he looked courtly, but if I was honest with myself, he looked so hot anyone near would faint from heat stroke from blushing so hard. Myself included. My thoughts turned filthy and I couldn't help but remember that night outside the cave when he'd put on a show for me. Licked his seed from his fingers with a long, black tongue that I couldn't stop fantasizing about.

I stopped to pat Hifasa, who purred at my touch. Using the distraction to get my heated cheeks and hormones under control. She playfully swatted at the fur tails on Rhuger's boots and he chuckled, scratching her behind the ears before leading me away.

As if he knew I'd rather spend all day with Hifasa than go to these games.

"So, what's that feather in your hair? It's beautiful." I asked, looking for a distraction, *any* distraction.

"Och, it's a seud iteach. Made from the feathers of an eun'bogha-froise." He explained. Rhuger noticed my blank expression and continued with his explanation. "The eun'bogha-froise is a bird whose feathers look like a rainbow. The colors shift and dance in the light. These birds chase rain storms and are often seen as the sun breaks through the clouds. They dance amongst the rainbows that appear. It is what the market is named after."

"They sound beautiful!" I smiled up at Rhuger and he cleared his throat.

"They are lovely. I'll take you to see them the next time it rains."

"I'd like that very much." I was so excited to see birds who danced in the sun and rain and rainbows. Such a peaceful, pure, and delightful thought. A part of me wished it would rain today, so Rhuger would whisk me off to go see the birds instead.

As we passed stalls and food vendors and groups of orcs, I noticed a trend. Either the orcs wore their finest, or they were dressed like they were going to war. Noticing my gaze flicking over the differences in dress and how I shied closer to him as the orcs dressed for war ogled me as we passed them, Rhuger bent down to whisper near my ear.

"The orcs not dressed well will compete today." The shiver that ran down my spine was distracting. *He* was distracting.

"And you're not competing, then?" I asked, attempting to distract myself from how distracting he was.

"Och, no. I'm your bodyguard. Keeping you safe is more important than competing." He gave me a lopsided grin that made my toes want to curl in their ridiculous slippers. "Not much incentive to compete. It's a means for orcs to prove their prowess and show off for the females."

"And you don't need to show off then? Surprising—you show off all the time." I told him dryly. He tipped his head back and laughed, his grin open and his powerful throat exposed. Entranced, I watched as his Adam's apple bobbed.

"I've competed in the past. I have nothing to prove." He chuckled as we strolled towards the square.

"Did you win?" I asked. "Win the hearts of the ladies?"

"I won last year." He stated with a half-shrug. "I did it to prove my worth to Rìgh Thorn as a warrior. Not for the lust of the crowd."

"Oh," I muttered. My emotions were tumbling around like rocks in a dryer. Why did I want to know about his love life so badly all of a sudden, and why couldn't I seem to ask the right questions?

We passed through the city center and out towards the nocrys stables where a nearby field had been taken over by the tournament. Banners fluttered high in the breeze and the clamor of the crowd was loud, even from afar. I had to swallow my distress. I couldn't afford to balk now.

As we approached, the crowd blocked most of the setup. The place was thick with orckin, mostly males and some females. Even the orclings were present. Either holding onto their mothers' skirts or weaving between the legs of tournament goers as they played their games. A smile tugged at the corners of my mouth as I watched them while we passed toward the back of a raised dais.

People stopped and stared as we passed. I couldn't fault them, though I was self-conscious as hell. I mean, my bare thighs were jiggling as I walked and the dress left very little to the imagination. Rhuger must have sensed it because he moved to my other side, blocking their view and baring his teeth at them. They quickly turned their attention elsewhere, and I heaved a relieved breath.

"Thank you," I murmured and smiled up at Rhuger. He gave me a brusque nod and held his head high again, eyes scanning the crowd for danger. As if anyone would try something with him at my arm. They'd have to have a death wish.

The crowd was slowly making its way onto the bleachers as we reached the stairs to the dais. Rhuger swept an arm out, an invitation for me to take the stairs ahead of him. So I did, attempting not to step on the fabric of the front panel as it slithered and pooled beneath my slippered feet on the stairs. I was so focused on not tripping that I didn't notice the wind picking up.

A gust blew past us and, in slow motion, I could feel the back panel of this ridiculous gown blow away to the side. The horror that I was about to moon the clan pooled in my gut. I would be too late to snatch it back into place!

Feverish hands grasped the outer sides of my thighs, high near my ass, thumbs close to my lady bits. I looked over my shoulder, eyes wide. Who'd grab me like that?

Rhuger stood behind me where we'd frozen on the steps. His hands were holding the back panel of my dress against my thighs and he was looking away, his cheeks and ears neon green. His gaze slid up to meet mine and the heat I saw there made need coil low in my belly. Rhuger must have smelled the shift in me because his heated gaze turned molten. The near-hopeless edge it normally held now tempered to something akin to a promise.

Time sped back up. The gust died, and Rhuger released my thighs as if they burned him. He stood straight, chin lifted high as the proud warrior he was, gazing ahead as if nothing had happened. The color staining his cheeks was the only evidence. Well, that and whoever else in the clan had witnessed him protect my modesty while also copping a feel. At least he'd been the only one to see my full moon.

Wait. FUCK! He'd gotten an up-close-and-personal view of my dimply, cellulite-riddled, stretch-marked *ASS*! I was internally screeching in mortification. It was one thing to see my pale ass from afar, glowing softly like the moon on a hazy autumn night. It was another *entirely* to point a high-end telescope at its pock-marked, blinding brightness! Lo, the beacons are lit! Gondor calls for aid!

He saw my ass!!! Gods spare me. If I'd chosen that most inopportune of inopportune moments to *fart,* I would have given my hot orc bodyguard *pink eye*! Did I, deep down in my smutty little heart of hearts, *want* him to see my ass? Sure! Like nature intended. IN THE GODS DAMNED DARK! *NOT,* pray tell, *under these conditions*!

Taking my cue from said bodyguard, I faced forward and held my head high with my shoulders back and spine straight. Every outward sign declared that I was Rìgh Thorn's granddaughter while inside, I was screaming into the void. I took to the last few steps with purpose and strode out onto the covered dais as if I owned it. Spotting my grandfather's towering form, I made a beeline toward him.

He'd seen my ass!

There was a small gathering of councilors, elite peers, and their attendants. Everyone was dressed extravagantly. The females dressed with elaborate belts that cinched their waists like mine, and their necks and hair were dripping with precious stones and small pearls. While I strode past them with only flowers in my hair, body chains, and the fidget spinner necklace Rhuger had gifted me with its single pearl. I was glaringly out of place, but I was too wired on code-red anxiety to care.

Grandpa Thorn was resplendent in fine clothes, dyed the shifting colors of the Pacific, and trimmed in silver and grey fur. He was speaking to his councilors when we approached. He paused, took me in, and a warm grin split his beloved old face.

"Chestnut." He called, arms wide as he folded me into a bear hug. After near crushing me to death, he pulled away, hands on my shoulders. "You look lovely."

"I'm afraid a stiff breeze will snatch this damned thing away," I muttered under my breath. "I nearly mooned half the clan climbing the stairs."

Grandpa Thorn frowned at that and cast a look over my shoulder at Rhuger.

"I did not allow that to happen, my Rìgh," Rhuger said deadpan, and I had to give him credit. Not even the teensiest bit of that bright green tinted his annoyingly perfect cheekbones. Meanwhile, an internal mantra of '*He saw my ass!*' played on repeat like demented circus music in my head.

Grandpa Thorn muttered something under his breath and steered me away towards the area with the chairs meant for us. One councilor was having a hard time keeping his eyes in his head and Rhuger growled harshly at him. He startled and looked away, but not before Grandpa and I scowled at him.

I mean... It was one thing for *me* to scowl at the counselor. It was *another* for Grandpa Thorn to. I mean, wasn't he the one who sent me this diaphanous affront to my modesty?

When we got to our chairs, I sat down, making sure my hands plastered the fabric across my ass as I did so. And that the front panel stayed firmly clamped between my thighs. I didn't trust the thin chains not to snap if I clapped my thighs together, let alone keep the front of my dress in place if another stiff breeze came my way.

Rhuger stood behind my right shoulder and Grandpa Thorn sat to my left. Grammie Ruksala tottered over to the chairs, her walking staff in hand. She wore something similar to what she did the last time, obviously not giving two shits about what people expected. Her dress was a deep grey this time and her cardigan with its many pockets was a goldenrod yellow. The little critter I'd spied in a pocket before was peeking out at everyone with wide, slitted eyes, its rounded ears flat against its skull.

As she passed me to take her place on Grandpa's other side, she gave me an exaggerated wink and a knowing grin before Grandpa Thorn looked at her and she wiped the expression from her face. Looking all the world like a harmless little old lady as she made her way to her cushioned chair. Grandpa squinted at her, his mouth a thin line, not buying it for a second.

I was confused as all get out. What was going on between Grammie Ruksala and Grandpa Thorn? I was going to need to go talk to my family's matriarch to sus this out. Because I knew Grandpa Thorn would deflect the conversation if he didn't want to talk about it. But really, I needed to talk to her again, anyway. To get to know her better, if nothing else.

The councilors sat in chairs behind and around us. The one that ogled me, thankfully on the other side near Grammie Ruksala. He'd started staring at me again, and I had to suppress a cackle as she whacked him over the head with her staff, berating him. The others had the decency to look elsewhere.

As the crowd closed in around the arenas, sitting in bleachers or standing along the sidelines, Grandpa Thorn stood. Immediately, the crowd fell silent. He strode forward and opened his arms wide.

"People of Oc'Dellor!" He boomed and people cheered. "Today is the day in which sixty of our best warriors fight for honor, creed, clan, and the admiration of our cherished females!" More cheers rent the air and I had to resist the urge to plug my ears with my fingers. "Today, we honor our clan. We honor our ancestors. And we honor our future!"

Orcs were cheering and pounding on the wood of the bleachers and railings. My shoulders crept up towards my ears as if they could block the sound. Then, I felt warm hands slide to either side to cover my ears. I could still hear what Grandpa Thorn was saying, but most of the other sounds were blissfully muffled. I sighed, shoulders slumping in relief. There was no doubt in my mind who it was, and I relished the warmth of his skin against mine.

If I couldn't be with him, this was enough. It had to be enough. Tears stung my eyes, and I blinked them back.

"And the winner of the games will receive the grandest prize I can offer!" Grandpa Thorn called out over the hushed crowd. "A kiss from my sweet granddaughter!"

The crowd exploded and I could swear I heard a choking sound from behind me. Rhuger's hands slid away from my ears. I glanced over my shoulder and saw Rhuger whisper frantically with Sigg. Sigg just caught my gaze, nodded, and came to stand behind me as Rhuger sprinted off.

I paid little attention to the rest of my grandfather's speech. Too anxious over where Rhuger went without a word. What could have possibly been so urgent for him to leave me in Sigg's care? Not that I didn't trust Sigg to protect me, too. This just hadn't happened before. The unknown made me anxious.

I turned around to face the arena as my grandfather wrapped up his speech. The crowd cheered loud enough that I winced. So many male orcs ogled me where I sat next to my Grandpa Thorn's chair in that stupid revealing dress. I hated it.

The crowd died down. The servants organizing the events matched up orcs in the six arenas and soon they were all a flurry of clashing weapons. With everyone sufficiently occupied, I addressed the elephant in the room.

"*Excuse me?*" I near growled, my voice strangled as I leaned out to catch my grandfather's gaze. He looked sheepish as he flicked his gaze to mine. "You could have *asked* me if I'd offer a kiss."

"Well, chestnut, it was a sort of spur-of-the-moment thing." He mumbled, and I didn't buy the lie for a second. "If you think about it, you are now a definite prize that any of these orc warriors would die for. Your honor will be held in high regard and you will be protected by all, not just that Oc'Turin."

"This is because of what happened when I first got here, the dorcha'aon," I said flatly. "And because of what we spoke of the other day."

Him giving me two weeks to find a mate or be handed over to the slimy Rìgh Orok. Or lots of orcs would die and it would all be my fault. Not that he'd said it would be my fault. But it'd be the reason it happened and I couldn't have that on my conscience. Grandpa wasn't pleased with my progress, so he was moving things along, despite him not giving me that list he'd promised.

"Och, you ken the importance of this, then." His stare was hard. "I will not risk you so again."

I understood, all right.

Overbearing old goat.

"You still should have asked me." I bit out. "You do not make my decisions."

"This is not Earth, chestnut. Time is wasting." That was all he said before turning to watch the six arenas before him, dismissing any further discussion on the matter.

He didn't have to tell me twice that this wasn't Earth. This whole place was something so far removed from what I was used to, it was difficult not to cry. And that I was now bound to be mated unless the Oc'Veltas delivered a miracle assist to reopen the gate. So I gritted my teeth and crossed my arms under my chest, determined not to do anything but show a unified front to the orcs.

I let the roars of the crowd draw my eyes to the scene below. A monstrous orc, the size of the womb-splitter from my first day on Talam who was peppered with scars, swung a massive bar mace the size of a small tree at a lithe orc who dual-wielded smaller maces that looked like shestopyors. The smaller maces with their six sharpened flanges both sliced and bruised as they connected. One hit by the bar mace and the slender orc would be crushed. But if the smaller orc could avoid the bar mace and land smaller wounds, he would come out on top.

It was death by a thousand cuts. The strategy was cunning, as evidenced by how the larger orc was wearing himself out. I admired it but found my gaze wandering over each of the arenas. It seemed flesh wounds were allowed, but the orcs were specifically avoiding blows to the head and groin.

"Sigg?" I called over my shoulder, refusing to engage in conversation with my grandfather again.

"Yes, Neamhnaid?" Sigg asked. That damned honorific made my eye twitch.

"How are these games scored?" For the life of me, I couldn't quite grasp how the games were to be won.

"Each of the six arenas is for a specific martial skill. Mace, sword, axe, hand-to-hand, spear, and bow. All the martial skills except bow are one-on-one. The bow is conducted as a group and each must fire until the other arenas have completed their matches. The contestant with the best overall accuracy wins. Then the contestants are sent to the next arena."

"So bow is dedicated for endurance?" I asked.

"Yes." He said, surprise tinting his tone. "There are ten contestants per arena—the last orc standing wins." His eyes were alight watching the games. He enjoyed these things.

"Do you compete in these?" I asked him, curious why he'd held back.

"Och, no. My role as nocrys trainer is too valuable to allow me to enter the games." He shot me a kind smile.

"Oh." We watched as the lithe orc finally felled the massive orc with a deft sweep to the hamstrings. The winner lifted his maces high and whooped. The crowd went wild.

Realization dawned that it was Asterun. As if I'd called him, he turned in his preening to the crowd to cast me a saucy wink. I couldn't keep the scowl from my face, as I did *not* want to kiss that arrogant asshole.

I couldn't muster the courage to ask where Rhuger was.

"So how is an overall winner decided?"

"The six orcs with the highest scores overall will advance to the last bout." He smirked, and my eyebrows shot up. He was enjoying explaining this to me and he was an excellent teacher. "In the final bout, the orcs choose their weapon and they battle one another. The last orc standing will win your kiss."

The way he said that, like he knew something I didn't, hit the 'danger' button in the back of my mind. I thanked Sigg and turned back around to watch the sword bout. My eyes jumped from bout to bout before shifting my attention towards the bow arena.

I nearly leaped out of my chair.

"Rhuger!" I gasped, utterly shocked. Sigg snickered behind me and my grandfather growled, but I ignored them.

Because there was Rhuger, bare-chested in his elaborate kilt and boots, with a look of utter concentration on his face. He stood in a line with nine other orcs of varying sizes and colors. A barrel—*barrel*—of arrows stood next to each contestant. They were all aiming downfield at a row of wood and straw targets, snagging arrows and firing them as quickly as they could.

Some orcs were firing as quickly as possible—as if firing the entire barrel of arrows was their sole purpose. Others took their time, making each arrow count. And between these two strategies was Rhuger.

He would reach into the barrel, grasp an entire handful of arrows, take his time aiming, then fire arrow after arrow from his fist in rapid succession. His arm holding the bow never wavered. Then he would reach into the barrel again and start the process over.

Looking downrange, I could see that the orcs who were firing quickly were often missing the target entirely while those who aimed well had well-placed arrows but still lacked the volume of the former.

The center of Rhuger's target was bristling with arrows. Some of them were even split into pieces by their fellows.

It was making things flutter low in my belly, watching the sheer, controlled, and deadly precision of his ability. I'd been so entranced that when the horn finally blew to call a ceasefire at the range, I had paid no attention to the other events. The winners were called for each—Asterun won the mace, a hulk of an orc with light and dark green striped skin won the sword, an older orc with grey hair won the axe, a heavily scarred orc that would have put any human body builder to shame won the hand-to-hand.

When it came time to announce the bow, my ass cheeks were barely gripping the edge of my chair. The announcer walked down the line of archers and stopped in front of Rhuger. He lifted his arm in the air. Rhuger was blowing like a bellows, sweat pouring off of him. He looked at me then and our eyes locked across the field. He grinned crookedly, sharp teeth flashing white even from so far.

Heat flooded my face.

Once the cheering died down, the contestants all rotated haphazardly, which made little sense. But who was I to judge? My eyes couldn't look anywhere but where Rhuger stalked to the sword arena, head held high and a swagger in his step.

"Stop staring at the Oc'Turin like that, granddaughter." My grandfather ground out. "You aren't supposed to show favoritism in something like this."

I looked at him, deadpan. Then I scrunched up my face and stuck out my tongue at him. My grandfather looked properly affronted before I turned back to watch Rhuger, my eyes drawn to him like steel to a magnet. My grandfather might command me to kiss the winner of this damned thing, but he sure as hell couldn't command me to look away from my bodyguard.

If the games were a place where males could show off to inspire the females' lust, it was little surprise he'd want to join in. It made me feel strange thinking that he might go off with another female once the games were over. My chest constricted so hard it hurt. Frowning over at where Rhuger was upending a bucket of water over his head, water sluicing off of him obscenely as the first sword bout commenced. I couldn't help but rub my chest.

As if my pain called to him, Rhuger turned and rubbed a hand down his face to rid it of the water, eyes locking with mine for a moment. He cocked his head, silently asking me what was wrong. I just shook my head, and he nodded in confirmation.

An obnoxiously loud female caught his attention then and flashed her breasts at him. He stiffened and looked sharply away while the other orcs all leered at the bold female. She kept trying to get his attention, but he just shook his head and ignored her.

Confusion churned in my guts. He was ignoring a perfectly willing female? Why?

He... couldn't possibly be competing to win my kiss, could he?

The thought detonated in my chest, and everything inside me began warring. How could I be so vain to think it was about me? What if he wanted to win my kiss? Was he really willing to call down my grandfather's wrath? Would he be able to win, or would I have to kiss someone else? What if he *did* win, and I had to kiss him in front of the entire clan?

I began screaming internally.

"You seem confused," Sigg stated. I turned to look up at him and his kind eyes.

"Why did Rhuger join the games? He left so suddenly..." I asked, unsure of how to possibly phrase what my heart was demanding to know. I swallowed thickly around my own tumultuous emotions.

"Och, he wants to win, of course." Sigg's grin split his rugged face, and he winked at me.

Stunned by what I realized was ardent wishing mixed with hope, I felt my face heat as I turned to see the winner of the first sword bout stagger off the arena with a gash on his thigh. Rhuger stood, shaking out his arms and cracking his neck. He stalked over to a rack of swords and claimed one. He deftly tested its weight by swinging it around him in a series of flashing steel arcs. Seemingly pleased, he prowled to the center of the ring to meet the announcer for that ring and his opponent.

Dread drenched me at the massive orc who took to the ring. He was easily the size of the womb-splitter. Well over eight feet tall and built like a mountain. He loomed over Rhuger. Then I recognized him. It was *Hisouk*.

Rhuger didn't seem fazed in the slightest.

CHAPTER 38[*]

RHUGER

When Rìgh Thorn had offered a kiss from Amelia as the tournament prize… I'd flipped all the platitudes and refusals to compete a rude mental gesture before stalking to Sigg.

This was my *one* chance to garner a kiss from Amelia without incurring Rìgh Thorn's wrath. My chance to prove my worthiness in his eyes, and regain his trust. My one chance to see if she tasted as sweet as she did in my dreams. To see if it would call forth the mating marks.

I knew the moment I laid my eyes on my brother what he was scheming. He wanted Amelia, her knowledge, and her ties to the Oc'Dellor lineage. I knew Asterun would be more determined to win the tournament, and possibly Amelia's hand. With my current standing, having the mating marks appear would be the best possible outcome. Then my claim over her couldn't be contested.

It didn't take a genius to piece together that Rìgh Thorn would use the Mating Tournament as an opportunity to show Amelia the orc males. To secure her a mate amongst them, to avoid the political upheaval that would come should she refuse to become Rìgh Orok's mate. Because Rìgh Thorn, no matter how much he loved his granddaughter, would put the lives of his people before those of his family. And Rìgh Orok was vile enough to go to war for something he wanted.

Someone *I* wanted.

And I would do whatever it took to become an option now, after yesterday. No matter how long of a shot it was. Because between Rìgh Orok and Asterun, neither would be good to her. Of Sigg and Hisouk, neither would love her. I couldn't trust anyone else to love her as I did. So I'd do it myself.

"Sigg. I need your help." I hissed low near my friend's ear. Amelia and the others could not overhear given how loud the crowd was. Though I saw Rìgh Thorn frown at me in my peripheral vision.

"What do you need, brother?" He asked, a smirk quirking the blond orc's wide mouth. As if he already knew.

"Please guard Amelia for me while I join in the competition. There's still time for me to join the bow. I know they're one short." My heart thundered in my chest, hoping that my friend and brother in arms wasn't in the mood to tease me mercilessly. That he wasn't so dead set on his bid for her, he'd deny me this chance.

"Och, go win so we can all stop groaning over how you moon after her." Sigg tried to keep a straight face as he nodded over his shoulder. "I'll watch over her for you."

I clapped Sigg on the shoulder and sprinted past him. I could hear Amelia's small noise of surprise as I left her. But she was in excellent hands. Sigg was honorable.

With no time to waste running back to my home tree to get my fighting clothes and weapons, I ran to the bow arena. The orc attendant in charge of that arena gave me a flat stare, eyebrows raised at me as I skid to a stop in front of him.

"You've chosen to compete?" He asked with a slow drawl. Completely unsurprised that I was showing up last minute. Did he know? Did *everyone* know how I felt about Amelia? Was I *that* obvious?

Fuck.

"Och." was all I could manage.

"Well, get in there then." He shook his head and shook a thumb towards the arena and the orcs who were currently lining up.

He didn't have to tell me twice. I hopped the low fence they'd erected and ripped my shirt off over my head. I stalked over to the weapons rack where the bows were stored. There was only one left. I snatched it and jogged over to the last open position.

The other orcs groaned when they realized I'd joined. Most wincing or shaking their heads. They knew already that the match would be mine. After all, the Oc'Turin training I'd endured growing up was far more severe than the training the Oc'Dellor received. These orcs hadn't needed to shoot arrows from dawn until dusk on the equinox each warm season as I had.

A call rang out from the attendant for us to prepare. I stood before the last target and cracked my neck before releasing a long, low breath. Centering my mind and will, even as my heart cried out for Amelia. She was the star to which I charted my course, and I knew my heart would not guide me astray.

Another call to arm and fire. The surrounding orcs started firing, and yet I held back, waiting for the wind to shift. As if the Source itself and all the gods were smiling on me, the wind died with hardly a whisper. I plunged my hand into the barrel beside me and grasped a fist full of arrows. Another trick learned at the brutal hands of my childhood trainers.

I raised the bow. Knocked the first arrow. Pulled back the bowstring, the bow creaking at the strain. Aimed. Released my breath, and let the bowstring slip from my fingers. The arrow shot from my bow, and though it wove through the air in a serpentine fashion, I knew it would strike true. It did. Dead center. And I sent the next arrow to cleave the first one in half.

The entire archery event whistled past me in a blur of fletching and twanging strings. All that I focused on was my breathing, grasping the fistfuls of arrows, drawing the bow with my back muscles, and letting fly arrow after arrow in rapid succession. Just to repeat it over and over and over.

I could have sworn I'd heard Amelia call my name at some point.

When the event was called, it was little wonder I'd won. The rings of the target couldn't be seen, it was a bristling nest of arrows. The others didn't have nearly as many arrows, nor were they as well placed as mine.

The attendant came to me and raised my arm, acknowledging that I was the winner of this event. I looked up just then and caught Amelia's gaze. She was staring at me in utter awe, perched on the edge of her seat. I grinned crookedly as sweat poured from me. I could see her blush from across the field.

The moment when the breeze had blown up the back of her dress before my eyes replayed in my mind. How the lush globes of her neamhnaid ass had flexed and jiggled as she took the stair before her. How her flesh was creamy and soft, with little precious dimples and marks that begged to be bitten. And the little thatch of curls at the apex of her thighs set my blood to singing in my veins. Demanding I lay her down on the steps and explore what wonders those crisp curls concealed.

But then my heartbeat skipped, and when it beat again, my sense returned. I'd grasped the flyaway dress panel and nearly spanked her with how swiftly I slapped the fabric back into place. Covering the sight that would haunt me until I could make her my mate. Make this vision a reality.

I looked away from her, desperate to ease the lust that was swiftly replacing the thrum of physical exertion, and noted that the orcs in charge of the bow event had completely replaced my target instead of just pulling free the arrows. I laughed. It felt good to show off my prowess. Especially to the female who owned my heart.

They then directed me to the sword arena. When I got there, I snagged a bucket of water to dump over my head. A prickle of awareness washed over me. As I wiped the water from my eyes, I looked towards the dais where Rìgh Thorn and Leanabh Banrigh Amelia sat in positions of honor. The look on her face made me pause. Something was wrong.

I tilted my head, a silent question if she was okay. She shook her head and smiled at me. It looked forced, but I nodded anyway. I'd have to ask her what troubled her when the event was over. Perhaps she hadn't had a choice in offering a kiss to the winner.

I swore then that *when* I won, I wouldn't force her to kiss me. She shouldn't be forced to do anything like that if she didn't want to. The thought that Rìgh Thorn had given her kiss as a prize without her consent tinged my vision red.

A female voice called my name, and I turned to look, instinct kicking in as if it were Amelia. The redness coloring my vision ripped away.

It wasn't her.

"Rhuger! Win for me!" The female cried.

A female I'd rejected in the past flashed me her breasts and I stiffened. Not in desire, but in affront. I whipped my head away from her, refusing to look at her again.

"Rhuger, look! I will bed you if you win!" I shook my head and ignored her squawking.

"I'll bed you, Arra!" an orc taking part in the sword called. Other orcs jeered and made lewd comments.

I'd turned down the bold Arra multiple times now. Not that she wasn't pretty. She was. But she didn't sing to me as Amelia did. No one did.

And I wouldn't settle for anyone else. Even if I won Rìgh Thorn's approval, if Amelia refused me, I would still hold true to her for the rest of my days. Loving her from afar as I protected her.

I knew so in my very bones.

I stalked away towards the sword rack and snagged a sword, testing out its balance, swinging it around my body in a flourish. The temptation to show off for Amelia was too strong to deny. The need to earn her approval was impossible to quell.

The third bout arrived, and I was called forward. I hopped the railing of the square space designated for the sword event and stood at the marked location on the ground. My opponent entered the arena, and I paused.

It was Hisouk. I was surprised to find him competing. He'd only ever wanted his cridhe, so perhaps it was for glory. He was a good fighter despite being a gardener, for sure, and his reach and strength aided him greatly. But he wasn't the fastest, nor the most cunning of the Oc'Dellor fighters.

I was.

We took our places on opposite sides of the arena. Hisouk cracked his neck and rolled his shoulders before lifting his sword. I sank into a fighting crouch, presenting him with my side, making myself as small of a target as possible. Moments stretched out between us.

The attendant shouted, and Hisouk and I leaped into action. Hisouk ran for me, his steps shaking the earth beneath my feet. I kept myself low as I danced forward on the balls of my feet. Hisouk raised his sword high and brought it down in a crushing blow.

If I'd been untrained, the blow would have felled me. Cut me right in half.

But I'd seen far more war than most of the orcs competing. So I slipped to the side as the blade whizzed past my shoulder and advanced for his unguarded side. He evaded the thrust of my blade, to my surprise. Hisouk had been training. I retreated from his defensive slash. I grinned at him and he smirked back at me.

"Not going to be so easy this time, Rhuger." He called, and I laughed, delighted.

"Show me what you've got, Gentle Hisouk!" I taunted and crooked a finger at him. Hisouk's face grew grim, and he strode towards me, his sword flashing in arcs on either side of his body. A defensive tactic that wouldn't work.

But I'd play.

When he came at me, I didn't take him down as I would have otherwise. Instead, I retreated and dodged his slashing arcs. Hisouk feinted a sword attack, and I fell for it. His secondary attack nearly broke my guard it was so strong. The blow cost me and I landed on my back in the dirt.

The crowd roared. It wasn't often someone knocked me on my ass.

I tucked my legs up to my chest and executed a kickflip, righting myself and landing on the balls of my feet in time to parry Hisouk's next attack. The roar of the crowd was deafening as we exchanged blows. Hisouk, not used to war, was tiring. I'd barely broken a sweat.

His last swing was low, an attempt to sweep my legs out from under me. I hopped it easily. His next attack was a thrust, and I raised my sword to meet it. Steel met steel, and I allowed his blade to shed against mine, sparks flying as I pivoted and advanced. The hilts of our blades collided. With a deft twist of my wrist, I sent his blade flying from his grip.

The crowd was deafening as I held my sword tip to Hisouk's panting throat.

"You've gotten better, friend," I smirked at him.

"Still not good enough to beat you." He growled as his chest heaved. "Yet."

Hisouk's smile matched mine as he raised his hands in defeat.

The attendant announced me as the uncontested winner of the bout, and the next pair took to the field as we left it. I returned my sword to the rack. A glance at the dais rewarded me with Amelia's slack-jawed expression and Righ Thorn's thunderous one. He knew I'd made the bout showy and didn't like it. Didn't like how I'd impressed his granddaughter.

I smirked and ducked my head.

Trying not to grin like an idiot, I got some water and waited, doing my damnedest not to look at the dais. I impressed her. I'd been afraid she'd find me monstrous for my martial skill. This wasn't the same as fighting on a battlefield, freeing orckin of their limbs and heads. But if her awe was any sign, maybe I didn't frighten her. Perhaps I had a chance with her after all. I wanted to punch the air in victory.

The fourth bout was over quickly. A young orc who'd barely started his training had gone up against a veteran. The youth had speed and energy—but that was nothing in the face of the decades of experience the older orc had behind him. It was over in four moves. The older orc slapped the youth's shoulder good naturally and offered to train him.

The fifth bout took the longest. So while that played out, I looked around the other five arenas and the current bouts. The bow wasn't much to speak of in terms of competition. I'd likely win the highest score in the bow out of all the competitors. Uther, having just lost his mate, refused to compete this year, and he was the only orc in Oc'Dellor capable of beating me in that event.

The mace, hand-to-hand, and the axe all had competent fighters so far. It was the tall, lithe orc who was currently fighting in the spear arena who worried me. It was Asterun. The best fighter of the Oc'Dellor besides Uther. And a total pain in my ass.

I didn't like the way I'd seen him stare at Amelia these past few days. I liked it less that he thought he was entitled to Amelia's hand. If I wasn't her bodyguard, and if I hadn't killed Tintain that first night, he would have definitely approached her. The thought of her potentially willing to bear his touch made my guts writhe.

I hated the air he breathed.

The bastard won the spear match and smirked at me from across the field. The challenge was clear. He was aiming to win Amelia's kiss, too. Not just the tournament and Rìgh Thorn's approval.

I snarled.

They announced the fifth bout of the sword. Of all five bouts, mine had been the most impressive, and thus, as the victor of that bout, it granted me the most points of all the competitors in our event. I didn't even wait for the attendant to finish announcing my win before I prowled to the hand-to-hand ring.

I'd be damned if I let Asterun win and get his slimy tongue

anywhere near Amelia's perfect lips.

CHAPTER 39*

AMELIA

"He's so good," I said, watching as he walked away from the sword arena to sit in wait for the hand-to-hand.

"Rhuger has been trained in war since he was a child." My grandfather growled, thick fingers combing through his beard as he contemplated the field before him. I could have sworn that was the first time I'd heard him use Rhuger's name.

"He has?"

"Och, he's served the Oc'Dellor well these past years, even against his own kin."

"You don't seem to like him much," I commented, looking at him.

"I don't have to. I respect him, though." Grandpa Thorn's gaze was sharp as he flicked his eyes toward mine.

That was... big. Grandpa rarely admitted respect for anyone unless they truly deserved it. He was just that kind of man—er, orc.

"Do you think he'll win?" I asked, curious.

"Och. His only true competition comes from Asterun as he's the Master at Arms's apprentice." Grandpa Thorn pointed far afield at the absolute pain in my ass.

Asterun was squaring off with an orc in the axe arena. Each wielded two one-handed axes in a whirling dance of traded blows and vicious swipes. But I couldn't bother to watch him for long.

My gaze flicked back to Rhuger, where he was just entering his bout for the hand-to-hand. The orc he was facing wasn't the biggest or swiftest, but he was built like a pit bull. Stocky, packed with dense muscle, and sporting a meaty block of a head. His skin was one of the few I'd seen that was nearly black, and it glistened with a slight purple sheen in the sunlight.

The announcer called, and the fight began. Rhuger sprung, jumping into the air and delivering a devastating haymaker that took his opponent to the ground. Rhuger danced away on the balls of his feet, hands loose at his sides as he waited to see if his opponent would get up.

To everyone's shock, the dark-skinned orc got back up, lifted his hands in defense, and advanced. Rhuger brought his arms up just in time to block a right hook that nearly bowled him over. But he capitalized on the moment and kneed the orc in the gut.

They became a blur of controlled strikes, kicks, and grappling moves. Rhuger had the height and speed advantage, but no matter how many times he knocked the orc down, he just *kept getting back up*. More than once, he'd landed vicious blows and had nearly sent Rhuger to the ground.

I gripped the arms of the chair in my hands, claws sinking into the wood as I watched the orc I loved, my bodyguard and friend, stand his ground against one of the best fighters I'd ever seen. I could barely breathe or blink as my heart battered against my rib cage.

"Esheth is a rare fighter." My grandfather said. "Very few have ever beaten him in the ring. It's his chief strength, his endurance. He's competent in the other martial skills, but nowhere to the degree of his hand-to-hand. This might be the bout that Rhuger loses."

"It's true. I've only seen him get beaten once. He usually wears out his opponents and then strikes a finishing blow." Sigg commented from behind me.

"Rhuger will beat him," I stated with conviction. And I believed it.

As if I'd willed it so, Esheth swung and Rhuger ducked. In one fluid motion, he scooped Esheth's back leg in his hand and lifted it up high as he stood. Esheth landed face-first in the arena's dirt. Rhuger released his leg and his body crumpled to the ground. He didn't get up again.

The announcer called the match in Rhuger's favor and they carried the unconscious Esheth to see the medics off to one side. Rhuger tilted his head back, took a deep breath, and walked to the next arena. He had blood running down his mouth and chin from his nose but otherwise seemed unhurt.

"Seems you were right, Neamhnaid." Sigg laughed as he leaned against the back of my chair. Relief washed through me as I smiled up at Sigg. "If he wins the most points in one more arena and wins the rest of his matches, he'll make it into the top six."

Gods preserve me. I fervently hoped he won. I swore to myself as I watched him upend another bucket over his head and cleaned the blood from his face that I'd tell him how I felt. Regardless if he actually won or not. I only hoped it wouldn't ruin our friendship.

RHUGER

My fist connected with my opponent's jaw in a vicious uppercut that laid him flat on his back. The orc staggered to his feet and raised his fists again. We'd been trading blows for a while now and no matter how many times I knocked him on his ass, he got back up. I respected him for it. Usually, my jumping punch knocked out an opponent in one blow.

We were both pouring sweat and covered in dirt and blood. My nose was broken and his eye was almost swollen shut. If neither of us could win, it would be a draw, and losing even one event would keep me from making it into the top six. It wasn't something I could afford.

I grasped my nose and yanked, setting it and sending a fresh trickle of blood gushing from my nose down my chin. Spitting a wad of blood onto the ground, I kept my gaze locked on him. He charged and swung. Ducking under his hook, I snagged his foot and lifted hard and fast as I stood again. His balance, already threatened by his swing, failed him completely. He landed face-first in the dirt, his legs crumpling to the ground a second behind his head.

Turning, I brought my fists back up, ready to watch him miraculously regain his feet. But my opponent lay unconscious on the ground. He still breathed, his wheezy huffs of air stirred the dust by his mouth. I let my arms drop to my sides as the attendant called the bout.

There was plenty of time before the mace, so I dumped more water on myself, drank my fill, and sat in the shade of a barrel. I could feel my nose already healing and it tickled, making me want to sneeze. Checking the back of my knuckles where I'd torn the flesh there against the fighter's teeth, I watched the pink muscle and tendon stitch back over my knuckles, my green skin softly closing in around it.

All these years amongst the Oc'Dellor, and only Uther had realized how quickly I healed. How it wasn't natural. Wasn't normal. Everyone else just attributed my resilience to my Oc'Turin training.

Which was partly true. But like the honorable orc he was, Uther had said nothing to no one. Not even Rìgh Thorn. Uther was the one to tell me that my healing ability must be a trace gift from my father's people. Whoever they were.

Normally, it made me uneasy, healing so quickly it was like cheating death. I was built differently and sometimes it felt like a curse. But on days like today? When important things hung in the balance? I was thankful for it.

Leaning my head against the barrel, I closed my eyes and waited for my bout in the mace arena.

"Rhuger!" a voice called some time later. "You're up!"

I cracked open an eye and saw the attendant waving me over. With a grunt, I got to my feet and prowled to the weapons rack. Some of the maces were already drenched in blood from previous bouts. My gaze raked over the available maces, some with spikes or bars, others bulbous or shaped closer to a war hammer. I reached for a pair of six-winged maces still smudged with blood.

After testing the balance of the maces with a few swings, I entered the arena and waited for my opponent, holding my maces at my sides. Cheers went up as thunderous footsteps shook the ground beneath my feet. I flicked my gaze up to gauge my opponent and paused.

The orc was immense, definitely of Oc'Blyre ancestry, with his pronounced tusks. He was battle-scarred and had a wicked scar that ran from his hairline down over his brow and cheek to split his upper lip. He wore a leather kilt, greaves, and bracers that protected his striped skin. The orc held a massive morning star mace with a spherical head covered in spikes with a shaft nearly as long as a spear that had a weighted end.

I couldn't help but grin as I spun the maces in my hands. The biggest challenge for me with these bouts wasn't the fighting. It was ensuring I didn't land any killing blows. And this was going to be the biggest challenge so far, as this wasn't the first time I'd ever gone up against an Oc'Blyre with a mace like that. And the times I had? It'd taken me less than five moves to leave them dead in my wake.

"This should be good. Finally, a challenge." The scar-faced orc grinned back, revealing those tusks.

"I was just thinking the same," I replied, holding my arms wide and offering him a slight, mocking bow.

The attendant barked a call, and the bout began. The orc swung his enormous battle mace around himself, building the momentum he needed to end me. Getting in close and fast was the only way to finish this quickly. Otherwise, I'd have to wear him down, and Source only knew how long that would take.

Timing his swings, I made to dodge under his guard. But he was far more agile than I'd given him credit for. He spun, swinging the battle mace with him, increasing the speed of his stroke, and aimed low. I jumped high enough to clear the mace head, but before I could recover, he'd advanced as his second swing came whistling towards my head.

I used both maces to strike his. The glancing blow sent his mace head wide, but one spike hooked between the flanges of one of my maces and sent it flying from my hand. I grimaced and tracked its fall in my peripheral vision as my opponent adjusted the arch of his swing, correcting it as he advanced again. This time, I dodged and rolled under his swing, popping up at his unprotected back.

As before, he spun on the ball of his foot to face me once more. Bringing his mace hurtling through the air, I rolled out of his reach and snatched my fallen mace before whirling to face him again. Side-stepping to get within range of me, he made a massive, circular swing, raising the battle mace up in an arch to bring it straight down on top of me.

I slid under his swing on my knees, lifting my maces high in an x-block. My block caught the shaft of the battle mace, but gave under the momentum of his swing, laying me back on my knees almost to the ground as I struggled to keep the block. The spiked head of his mace crashed into the ground above my head in a rain of dirt and rocks.

My opponent attempted to pull his battle mace free, but it was stuck fast. We shared a glance and knew it was about to be a battle between strength and agility. In a lightning-fast move, I slid the heads of my maces apart slightly, pushed the shafts of my maces against the shaft of his until my knuckles brushed it, then heaved them back. The flanges in my mace heads bit deep into the wooden shaft of his battle mace. With a roar, I arched my back, tightened my back muscles, and snapped the shaft of his mace in half.

Surprise lit his face as his mace fell to pieces in his hands. I used the momentum from splitting his mace in half, whirled from the waist, and as he fell forward, struck his shoulder and knee. The flanges sank into his joints with sickening crunches, shattering the bone and cartilage. He howled as his leg buckled and he fell onto his good side.

Ducking out from under the broken shaft of the mace head where it was still sunk into the ground, I spun to my feet and held my maces at the ready. My back, shoulders, and pectorals screamed from the exertion it took to break the thick shaft of the battle mace. Breathing heavily, I waited a moment as my opponent snarled into the dirt of the arena, his blood pooling under the wreck of his knee, his arm hanging limp at his side.

"Match is over!" called the attendant, raising an arm towards me. "Winner is Rhuger!"

Medics were already swarming my opponent, getting him

stable enough to move. I grimaced. I hadn't intended to hurt him so badly. He looked up at me then and gave me a solid nod. Acknowledging my win and letting me know there was respect between us. I nodded in return and backed toward the weapons rack.

After I put my weapons back, I moved to the next arena I was directed towards. I'd made it. Four out of six wins. Three of six, so far, with the highest scores. It would take some time for the remainder of the mace bouts to finish to find out who'd won the most points out of that section. But even if I didn't reach the most points in the mace, all I had to do was win one more fight and I'd be in the top six.

I snuck a glance at the dais as I wiped my mouth with the back of my fist. A shivering thrill ran over my skin as my gaze met Amelia's. She'd been watching me this whole time. Her sweet, rounded face with its freckles like stars followed me as if no one else existed in the tournament.

Knowing my cridhe couldn't keep her eyes off me as I fought to win her kiss left my loins aching in need. Nothing would stand in my way of claiming that soft pink mouth of hers. Of letting her know with my lips on hers how I felt about her, as I still couldn't find the words to tell her.

AMELIA

Rhuger had decimated the gargantuan orc with the pole mace. Broken him so he wouldn't be able to fight for a good long while, if ever again. I should have been scared. Should have been terrified of what my bodyguard was capable of. Of just the small vignette I was seeing in his years of being a soldier, being a warrior.

But I wasn't.

As Rhuger glanced my way, checking on me even as he strode

to his next competition, I realized why. Yes, he was my appointed
bodyguard. Had saved me quite a few times now from certain death.
But I knew, in the same way, that I knew the suns would rise and set,
knew the seasons would change and the tides would rise and fall, that
he would do nothing to hurt me. At least not intentionally.

And some dark part of me that loved the morally grey antihero
and villain characters delighted in the sheer power he commanded.
From others, from his body, from the very weapons in his grip. It was as
if he was on an entirely different level from his opponents. Like his
father had been some primal god of war.

The last two martial skills Rhuger fought in flew past for me.
The roar of the crowd became too much to bear for a while, so I had to
hold my hands up to cover my ears. I dimly remember someone
bringing food and drinks, but my focus was locked on Rhuger.

He whirled a spear around his body within the arena,
exchanging blow after blow with his opponent, who was skilled and
held his own. But in the end, Rhuger had hooked an arm around his
opponent's spear, twisted it to his side, locking it against his back, and
slid his spear to halt a breath away from the other orc's throat. His
throat bobbed and a thin trickle of blood dribbled down his
collarbones.

The axe took seconds. Rhuger's opposition was young, maybe
in his late teens, and lacking the experience necessary to last against
my bodyguard. Rhuger had advanced, twin axes swinging. One axe had
bitten deep into the edge of the wooden shield the other fighter had
strapped to his arm. Rhuger yanked, ripping the shield apart, and in the
same movement, swung his other axe, knocking his opponent's axe out
of his hand. The poor kid had dropped his shield and held up both
hands in surrender, eyes wide and face pale.

Rhuger had ruffled his hair, saying something to him before
stalking off to get some water. That small sweetness and camaraderie

with someone far younger than him warmed something in my chest. Rhuger glanced at me again as he got another ladle of water from a bucket. And it was as if I could breathe again. My hands slid from my ears to rest on the arms of my chair once more.

"Now the top six fighters will fight here in the arena below the dais. Each will pick their own melee weapon. The last orc left unbloodied wins the event and your kiss." Sigg explained, his arm braced over the back of my chair as he spoke down near my ear.

"If they're already bloodied, how will they know?" I asked, exasperated.

"Each contestant has an announcer look over their current wounds and keep a close eye on them for the entire bout. The medics will look at them beforehand and patch them up, so new wounds will be more obvious." He said, pointing to where the knot of fighters was being looked at by some medics. "It's only till first blood, as some fighters could last all day if left to fight until someone dropped or died."

I knew who he meant. Rhuger stood with an attendant who was making notes on a board as he circled Rhuger's sweat-drenched and dirt-covered form. No one had gotten through all the trials without at least some bruises, scrapes, and minor gashes. One of them had lost a finger and was just binding it up as if it had been nothing.

The crowd was going wild as the lead announcer called forth the six fighters who would enter the final round. "Asterun! Shohtun! Gregal! Rhuger! Belic! And Hisouk! Report to the grand arena!"

CHAPTER 40*

AMELIA

"*Hisouk?*" I asked in utter bafflement.

"Och, he did well for himself in his other fights." Sigg was laughing behind his fist. "You know, the ones in which he wasn't fighting Rhuger?"

I turned and looked at Sigg in bleating panic, face red as a beet. Sigg tipped back his head and howled his laughter to the beams of the canopy over the dais. Several elites of the clan looked at him with barely veiled distaste. Evidently, it wasn't the *done thing* to guffaw so boisterously. But Sigg gave no shits, and neither did I.

"No need to explain, Neamhnaid." He chuckled, barely getting his face and laughter under control. "We all know who you'd like to win the tournament."

"Sigg." Grandpa Thorn's tone bit like steel and his gaze was forbidding. "Stop encouraging her."

"Yes, my Rìgh," Sigg replied, a slightly mocking tone limning the serious words.

I rolled my eyes and turned back to the arena at the feet of the dais. The six fighters lined up facing us, their gazes flickering between their Rìgh and me. The prize. *Ick.*

Rhuger's gaze never wavered from mine. He gave me a subtle wink and a small half-smile. I flushed and fought to keep from ducking my head. I had no idea what it was about him, but he flustered me just by breathing. And when I was already out of my element? It was even harder to hide the reactions I had to him.

Grandpa Thorn stood then, stalked to the edge of the platform, and held his arms wide. The crowd went wild, cheering for what they knew would be *the* bout of the year. Eventually, the crowd calmed and my grandfather's booming voice echoed across the tourney.

"Good orckin of Oc'Dellor! Today is a fine day to celebrate the virility and strength of our males! Before us are the six fiercest warriors our clan has to offer!" The crowd went wild, and the females watched with avid interest at the railing. A lot of them were eyeballing Rhuger.

I hated it.

"It is now time for the last bout! Each male is allowed a weapon, except the bow, and the last orc unbloodied within the arena will be named the victor! May the gods grant you their favor!" The throng of orckin continued to cheer, and the six contestants bowed with their fists to their chests at the dais. Grandpa Thorn gave them a magnanimous gesture, and the fighters peeled off to the weapons racks.

Asterun immediately went for twin daggers that were long enough to be short swords. The one with the missing finger, Belic, picked an axe and a targe shield. Gregal, an orc almost as large as Hisouk, who was covered in hundreds of scars, chose a war hammer whose head was nearly as large as Gregal's. Hisouk chose a massive morning star mace whose spiked head dangled from the shaft by a thick chain. The whip-thin orc, Shohtun, snagged a spear with a bladed end. Last was Rhuger, whose gaze had been systematically roaming over the weapons and the ones his opponents had chosen. Without hesitation, he strode to the sword rack and picked up a plain falchion.

Each orc was playing up to their strengths. Asterun was incredibly agile and having twin blades gave him twice the opportunity to slip in and nick his opponent. Belic was armed for a balance of defense and offense, the only orc to choose something that could be used as a weapon and a shield. Gregal obviously relied on his sheer strength and size, so a war hammer was fitting. Hisouk had the power to wield the morning star mace with deadly efficiency. The longer range and quick reactivity of the bladed spear seemed ideal for the willowy Shohtun.

And Rhuger? Well, he could have grabbed a boot knife and done severe damage, so an effective sword like a falchion was like giving a butcher a chainsaw. He'd picked it up off the rack, hefting it and testing its balance, executing several swinging maneuvers to get a sense of the blade.

When all the contestants had their weapons, the attendants directed them to six marked places in the square ring before the dais. They placed Rhuger with his back to the dais in front of me and I had to suppress a shiver as I watched a bead of sweat slide down the long muscles of his spine. I shook my head. Here he was about to take on five highly skilled fighters and I was being a thirsty bitch.

The crowd quieted as the lead attendant stepped forward and tossed a weighted cloth high. I held my breath as it plummeted to the dirt of the arena floor, the cloth a fluttering banner trailing behind it. The weighted cloth hit the ground in a puff of dust and it was as if the entire world shifted.

The six fighters turned razor-sharp in their focus and energy. One heartbeat thundered in my chest, then two, before anyone moved. Then pandemonium ensued. The arena was a blur of limbs and weapons as all six fighters engaged one another.

Shohtun was the first to move, whipping his bladed spear to his side and lunging at Rhuger, who was next to him in the circle of fighters. I watched in horror as the hefty blade sliced through the air toward Rhuger's unprotected left side, his sword in his right hand. There was no way he could deflect it. He was going to get skewered, and I couldn't look away.

As if he had *all* the time in the world, Rhuger noticed Shohtun and, as the blade was mere inches from him, he just *stepped forward*.

The blade skimmed his shoulder blades, nearly snagging on his braid. In lightning-fast succession, Rhuger turned towards Shohtun, grasped the shaft of the spear, locking it against his body, and brought down his falchion against the shaft, splintering it into two jagged pieces. Shohtun's momentum was his downfall. Rhuger lifted his sword arm and rammed his elbow into Shohtun's face.

Blood spurted from his nose and mouth as he staggered backward. His expression was one of shock as he spat out a tooth and walked off the arena floor. But Rhuger wasn't even paying attention. He'd already stepped toward Belic, whose axe was whistling down in a deadly arc toward his shoulder.

I gasped and dug my claws into the arms of my chair as Rhuger's dark laugh rumbled over the crowd. The male was facing dismemberment and was laughing like it was the most fun he'd had in ages. I wasn't sure if I should be afraid or not, but my pussy had its own ideas and flooded my seat at Rhuger's display of deadly efficiency.

RHUGER

Shohtun was no challenge. He'd thought to catch me unawares in my peripheral vision on my prone side, thinking his extended reach would save him. He'd been wrong, and I'd left him spitting out his teeth.

Belic, on the other hand, was going to be an irritating problem. The only orckin to choose a shield as part of their weaponry, he had the added advantage of a defensive object. I heard his axe slicing through the air and pivoted on my left foot. I slid out of the way of his axe swing and presented a smaller target as I retreated a few steps.

A glance let me know Hisouk was fending off both Gregal and Asterun. He was doing an admirable job of it. My friend had come a long way from where he'd started a few years ago. I was proud of him. But there was no assisting him in a fight like this.

So I turned my attention back to the male who charged me, slamming into me with his shield. I fell to the ground and rolled out of the way of his axe swing, which would have severed my shoulder had I not moved. Rolling to my feet, I executed an underhanded swing to block Belic's strike and maneuver his axe head away from my body.

We traded blows, his axe and shield against my falchion. Belic used his shield as a weapon with devastating efficiency. For each axe swing, I evaded or blocked, his shield would be there to push me back. He even attempted to crush my throat with the iron edge of it, punching his shield forward in a vicious jab. Dropping to my knees, I narrowly missed it, feeling the passing of it overhead as it brushed my hair.

I spun on my knees as I maneuvered to my feet and swung at his legs. The male jumped, cleared my sword, and landed lightly on his feet. He swung his axe downward, and I pivoted, lifting my sword up crosswise against my side from head to hip. The axe glanced off my blade, not even leaving a nick in the steel edge of my sword.

There was a reason why falchions were some of my favorite blades. Most swords were made to stab or slice. A falchion did that *and* hacked through whatever stood in your way like an axe. Be it a neck, armor, or shield. The thicker end of the blade held a gentle, wicked curve, not unlike my cridhe. This weighted curve put more power behind each swing, and more deadly force into each landed blow.

I swung my sword down and outward to block Belic's next attack. On the backswing, I swiped at his unprotected knees and he retreated. Re-centering himself, he glared at me over the rim of his shield and hefted it into place. Standing tall and presenting a smaller target, I beckoned him forward with a jaunty grin and a crook of my finger. Belic beat his axe twice against his shield and advanced.

He attacked with swing after swing of his axe. Pressing the advantage and attempting to herd me to the outer edge of the arena. If I stepped over the line, I'd be out just as surely as if I'd bled. I let him press me toward the edge, blocking his swings with the edge of my blade. The crowd roared for Belic and a victorious glint flickered in his eyes.

One that wouldn't last.

I dodged his next swing and tumbled a roll forward past him. Popping up onto the balls of my feet, I spun in time to see Belic swing his shield arm wide behind him to block any potential attack and possibly strike me as he turned to face me once more. His shield arm was still in mid-swing, his back now to the edge of the arena.

It was as if time slowed, and I had an eternity to make my next move. The shield was composed of vertical boards bolted together with an iron outer ring to keep it all in place. A durable defense capable of deflecting most attacks. But not mine. I swung my sword in an overhand arc, putting all of my body's power behind that swing.

My falchion bit through the thin iron edge of the shield like a scythe through grass. The hefty end of the blade slid through the vertical space between the two outer boards of Belic's shield with an audible *thunk*. The crowd roared, thinking that my sword had gotten stuck fast, that Belic would soon nick me and I'd be out of the running.

But the pale cast that overcame Belic's face and the slight widening of his eyes told me he knew what was coming. In the heartbeat between one move and the next, I grinned at him, a feral flash of teeth that spoke to the battle lust that thrummed in my veins. Battle was my birthright and one that I'd earned. And few could stand against me and live.

With a hard wrench of my sword and a forceful twist of my wrist, the falchion forced free the outer board of Belic's shield. The iron band squealed as it bent and the wood panel ripped free from the bolts to fall to the ground of the arena at Belic's feet in a puff of dust. Belic attempted to retreat, to shuffle back so he could regroup, but I pressed the attack.

With the iron band severed, bent uselessly where the outer board had been, it compromised the shield. In two swings, it lay in splinters at his feet, the straps, iron band, and rivets that kept the shield together nothing more than a dangling mess from his forearm. Belic raised his axe, ready for my next attack, even with his back heel mere inches from the edge of the arena.

With calculated precision, I swung my sword, knocked his axe from his hand, and thrust my blade toward Belic's face. Halting just as suddenly as I'd moved, I saw my reflection in Belic's horrified gaze. The tip of my blade was so close to his eye that his eyelashes brushed it when he blinked. The sword did not move, and Belic did not breathe. A deft flick of my wrist and the tip of my sword cut a small slice in Belic's cheek. Blood welled and slid down to drip from his jaw.

I swept my sword down and away and Belic chuckled, shaking his head as he stepped back over the line and out of the arena. The male had a good sense of humor and honor. Unlike the male whose light, rushing footsteps brought him nearer to my blade, and my victory.

Swinging my sword as I spun, I met Asterun's daggers and sparks flew as steel shed against steel. His eyes were feverish and hateful, filled with an arrogance he had not earned as we passed one another. Hisouk and Gregal were out of the running. It was now just Asterun and I battling for Amelia's kiss.

I would not lose.

AMELIA

"I've never seen him fight like that," Grandpa grunted in grudging approval as Rhuger battled Belic with lithe grace. "With such focused determination. He's never fought like this, not even when we've been on the battlefield."

"How long have you known him?" I asked, curious as we watched Rhuger battle like an orc possessed. My grandfather seemed to know a lot about Rhuger and it was suspicious.

"Most of his life." Grandpa Thorn was rubbing at his beard with his thick fingers, lost in thought again.

That was interesting. Rhuger had to be *someone* for my grandfather to not only know who he was out of the thousands of orckin in the clans but to have monitored him for so long. There was a pattern here I was only now seeing the edges of. A long pattern of history between Rhuger, my grandfather, and the clans.

No one would explain it to me, even if I asked, so I would watch and wait for the pattern to reveal itself. Because if I'd learned nothing else so far in my life, it was that people lie, but patterns do not. And with enough time, any pattern and any deviations from it would become clear.

Flicking my gaze back to the arena, I watched as Gregal struck

Hisouk, who stumbled back over the edge of the arena, knocking him out of the running. Hisouk cursed as he looked up at me with an apologetic expression. He nodded and strode away.

Why had he looked so sorry?

With Hisouk out of the way, it didn't take Asterun long to bypass Gregal's guard and leave a smiling gash on his bicep. Gregal, pissed off, threw his weapon to the ground and stormed off of the field. Rhuger had just wrecked Belic's shield and whipped his sword up to his eye. In a quick movement, Rhuger left a bloody cut on Belic's face, knocking him out of the running. As Belic retreated from the arena, there were only two fighters left. The crowd waited with bated breath as the apprentice to the Master of Arms and my bodyguard were about to go toe to toe.

Asterun ran at Rhuger's unprotected back, daggers ready to slash and maim. His attempt at stealthily taking out my bodyguard failed as Rhuger heard him coming and turned, blocking Asterun's dagger and shedding sparks as they passed one another. They turned to engage and their traded blows came faster and faster until they moved in a blurred dance only they could see.

Asterun's greatest asset was his speed. But it didn't seem to matter against my bodyguard, who only increased his own pace to match that of his opponent. Sitting here, watching Rhuger throughout the tournament, something clicked. He was made for this. For battle and war.

The light that sparked in his eyes and the grin that split his face as he fought was not entirely sane. He delighted in conflict and destruction. And as someone who valued peace and creativity, I should be terrified of him. Terrified of what he could do to me.

Instead, I couldn't keep the filthy thoughts of what he could do to me off of the battlefield out of my mind. A war of a different kind as teeth clashed in fervent kisses and desperate hands ripped clothing free of feverish skin. Gulping, I forced out those thoughts so my scent of arousal wouldn't reach anyone. The only person I wanted to scent how damned horny I was currently was lunging at his opponent, sword tip narrowly missing Asterun's throat.

Asterun spun out a low kick, grasping a handful of dirt in his hand at the same time. As Rhuger stepped back, Asterun let the dirt fly into Rhuger's eyes. Rhuger danced further back, but not far enough. The dirt caught him in the face and he rubbed the heel of his hand against his eyes as he held up his sword in defense.

I hissed.

"Cheat!" I barked, and my grandfather's hand landed heavily on my shoulder.

"This is fair play, chestnut." When I looked at him in bewilderment, he explained. "The arena is fought like the battlefield. If an orc cannot handle a little dirt in the face, he's not worthy to win or to live."

Rhuger danced back on the balls of his feet, rubbing his eyes with the heel of his hand and holding his sword in a defensive position. Asterun pounced, capitalizing on the opportunity. Rhuger successfully blocked a few swipes of Asterun's daggers, but couldn't see out of his left eye. Rhuger pressed forward in an attack and that's when it happened. Asterun ducked low and spun to Rhuger's left, steel flashing in the afternoon sun.

A gash opened up on Rhuger's thigh. He hobbled a step, stunned, and finally wiped the dirt from his eye as blood dribbled down his thigh just below his kilt. Asterun shot his arms into the air and the crowd went absolutely feral. The champion's grin was fit to split his face in half and Rhuger handed his sword off to an attendant before stalking, not limping, over to Asterun to clasp forearms with him in a show of camaraderie.

Asterun leaned toward Rhuger to speak in his ear and I watched Rhuger's expression morph from studied politeness to unleashed rage. Pulling away and releasing Rhuger's forearm, Asterun threw him a self-satisfied smile akin to a cat after it's caught and eaten a bird.

All I could truly focus on was the sheer volume of blood that was coursing down Rhuger's leg and boot. I was stunned he was still conscious, let alone still standing like nothing was the matter. Rhuger's silver and onyx gaze flicked up to mine, his expression a strange mixture of panic and fury. I looked down at his leg and then back up into his eyes, knowing full well my expression was one of worry. He shook his head, sighed, and offered me a self-deprecating smile along with a shoulder shrug.

Worry still knotted my guts, just as panic still lingered in his eyes as the combatants filed back out onto the field in front of the dais. Asterun was grinning, and I blanked my expression. It would rankle my clan to publicly disgrace the bastard after he'd won the tournament. Even if I didn't think his victory was a fair one. I didn't want to upset the people on their celebration day, so I'd do as I was told.

Didn't mean I had to like it.

"We have our champion!" Grandpa Thorn boomed over the tourney, gesturing to Asterun. "This year's champion is Asterun Oc'Eirun!"

With everyone distracted by my grandfather, Sigg leaned down near my ear.

"Once the prize kiss has been given to the winner if a lady wishes to kiss another fighter..." He murmured and I turned my head towards him to let him know I was listening while I kept watching the scene below. "She could claim them as her champion..."

That caught my interest.

"Champion?" I asked Sigg quietly so my grandfather, who had stood and was waiting for the crowd to calm enough for him to speak.

"Och, a lady's personal champion. It doesn't *have* to be the winner. It is an old custom and oft forgotten." The mischief in his voice was obvious. But gotdamn if this guy wasn't being a good wingman to Rhuger. And allowing me to honor who I thought the true winner to be.

"It's time for the prizes!" Grandpa Thorn shouted and turned to me even as attendants rushed to stand at the base of the dais. Each holding a pillow with some trinket or another placed atop it. The expectant look on my grandfather's face nearly had me growling.

Oh, I'd kiss the cheating orc, all right. Just not how anyone expected me to.

So I stood and carefully made my way down the stairs to the arena floor, careful not to let any stray breeze compromise my dubious modesty. I was going to burn this damned dress as soon as possible. I strode to where the attendants gathered in front of the contestants. Asterun was front and center, chest puffed out, and head held high.

Nerves ate at me as the gazes of the entire clan rested on my shoulders. I didn't know what I was supposed to do or how I was supposed to act. No one had bothered to explain. Panic bubbled up inside of my chest, a strangled scream desperate to get out. I swallowed it instead as I stopped below my grandfather, where he stood, larger than life on the dais.

"My granddaughter Amelia's kiss, as well as the usual prizes, goes to Asterun!" my grandfather called, and the crowd cheered.

I glanced nervously at the attendant nearest to me. He smiled gently and nodded towards Asterun, a quiet sign it was time for me to pucker up. Nodding my thanks, I held my head high and stepped in front of Asterun, who offered me a courtly bow.

"Hello, Neamhnaid. I believe I've won your kiss." He said, amethyst and obsidian gaze sparkling in triumph and heat. It was like he was attempting to smolder, but didn't have the right stuff to pull it off. It was plastic, fake, just like his personality.

"I believe you did," I replied flatly, face still as blank a mask as I could keep it.

I didn't want to kiss him. Didn't want to touch him, either. The only orc before me I felt comfortable touching was Rhuger. And he'd come in second.

Swallowing the bile that crawled up my throat, I stepped forward and reached up to grasp his face in my hands. Asterun bent down slightly, smirking as he did so. I brought his face toward mine, and he closed his eyes and pursed his lips, prepared for me to kiss him in front of the entire clan and the male I'd lost my heart to.

At the last second, I jerked Asterun's head to the side and planted a feather-light kiss on his storm-grey cheek. Releasing him as quickly as I could while still being polite, I backed up a few steps to put space between us. I didn't want him attempting to claim what he assumed was his. The cheering seemed to die out as Asterun's eyes popped open in surprise.

The orc looked disappointed. I couldn't care less. He'd cheated in my book, regardless of how the rules worked. Of the two, Rhuger's skill was of a higher caliber.

The orckin of the Oc'Dellor were confused but clapped politely, anyway. It seemed they'd expected me to kiss him on the mouth but hadn't bothered to tell *me* that. Eventually, the crowd died down. And that's when I raised my voice.

"I'd like to claim my own champion." The noise died immediately. I suddenly felt wary—but I'd already committed to what I was going to do. I swear I could hear Grandpa Thorn's teeth grinding from the dais behind me. Rhuger's expression was shocked as I turned to look at him.

RHUGER

Watching Amelia approach Asterun to give him a kiss wrenched my gut until I thought I'd throw up. I wanted to reach out, to grasp her arm and stop her from giving it to a male who wouldn't cherish what she was about to give him. She shouldn't be kissing him. Shouldn't have to kiss anyone, to begin with.

Instead, I fisted my hands at my sides, my claws biting into the palms of my hands. I could feel the blood trickle out from between my fingers. Feel the blood coursing down my leg from the gash Asterun had left me with, the flesh already knitting back together. I used this physical pain, and clung to it, as I braced myself for the emotional pain I knew would strike when her lips met his.

Amelia stood before Asterun. His grin was sly, self-assured, and cocky. I hated it. He granted her a sweeping, courtly bow and grinned up at her from under his lashes. It was a bit I'd seen him use plenty of times.

"Hello, Neamhnaid. I believe I've won your kiss." He said. The gathered orckin were cheering. Their victor, their warrior, was about to receive his rich reward, a reward he didn't deserve.

"I believe you did." came her flat reply.

Her expression was a blank mask as she took his face in her perfect little neamhnaid hands. It took everything I had not to shred him to ribbons, the cords in my neck taught as I ground my teeth. Agony lanced my heart as she pulled his face in toward hers. Asterun closed his eyes, puckered his lips, and leaned in.

But at the last moment, she turned his head to the side and kissed his cheek.

Asterun's eyes popped open in surprise. Amelia pulled back quickly and released his face before stepping back. The cheering died down and there was confusion. Orckin murmured low, but she'd technically done as asked. Polite clapping rose within the tourney, acknowledging her gift.

She should have kissed him on the lips. But my wickedly sharp cridhe had been told to gift the winner a kiss. No one specified what kind. Relief was like a war hammer to my gut and I felt dizzy with it.

But then my sweet pearl did something *no one* could have expected. She turned to the crowd and waited for the applause to die down. When it did, she spoke, projecting her voice so everyone could hear.

"I'd like to claim my own champion." Her voice rang out clear as a bell, as the chiming crystalline acorns of the Craobh na Beatha. The entire tourney went immediately silent. Not even the wind dared to blow. She turned to look at me then, and I froze in disbelief. "I'd like to claim Rhuger as my champion!"

Saying nothing more, she stood before me in that damnable excuse for a dress, grasped my face in both of her perfect hands, and stood on her tiptoes. For half a thought, I wondered if she'd kiss my cheek as she'd done for Asterun. But then that bowed mouth of hers brushed mine, and my heart stopped.

The kiss was chaste, a firm press of lips that lasted an eternity and only a second. But my body's reaction was anything but. My hands twitched at my sides, desperate to sink into the pillowy softness of her rounded body. Blood rushed from my head to my groin so fast that I saw stars. And a searing need lit every nerve in my being.

She pulled away, dropping back onto her heels, and I nearly

pulled her to me, unwilling to let her go so soon. Desperate to claim her mouth and sink into her softness. A softness I'd unknowingly craved all of my life.

But I let her go.

My hands trembled at my sides as she retreated, a fierce blush riding high on those freckled cheeks. That single chaste kiss burned, leaving a tingling sensation that my body demanded more of. As I stared into her strange uisge-beatha eyes that rose to meet mine, the slowly dawning clarity I'd been experiencing since I'd met her shifted into sharp focus.

There was no denying it now. There was absolutely no way I could ever be parted from her or live without her. Wherever she went, I would follow. I still doubted I was worthy of her, confused why the Source would gift me such a treasure of a female as my one true mate.

But no matter what the Source decreed, the choice to be with me, to be my mate and my cridhe, would always be hers.

CHAPTER 41*

AMELIA

Once I'd passed out the other rewards for the various fighters and events, I returned to the dais, exhausted and overwhelmed. I hadn't expected to hand out prizes either, but an attendant had appeared at my elbow after I'd bestowed the kisses with the first round of awards so I couldn't exactly say no. *Everyone* was looking at me as if I'd grown a second head. Looked at Rhuger with surprise on their faces. Asterun was pointedly looking ahead, a tick working in his jaw as he kept his head held high. And Rhuger, well, he kept his gaze on the ground and refused to look at me again.

What had Sigg gotten me into? What did I do wrong now? No one outright yelled at me, but I kind of wished someone would. It'd feel less damning.

Back on the dais, whispers and the narrowed gazes of the councilors and peerage followed me to my chair. Grammie Ruksala waved me over to her, and I bypassed my chair to go stand before her. She waved me down to her level, and I bent at the waist until she was within reach.

"Don't fret, girl, it will all work out." Grammie Ruksala said as she patted my cheek.

"I sure hope so," I whispered, tears threatening.

"Hold down the back of your dress." She commanded in that same grandmotherly tone.

"What?" I asked and hurried to do as I was told. The second I'd held the fabric of my sorry excuse for clothing against my thighs, the wind picked up and flapped the back panel around like a war banner. I felt my face heat and a look of horror overcome me as I stared at Grammie Ruksala. She'd just spared me from mooning the entire clan *again*. "Thank you." I croaked.

"You're welcome." Her gap-toothed smile was warm and made me miss Grandma Ruth in a piercing way. "Now you'd best get gone and change into something more practical."

"Okay, Grammie Ruksala, thank you."

"Good lass." She said and shooed me away towards the stairs.

Grandpa Thorn appeared and grabbed my upper arm as I made to leave the dais. I scowled up at him, and he gave me a knowing look. I turned back to him and he let my arm go, guiding me instead over to an empty part of the dais.

"We need to talk." He said.

"Do we now?" I replied, upset about having to kiss someone, to begin with. Upset about how Sigg seemed to have thrown me under the proverbial bus. Hell, I was upset about the dress.

"Don't sass me, chestnut." He snapped. "This is important. Tomorrow, you *must* choose someone and mate with them. Rìgh Orok *will* be back the following day for you. And unless you've mated, I can do nothing to deter him without risking war."

"You're not mad I kissed Rhuger?" I asked, confused.

"Oh, we'll talk about that eventually, but right now it's rather low on the list, chestnut." Grandpa Thorn was exasperated as he tried to keep his composure.

"What about the Oc'Veltas? Did you hear from them?" I asked, returning to the topic at hand even though I was baffled by my grandpa's refusal to get all up in arms over claiming Rhuger as my champion.

"Our messenger returned empty-handed. They didn't believe someone had come through the Geata." He said his lip curling in distaste.

"I could just *try* to see if it'll work again." I offered.

"Ruksala said it wouldn't work if you tried." He murmured, looking to where my great-grandmother was talking to Rhuger.

"I've given you all the time I can. But you *must* decide. Or I will decide for you." His tone turned forbidding.

"Excuse me?" I asked, rage burning in my gut. "You will do *no* such thing! It is *my* life that's at stake here. You are asking me to make this life-altering decision in an impossible amount of time!"

"It *is* a possible amount of time. You just choose not to and risk the entire clan! Just *bed* someone and get it over with. You don't have to stay mated to them for long if you don't want to. But you *must* mate with someone."

"*I am not built that way.*" I breathed. "One-night stands and flings aren't something I can *do*. I've *tried* in the past and have *failed*. I am not *made* for casual sex, Grandpa."

"Then what kind are you made for?" He asked.

"I have to *love* them." I sighed.

"If there is anyone you have *any* feelings for. Even if you just

like them enough that it can grow into love, you need to pursue it."
Grandpa Thorn eyeballed me.

"Whatever happened to that list of approved males you were
going to give me?" I asked, exasperated.

I knew precisely who I'd choose if he was willing. But I also
knew if he wasn't on Grandpa's list it would be hopeless.

"There is no list." He admitted with a sigh as he rubbed his
eyes. "I hoped that would spur you to find a mate."

"I'm... I'm done." I said, backing up with my hands up. "This is
all ridiculous and Grandma Ruth would browbeat you for what you're
asking of me. You're asking me to relive the worst experience of my
life."

"Whatever you endured at the hands of your ex-husband. Rìgh
Orok will be far, far worse." The fear in Grandpa Thorn's eyes made
terror clench in my gut, snagging deep and tearing at my soul as black
memories battered at the back of my mind. I felt myself mentally falling
backward into the dark clutches of those memories. Felt the color drain
from my face as I was suddenly freezing in the sultry heat of the
afternoon.

"Pearl? Are you alright?" Broad, warm hands grasped my face,
and turned it so I met silver and onyx eyes framed by sinfully long
lashes. Eyes I dreamed about.

I opened my mouth to speak but found I was voiceless. Instead,
tears trembled on my lashes, threatening to spill. I sucked my lips
between my teeth, fighting to keep my hands at my sides. Instead of
bringing them up to cup the scar-flecked backs of his hands, pressing
his palms tight against my cheeks and closing my eyes. Letting his
touch banish the dark.

"What's going on?" Rhuger asked.

"There's no chance for her to return through the Geata. Rìgh Orok will come for her the day after tomorrow if she hasn't taken a mate. He's sent a message ahead." My grandfather's voice was a low rumble as he stood with his arms crossed over his chest. "I told her that if she doesn't choose tomorrow, I'll choose for her."

Rhuger looked at my grandfather in horror. I watched as Rhuger's skin paled considerably and a tic worked in his jaw. I looked down at the ground, ashamed and hopeless. Unable to look Rhuger in the eye lest he saw what I felt for him. If it were to happen, I wanted Rhuger to be with me because he loved me. Not because he felt he was doing me a favor.

He may have flirted with me a lot and even put on a show for me outside of the traveler's cave, but that was before he knew who I was. Before he'd been made my bodyguard. Duty and my position seemed to have tempered his flirting, and he'd deflected anything resembling an advance from me.

I didn't have to be told that if I went with Rìgh Orok, Rhuger could not go with me. I couldn't stand the thought of being without him. To face the horrors of the Oc'Turin court alone.

"See her back to her tree home and make sure she stays there until tomorrow." My grandfather said to Rhuger, then his gaze flicked down to mine. "Think carefully. I'll expect your answer in the morning."

My gaze shifted, blurred, as my mind took a proverbial step back. The world around me suddenly didn't feel real. Like I was in a waking nightmare I couldn't escape from. I knew I was dissociating, but I couldn't help it. It was just too much.

Rhuger's hand found my shoulder, a spark of light in the grey my world had become. I only vaguely remember the walk back to my home tree, snippets of awareness while in auto-pilot mode. Orckin were cheering and dancing their way to the city center, and the party that would start along the glittering, colorful market. The fighters were fawned over, no matter how well they'd done.

A female came up on Rhuger's other side and slid her hand from his neck down his chest and arm, gaze sultry as she walked backward, keeping pace with us. How *dare* she touch him? I bared my teeth at her and made an ugly sound in my throat. The female looked startled, her gaze sliding down to where Rhuger's hand laced with mine. She just shook her head and laughed as she wove away through the crowd.

"What was that?" Rhuger asked me and I looked up into his beloved black and silver eyes. His brows twitched upward in surprise.

"I..." I began, stepping back into the present as my face heated. Shit, I'd promised myself I'd tell him how I felt no matter if he won or lost. I found myself tongue-tied as I struggled to push the words past my lips.

"Why did you choose me as your champion?" He murmured the question as we moved out of the celebrating city center and down an avenue that wound under the sheltering arms of Baile Coille's home trees.

"Do I need a reason?" I asked, looking ahead, hand going a little sweaty in his.

I had absolutely no idea what I was doing. Navigating how relationships should work had always been challenging for me. I gave too much and demanded too little. When I decided on someone, it was all or nothing, and most people couldn't understand it. Drawing and redrawing these lines between us was exhausting. Maybe it didn't matter, maybe I didn't have to do anything but be honest with myself, with him.

"You don't understand, pearl." He ground out. "You should not have claimed me as your champion."

"Why?" I asked, confused. Feeling those lines slipping from my fingers as I mentally released them. Leaving nothing between him and my heart. "Sigg said I could choose my own if I wanted, besides the winner. I thought you should have won. The bit with the dirt in your face was underhanded."

Rhuger tilted his head back and snarled up at the sky. I jumped, pulling my hand from his as we stopped at the base of the knoll where my home tree stood.

"Sigg. Source damned meddler." He growled before looking back down at me.

"Was the kiss that bad?" I asked nervously and picked at my nails. It had been a while since I'd kissed anyone. My ex-husband had stopped kissing me long before I'd left. Years ago. Perhaps I really was a terrible kisser.

"Och, no, pearl. The kiss was..." His cheeks suddenly flushed bright green, and he swallowed hard. "It was lovely."

"Oh. Good." Awkward. But my insides danced with joy. At least it hadn't been terrible.

"You still should not have done that," Rhuger murmured, brow furrowed and gaze lit with something I didn't understand.

"Why?"

"Did Sigg tell you why that old rule is still honored?" He asked.

"No?"

"I thought not. It was implemented so that a lady might not be looked down on for kissing another if she had a mate or an intended competing for glory." His voice and expression were tight, a tic working hard in his jaw.

I was quiet, processing.

"By choosing me as your champion and rewarding me higher than the winner of the games, you implied..." His words were choked short.

Like a brick to the face, it hit me then.

I'd implied there was more going on between the two of us than there was.

"Oh gods, I'm so sorry Rhuger." My hands flew to cover my mouth, and I blushed so hard it felt like even my shoulders were red.

"Sorry you kissed me or sorry you implied I was your intended?" His gaze held a certain heat that I couldn't interpret.

"I'm sorry if I overstepped and created an unpleasant situation for you." I groused, not sorry at all about the kiss. When I crossed my arms, Rhuger's gaze fell to my chest. Blushing hard again, I refused to move. His gaze flicked back up to mine, and I held my breath.

"Don't you care what they think? What Rìgh Thorn thinks?" He asked, confusion written on his face.

"No?" I was confused too. "Why would I care what they think? It's my life, not theirs. If people want to misinterpret my actions, that's on them. You know my intentions, and that's good enough for me."

"You really should care, pearl." Rhuger rumbled, his hands going to rest on his narrow hips. "It might have jeopardized you finding a mate before Rìgh Orok comes back for you!"

"Why is it that every man in my life, every male, tells me what to do and thinks they get to control me? My ex-husband, Grandpa Thorn, Rìgh Orok, and now you too?" The words snapped out, bitter in their truth. That yawning chasm inside that I kept trying to patch over —that feeling of helplessness and despair—roared to life. "Why must everyone assume I know what your rules and etiquette are with no one bothering to explain? *All* I get are half-assed reasons."

"Amelia..." Rhuger began, reaching a hand towards me, pain etching his face. As if he could sense my inner turmoil.

Rhuger took a step toward me. I took two backward toward the stairs at the base of my tree. *His* tree. Was nothing truly mine? Was I not even my own, anymore?

"I'm sorry for making things difficult for you. For not knowing what it meant for choosing you as my champion. If anyone asks, I'm okay with you telling them I didn't understand. I am ignorant. I'm doing my best to learn as much as possible, so I'm not. But it's not enough, is it?"

The chasm that lurked under the surface of my skin yawned wider, howling.

"I'm not enough," I whispered.

"Amelia-" I spun, not giving him the opportunity to say whatever platitude was on his lips, and ran up the stairs to his home tree as if chased by the hounds of hell. Panic began bubbling in my veins and I took the stairs two at a time. The chasm darkened my vision, and I barely made it to my door before a sob choked me.

Again. It was all happening *again.*

Scrabbling for the door handle, I ripped it open, ran inside, and slammed it behind me. I couldn't seem to breathe, couldn't get enough air inside my lungs. Rough coughing, sobbing and harsh panting were the only sounds in my small home.

But it wasn't even truly mine, was it?

Barking a rough cry, I ran to the bed and flung myself atop it. Grasping a pillow, I shoved it against my face and began screaming into it. Wave after wave of panic and despair and heaving hollowness washed over me as I finally let everything out with wretched sobs and muffled screams.

Because there was a bitter truth to what I'd said. I wasn't enough for my ex-husband back home on Earth. And I wasn't enough to be a lady to these orcs here, no matter how hard I was trying. To be what they expected me to be.

Talam, this world, was a wondrous place. But navigating the archaic customs and alien ways had proven how different I was. How I didn't fit in.

And gods, how I just wanted to belong *somewhere.*

RHUGER

I'd fucked up. Somewhere between my sense of duty and Amelia's position and knowing she was my cridhe, I'd let time slip through my fingers. Instead of wooing her as I should have been doing, I'd pushed aside anything resembling interest from her. And then I'd gone and tangled my surprise at having her choose me as her champion with our situation until I'd hurt her. There was always clarity in hindsight, and hindsight was telling me I was a thrice damned fool.

I'd heard her crying from the base of the tree. The self-hatred that erupted in me tinged my vision red, and I punched the trunk of the tree until it faded. When it did, my fist was a mangled wreck, and I'd punched through the outer bark of the tree, bloody chunks of bark littering the moss.

Flexing my fingers, I panted as I watched the tendons, muscles, and skin knit back together over my knuckles. Fresh scars crisscrossed my knuckles and fingers. A permanent reminder of how I'd fucked up.

Why was I so determined to self-sabotage with Amelia? What was Rìgh Thorn thinking, forcing her to find someone, or he'd choose for her? How could he possibly *think* he had the right to choose on her behalf? And why had Sigg, who'd *just* declared his intentions for Amelia, given her the one course of action that would *ensure* she kissed me? A kiss that...

Fuck that *kiss*. Such a chaste thing, just a light press of her lips against mine. But my body had roared to life like it was the most erotic thing imaginable. Her mouth was so wondrously soft, pliant, plush. Tender and gentle in a way I'd never experienced before. As if she cared and cared deeply. For me.

I raised my scarred hand to cover my mouth as my face exploded in heat. A heat that was mirrored in the throbbing in my cock and the thrumming in my veins. The vicious, primal need to rush upstairs, throw those lovely thick thighs wide, and feast on her until I was full before I plowed my luscious cridhe was almost too much to resist. I needed to hear her scream my name as she came undone beneath me more than I needed air.

"Rhuger!" a jovial voice called. My head snapped to where Rorich was making his way to my tree home. "You did outstanding at the tournament! I'd expect nothing less from a legendary warrior such as yourself."

Rorich's happy, grinning face, still slightly rounded from youth, went from jovial to concerned in a matter of heartbeats. I could only imagine what my expression must have been like. Crazed and bordering on insane, most likely.

"I need you to stay here and watch over Amelia." I rasped, voice gone hoarse and gruff with rising desire. "Don't let her leave her house."

"Okay, where are you going?" Rorich asked as I stalked past him towards the little stone bridge that spanned the babbling brook and led towards Baile Coille proper.

I didn't answer, couldn't answer. So I sprinted, my booted feet slapping the cobblestones as I hurtled through Baile Coille, desperate to escape. Because I knew what would happen if I stayed. I'd give and give and give. And then I'd take and take and take until dawn. Until the suns burned out for all time.

Until my heart gave out and beat its last.

CHAPTER 42[*]

AMELIA

Dusk had arrived by the time I'd stopped falling apart. I felt empty and wrung out as I stared at the ceiling, tracking how the light changed against the wooden beams as night fell. My nose was stuffed, and I'd somehow managed to rip my dress, but I hated the damn thing, anyway.

Memories of how Rhuger had looked at me while I was wearing the flimsy bit of cloth and how he'd seen my ass when the wind had picked up on the stairs flickered behind my eyelids each time I blinked. And I swear I could feel his warm hands against the backs of my thighs in a ghostly echo.

I'd fucked everything up. I had no list. No prospects outside of the one male I truly needed. And only tonight and tomorrow to find a willing partner I could stand, bang, and get myself knocked up by.

I sat up on the edge of the bed and finished tearing the ridiculous dress from my body. The flowers I'd hastily shoved in my hair this morning fell at my feet on the dark floorboards. I snapped the thin chains from my neck, waist, and thighs. Wrapping them all up in a ball, I tossed them in the corner.

Sitting there naked, I wrapped the last bits of my heart around myself and got to my feet. I rummaged in the trunk and pulled out my bra, panties, a tunic, and some leggings. With mechanical, practiced movements, I got dressed and shoved my feet into my boots.

If tonight was a party, and a mating one at that, it would be my best opportunity to find a mate. Hopefully, getting drunk would make pretending whoever I ended up with was Rhuger easier to bear. Because I knew I'd never be able to otherwise.

Dressed, I strode for the door and opened it wide. Ready to face Rhuger and his insistence that I not go to the after-party as I'd been instructed. For once in my life, I couldn't care less about what I was supposed to do. None of this fit into a path forward that didn't end up with me in pain. So I'd go for the one where I at least have a *chance* of numbing it.

But when I got outside, Rhuger wasn't on the deck. And when I went down the stairs, he wasn't below either. Instead, Rorich stood guard, looking anxious. He looked up as I reached the bottom of the stairs and his eyes went wide.

"Amelia, you're supposed to stay inside tonight." He admonished.

"Where's Rhuger?" I asked, voice dead and inflectionless.

"I'm not sure. When I got here, he ran off. Said he'd come back later." Rorich shrugged.

"Of course he did," I murmured. Remembering how he'd asked me what my territorial streak was all about earlier. Perhaps he *had* wanted her advances and gone to find her again. Couldn't say I blamed him. She was gorgeous. My feet moved as I headed towards the city center and a fate I didn't want. "I'm going."

"Amelia, you *can't!*" Rorich said as I stepped past him.

"I'm *going*, Rorich!" I snapped, whirling to look at him.

"Then I have to go with you," Rorich muttered, a silver blush riding high on his cheeks.

"Do what you want." I sighed and continued walking towards the city center. Knowing it wouldn't be hard to find the after-party I wasn't invited to. Even if I hadn't seen how the market had been decorated, all I'd have to do was follow the partying and moaning.

We passed several couples and groups mating everywhere from decks to stairs, up against tree trunks and buildings, and even leaned over the stone railing of a bridge. The moaning, grunting, and slap of flesh against flesh as music wove through the city was a stirring symphony, making me wish for things I couldn't have.

I glanced over my shoulder to check on Rorich and he was staring at my feet as we walked, body stiff and shoulders hunched up to his ears. The poor guy was having a hard time. I felt a pang at dragging him into this, but I was out of options.

The city center was filled with partying orckin. Most were naked but others were clothed and they danced, undulating to the music made by a gaggle of musicians on a stage. Food and drink were set up on tables to one side. Pausing, I watched as orc after orc snagged cups from a table and downed them before someone refilled them. There were also casks of the usual alcohol, so I made a beeline to the tables, Rorich following close behind me.

I got into the fast-moving line and ignored the stares I got. I was going to need quite a few drinks before I could stomach anyone touching me. If I could at all.

"Amelia?" a voice called in shock and I turned to find Sigg looking at me in bewilderment. "What are you doing here? Where's Rhuger?"

"Hell if I know," I said, raising my chin and unable to keep the bitterness from my tone. "I'm here to find a mate, like my grandfather instructed me to do."

Sigg's mouth opened and closed in confusion as he looked around. As if trying to spy his friend somewhere behind me in the crowd. Instead, he spotted my other guard who stood next to me, eyes wide as saucers, looking all the world like a lost kitten in a den of wolves.

"Rorich, what are you doing here? You're not of age yet." Sigg's voice rumbled as he stood beside us, arms crossing over his broad chest.

"Amelia insisted she come. I couldn't let her come alone." Rorich stuttered, eyes snapping wider as a naked female strode past, dragging her fingers along the collar of his shirt. He turned as pale as the moons overhead and gulped hard.

"Get out of here, Rorich. I'll watch over Amelia until Rhuger comes for her. Since I know I can't force her to leave." Sigg's wry expression made me scowl.

"Alright, if you're sure?" Rorich asked, getting more and more skittish by the minute.

"Och, off with you."

Rorich didn't need to be told twice. He turned tail and ran off as if the hounds of hell were after him. Poor guy hadn't been ready to see so much naked flesh. Neither had I, but I wasn't about to flee now.

"Why are you here, Amelia?" Sigg asked me. Using my actual name instead of the nickname 'Neamhnaid'.

"I'm supposed to find a mate, right?" I swallowed and tried not to let that howling tempest in my chest pull me down. "Maybe if I get drunk enough, I'll find one."

"Amelia..." Sigg began, frowning at my statement.

But I didn't let him finish and strode over to a table laden with drinks. Orckin were downing the small cups before heading into the Rainbow Market, which was now boarded up and lined with couches, cushions, and glowing lanterns. Seductive music wove through the crowd that had gathered. Bodies were already naked, already gyrating and thrusting in time with the music. I realized belatedly that this after-party was a clan-sanctioned orgy. Before I could second-guess myself, I snatched a cup and downed it.

"Och, shit." Sigg grimaced, appearing at my side. "You should not have drank that."

"Why? Ladies can't have alcohol?" I muttered bitterly. Snatching another cup, I tipped it back and downed it. It had a strange herby flavor and it bit like whiskey.

"No... it's not that. You just downed two glasses of luibh gaoil." His wariness piqued my curiosity.

"What the hell is luibh gaoil?" I asked.

"It's something for those taking part in the parties to drink. You won't be taking part." Damn orcs beating around the bush, like always. Expecting me to understand.

"Won't I?" I snarled. Sigg looked taken aback, and I suddenly felt bad. "Sorry, I am clueless about *all* of this. If you can't explain it better to me, so I understand, please help me find Sharn."

Sharn hadn't steered me wrong yet. I knew she'd tell me what the hell this stuff was. And what it *meant.* I couldn't help but be a salty bitch after today.

"Follow me. I'll help you find her." He muttered, and I set down the cup. He turned and led the way through the crowd, his height allowing him to peer over the heads of others. Something that, for the first time in my life, I was too short to do.

It didn't take long for me to lose sight of Sigg in the milling crowd. Orckin were laughing, dancing, and sharing kisses and pleasure openly. One female had two males rutting her at once. The one on top sucking the cock of a waiting third as the female wailed her pleasure. Glancing around, I noticed that similar groups were coming together. And watching females getting railed and males satisfying one another until it was their turn was... affecting me.

"All alone, lass?" A voice called from behind me and I whirled. It was Asterun. He grinned down at me. His strange purple eyes looked like they were glowing in the flickering lights. "I see you've been drinking luibh gaoil, Neamhnaid." He crooned. I jerked my head back as he leaned down towards me, eyes on my mouth.

"And? What do you want?" I snapped, and he chuckled. My body... well... *reacted* to that dark laugh of his. Heat flooded me and suddenly my skin felt feverish.

"Och, has no one told you? Sweet thing, it imitates the mating frenzy." He murmured, licking his lips. I stepped back, away from him and his scent, which suddenly, I liked. I licked my lips, mimicking him, trying to get my body under control. He stilled, eyes burning as he focused harder on my mouth. "Such a strange color, your tongue. I wonder what it tastes like."

A sudden explosive throbbing started at my core, and I felt moisture slick the insides of my thighs. I gasped. I'd never felt lust like this before in my entire life. It felt like I'd die if I didn't get a cock inside of me *now*.

"Ah, Neamhnaid, you smell so... *delicious*..." Asterun's eyes fluttered as he inhaled, breathing me in.

I was suddenly focused on how long his lashes were and how he curled his lip, licking his canine with his Black Tongue. My thoughts drifted to what it would feel like to have an orckin tongue on my body.

Down my throat. Between my legs…

"How about giving me a proper winner's prize?" He breathed and reached for me.

"That won't be necessary." Growled a voice behind me just as an arm snaked around my waist and jerked me back against a wall of muscle. I looked up and Rhuger stood staring at Asterun with a murderous gaze.

"Rhuger!" I gasped and felt his heat against my back like a brand.

"I just came to claim the rest of my reward. If she's drunk the luibh gaoil, then she's willing." Asterun bared his teeth at Rhuger, standing with his chest puffed out and head held high.

"No, I'm not!" I snapped, but both males ignored me.

"You know what happened to the last orc who tried to touch her, Asterun," Rhuger growled, and the sensation of his rumbling made my skin sing. A hard throb wracked my core, eliciting a broken mewl from me.

"Well, we can't let her suffer. I'd be willing to share her with you, Oc'Turin." Asterun offered, eyes narrowed, obviously not willing to let his delusional claim on me go.

"I don't share. And she won't suffer." A tick worked in Rhuger's jaw, and his hand splayed over my stomach. I wish he'd slide those long, thick fingers beneath the waistband of my pants and…

"I don't share either!" I snarled. Both males continued to ignore me. I continued to fight the haze of lust that I couldn't shake. Because honestly? Being shared didn't sound so bad right now.

"Och, and you'll see to it, will you?" The shorter, slimmer orc sneered. Gods, he'd be good-looking if he didn't sneer like that all the time.

"Aye," Rhuger stated, voice clipped.

"You know what Rìgh Thorn would do to you if you took to her bed." The knowing look Asterun gave Rhuger spoke volumes in a language I couldn't read for shit.

"Who said I'd be taking anything from her? I know I'm not worthy to mate her." Rhuger's voice was calm and cold.

I started panting, fingers clinging to Rhuger's muscular forearm as I tried in vain to hold against whatever fire the luibh gaoil had lit in my veins. My mind felt like it was being held still in a bowl full of jiggling jello that was the rest of the world, even as my senses sharpened.

"Then how do you expect her not to suffer?" Asterun groused.

"If you need to ask me that, then you don't know your way around a female." Rhuger's dark laugh raised a flush to the other orc's cheeks. And it sent a spine-tingling rush of heat down my body to pulse between my legs.

"You can't keep me from her Fògradh." He snarled. I was too lost in the pounding between my thighs and how heavy my breasts felt to argue.

"Can't I? I dare you to try." Rhuger growled, grasping me tighter and causing my breathing to hitch. I bucked back against him, unable to control myself. My ass met his groin, and I nearly moaned at the hardness I felt there. The length of him I'd seen him stroke as he'd said my name in release that night outside of the traveler's cave.

"What's going on here?" Sharn demanded, slipping between nearby orcs to stand next to us. Rhuger's gaze flicked to my friend, and he shoved me toward her harshly. I stumbled, and she caught me before I face-planted. "Rhuger!"

But Rhuger had already turned to Asterun and roared. The

sound was so primal it nearly undid me and I moaned softly against Sharn's shoulder. Asterun hissed and pounced. He landed a solid jab on Rhuger's cheek, and I cried out in alarm through my lust-addled brain.

"Not his perfect face, *you gotdamned expired coupon!*"

Sharn held me tightly, keeping me upright as Rhuger took the hit, spun with the momentum of his opponent's blow, and landed a haymaker to the back of the orc's head. The orc went down and Rhuger jumped atop him. Asterun was stunned but recovered quickly, rolling onto his back. The two orcs tumbled over one another, trading blows as the crowd made room for their fight. Some even cheered and laughed as if this were normal.

Well, perhaps for a spicy after-party worthy of a sex club, where procreating was the goal, it *was* normal. All I knew was that watching Rhuger pummel the shit out of Asterun was doing *things* to me even more than when he'd fought in the tournament. Like, 'put a baby in me now' kind of *things*.

Rhuger pinned Asterun underneath him and got him into a kimura lock so his arm was inches from being wrenched from the joint. Asterun shouted, pinned face-first on the ground as Rhuger adjusted his grip so he could bend closer to Asterun's face.

"She is not for you," Rhuger growled into the grey, pointed shell of Asterun's ear.

"Fuck you!" Asterun spat and Rhuger pulled back further on Asterun's arm, making him cry out.

"You only wish." Rhuger chuckled and, with a sickening pop, dislocated Asterun's shoulder.

Asterun roared his pain into the unyielding cobblestones. Rhuger pulled his arm back and let his fist fly, delivering a devastating haymaker to the back of Asterun's skull. When his fist made impact, Asterun jerked and then slumped, unconscious. Rhuger released his dislocated arm and stood, inspecting his knuckles.

Glancing between the two males, their state was starkly different. Asterun looked beaten and bloodied while Rhuger was banged up with a few bleeding gashes. But nothing remotely as bad. It was like he was made of something different from other orckin. Allowing him to walk away relatively unscathed compared to his opponents as they lay wrecked at his feet.

Rhuger looked up at me then from under his lowered brows and the bright silver of his gaze felt like an arrow to the heart. He prowled over to us and my heart beat itself senseless against my ribs as my pussy throbbed in need. Sharn had to hold me upright as my legs were shaking so badly I'd collapse on my own.

"Give her to me." Rhuger rumbled at Sharn, voice filled with unquestionable command. Gods, if he spoke to me with that tone, I'd come moaning right on the spot.

"What are you going to do?" Sharn asked, a hard clip to her tone.

"I'm going to take care of her." He growled. "Or are you going to fight me over this, too? She is my responsibility."

"Oh, you're going to take care of her, are you?" Sharn's sardonic tone bit.

"She hasn't claimed me as her mate. I'm only giving, not taking. I swear this to you." His voice grew darker, gaze wild. "If you don't let me take her, she'll soon make a spectacle of herself, and I won't be able to keep her safe. You know this is the truth."

Sharn looked between the two of us, studying me as if gauging my state. A moan escaped my lips, and I sagged as my pussy clenched desperately at nothing, needing to be filled. Her mouth flattened into a thin line before she passed me off to Rhuger.

His body was putting off so much heat it drew me like a magnet. And gods, *his smell*. He'd always smelled so good to me, like spice and pomegranate, but with the luibh gaoil in my system, he smelled downright *delectable*. Unable to help myself, I leaned in against him and licked his chest where it peeked out between the laces of his black tunic. His hiss and how his powerful hands clutched at me so I'd stay upright on my wobbly legs were like gasoline on the fire in my belly.

"Don't make me regret this, Rhuger." She snapped and turned, leaving us alone.

Rhuger watched her go, a heavy sigh escaping him. I didn't want him to feel sad. I wanted to make him feel good. Because, gods, he made me feel downright euphoric.

I stood up on my toes and wrapped my arms around his neck. With a desperate jerk, I yanked him down to me. He stiffened, his attention brought back to our current predicament and how I was shamelessly grinding against him.

"Rhuger..." I moaned.

His silver and black gaze was molten as it met mine. Fuck, I just wanted to climb him and wrap my legs around his waist. Wanted him inside me so badly and for him to never stop fucking my brains out. I rubbed my body against him, my nipples hard little pebbles against his rock-hard chest. The fabrics of our clothes were too much. I wanted all of his naked green flesh against mine. Wanted to feel him all over me, inside me, pounding me into oblivion.

"Pearl..." He rumbled, a pained, desperate tone limning his pet name for me. I gasped as the vibrations from his growl tickled my oversensitive nipples. Desperate to kiss him, I pulled myself up enough to claim his mouth with mine. He protested for a moment before stilling. His eyes rolled back in his head as he moaned into my mouth.

It was like the leash he kept himself on snapped, and he clutched me to him hard, his long black tongue slipping between my lips to dance with my smaller pink one. I moaned into his mouth as he growled into mine. The taste of him flooded my senses, and I melted against him. This must be what ambrosia tasted like, like him, like heaven.

With a jerk, he pushed me out at arm's length, shaking himself all over like a dog. I clutched at his massive arms and panted heavily, a blush riding high on my cheeks. My legs were trembling, and I could feel how wet my pants were between my thighs. One kiss. One kiss from him was all it had taken to get me this close to orgasm. *Shit.*

"Rhuger..." I mewled and reached for him. He only shook his head.

"Amelia, you've been... drugged with the luibh gaoil. What you're feeling are the effects. I'll take you back home and help you through this. I-"

"Rhuger... I feel so hot..." I whimpered, cutting off whatever he was saying. My skin felt like it was on fire, the simple fabric of my shirt and pants too much to bear on my over-sensitive skin.

I reached down and snagged the hem of my tunic and began tugging it up over my breasts. He drew in a sharp breath, eyes riveted to my bra. Rhuger hissed and let out a string of curses in Black Tongue too fast for me to decipher before grasping my shirt and tugging it back down. His ears and cheeks were bright green.

"Amelia, this isn't you, okay? This herb mimics the mating frenzy, to help produce orclings." His voice had gone deep and rough and it felt like a hand on my skin.

I ignored what he'd said. So overwhelmed with need that I just reached helplessly for his hand. Grasping his wrist in both of my smaller hands, I yanked it towards me. His large warm palm cupped my breast and feeling it there was pure, horny bliss. Sighing, I pressed it to myself harder, wanting the friction of his calloused palm against the sensitive tip of my breast.

"FUCK." Rhuger barked, squeezing his eyes shut. My breathing hitched, and with a snarl, he burst into motion. He swept me up into his powerful arms and bolted away from the gathering. I had no idea where he was taking me. And I really couldn't find it in me to care.

Twining my arms up around his neck, I kissed him everywhere I could reach. Panting and moaning into his neck, I was able to zero in on the soft lobe of his ear. I took it between my blunt teeth and began sucking on it like it was his cock.

"Stop it, Amelia." His harsh growl didn't even penetrate my lust-addled mind. He'd have to penetrate me with something a whole lot harder to get me to listen.

"Please... Rhuger... I need you..." I groaned between breaths into the pointed shell of his ear. I barely registered him leaping up some stairs, and I dug my little claws into his shoulders as he shifted me in his arms and kicked open a door.

My door. Well, technically *his* door.

He stomped into the tree house, the cadence of his walk full of urgency and demand. Who would have ever thought hearing someone's footsteps could be *sexy*?

Rhuger hooked the door with his foot and kicked it closed without hardly breaking stride. He prowled over to the bed and chucked me onto it. He straddled my legs, breathing hard, his eyes wild. A rough growl shuddered out of him.

"Amelia. You are making this incredibly hard-" He began, gritting his teeth.

"I bet I am..." I reached a hand up to his thigh, just under his kilt. Rhuger hissed, snatching my wrists and pinning them above my head amongst the pillows where they couldn't go exploring. His expression grew stony as his molten silver gaze bored into mine.

"What do you want, Amelia?" The utter *demand* in his tone was enough to set me writhing beneath him.

"I want you." I breathed. Rhuger shook his head at me, his braid snaking over his shoulder onto my chest. I wondered what all that lovely hair would look like curtaining us against the world. How it would feel against my skin as he fucked me. I couldn't help the small cry that escaped my mouth at the thought.

"I need you to tell me that without the herb in your system." He moved like he was going to get off of me and I panicked.

"Please! Don't leave me like this!" I couldn't stop the tears then. Too many times my ex-husband had left me wanting and aching and needing touch. Refused me even a simple hug for weeks on end. Used one of my love languages against me as punishment. I was beyond desperate right now. To be left like this, with an unknown horny red bull concoction in my system, was terrifying.

Rhuger's eyes snapped to my tears, and he froze.

"I wasn't planning on it, pearl." He swallowed hard. "If you will let me, I will give you relief until the herb is out of your system..."

"Yes! Please!" I squirmed under him and his gaze shifted from defiant to something darker, sharper. He bent his head down to mine, silver eyes glowing like twin moons in the dark expanse of his gaze.

"Yes what, Amelia? Use your words..." He crooned mere inches from my mouth.

"I need you Rhuger, I need your touch and your taste and if you don't fuck me, I'm going to lose my mind!" Wriggling, I moved my legs out from under him and wrap them up around his hips. I ground shamelessly against the hard length beneath his kilt. Evidence that he wanted me, too.

"*Good lass.*" He hissed out before transferring both of my wrists to one hand.

He snatched my face in his free hand and began devouring my mouth. It wasn't delicate and sweet. No, this was a kiss filled with longing and hunger and unfulfilled need. I met his mouth, his tongue, stroke for demanding stroke as I ground as hard against him as he'd let me. Then, with a snarl, he pulled away, releasing my face to reach down and rip my tunic off me, shredding it to ribbons with his claws.

FUCK it was hot.

His chest heaved as he stared down at my breasts, where they were cupped in the dubious protection of my lacy bra. Oh, so gently, Rhuger slipped a clawed finger just beneath the lace and glided it along the curve of my breast. I gasped and arched my back up, jutting it into his hand.

"I'm going to devour you." He growled and my pussy quivered at his promise. "The more you beg me, the more I'll give you. If you want me to stop, you tell me, yes?"

"Yes, Rhuger." I rasped.

"Good girl." His lip curled as his gaze raked over my partial nakedness. "Now take this off. I'd rather not shred such a pretty thing."

With that, he released my hands from where they were pinned above us. I snaked a hand behind my back and twisted the eye hooks, popping the closure open. I snatched the bra from my chest and tossed it to the floor, baring myself to Rhuger from the waist up. My chest was heaving with my harsh breaths, breasts jiggling, but I wasn't self-conscious in the slightest.

Rhuger ran a hand up from the soft rolls of my stomach,

between my breasts, to my throat. He gently cupped it, squeezing gently with his fingertips, eliciting a gasp from me. Then he dragged his hand down to cup one of my breasts, teasing the nipple. I gasped and bucked my hips against him. He thrust his hips down *hard*, pinning mine to the mattress. I moaned long and low at the luscious pressure right where I needed it most.

"Lovely." He rumbled before bending his head down and taking my other nipple into his mouth.

And slay me. His tongue was so slick and long, with a strange bumpy texture over the top that rubbed over my peaked nipple. I cried out sharply, thrashing beneath him. Rhuger paused his ministrations and looked up at me under his lashes. I could barely see his irises. His pupils were so blown out.

"Did I hurt you?" He murmured in question.

I shook my head vigorously no.

"Use your words, pearl." He demanded softly.

"I-I'm really sensitive there..." I whispered, suddenly shy.

He growled so loud and possessive then, that I flinched. Locking his molten gaze with mine, he slowly lowered his head. His long sinuous black tongue snaked out of his mouth to wrap around my nipple before giving it a good long laving. I groaned at the sight and feel of his strange tongue tickling one of the most sensitive parts of my body and thrust my breast further into his mouth. If I bent my spine any further, I'd snap it.

Rhuger chuckled darkly before moving over to the other taut peak. Teasing, licking, nipping at it until I was thrusting my hips against his as hard as I could.

"Hold on to the bed, pearl." He growled, and I immediately obeyed, grasping part of the headboard above me.

He smiled crookedly, a devastating thing to witness. Then he turned his attention to my chest and began kissing a trail from my collarbones down to my belly. His clawed hands gently raked against my sides as I squirmed and gasped under his touch. Rhuger's hands reached my hips, and he roughly yanked my pants down. He paused, seeing the lacy underwear that matched my bra. They were *completely* soaked through.

With a rough, desperate sound erupting from his throat, Rhuger ripped my pants completely off my legs. Grasping my thighs with his huge, calloused, clawed hands, he threw them wide. His expression was hungry and feral as he gazed at my soaked panties, the wetness that slicked the insides of my thighs almost down to my knees.

Kneeling between my legs, he ran one of his thick fingers down my sopping wet crease through the thin fabric of my panties. He brought it up to his mouth and licked it. His eyes rolled into the back of his head as a broken moan shuddered past that perfect, sinful mouth of his. As if I were the best thing he'd ever tasted.

Rhuger bent down and took my whole mound into his mouth. He groaned loud and long, sharp teeth scraped lightly against the fabric as he tongued the wet fabric. When I bucked against him, he curled his arms up underneath my hips and locked me into place so that I couldn't move.

"*MINE.*" His feral growl against my pussy nearly sent me over the edge. Rhuger's eyes were glittering black pits, and the tight leash he kept on himself seemed to slip further. "I am going to lick the soul right out of you."

CHAPTER 43[*]

RHUGER

Gods, what had I gotten myself into? What unholy bargain did I make with Sharn? To sate my cridhe with only my hands and mouth, not the entirety of my body as my instincts demanded. It was an impossible nightmare made flesh.

But, *fuck*, she smelled so damned good. The little undergarment drenched in her wetness was a cruel siren. So when I'd thrown her juicy thighs wide, her desire perfumed the air. I caved and knelt at the altar of her body as I'd said I would and took her mound into my mouth. It took everything I had not to shred the lacy under thing with my teeth. Instead, I scraped them against the fabric and shuddered at the tidal wave of hunger that crashed over me.

As my tongue met the soaked fabric over her crease, her taste exploded on my tongue. Sweet with a slight tang that drew a ragged groan from my throat. Amelia bucked under my mouth, her swollen, needy core so sensitive to my touch, my breath.

"*MINE,*" I growled low and long, hooking my arms around her hips and locking her in place so she couldn't wriggle free. I looked up at her then. Over the soft rolls, curves, and mounds of her body, decorated with pale stretch marks and freckles like a masterpiece, to those uisge-beatha eyes that I loved so much, hazed over with lust. That perfect little pink mouth opened in a lovely o-shape as she panted. "I'm going to lick the soul right out of you."

Her shuddering moan at the filthy words that dripped from my damnable mouth nearly undid me. Nearly snapped the leash I was desperately straining against and holding on to. I returned my attention to the feast before me. Slipping my tongue under the edge of her panties, I moved it aside so I could hold it open with a finger.

I stared down at the small thatch of dark curls that had incised me at the tournament when her dress had blown up. The entirety of her crease, her curls, and her trembling inner thighs glistened with her slick, desperate need. It was the loveliest, headiest thing I'd ever witnessed.

I'd never bedded a female. But that didn't mean I didn't know what to do. I'd grown up watching and listening to mating couples and the bawdry stories the males told. Once I arrived at the Oc'Dellor, I sought the Academy's wisdom, the school Rìgh Thorn had established. It held classes for males seeking mates. Taught them the basic principles of mating, techniques to bring females to orgasm to stimulate their fertility, and how to care for a female and orclings. I'd taken every class available and received top marks.

I was so damned glad I had. Because I was going to worship her all night and use every trick and technique I'd ever learned to do so.

Breathing over her mound, a small sound escaped my cridhe. Elongating my sinuous, curling tongue. I licked her entire crease from base to top. Amelia gasped and tried to jerk in my grasp, so I sunk my claws gently into the pillowy softness of her thighs, reminding her without words to be a good girl for me and hold still. She did.

The leash broke. My instincts roared to life at how her body responded to mine, a perfect push and pull of the tide and the moons. I planted my face between her thighs and roared. Amelia cried out but didn't move. So I rewarded my good, sweet cridhe with all the wicked lust I possessed.

I began licking every crease and fold of her, every dip and rise, learning her with my tongue, my nose, my chin. Gods, she tasted divine. And the sounds she made as I explored her were enough to drive me mad. Soft gasps, breathy moans, and sharp cries. The last escaping that perfect bowed mouth whenever I lavished attention on her clit.

Glancing up, she had her arms over her chest, their soft swells pressed against her rib cage under them. Fuck, how I wanted to scrape my teeth against all that softness. Amelia was watching me with the most delightfully lewd expression on her face, and I'd barely even started. I reached up, still teasing her dripping core with my tongue and grasped one of her small hands, and brought it down to place at the back of my head.

"You're going to want to hold on for this." I rasped, voice gone deep and rough.

She seemed confused, and the expression was precious. With my gaze still locked on hers, I slipped my tongue inside her. Amelia let out a warbled cry and threw her head back into the pillows, her luscious body arched and trembling for me. Her other hand joined the one in my hair, her tiny claws tangling in the strands.

Satisfied, I focused again on my feast. Closing my eyes, I lost myself to it. To her.

Her core was tight, even for my tongue, so I worked it inside her and growled. A flood of her juices surged into my mouth, more intoxicating than luibh gaoil. Swallowing her down, I moaned and clutched her tighter to me. As I slid my tongue in and out of her quivering core, exploring where she liked my tongue most, I rubbed my nose against her clit.

Her thighs trembled against the sides of my head, and her soft cries changed to open moaning. Her hips twitched, and her walls closed in on my tongue, so I replaced it with my fingers, claws retracted, and moved my mouth to her clit. I took it into my mouth and sucked and flicked my tongue against it. Amelia threw her head back and screamed my name to the rafters as she climaxed.

The feel of her clamping down on my fingers had me snarling and nearly spending as I continued caressing her. Beyond desperate to give her another orgasm, and another, and another. As many as I could until my body betrayed me and I came under my kilt. So I didn't stop sucking and licking, pumping my fingers in and out of her even as her juices flooded my palm.

Amelia didn't even come down from her first orgasm before the second hit. She tried to hold still, but her body had other ideas, and she bucked against me, pressing the back of my head into her pussy. I slowed and softened my movements this time, letting her come down gently. The luibh gaoil made her desperate and hungry but also sensitive. And I wanted her to enjoy everything I was going to do to her.

When she finally flopped against the bed, trembling, I released her with a dark chuckle.

"Rhuger..." Amelia panted my name weakly, her little clawed hands cradling my head against her.

Sitting up, I stared at the twitching, lust-drunk goddess in my bed. Her face and chest were flushed, her thighs splayed wide, and a fine sheen of sweat glistened on her neamhnaid skin. And the wet spot that spread on the blankets from the pleasure I'd given her ignited a fierce satisfaction in me I'd never known.

"I'm not done with you yet, pearl. You're going to bloom for me." I said, my cock hard and aching for me to plant it inside of her and rut her until our hearts gave out. I would. Eventually. But not right now.

Gently, I helped her close her thighs together and slid my hands up her long legs, to her hips. I slid my fingers under the sides of the delicate black undergarment she wore. Letting my claws slide out slightly, I scraped them gently down her thighs as I pulled them from her. She shuddered and whimpered, hiding her mouth with her hands as her soft brown waves created a halo about her head.

Gods, she was gorgeous.

I tossed her panties to the side, grasped her hips in my hands, and hoisted her up. She squealed and flailed her arms, searching for purchase as I threw her thighs over my shoulders where I knelt on the bed. Her head and shoulders rested on the mattress, her forearms and hands holding onto my thighs firmly over the kilt. She was so damnably *close* to where I needed her most.

But I'd made promises I was honor bound to keep. *FUCK*!

Wrapping my arms around her torso, I pressed her back and ass against my body. Arms and hands sinking into her plush curves. I looked down at her startled expression and let out a breathy, shaky growl that broke against my need for her.

"Be a good lass and scream for me," I demanded, sinking my mouth into her ripe cunt. I licked her in one long stroke. Flicking the tip of my tongue against her clit, I elicited a lovely cry from my cridhe before I delved my tongue deep into her core.

I'd been gentle before. I wasn't now.

Now I was a ravenous beast as I fucked her with my tongue, never more thankful for its length and dexterity than I was at this moment. Growling low, my tongue vibrated as it pumped in and out of her. There was a spot inside her that made her moan harder each time my tongue pressed against it. So I did what any good lover would do. I kept pace, building her pleasure in all the places her body craved.

If she didn't crush my skull between her lovely thighs, then I wasn't doing my job right. So I shifted her delicious weight in my arms and cupped her mound with my hand, rubbing her drenched clit with my fingers as I drank her down. Amelia quivered in my arms, her long legs pressing in on either side of my head. Her cries came faster as she neared her release, her chest heaving with her harsh panting.

"Rhuger!" she cried and gods, even my name on her lips, staggered me towards climax. "I'm going to come..."

And then she did. Eyes locked with mine, she wailed my name and dragged her little claws down my thighs, leaving slight scratches behind. The meager pain mixed with the intense pleasure of watching my cridhe come undone made me nearly burst. Her thighs clamped down around my head, and she gasped, body rolling against my hold as I continued to fuck her with my tongue.

As I gently brought her down from the height of her pleasure, panting and shaking, desperate to plant myself inside her and never leave, she slid her hand up under my kilt. Her small fingers grazed my cock where it pressed against her back through the leather. I let out a long, ragged moan against her core, causing her to shiver.

Hissing, I flipped her over onto her belly on the bed as if she weighed nothing. If she touched me like that again, I wouldn't be able to hold back from her. Would break my promises.

"This is about you, not me." I rumbled, pressing my hand down on the small of her back so she wouldn't flip over.

"But I want to taste you Rhuger! Touch you!" She cried, lush legs kicking in a vain attempt to fight me. All it did was fan the flames of desire that roared in my veins. Her velvety plushness jiggled and made me wonder precisely how her body would quake as I ruthlessly pounded into her from behind.

"Not tonight," I growled, sitting up on the edge of the bed.

I dragged her over my knees so her chest was against the mattress and her perfect, plump ass jutted up into the air over my thighs. A piercing lance of lust made me light-headed as my cock strained against my kilt against her soft stomach. Source damn me, but I wanted to know what it felt like to be buried between her thighs.

"Why not!?" she wailed, unable to stop herself from rubbing against me. Her sensitive skin needed friction like her lungs needed air. She kicked again, her ass rippling with the movement, and I thrust up against her stomach, unable to stop myself. I knew I was leaking like a busted pipe under my kilt, all over the mattress and floor. But I couldn't find it in me to care.

Pushed to the edge of madness, my ragged breathing sounded more like the growls of a wild animal. That's what she made me want to be. The beast who rutted the gentle beauty. Claimed her. Sated her. Possessed her.

So, against my better judgment, I told her exactly what I wanted to do to her.

AMELIA

"When I take you, you're going to be begging me to fuck you blind, and you're going to need my cock in you so bad you won't need the luibh gaoil. And then..." Rhuger grasped my ass with his large warm hands, nails sinking in slightly. I moaned as he kneaded my ass, cupping it and letting his palms wander up and down my waist to my thighs. Memorizing their shape. As if he alone had every right to do so. As if I were *his*.

Fuck, did I want it to be true.

I was so desperate for him I'd take whatever I could get. Whatever this luibh gaoil was, it demolished all the inhibitions I had about sex. All I wanted to do was straddle his hips, sink down on his war club of a cock, and fuck him till I milked him dry. He kept denying me what I craved so badly, that hearing him talk about how he was going to pile-drive me rode a fine line between rage, desire, submission, and pain.

"I'm going to fuck you so hard-" He slapped my ass with a loud crack. I yelped before moaning as he gripped my ass again. His breathing was ragged, his voice trembling as he told me how he wanted me.

"And so good..." Rhuger's massive hand slapped my ass again, and I choked out a sobbing cry into my fist. Shit, it felt amazing when he spanked me. I didn't even know I *had* that kink, damn it.

"I'll ruin you for any other cock for the rest of your days." Rhuger retraced his claws and slipped his long, thick finger into my sopping-wet pussy, pumping it in and out of me roughly. I cried out and squirmed, needing more. More of him inside of me. *NOW.*

I wanted to tell him to ruin me. Take everything he wanted, knowing full well he'd give me everything he had in return. I delighted in that dark edge he had, the one that wasn't tender, but rough, primal, and demanding. Fuck, I just wanted him to bang me like a screen door in a hurricane. But nothing came out of my mouth but lewd sounds fit for a porno.

"And if you're a good lass, I'm going to bend you over that railing outside," He added another finger and picked up the pace, practically slapping my ass with the heel of his hand. Nearly spanking me with it and teasing my newfound kink. "And I'm going to fuck your brains out in front of all the clans and there will be no doubt that you are *MINE*."

His voice rasped over my too-sensitive skin and I shuddered as I moaned, coming close to release just from the filthy words that dripped from his sinful mouth. Imagining what he was describing was ratcheting my lust up to a whole new level. His fantasy became mine, and I struggled not to come yet.

Rhuger fisted his free hand in my hair and tugged. I gasped and bared my throat, head tilted all the way back. His growl of approval dragged a sobbing wail from me.

Snarling, he pulled his hand from my pussy, flipped it, and shoved three fingers inside of me, his thumb sliding over my clit each time he pumped his fingers. The orgasm built fast, and with a flickering of his three fingers over that sweet spot inside of me, I screamed my orgasm.

RHUGER

"Rhuger!" she screamed my name from her exposed throat. She thrashed, all that lovely mounded flesh rippling and inciting me until I'd bared my teeth. I didn't even let her finish her orgasm. She was going to get another, and she was going to get it right fucking now.

I let out a dark laugh as I hoisted her and sat her on my lap so she was straddling my thighs. I pulled her roughly against me, her back against my chest. Spreading my legs, I spread her thighs wide so I could play with her, make her sing for me.

I rocked upward against her ass as I breathed raggedly into her ear. Letting her feel precisely what she did to me. How desperate she made me. How badly I wanted her and all of her softness.

She moaned long and low at the press of my cock, grinding her ass against me. Her back arched as I murmured to her in Black Tongue, face pressed into the soft waves of her hair. We rocked together like that for a bit, my hands roving all over the soft landscape of her body, hers reaching back to sink into my hair as she opened herself to me.

Source damn me for eternity, it felt so *good*. Even better than the orgasm I'd had outside of the traveler's cave as she'd watched me pleasure myself. If it felt this good just touching her, pressing against her, I couldn't even fathom what it would feel like inside of her.

"I want your cock inside me so bad, please!" Amelia begged as if reading my mind.

She turned her head and left a sweet, trailing kiss on my cheek. Closing my eyes, I groaned and claimed her mouth. My hands teased her nipples, causing her to buck backward against my erection as our tongues danced.

Releasing her mouth, I panted as I looked down at the female who was not only my soul-bound partner but the one person who saw me, treated me kindly, and held my wreck of a heart as if it were the most precious gift she'd ever been given. Her whiskey eyes glowed, drawing me in where I gratefully drowned.

I wanted to treat her with the tenderness she treated me. Say the right things. Be the gentle lover she deserved.

But all I had were my wicked thoughts, my hungry body, and my desperate soul. I wasn't made for that kind of love. I was too rough around the edges. Too broken. I was a penitent, a wretch, begging her for grace and love with all that I was.

"I have to ready this tight little pussy of yours for my massive cock." Snarling words tore from my throat that were far from what I wished I could say. "I need to stretch you wide before you can take me without pain. So tonight, you'll take my fingers inside of you. Or my tongue. Until you are spent and the herb is out of your system."

I slid my hand from her breasts, down over her belly to where she was drenching my kilt in her desire, then shoved the three thickest fingers of my hand deep inside of her slick heat roughly. She gasped, spreading her legs wide over my lap to give me better access. Silently asking me to give her more, to go deeper. Such a *good fucking girl.*

I slid my hand over her chest to knead her breasts, teasing and pinching her sensitive nipples as I pumped my fingers in and out of her. The wet sounds of fucking her with my hand mingled with her desperate moaning and the sound of flesh meeting flesh drove me beyond sanity.

She was practically bucking off of my lap now. I had to bite down on the meaty part of her shoulder *hard* without breaking the skin to get her to behave and hold still. She cried out, her walls clenching down on my fingers as she nearly came. It seemed my pearl enjoyed being bitten. Good thing I relished sinking my teeth into her.

I released her shoulder and bent towards her ear, one hand fucking her as hard as I could, the other grasping her soft belly, holding her right where I wanted her. I rocked up, thrusting my aching cock hard against her ass, letting her know what was waiting for her if she wanted it. "And if you still want this afterward, I'll plant my cock inside of you and rut you until you beg me to stop."

"Don't stop! Don't stop!" She cried, writhing in my lap. I could hear the change in her breathing, a hitch that told me she was moments away from climaxing.

"Now, come for me!" I snarled into the delicately pointed shell of her ear, nipping her earlobe.

Like the good lass she was, she obeyed. Throwing her head back over my shoulder, she screamed my name as her walls clamped down on my fingers. Her orgasm had her rolling her hips, her lush ass pressed back against my groin *hard.*

Fuck, how I wished it was my cock she was clamping down so hard on instead of my fingers as she continued to writhe and cry out in my arms, riding out her pleasure. So that's precisely what I imagined. Being sunk completely inside of her as she milked me, my knot locking me in place precisely where I was meant to be. All the orgasms I'd given her making her fertile and ripe. Ready for the seed I'd pump into her womb until the soft curves of her belly tightened and swelled with our bairn.

Grazing my teeth against her neck, I resisted the urge to sink my teeth into her lovely neamhnaid skin until she bled, marking her as mine. Instead, I thrust upward against her grinding ass, roaring against her shoulder. My knot constricted and my cum splattered against the floor in a rush.

I rested my forehead against her shoulder where I'd bitten her. Panting hard and suddenly loose-limbed and languid. I cradled her against me, hoping one day it could always be like this between us. The tenderness mixed with the brutal mating. As we sat there, trying to catch our breath as we returned to our bodies from the heights of our pleasure, I couldn't help but chuckle.

"What?" Amelia asked, turning her head to place a kiss against my temple. Such a chaste thing after such depravity. She rested her hands against the one I'd pressed into the rolls of her soft belly.

"That's the first time I've come just by pleasuring another. You are a wonder, my pearl." I rasped, pulling back enough to see those lovely uisge-beatha eyes that intoxicated me so. She gifted me with a small smile.

My cridhe mewled as I gently slid my fingers from her core, now wrinkled from her pleasure. I helped her off of my lap, her legs quivering so badly she couldn't do it on her own. Once she lay down, I pulled up her blankets and brushed the soaked waves back from where they stuck to her cheek.

I got up and went to the kitchen, filling a mug full of water for her. When I returned, I sat down on the edge of the bed and gently lifted her head from the pillows.

"Drink, pearl," I murmured, and she obeyed, her tiny hand covering the back of my palm as she swallowed the water in long droughts. When she'd finished it, I set the mug on the floor and lay her head back down amongst the pillows. "Sleep, I am here."

Amelia gave me another soft smile before her eyes slid closed. She was asleep within moments, but she refused to let go of my hand, even in sleep. So I lifted it to my lips and brushed a tender kiss against her knuckles.

Gods, it was the truest test of will to only sate her, help her through having the luibh gaoil in her system, and not fully mate her, claim her, and save her. But it wouldn't be right to do that, to take advantage, without her consent while of sound mind. I only hoped that when she was free of the herb, she would still have me. It was a blessing that I had had none of the luibh gaoil myself.

Otherwise, nothing but the Source itself could have kept me from claiming my cridhe.

CHAPTER 44*

AMELIA

I woke up with a throbbing ache in my belly. Glancing down, I could see Rhuger's head already between my thighs, his massive shoulders tucked up tight under my thighs, feverish hands gripping my hips, keeping me locked against him. He groaned, kissing my inner thigh gently, his breath fanning over my swollen, hungry flesh. It was so damn erotic I let out a small cry, fists gripping the sheets.

"I can't... I can't, pearl." His voice was thick and gravelly, rumbling over my skin.

"Can't what, Rhuger?" I breathed, body writhing in his hold. Desperate for anything he'd give me.

"I can't... keep going without... release." His gaze was molten, his pupils blown out to where his irises were almost engulfed with black. He'd only come once when I'd been on his lap. Since then, I'd napped and woken horny as fuck multiple times. And each time, he'd sated me until I passed back out. But he hadn't come again.

"How do you want to come?" I breathed, voice catching. I hoped he said he wanted me. Because I wanted him inside me so badly,

I could barely see past the thought.

"As much as I would like to spend *on* you... or *in* you... I can't have my scent on you." He snarled, teeth teasing the inner flesh of my thighs. His long Black Tongue laved the wetness there, moaning like it was the best thing he'd ever tasted. Even after all the times he'd gone down on me, it was like he couldn't get enough of how I tasted.

"Why?" I shuddered under the ministrations of his tongue and mouth.

"I'm not your mate. And I have sworn to only ease your hunger until the herb is out of your system. Not my own." His voice was oddly flat, even as he teased my clit with the tip of that damnably long, black, ribbed tongue.

"So, how else would you like to come?" I panted, trying to stay focused. He'd been pressed against my back the last time he'd come. So I hadn't been able to see what expression that perfect face of his had made when he'd orgasmed. It was a sight I was fucking determined to see while I could.

His eyes slid to my panties, where they lay on the floor by the bed. I could almost see the light bulb go off in his head. Rhuger's gaze sparked as he gave me one last, long lick along my core before shoving away from my hips as if I burned him. I throbbed in his absence.

Rhuger stumbled from the bed. The giant graceful orc who moved with the smooth litheness of a predator actually *stumbled* from my bed. He reached down and snagged my panties off of the floor before retreating to the entire opposite side of the tree house. Like he had to keep as much space between us or he'd fail his vows not to fuck me unconscious.

Did that mean he wanted me as badly as I wanted him? I could only hope. And hope he kept his promise to fuck me blind after the herb was out of my system. Because hot damn, it had been *so damned long* since I'd been desired sexually. Or in any capacity, really. Evidently, it was something I craved when it came to intimacy.

And I'd never been more open and emotionally intimate as I was with Rhuger.

He slumped against the wall, eyes glittering black pits beneath his lowered brows. Rhuger's expression was slack as he panted hard, chest heaving and glistening with more than just sweat. And the sight of him so close to coming undone was enough to set me squirming on my bed.

I couldn't take it anymore. The luibh gaoil could be damned. I didn't need it to feel this horny for him. I'd just been denying it this whole time, like a fucking moron.

I let my hand snake down between my thighs, fingers shaking as I started to rub circles around my clit. Rhuger's stare as he stood frozen watching me touch myself was enough to set me moaning. The primal hunger and focus had me doing something I'd never done before. I did for him what he'd done for me. I put on a show. So he could witness what he did to me. How badly I wanted him.

I arched my back and fondled my breasts with my free hand as my hips rolled to meet my hand. Shamelessly, I stared at where his cock strained against the leather of his kilt as I teased myself. Wondering what he looked like up close. Wanting to taste him and swallow his cum as he shot it down my throat. Needing him to fill me in more ways than one.

"Pearl." Rhuger's rasp cut through my panting and I met his gaze. "Turn to face me. Prop yourself up on your pillows. Let me watch you pleasure yourself."

I'd never scrambled to do anything faster in my life. I tossed pillows against the wall and flopped back onto them. Then slowly, while he watched, I opened my sticky thighs.

Rhuger grasped my panties in his fist and rubbed his face in the still-damp fabric. He moaned and opened his eyes to searing slits, black tongue slithering out to lap at the wetness that still clung to my panties. Watching me, he reached down to rub along the tented length at the front of his kilt.

I let my thighs flop completely open and started undulating my hips so he could see how I was touching myself. Let us both imagine what it would feel like for our bodies to meet and part and meet again, like the waves against the shore. It was pure, sweet torture.

Rhuger clenched my panties between his teeth, a tic working in his jaw. With a desperate urgency to his movements, he nearly tore through the reinforced leather of his kilt in his speed to rid himself of it. A dark spot in the leather where his cock tented his kilt reminded me of exactly how much cum he produced as memories from outside the traveler's cave fluttered behind my eyelids. Finally unbuckling the kilt, he let it fall to a heap at his feet.

I moaned loudly when I saw him, my core throbbing incessantly. He was just as I remembered. Thick and long and curving up towards his abs proudly. And dripping pre-cum down his twitching shaft to plop on the floorboards at his feet. He was still too far for me to see the details of him, but he was exquisite regardless. I fought to keep my legs open, and not to squeeze my thighs together as I picked up the pace with my fingers.

Rhuger's panting breaths shuddered out of him as he took my panties and began stroking himself with them. As he moved them over his shaft, they grew wetter with the addition of his pre-cum. Glancing down, he adjusted them so the groin of the panties that had covered my pussy now covered the reddish tip of him. The closest he could get to my core without actually being inside it. His seed bloomed past the fabric of my panties and he hissed, throwing his head back against the wall as he worked himself with the soaked fabric.

"Pearl. Be a good lass for me and stick your fingers inside your sweet cunt. Pump them in and out and think it's me." Breathing ragged, voice hoarse, Rhuger told me what to do.

"Rhuger..." I whimpered and did precisely as he asked. His growl of approval had my hips jerking in response. I was already so close as we pleasured ourselves together.

"Good lass, you're doing so well." He praised me and my thighs quivered. I didn't know what it was about wanting to please him and having him praise me, but gods be damned, it was like pouring gasoline on a bonfire. Then he asked a question that nearly drove me beyond sanity. "Do you want to come together?"

I bit my bottom lip and fought off my orgasm, now driven to come with the male that had so quickly become my everything. Nodding, I swallowed hard, not trusting my voice, not trusting myself not to cry at how perfect this was. How perfect *he* was.

"Use your words, Pearl." He demanded in a low growl, looking up at me from under his brows as he shifted to grasp his cock with both of his hands.

"Yes!" I gasped.

"We'll count down from ten..." Rhuger breathed, fevered gaze locked on my body, on my movements, on my face. "Ten... oh, pearl, you're so fucking gorgeous."

Shit. If he kept praising me like that, I wouldn't last till zero. I closed my eyes and sucked my lips between my teeth, biting down and using the pain to stay present, and not fly into release.

"Nine... do you have any idea what you do to me?" He asked me in a broken snarl. I opened my eyes again and looked at the feral expression on Rhuger's face. "Eight... Seven... Look at what you do to me. Watch me fuck my fists."

Gods damn me, I did. He'd bared his teeth in a desperate snarl as his hips snapped forward in a crazed rhythm to meet his fists where they clenched my panties. The sloppy, wet sounds of him pumping his cock mingled with the juicy noises I made left me shuddering. It was so close to what I needed, yet not enough. It would never be enough until he was inside of me. And even then, I feared a lifetime of lovemaking still wouldn't be enough to quench this gods damned thirst.

"Six... ugh, I wish this cloth was your tight little cunt." He hissed, his throat bobbing as he swallowed hard. At this point, I couldn't stop gasping and groaning, keeping myself from the edge of release with the last shred of my will, even as I fucked myself with my fingers. "Five... so close, pearl, you're almost there..."

Shit, shit, shit, shit!

"Four... Three... You're doing so well, gods pearl. Two...." Rhuger rasped, I was moaning and sobbing, trying to hold back long enough to make it. I wanted to come with him so damn bad. If this was as close as I'd get to sex with him, I'd take it.

"Rhuger... Rhuger. *Rhuger!*" I cried his name repeatedly like it was my mantra.

"One." He snarled the word, and I felt my world draw down to the feel of my fingers inside of me, the heel of my hand against my nub. Imagining that it was him doing these things to me. Rhuger inside of me with that damn war club of a cock.

"Zero!" Rhuger barked and thrust one last time into my panties, back arching and eyes riveted to mine as he roared his release. I was half a heartbeat behind him and came up off the mattress completely with the force of my orgasm.

I couldn't scream, I couldn't make a sound. Hell, I couldn't even *breathe*, the climax hit me so damn hard. Repeatedly, my body came up off of the mattress. Finally, I could draw in air and a shuddering wail escaped my lips. My head pounded as my body continued to writhe and ride out the orgasm that just... kept going.

Rhuger's dark laugh broke through and I caught his gaze again, hips still spasming.

"I take you enjoyed that, did you Pearl?" His voice was hoarse, and he was milking the last of his spend from his cock. The puddle of whitish liquid at his feet was... astonishing. The last of the orgasm fell away, and I dropped back down onto the bed in a limp pile. "I didn't know a female could shoot her juices from her cunt like that..."

"Oh, my god..." I exclaimed as I slammed my shaking thighs together and covered my face with my hands.

"What's wrong?" Rhuger asked, worry in his voice. I heard him buckling his kilt back on, then his hands were on my face, attempting to move my hands away.

"I squirted! That's so embarrassing!" I cried and refused to let him pull my hands away.

"Is it... wrong? Painful?" He asked.

"Noooo... It just... It's not something all human women can do. They have to be really aroused and horny and climax really hard to do that." I mumbled, wishing I could just disappear. My face felt hot enough to fry an egg on.

"So I made you really aroused and horny and you climaxed that hard?" The amusement in his voice was hard to miss.

"Yes! I've never done that before..." I admitted, not sure if having him so pleased sounding was a good thing or not.

"This is something your ex-husband never accomplished, then? Made you come so hard you squirted?" His voice had an odd note in it. A warmth I couldn't place.

"Yeah…" I mumbled into the heels of my hands. I heard him chuckle and dared to move my fingers so I could see his expression through them. His shit-eating grin was so damn smug.

"You liked it then. When I praised you. When I got off watching you." Not questions, just statements.

"Yes…" I shuddered and felt my face grow even hotter if that was even possible.

"Delightful," Rhuger murmured, his lopsided smile devastating.

RHUGER

I was a thrice-damned fool and a wretch. Looking back, I'd known almost immediately that Amelia was my cridhe. My immediate draw to her had been undeniable. But I had blinded myself to the truth of it. Allowed positions and roles to get in the way of what mattered most.

Of all the years and all the male pleasure mates I'd had, it was nothing compared to this. Nothing could have possibly prepared me for what it would be like to share such intimacy with my cridhe. How just her taste, her cries, her soft body beneath my hands and mouth could send me soaring. The feeling of wholeness that engulfed me every time she touched me seemed to pull together the remnants of my soul.

I'd come more than once after we'd come together while pleasuring ourselves, kneeling on the floor at the edge of the bed. With her thick thighs flung over my shoulders and her hands in my hair as I devoured her. Days ago, when I was taunting her as we crossed the stream on the tree, I'd told her I'd worship her if she'd let me. Now she had, and here I was, praying before the moon goddess who held my wretched heart and soul in her tiny neamhnaid hands. Worshiping her as she deserved.

Whenever she'd fall back, satisfied for the moment, I'd get us water and fruit. Would lie down beside her and watch her sleep, or whisper to her in Teanga Dhubh while she gently stroked my face with the sweetest smile.

At one point, she even sang for me. A song about a moon and stars, about kisses, and being the one she worshiped and adored. The one she loved.

Something broke in me then. Some scabbed over, festering wound she lanced with her song had me blinking back tears. Had me swallowing down the emotions that churned within me like a storm.

"Oh, Rhuger... It's okay, let it out." She whispered, cupping my face in her hands, eyes full of understanding.

"I don't want you to see me cry. I don't want you to think me weak." Biting the inside of my cheek, I tried to let the pain and blood center me. But I was beyond it now.

"How could I ever think of you as weak? You're the strongest person I know. And it takes strength to cry, to allow yourself to feel and process and release." She murmured, her brows pulled together. "I promise, I won't think less of you. It's okay to cry, darling. It's okay, I'm here."

A ragged sound escaped my throat. Her uisge-beatha eyes widened before she pulled me to her. Pulled my head down to her chest where I could hear the steady beating of her heart. Amelia hummed to me and rocked me as if I were an orcling. Ran her hands over my head and rubbed soothing circles on my shoulders. But it was only when she kissed the top of my head that I broke.

I hadn't been shown such tenderness since before my mother died. I never expected to experience it again for the rest of my days. Yet here I was, in the arms of my cridhe. Knowing every moment without her had been worth it to get here.

And also knowing this might fade like mist in the dawn once the luibh gaoil wore off. Because she wasn't fully orckin so she didn't feel like we did. She likely would never show the mating marks that would bind us together as one for the rest of our lives.

After my tears ran dry, we slept for a time tangled together. Until, inevitably, she began panting and moaning in her sleep. The luibh gaoil demanded sex, climax, and seed. So I slid my hand between her thighs, past the damp curls, and slipped my fingers inside of her.

I watched her eyelids flutter open and her eyes focus on mine as she whispered my name in the dark, a soft demand. So I dipped my head and claimed her mouth with my own. Drank down her sweet sighs and soft cries as I brought her to another quivering climax with my fingertips.

Even if this night was all I had with her, it was worth it all.

CHAPTER 45

AMELIA

"You didn't have to do that to me all night, you know," I whispered into the morning sunshine. My voice was hoarse from a night of screaming as I pushed my rat's nest of hair back from my eyes. Rhuger was lying beside me on the bed, sunlight igniting a halo around his head and limning every perfect inch of him.

"I know." His grin was absolutely wicked as he sat up on the edge of the bed. "I enjoyed it."

"You... you woke me up already... doing stuff to me." I knew I was beet red as I hid most of my face in the pillow we'd shared.

I couldn't keep my eyes from his, worried perhaps he hadn't wanted last night as badly as I had. The luibh gaoil had just made clear what I'd known all along. That we were two parts of the same soul. I just hoped he realized it one day, too.

"You'd granted me permission to slake your lust until the herb was out of your system, pearl." He murmured, an unreadable expression on his face. "I admit I took advantage of the situation, as there would likely never be another opportunity. I wanted something to remember."

"Why wouldn't there be?" I asked, confused. Heart hammering at the idea he wanted to *remember* last night.

"Why wouldn't there be what?" He asked as he looked away from me and started lacing up his boots.

My cheeks heated. I hated he was making me say it, but... it was part of the consent thing he had. Being open about wants and needs. Wasn't it?

"Another opportunity." The words fell into the morning sunlight like stones in a river.

Rhuger froze, then released his boot and sat back up. He turned his head, his messy braid shifting against his scar-flecked spine. Rhuger's expression was completely stunned. He blinked once, twice, but it was like I broke his brain with those two words.

"What is the luibh gaoil, anyway?" I asked, changing the topic and looking down at my hands, where I was picking at them in my nervousness. I'd had other people explain it, but I wanted to hear it from him. Hear what he thought about it.

"It's a fertility herb infused uisge-beatha." He muttered, looking away from me. "It mimics the mating frenzy that overtakes cridhe pairs, allowing the female multiple orgasms. The more orgasms a female has, the more likely she is to conceive. Orckin need to be careful, too much of it or drinking it without a partner to help you through the frenzy often leads to madness."

"Oh. Well, lucky females." I laughed, and he looked over at me, confused. I wasn't worried about going mad as I'd passed that threshold long before drinking the luibh gaoil.

Since I'd placed that broken acorn crystal in the empty divot in Grandma Ruth's sea cave and wound up here on Talam. Since my reality turned inside out and upside down when Rhuger had taken my hand in that cave like it was as natural as breathing. He'd hinted that I might be his cridhe. Was that why every single aspect of last night felt so right? Why it felt as if we'd been together our whole lives rather than just two weeks? Being with him was easy as my hand sliding into his, our fingers entwining as if made to fit together perfectly.

All I knew was that this was swiftly becoming a topsy-turvy dream I hoped I never woke from.

"Lucky?"

"Well, back on Earth, it's common that women don't even reach one orgasm with their partner, let alone many." Shrugging, I stopped picking at my fingers and met his gaze again. Trying *really* hard to not blush hot enough to combust as I attempted, and failed, to keep from remembering precisely *how many* orgasms he'd given me last night. I'd lost count after ten.

"You came many times. Was that because of your orc blood, then?" He asked, curious.

"No idea, but human women are capable of as many orgasms as their partner can give them. Most men just don't know what they're doing or don't care." I shrugged as I sat up, holding the blanket to my chest. I winced at how my thighs stuck together, how my low back ached, and my body was sluggish to respond.

"They don't care about their partner's pleasure?" He demanded, incredulous. Standing swiftly, he stalked to the sink in the kitchen. He wetted a cloth and warmed it over the heating stones. "Even the Oc'Turin make sure their females reach orgasm."

"Human women don't need to orgasm to conceive. I know for a fact that all of womankind wished it was like that, though." Rhuger brought me the warmed damp cloth, and I blushed. "Thank you..."

"It's nothing." He murmured, deep in thought. I took the proffered cloth, our fingers brushing briefly. I felt that touch all the way to my core. My mind recalled all the things he did with those fingers throughout the night. Despite how I ached between my legs, lust still heated my belly in a searing flash.

Rhuger inhaled sharply, face suddenly a tight mask. He jerked his hand away as if I'd burned him. He took a few steps back from me, fists clenched at his sides, boots not even fully laced yet. His shirt was still in a heap by the door.

"I should go." He said curtly, before stalking quickly to the door, snatching up his black tunic as he went. "I must tend to Hifasa. Stay here. It's not safe for you outside yet."

Before I could reply, he'd swung the door wide, taken a bracing breath, and stomped through it. The door slammed. I jumped, stunned.

"What the hell was that about...?" I muttered before I moved the sheet aside and began cleaning my own juices from my thighs. Some of it was flaking where it had dried against my skin. My pussy throbbed, and I realized the herb must still be in my system if I could still feel horny while simultaneously *this* sore.

Or maybe it was just my reaction to *him*.

RHUGER

Source damn me to the fiery core of Talam. I swear I'd thought the luibh gaoil was out of her system come morning. I couldn't smell it mingled with the heady scent of her while I watched the warm beams of sunlight set her neamhnaid skin aglow as she slept beside me.

I'd only dozed in brief intervals, too desperate for every moment I could spend with her like this. Not just the physical intimacy, though that had been beyond anything I could have dreamed of and we hadn't even fully mated. No, it was tender moments like this. A fleeting gift I clung to with every fiber of my being.

Because I was afraid that when she woke, she'd be free of the luibh gaoil, and not want anything to do with me. Angry that I hadn't told her about the luibh gaoil. That I had touched her, tasted her, devoured her without her choosing it uninhibited by the herb. Perhaps angry that I had enjoyed myself within the constraints of my word.

I should have told her about the luibh gaoil. Should have somehow found the will to stay and keep her inside the house. But I'd been too tangled up in emotions I could no longer control. Emotions I'd had a death grip on since I was a child. Because if I didn't control them, and keep them on a short leash, either others died, or I was left broken. So I'd fled like a damned coward.

Before Amelia had arrived, everything was clear-cut and simple, predictable, even if it had been dangerous and devoid of joy. But once she'd appeared on Talam? She'd done nothing but get into trouble constantly. Was completely unpredictable in what she would say or do. Was too full of emotion for her own good and incapable of hiding it. The most damning of all was her ability to see through every defense I'd ever erected around my heart, see the truth of me, and draw out feelings I'd forgotten I was capable of.

And then she'd said those two words that completely shifted the trajectory of my destiny. "Another opportunity." Her words might as well have been boulders as they crashed into my hard skull.

Source preserve me, I couldn't formulate a coherent thought. Just automatically chatted with her and got up to get her a warm wet cloth to clean herself while my thoughts spiraled out of control. And when she'd taken the cloth from my hands and our fingers had brushed? The sudden burst of her aroused aroma, now so ingrained into my being, perfumed the suddenly too-cramped space of the house and set my teeth on edge.

Some feral instinct roared at arousing my cridhe, my body responding just as sharply to her touch as she had. My vision tunneled as I fought myself and jerked away from her. Fought to keep my word not to mate her like the depraved animal I was.

"I should go." Grinding the words out between my teeth, I backed away from her toward the door. "I must tend to Hifasa. Stay here. It's not safe for you outside yet."

I lied. Opening the door, I took a deep breath of the fresh morning air and stomped outside. I let the door slam behind me and fought a wince. I hadn't meant to leave like that, but if she somehow still had the luibh gaoil in her system, I didn't have it in me to keep my word.

Each orgasm I'd given her had driven me closer and closer to the edge of madness as if I'd drank a vat of the luibh gaoil myself. My control was threadbare as it was. Hearing her scream my name in release one more time, no one and nothing would keep me from claiming her in every wicked way imaginable.

The crisp morning breezes of Baile Coille filled my lungs and scattered the remnants of Amelia's scent, clearing my head. I bent down and snagged my swords from where they lay on the top of my gear and my bow. My body demanded movement, exertion, and strain. So I'd give it what it wanted in the training yard since I couldn't in Amelia's bed.

"Good morning, Rhuger!" A cheery voice called. Glancing over the railing, I saw Rorich waving up at me from where he'd just crossed the little bridge over the nearby stream.

"Morning," I grunted, suddenly skittish and guilty as if he'd caught out at something shameful. And perhaps he had.

"Did Sigg find you last night?" He asked as I met him down at the base of the home tree. He looked sheepish and scuffed his boot on the moss. "I'm sorry I didn't stay with Amelia. I'm not allowed at the party yet and, well, she refused to stay here."

"I found Amelia. She's inside. Don't let anyone in for now unless it's a female, understand?" I gave him his order, and he nodded. But not before he inhaled and froze. A silver flush brightened his cheeks just as his face twisted in polite confusion.

I smelled like sex. But not mating. If Amelia and I *had* mated, our scents would have combined into something easily identifiable. That we hadn't mated and resisted the siren song of the luibh gaoil wasn't common amongst the orckin. Leaving a *lot* open to interpretation that could both save her and damn her. I needed to get ahead of this now before the gossiping started.

"She drank the luibh gaoil, not knowing what it was. I helped her through the frenzy but did not mate her." I explained flatly, my emotions churning in my gut as I fisted my shaking hands at my sides. "If I find Sharn, I'll send her here to get Amelia for the female's ritual. For now, I'll be at the training yards."

With that, I stalked off, not waiting for Rorich's assent. If I stayed anywhere within sight of where Amelia was, I wouldn't be able to resist going to her, mating her, and seeing if the cridhe marks would bloom across her mostly human chest. My head was so full of tumbling thoughts, I couldn't remember how I'd gotten to the kitchens, only that I came to standing with a bowl in my hand and Sharn's hand on my shoulder.

"You alright there?" She asked me, concern furrowing her brow over her sapphire eyes. Dark smudges made her eyes appear more deep-set than they really were. Evidence that she'd gotten no sleep, like most of the females who were of age and willing. I jerked a nod at her and looked away, cheeks burning bright green.

"I kept my word." The words were almost bitter as they hissed out between my gritted teeth. "I helped Amelia through the frenzy and did *not* mate her."

I stressed the word *not* with a cutting glance, daring her to call me a liar. But she didn't even take a cursory sniff to check. Why did I feel like an orcling caught sneaking sweets?

Because I'd devoured my sweet last night. And I was guilty of gorging myself.

"Good. How is she doing? The first time with luibh gaoil can be... Trying." Sharn's lip curled slightly as she grimaced at her own memories.

She'd told me one night, as we were both deep in our cups, that her first time drinking the herbed whiskey had made her nauseous. Not exactly the best state to be in when getting railed and throat fucked. She'd pushed the male who was priming himself for his turn in her mouth and vomited all over his groin and the face of the male beneath her. Neither male had flinched, had asked if she was alright to continue and at her ascent, finished.

She'd been so bitter when she'd told me that story. It wasn't until later that I realized that her bitterness wasn't necessarily because of the humiliation of vomiting on two males. But that she hadn't understood her own leanings until that night. That her first time hadn't been with someone she would have wanted. She'd never told me she preferred females, but to me it was apparent. Sharn could have said no to taking part in the after-party from then on out. But each year, she downed at least two luibh gaoil and joined in. I felt for her and was in awe of her willingness to help keep her people alive.

"She's resting," I whispered, remembering how lovely my cridhe had looked with her tousled waves. How they glowed around her rounded face, a riot of warm colors in the morning sunshine.

Gods, why hadn't she pushed me away? Why had she stared at me with shy adoration, as if she loved me? I craved what lay in her eyes, but it would have been easier had she exiled me from her bed. I was used to that.

"Could you do me a favor?" I asked, trying not to beg Sharn to spare me. It must have shown on my face anyway if her surprise was any sign.

"Anything." She said without hesitation.

"Could you please fetch Amelia for the female's ritual? I... I don't think it's a good idea for me to bring her."

"Why wouldn't it be a good idea?" She asked me, attempting to catch my eye, but I avoided her. "Rhuger." She tried to move around me to get up into my face, but I turned in the opposite direction with my bowl. "Rhuger, what aren't you telling me?"

"Nothing important," I muttered as I turned and avoided her again. She growled and stomped her foot at me in irritation.

"That's a load of nocrys shit." Sharn's mouth pressed into a flat line as she glowered at me with her hands on her hips.

"Thanks," I said, and strode away as quickly as I could toward the training yard, still with the bowl of porridge in my hand.

AMELIA

In the hour after Rhuger left, I'd stayed in bed, unable to do more than pull on a spare nightdress. My skin was still far too sensitive to wear anything more. And I ached *everywhere*.

As I lounged and stretched in bed trying to loosen my stiff muscles, I yo-yoed between kicking my sore legs while squealing into my pillow like a crushing pre-teen and staring at the ceiling, wondering why Rhuger had left the way he had. I wished he'd talk to me about how he felt, so I wasn't in the dark. But I got the feeling he didn't know himself, so how could I expect him to explain it to me?

I just hoped he'd agree to be my mate, even if it were short-term. I'd already decided to ask him. If last night taught me anything, it was that he felt something for me. Physical, emotional, or both, I wasn't sure. I didn't want to get my hopes up, but I wanted all of him for as long as he'd let me have him. Of that I *was* sure.

There was an impatient knock at my door and I nearly gave myself whiplash as I rolled over and stared at the door. My heart hammered in my chest and my mouth went dry, waiting for Rhuger to come in. Waiting to tell him my plan and ask him to be my mate. At least until Orok gave up.

"Coming!" I called when the knock sounded again, voice still raw and throat aching. Then chuckled because, well, I *had* come a whole fucking lot the night before.

I stood on quaking legs and used the furniture to brace as I made my way to the door. I just hoped it wasn't poor Rorich checking in on me. That poor kid had it rough last night, and I needed to apologize to him for dragging him into my mess.

Reaching the door, I braced myself against the door frame and opened it. Sharn was standing there in a dress, highly unusual for her, and looking a little worse for wear. There were bags under her eyes and her shoulders slumped, exhaustion etched into every inch of her.

"*OOF!*" Sharn cried, shaking her head as if she'd smelled something too strong to handle. Her eyes watered as she cleared her throat.

"What's wrong?" I asked. I had to admit, it surprised me to find Sharn visiting me after the party last night. Wasn't she sore, too?

"Your house smells like sex." She laughed. "Did Rhuger behave himself? He refused to talk to me when I saw him at the kitchens."

My face heated, and she smiled kindly at me.

"He... was amazing. We didn't go all the way or anything." I muttered, unable to keep the disappointment from my voice and the burn from my cheeks as I looked down at my feet.

"All the way?" She asked.

"Intercourse—er, mating?" I attempted to clarify. This was awkward.

"Ah. Good. He kept his word, then." She nodded as if relieved. "He's far more honorable than any other male would have been. You're lucky."

"Are you okay?" I asked, worried. "Was last night horrible for you?" I left the door open and hobbled to the kitchen to make us some tea. I motioned her to sit down at the table.

"Tired. And sore." She sighed as she sank down into the spare chair, wincing.

I placed the kettle on the hot sunstones. The water heated quickly, and I poured her a cup of tea. Bringing it to her, I couldn't help but grimace at the unhappiness on her face.

"I'm so sorry, Sharn," I murmured. She just waved me off and gladly accepted the mug of steaming tea. After a few bracing gulps, she sighed and set the earthenware cup down.

"I'm sorry too. It wasn't like it wasn't enjoyable. The males make sure that we are delirious with pleasure, so we have a better chance of conceiving." Sharn sighed as I sat across from her with my cup. "It just wasn't... fulfilling."

"Rhuger explained that about orc reproduction. That orgasm directly correlates to fertility." I offered, letting her know I wasn't wholly ignorant on the topic.

"They don't for humans?" She asked, surprised, as I sat down and grasped my cup.

"No. Human females don't need to reach a climax to conceive. Only males do."

"Lucky," she said dryly, and I looked startled.

"For my kind, it would be the other way around. Too often, male humans don't know where the clitoris is, let alone how to bring us to climax. They're too occupied with their own pleasure most of the time." Ghostly memories whispered in the back of my mind. Of nights in my ex-husband's arms, left wanting and confused. But the memories I'd made last night with Rhuger had turned those old memories into hazy echoes.

"Well, for females like me, the idea of having an orgasm with someone I don't want isn't all that appealing. I'd happily trade to conceive without dealing with the intimacy of sharing an orgasm with a male I don't want." Sharn's words didn't quite bite, but they held an old bitterness.

"I... hadn't thought about it like that," I admitted, stunned. The thought tumbled around in my mind as I tried to search for the right words. "I know what it's like to have such an intimate moment with someone and not want an orgasm. So I can see how, if you *had* to have sex with someone you didn't want, getting it over and done without the intimacy of an orgasm would be ideal."

"Thank you for your understanding." She smiled tightly. "Few females get it. They'd put up with any male as long as they conceived. We *can* say no, but there's this expectation and pressure to pump out orclings like a nocrys with a litter. Most females lock away their feelings and desires even as some hope they'll find their cridhe match."

"Well, that's a load of bullshit." I wrinkled my nose and shook my head. "Isn't the cridhe bond all about the heart and love and your one true match? How can you find that in someone else if you reject it in yourself?"

Sharn just stared at me for a few heartbeats, a strange understanding dawning on her lovely features. But as quickly as the expression bloomed, it faded. What use was accepting yourself if no one around you did the same in a world like this?

"I'd honestly mate with a human man if it meant I'd get pregnant immediately. I doubt human seed is that strong, though." Sharn chuckled, changing the topic.

"Maybe it is." I thought about it for a moment, head cocked to the side. "I mean, I wouldn't know. My ex-husband would *not* have made a good father. And he wouldn't have allowed me to raise a child without him. So I avoided getting pregnant at all costs. My mom only had me. She and my dad split up not long after and she didn't find anyone else she wanted a family with. So, unfortunately, I can't tell you either way if orckin females can easily get pregnant from human men or not."

"I'm glad you're rid of him." Sharn's tone was solemn, and I looked up at her. "He can't find you here. Not with the gate broken. Here on Talam, your mate would treasure you and your orclings. At least within most of the clans. I can't say the same for the Oc'Blyre or Oc'Turin. Rhuger is a special case."

"True. But my choices aren't my own, are they?" I asked sadly. "No females are here."

"It's what comes of being a part of a dying race." She raised her cup to me in salute and I clinked cups with her.

"We should head to the baths. The female's ritual is a tradition where we bathe together the day after." Sharn told me, getting up. "It gives us time to recuperate, gossip, and get clean after a night of debauchery. We use a special soap that removes any male scent from our bodies. That way, if a female conceives, it's easier to scent which male is the father."

"Well, isn't that handy?" I huffed a laugh and stood on wobbly legs.

"You'll want to put on the dress Manira gave you. You're going to be *far* too sensitive for anything else." Sharn advised, and I shamelessly pulled my nightdress off over my head and hobbled for my trunk.

A few minutes later, we were both easing our way down the stairs, holding onto the handrails for dear life as our legs shook beneath us. Rorich was very kind and helped us, acting as middle support for us to cling to. The poor kid even offered to walk us to the baths, probably to glimpse his beloved Manira. But we waved him off and clung to one another as we made the trek down the sleepy avenues of Baile Coille to the female's dormitory and the private baths within.

"How the hell did you make the trek here and back?" I asked, baffled. My knees were practically knocking together despite how the walking eased the cramps. How Sharn had managed it was a minor miracle.

"Not my first Mating Tournament, Amelia," Sharn smirked. We chatted the rest of the way there. About the tournament, the after party, and Sharn asked *way* too many questions about how Rhuger had *performed*.

When we arrived, the place was packed. Females, both mated and unmated, filled the dormitory. All of them were limping and exhausted. The ladies who were too young or too old to participate were helping those who had. Helped them undress and make their way into the baths.

"Are the baths going to be large enough for us all?" I asked, stunned by the number of females. There were far more of them than

I'd initially thought.

"They will. There are more caverns farther back. One of them is huge, enough to hold all of us many times over, with dozens of little waterfalls we can wash under." Sharn explained. "One of the few good things our foremothers did was claim these bathing caves for themselves."

"Where's Manira?" I asked, looking for my friend.

"Probably inside helping distribute soap and things," Inassa said as she appeared beside me. I jumped a little, and she offered me a small smile. "Manira's good with that sort of thing. I wouldn't know where to begin."

I nearly did a double-take. What happened to the snide Inassa I'd mouthed off at just a few days ago? Who was this amiable female who was *complimenting* someone she'd mocked? Could we keep this one?

"I'm not blind to others' good qualities, Amelia," Inassa said with a small smile as if she'd read my mind. Before I could reply, she'd glided, as gracefully as anyone could after getting railed all night long, toward the entrance to the baths.

"Who was that, and what did they do with Inassa?" I asked Sharn in a conspiratorial whisper. Sharn just gave me a shrug, also at a loss.

Eventually, we made it into the bathing caverns. Flickering lanterns led the way towards a tunnel to one side that opened up onto the massive cavern Sharn had mentioned. The waterfalls weren't so big that the sound drowned out the conversation, but they were big enough to shower under. Steam wafted across the water's surface as dozens of females laughed and chatted together.

The cavern was a marvel. Glowing mushrooms in a rainbow of colors filled the nooks and crannies in the worked stone. Moss created a soft carpet underfoot and soft light filtered in from holes in the ceiling high overhead. Lovely, little glass lanterns lined the walls and hung from hooks on the walls, brightening the darker corners. Floating candles and flowers rocked lazily in the waters of the bathing pool. A table was set up with refreshments and another with brushes, scrub poofs, soaps, and oils. Punctuating it all was a pungent smell, similar to pine and citrus.

A little knot of older orckin females was playing music, sewing, or doing something similar to knitting. Little girls splashed in the shallow end of the baths under the watchful eyes of their mothers. Some females quickly got clean and left, while others lounged in the hot water, nearly asleep. But overall, everyone was enjoying themselves in some capacity.

And presiding over the *ritual* was Grammie Ruksala. Sat on a small mountain of a pillow, she watched the gathered crowd with an absent smile. Something told me she was sneaking a peek at who'd get knocked up this year, as her eyes had that faraway, cloudy look.

But then her gaze snapped to mine and cleared. Her knowing eyes looked straight into my soul, and I stiffened. Grammie Ruksala only smiled her gap-toothed grin and waved us over. Unable to deny her, we walked toward her. She wore her usual dress, but her orange cardigan was off in the warm, damp heat. Her mating marks were on full display above her strapless dress. The lines were still crisp and discernable, even though they had faded with age. The ink flowed in a design that was made of bold strokes interspersed with delicate detailing. Ornate and powerful.

"No kit for you this tournament." Grammie Ruksala told Sharn. One eyebrow quirked up as she gave her a knowing look. Sharn paled slightly and looked damned confused, but said nothing.

"What about me, Grammie Ruksala? Will I have an orcling this year?" I asked.

Dread and hope battled it out in my belly. A dark-winged bird and a swarm of butterflies that made me nauseous with their dance. If I got knocked up, I wouldn't have to go to Lord Orok. But who knew who the father would be at this rate? Today was my last day to mate with someone. And if I didn't, Lord Orok might end up being the father of whatever child I had.

I was betting my future and the future of my potential children on Rhuger. On what seemed to exist between us.

"Oh, but that would be telling." Her grin grew sly, eyelids lowered as she chuckled and shook a gnarled finger at me.

That... Didn't make me feel any better. *Fuck.*

Sharn steered me away, and we shared a slightly alarmed look as we got to the table with the bathing products. Manira was there, and she looked at us with concern. I let go of Sharn and hugged Manira, who gave my back a soothing pat.

"Are you both okay?" She asked as I released her and stepped back with a sigh. "What did Fear a Chì Ruksala say?"

"She wouldn't say if I'd be having an orcling this year or not," I muttered, feeling like I was going to barf all over the bars of soap that was the source of the pine and citrus scent.

"She told me I wouldn't have an orcling this *tournament*. But not this *year*." Sharn's voice was flat, stunned, as she looked at us with fearful eyes.

No *wonder* she'd gone so pale. It seemed both of our futures were going to be sliding sideways like a jack-knifed big rig on ice.

CHAPTER 46*

RHUGER

"I heard our neamhnaid went to the after-party last night against her grandfather's orders." A gruff voice called from the weapons shed next to where I stood at the archery range.

I slackened the string of my bow and lowered it until the arrow was aimed at the ground. Then, flicking my gaze to the shed, I caught sight of Uther where he leaned against the doorway, his tiny son asleep strapped to his chest. Uther's gaze bored into me with extreme intensity.

"I also heard that you beat our tournament champion senseless over her. Then ran off with her like a thief in the night." His tone wasn't quite accusatory, but it was close. Uther was offering me an opportunity to explain myself.

So I said the only thing I could—the only true thing in all of this mess I'd made.

"She's my cridhe."

The silence that met my admonition was deafening. Uther didn't move a muscle. Just stared me down as his brows drew inward even further. Pulling at his facial scars and making him look something fierce.

"That's a high claim." He finally said dryly, clicking his tongue against his teeth.

"I know it in my bones," I replied. Now that I'd finally admitted it to someone, the burden of it fell away. I could stand a little taller and breathe a little easier. Didn't ease the roiling in my guts though.

The truth of it had been there the entire time. Behind everything, what I'd said and done. How Amelia had so quickly become the center of my world. Even down to how I was around others, less antagonistic and more relaxed. Everything had changed the moment she'd fallen through the Geata.

I'd never go back. Couldn't even if I tried. But I didn't know how to move forward either. I'd experienced nothing like this before. And I was afraid for the first time since I was a child.

Afraid to get it wrong, the tangled political web surrounding Amelia, that she'd get hurt by me or someone else angling for her, that I'd fuck everything up and she'd grow to hate me. But mostly, I was afraid of how strong I felt about her. Afraid of the desolate wasteland in my chest that housed dark spirits, ghosts, and all the monstrous aspects of who I was. Afraid that I wouldn't measure up to what she deserved in a partner. Too broken, harsh, and dark for someone like her.

How could I give her my heart without understanding it first? How could I interweave my life with hers into a single pattern when there was so much I'd buried deep inside? Where all of my darkness dwelled, a place someone as luminous as she should never have to tread.

"And you won't know for certain until you mate her. Which, by the smell of you, you resisted when you helped her through the frenzy." Uther's gaze shifted into something I couldn't place.

"I got her into that mess. The least I could do was get her out of it." I said bitterly.

"You haven't told her, have you." Not a question. Just a quiet, awed statement.

"No," I replied.

"I don't doubt she'd take you as her mate if you offered." Uther's statement hung in the air between us. "Even if you didn't tell her she was your cridhe."

"I don't want our cridhe bond to be born of an impossible, desperate situation," I whispered the aching truth.

"You want her to love you. Accept you completely, with no schemes getting in the way." Again, not questions, but statements of fact.

"I do. If things were as they should, I'd have time to woo her properly, truly meet her soul to soul." I knew it was a child's dream, a romantic fantasy that was far from the reality I was living. But that fantasy was the only thing that had gotten me through some dark times. Imagining courting my cridhe like the heroes in the old stories did. And it was the only positive example I had.

"Nothing's that easy, runt." Uther bit out, suddenly furious. "You have an opportunity none of us have had since Fear a Chì Ruksala and Rìgh Tyras. If what you say is true, then the cridhe bond hasn't disappeared from our people, only slumbered."

I said nothing. Just stared at him. Wishing I could convey the hopelessness I felt inside.

"I don't deserve her." The words burned and scraped as they exited my throat. There was a stunned silence. And like the masterful swordsman he was, he went straight to the core.

"It's not about *deserving*. It is about *accepting* and *cherishing* the gifts we are given *when* they are given." Uther pushed off of the doorframe and stalked toward me, face contorted in rage and sorrow. He stood before me and jabbed a finger straight into my chest over my mangled wreck of a heart. "Learn from an old orc and don't wait until it's too late to cherish it properly. Don't wait until that precious gift has slipped through your fingers and is gone."

With that, he slammed his shoulder into mine and strode back toward the keep.

"Go clean up. You reek of things you don't *deserve*." He growled over his shoulder as he left me alone in the training yard.

Like the females, the males had a ritual of their own in the baths. There was drinking, games, gossip, and rivalry. It wasn't uncommon for males who had bedded the same female to end up knocking each other's teeth out over who would be the father of her orcling. *If* she conceived, that is.

Since I'd never taken part in the after-party, I'd only gone to the ritual my first year in Baile Coille. It was easier to avoid the ritual altogether rather than defend myself against opting out of the clan orgy *and* refusing the advances of some males who thought I wasn't keen on females.

Honestly, it had never mattered to me what parts a person had or didn't have. All of it was enjoyable. The one thing that mattered was being understood and accepted. I'd stayed longer in relationships with pleasure mates than I should have because of it. And ended up broken over it.

But I'd never felt a pull to anyone here in Baile Coille. And some days, I wondered why I'd stayed all these years. Why I'd put in the time, beads, and effort into building a home tree for a mate I'd likely never have. I think some part of me knew that if I stayed and prepared a home, my cridhe would find me. And she had.

I didn't bother going back to Amelia's home tree, *our* home tree, to get my spare kilt and clothing. Because I knew I'd cave if I saw her right then. Despite the knowledge that she was my cridhe anchoring me, one whiff of her scent, one glance from those uisge-beatha eyes, and I would be done for.

So instead, I went straight to the baths.

Warm mist met me as I stepped through the carved tunnel toward the pools. The air smelled of male musk, soap, and salt. When I exited the tunnel and came to a stop in the caverns, everyone went quiet and stared. I tried to ignore them and stalked to where I saw Sigg and a few others lounging in one of the pools toward the back. The cave was lit by lanterns filled with sunstones and the glow worms that lived on the cave ceiling, giving the impression of stars in the dark.

I could feel their eyes on me, on the stain on the front of my kilt from where my cridhe had squirted her juices all over my lap as she screamed my name. The evidence of her desire wasn't the only thing that stained my kilt, either, and they could smell it.

As I passed, confused whispers followed me. Sigg turned to see what the silence was about, caught sight of me, and waved me over. I noticed as he registered my scent, his eyebrows popping up in surprise and then down into a scowl. Hisouk stood up from the pool where he'd been sitting beside Sigg.

"Put that away!" Sigg snapped, leaning away from where Hisouk's cock was dangling not too far from his face.

"Sorry," Hisouk mumbled and sat back down in the water. A rusty blush stained his cheeks even as he stared at me in concern. Hisouk wasn't as well-endowed as some of his other Oc'Blyre kin, but he was still an impressive size. And usually shy about it.

"What kind of mess have you gotten yourself into, you bastard?" Sigg hissed when I reached the edge of the bath. I yanked my shirt off over my head and unbuckled my kilt, dropping my clothes in a pile nearby. "I'd call you a *rutting* bastard, but it's clear you didn't get that far."

I cut a glare his way as I stepped into the water. Sigg was furious. I couldn't remember the last time I'd seen him so angry. And Hisouk wasn't much better, glowering at me. The water hit my hips and I waded over to where they sat along one of the underwater benches.

Sigg had taken part if the bite marks were any sign, but Hisouk hadn't. Both males longed for their cridhe. Only one used the after party as a diversion and to find his cridhe, the other refused to touch anyone until he found his. And here I stood in front of them, reeking of my cridhe's sweet scent. Guilt and shame were twin daggers in my gut.

Neither Sigg nor Hisouk would have hesitated to tell their cridhe about the bond as I had.

"I swore to Sharn I would only help Amelia through the frenzy." My words were flat.

"To the blackness beyond the stars with Sharn." Sigg spat. "You had the perfect opportunity to solve this entire problem!"

"It wouldn't have been right." Hisouk's deep, even voice rippled over the water as I stood there under their judgment. Sigg looked askance at Hisouk, who cocked his head and squinted at me. "She'd drank the luibh gaoil. But she didn't know what it was. Which means anything more than what Rhuger did would have been done without her clear-minded consent."

And we all knew what that kind of punishment would have awaited me. I would have saved the executioner the trouble and strung myself up by my innards if I'd betrayed Amelia like that. So I jerked a nod of acknowledgment to Hisouk, who hummed. Sigg's expression didn't clear, but it softened. A tick worked in his jaw as his gaze flicked from Hisouk to me.

"Did you at least tell her how you feel? Offer to be her mate, at least until this thing with Orok is finished?" Hisouk asked, leaning his elbows back behind him on the edge of the bathing pool.

"No." The word nearly choked me on its way out.

"Time runs out *tomorrow* morning." Sigg's voice lashed out low, striking true.

"I know."

"Then help us understand, Rhuger." Hisouk pleaded. "If you care about her so much, and want to be with her, why do you hold back from telling her? From saving her?"

I didn't open my mouth, just looked Hisouk in the eye, let him see what he would within my gaze. I'd known for some time that Hisouk had some small gift of sight. His eyes seem to cloud over, then clear as his irises blew out wide. He took a deep inhale through his nose and went ramrod straight as understanding hit him like a boulder to the head.

"What?" Sigg asked, looking between us with irritation.

I nodded at Hisouk in ascent. Letting him know he was right. So, he leaned over and whispered low and quiet in Sigg's ear. Sigg sat there frozen, staring at nothing, even after Hisouk had pulled away and run his hand over his face.

"How long have you known?" My friend's voice was oddly flat and inflectionless. When he finally looked at me, an unholy rage burned in his eyes. I couldn't open my mouth to speak. Just stared helplessly at my friend. "*FOOL!*"

In a splashing surge, Sigg stood and stormed out of the pool. I watched him snag his clothes and throw them on over his wet body as he left. Everyone in the cavern watched Sigg leave, then turned to gawk at me and this fresh development. Ignoring them, I turned back to Hisouk, whose expression was filled with disappointment.

"Sit. Clean yourself up." Hisouk ordered. For once, I obeyed.

We sat in silence as chatter from the other pools picked up once more. Snagging my braid, I began to unplait it. Dragging my claws through the snarls and tangles. The knots at the top of my head, where Amelia had sunk her fingers and claws into my hair as I'd feasted on her, were difficult to get out. Without needing to ask, Hisouk turned and began combing out the tangles with a comb and his fingers.

There was a closeness that the Oc'Dellor males shared that was starkly different from that of my home clan. The Oc'Turin made closeness about power and who held it and who submitted. Here, it was a simple camaraderie that I'd first taken as a physical interest. But I'd soon realized that was just how it was here. Males would often help one another groom and plait their hair, offer comfort and physical closeness that could stay platonic or become something more, and support one another in their day-to-day lives.

They realized something that the Oc'Turin hadn't. They were all in the same skiff, in the same situation. *All* of them were trying to either find a mate or their cridhe. And with so few females, they had learned to rely on one another for the things we all used to receive from our females. It was nice to have this with no pressure or power struggle.

When Hisouk had finished combing out my hair, I grabbed some soap and began my ablutions. I hadn't been surprised to find Sigg here. But I had been surprised to find Hisouk. But then I remembered. Sigg had mentioned that both he and Hisouk would take matters into their own hands and offer themselves to Amelia if I didn't. Offer to save her from my brother if I could not. It made sense that they would meet to decide who would offer themselves first.

Self-loathing and shame choked me.

As I lathered my hair, snippets of nearby conversation drifted to me. My bout with Asterun over Amelia had been noticed by more than just Uther. And when I'd left carrying her like the princess she was, cradled in my arms as she moaned into my ear, that was witnessed too. I grit my teeth and fought not to bare them, fought not to show any sign I'd heard. It wouldn't do for me to beat the shit out of these males over something true.

I couldn't help how hearing her name on their tongues made me want to cut them out at the root, though.

"What a dress! Did you see how the Neamhnaid glowed in that wee slip of a thing?" A drunk male asked in astonishment. Remembering the tournament and how my cridhe had been dressed more as a pleasure mate than a princess.

"Och, and how it would flutter at the merest breeze? Shame it never blew up high enough for us to see anything." Another male replied with a dark chuckle.

"Who even gave her that dress? I've seen nothing like it." A third chimed in. A clothier from the market, I remembered his voice.

"I did." Came a cultured, clear voice over the din of chatter. Not hollered, but low and clear enough that everyone heard.

It was the damned steward. The one who'd separated me from my cridhe for the tournament prep, so I wasn't there to protect her. I bared my teeth then, snarling low and terrifying the males nearby as I turned my head toward him.

"You what?" Asked someone, bewildered.

"There was a request made for a dress for the Neamhnaid, so I had the dress made to certain specifications." The steward said as he absently scrubbed his slim arm. "The Rìgh trusts me, trusted my judgment in the choice of dress for the tournament. I've petitioned the Rìgh for his blessing to mate her, as she has found no one herself."

My blood ran cold. The right bastard looked straight at me as if he could see into my soul. Then the fucker smirked at me. Taunting me by implying that he was good enough to mate her, but I wasn't. And by only helping Amelia through the frenzy without mating her, I was admitting the same.

Source knew, *I* thought it was true. But hearing it, having it implied, by someone else, someone unworthy to breathe the same air as my cridhe, set my blood *boiling*. My stomach nearly betrayed me as my body jerked from one extreme to the other in a matter of heartbeats.

"The Rìgh will announce her mate at dawn. And, given her pedigree, Rìgh Thorn will undoubtedly choose someone civilized of good breeding as her mate." The steward sat straighter and continued to smile at me. So certain in his victory over us all.

All because he came from a well-to-do family within the Oc'Dellor. Because of his position in Rìgh Thorn's court. Because he was *civilized.*

Unlike me, an exiled prince from a rival clan. Bred for war, thrived on the battlefield, and utilized barbaric tactics in the process. Too rough for someone so fine and soft like the Oc'Dellor's princess. Only good enough to protect her from harm, not love and cherish her as she deserved.

I turned and looked this ripe piece of nocrys shit full in the face.

"Amelia will choose for herself," I murmured low. A ripple of unease seemed to shake the orckin males, reminding them of who I was and what I was capable of.

"And what happens when Rìgh Orok comes for her tomorrow? What happens if she hasn't decided by then?" The steward asked haughtily, his thin mouth thinning further as he scowled at me down his prominent nose.

"Then I will protect her." I couldn't help but imagine all the ways I could torture and kill this steward who thought his position entitled him to what was *mine*. "And I will slaughter anyone who dares to take away her choice."

Dead silence descended on the bathing caverns. Only the muted sound of rushing water echoed in the space. They all knew I meant it. Whether it was a Rìgh, a steward, or one of my friends, if they attempted to take her choice away, I could and would destroy them, regardless of the consequences. She deserved that much, at least.

But I wasn't entirely selfless in this. I was selfish enough to kill anyone who tried to take away her choice while also hoping she would choose me. Because she was my cridhe and I was hers.

I turned my back to them all and quickly finished bathing. Refusing to look at Hisouk, I cleaned my leather kilt and stalked out of the pool, buckling the wet leather garment on as I went. I didn't bother to dry off, didn't bother to re-plait my hair, just snagged my boots and shirt and left with my head held high.

If I stayed even a moment longer with all of those eyes on me, eyes that belonged to males who saw my cridhe more as a prize to be won than a female with a beautiful heart, the leash I kept myself on would snap. And I'd leave the bathing pools overflowing with blood.

The fresh bite of the evening air hit me like a slap to the face after all that stuffy heat. I let out a rough roar at the moons overhead, ridding myself of the worst of my rage. I huffed a breath in the quiet that followed, all the insects and nighttime creatures falling silent. But the rage came back stronger.

Snarling and full of hate, self-loathing, anger, and despair, I made my way back towards my home tree and my cridhe. My footfalls were heavy as I plodded toward her like I was on my way to the gallows. Instead of home to the other half of my soul.

AMELIA

After Manira escorted me back to my home tree, Sharn being too tired to take me herself, I went inside the house and lay down. I could hear Rorich talking in excited hushed tones to the calm and collected Manira down below. I couldn't keep the small smile off my face at their unofficial courtship. They were so sweet together it almost hurt like a horrendous cavity.

When Manira finally left, I found I couldn't sleep. Even as the last of the evening faded to full nighttime, I couldn't close my eyes. After a while, I realized why. I was waiting for Rhuger to come home.

For whatever ungodly reason, I wasn't as afraid of tomorrow as I knew I should have been. I wasn't upset or scared. It didn't feel real. As if I knew that horrible outcome would never happen to me. Because I knew Rhuger would protect me.

It was late when I heard soft footsteps on the stairs. I got up on shaky legs and made it to the door, opening it to the light of the moons and the sunstone lanterns. Rhuger paused at the top of the stairs, his hair tied back in a pony with the bit of leather that usually held his braid together. I couldn't keep my damned eyes off of the long sheaves of his hair, dark as midnight, as they shifted along his back as he moved.

"You're awake." He said flatly. That's when I registered his expression. His brows were drawn tight over his shuttered gaze, his lush sinful mouth pressed into a fine line, and a tic worked in his jaw. Rhuger was tense, on edge, and unhappy. And that was putting it mildly.

"Yes?" I replied softly, confusion and worry warring for top emotion. "I was waiting for you. Where have you been?"

"I had things to take care of." Came his clipped reply as he stalked to his hammock.

My chest constricted. Could he have sought relief with someone else after he left? He hadn't allowed me to touch him, hadn't given in to mate me. Blue balls weren't something most men tolerated back on Earth in my experience. I couldn't imagine it'd be much different here.

What had I said or done to ruin things? My mind started spinning in circles, and I had to shake myself. I'd done that with Adam. I'd be damned if I ever let that happen again.

"Did I do something wrong? Something to upset you?" I asked, confused and trying to stay calm.

"No." He said, pointedly not looking at me as he sat in his hammock and pulled off his boots.

"You've been avoiding me." It wasn't a question. He stiffened.

"Not everything is about you." He snapped, and I jerked.

"I'm sorry," I murmured. "I didn't realize I did that." My guts felt oily. I wasn't sure how I'd tried making everything about me, but it was the last thing I wanted.

He seethed where he sat in his hammock, glaring daggers at me before yanking his boot off and throwing it hard against the wall of my house. I flinched, and he grimaced. He muttered something in Black Tongue, likely some curse I hadn't learned yet before he wrenched out the leather strip and started braiding his hair.

"I don't want to be a burden." I began, licking my lips. "If it would be easier to have someone else be my bodyguard, then I'd appreciate it if you could let me know who I could trust."

Evidently, that had been the *wrong* thing to say. Stupid *fucking me* pushing him away out of fear of losing him while simultaneously trying to offer him space.

"You can't trust *anyone* in the clan. At least none of the males. And unfortunately, we have no female warriors anymore." He snarled, lip curling as if he were disgusted. Was he disgusted with me or was it something else?

"Then give me a sword and I'll protect my gotdamn self." I know the look I gave him wasn't quite sane. "If you refuse me that, then I'll just rip out their jugulars with my bare teeth."

"You wouldn't last." Rhuger's sharp words hurt.

"Wouldn't I? If you think my grandfather's knife tricks are all I know, you're sorely mistaken." My voice rose as I shoved my fists onto my hips, pissed that he thought so little of me and what I was capable of.

"And yet they didn't help you when you needed them most." He spat.

Slapping me would have done less damage.

"Something is better than nothing." I bit out. "And you have *no idea* of what you speak."

"I killed an orc to spare you. Was there when you fell apart afterward. I think I have a damned good *idea*." The snarl that contorted his features was a knife to the gut.

I froze, face paling. Not from fear, but rage. He opened his mouth to speak again, his expression telling me he realized he'd gone too far. But I would be damned if I let him utter another fucking word.

Fury uncoiled in me—something I hadn't felt in years. With lightning-quick precision, I executed a perfect axe kick to his groin. He nearly caught it, but I was fueled with fury and he was caught off guard.

It hit. He howled, clutching his nethers.

I didn't give him a chance to recover. Instead, I lunged forward with a flying knee kick to his face, snapping his head back. And as he swung back in the hammock, I swept down and grasped his ankle in my fist. I heaved with every ounce of strength I possessed and over the lip of the hammock he went, the railing whacking him in the head on the way down.

A moment later, I heard the *whomp* of him landing on the mossy ground below along with Hifasa's yowl of surprise. He groaned. I stood, looking over the railing as he got up on his hands and knees, shaking his head. Hifasa swatted him for disturbing her sleep. He flipped over onto his back from the force of her attack, breath whooshing out of his chest.

Rhuger's dazed eyes met mine in the dark. I just cocked an eyebrow at him, flipped him the double bird, and sauntered into *my* gotdamn house. I slammed the door behind me hard enough to rattle the wall.

How had everything gone to shit so fucking fast?

CHAPTER 47

RHUGER

I'd fucked up *again*.

Laying where I'd rolled after Hifasa had batted at me for disturbing her sleep, I stared up at the clouds that were quickly obscuring the stars and the moons. We'd have a storm before long.

How did I consistently manage to say and do the wrong things? How in the blackness between the stars did I keep self-sabotaging with the one person I couldn't hide from and longed to be with? What would it take for me to tell her how I felt? See if she'd accept me as a mate, if not a cridhe?

Slapping a hand against my face, I snarled as I wrenched my nose back into place. Her knee strike to my face had been quick, impressive even. Amelia was far more than anyone, me included, gave her credit for.

I could feel her hot anger, her pain, and her disappointment as if they were my own emotions. A legacy of the cridhe bond. Her anger was a front for the wilting of her heart. A wound that was of my own making.

I should have never thrown what had happened with Tintain in her face. It had been a festering wound all this time, just beneath the surface. Because I knew what it was like to be forced to give what you didn't want to. And I loathed that she had to experience that kind of helplessness here on Talam when she'd already left those kinds of memories back on Earth. I had no idea if she'd forgive me, but I knew what I had to do.

AMELIA

Sometime later Rhuger came and knocked on my door.

Curious but unwilling to make the first move, I stalked to the door in my bare feet and night dress. I made sure he could hear me coming. But I wasn't in a good enough mood to see his face without punching it. So I didn't open the door.

"It's me." His voice was thick and defeated. It made me wonder if I broke his nose. "You were right. I should not have taken my distress and anger out on you. And I definitely should not have thrown what happened in your face. I deserved what I got. I apologize, Amelia."

I stood there facing the door, arms crossed, and processed. His apologizing and admitting he'd been wrong was, well, surprising. As was the sincerity in his voice. I wasn't used to that. I was used to getting gaslit into thinking it was somehow my fault. Biting my lip, I kept silent.

"If you'll allow me to continue to protect you like I swore to do, I will." His voice trailed off into the gentle noises of the night. "You surprised me, you know."

His tone had changed, something edging towards admiration and amusement.

"It's not easy for seasoned orckin warriors to catch me off guard like that." On the other side of the door, I could hear him berating himself under his breath. "I hope you'll forgive me, or at least allow me the opportunity to make it up to you... goodnight Ame-"

I opened the door then and looked up into his startled face. Surprised to see that it didn't look like I'd broken his nose after all.

"Did you mean all that?" I asked, swallowing thickly past my heart.

"Yes. I was angry. Not at you. About... other things. I shouldn't have taken it out on you, and I hope to earn your forgiveness."

"You already have it," I told him and he looked astonished.

"What? Why?"

"You're a person too. You're allowed to have bad days. We just need to figure out how to communicate better when things are off. Okay?"

He just nodded thoughtfully.

"You can always talk to me, you know," I murmured. "When you're angry or have a lot on your mind. I'll listen and I won't judge. Okay?"

Again, he nodded, slightly stunned.

"I didn't fight back against that orc because..." I started, licking my lips, needing to find the words so he wouldn't think less of me. Like I was a hypocrite for knowing self-defense, yet hadn't been able to defend myself when I needed it most. Of everyone, he understood me the best, and I wanted him to understand this too. "My ex-husband was someone I trusted implicitly. When he... forced himself on me... I was so shocked. Shocked at the pain, shocked at the broken trust, shocked that he would do that when he'd professed to love me.

"Once I'd been able to see past the betrayal, all I could think about was surviving the encounter. It was like all of my foremothers whispered in my ear to hold still so it wouldn't hurt so bad. That if I held still maybe he'd let me live. I was already broken inside so I laid still until he was done. I didn't fight back because I trusted him and loved him and he hurt me at a moment of vulnerability. I didn't fight the orc because... memories from what happened with my ex-husband flooded me and made me panic, made me freeze."

Finally able to brave a look at him, I flinched at the utter devastation on his face.

"Brave female." He swallowed thickly and I could have sworn I could see the faint glimmer of tears he was holding back. "Why do you tell me this?"

"Because I don't want you to think less of me," I whispered. "I hope you'll understand me better now."

"I don't think less of you. You survived. That's more than anyone can ask for." Rhuger told me, voice hoarse. I just nodded and stepped back into the home tree.

Unsure of what to do or what this all meant, I just stood there awkwardly. I didn't have to explain all that to him, I just knew I wanted Rhuger to understand me better before I left. Because tomorrow wasn't all that far away now. And neither was my new future. One with a cruel Rìgh who I was plotting to murder if he so much as touched me.

There was so much left unsaid between Rhuger and me, but I couldn't bring myself to tell him how I felt about him. Not now. Maybe not ever. And it *hurt*.

"Goodnight, Rhuger," I whispered.

"Goodnight, pearl." He murmured, brow furrowing. Something in his eyes told me he was thinking the same thing. That this was the end of whatever had been budding between us. That our time was up.

I closed the door softly, heaved a heavy sigh, and tried not to collapse into tears.

Bright flashes of lightning lit my room and rumbling thunder crashed overhead. I sat up in bed, breathing hard at being woken up so suddenly. Just then, the heavens opened up and torrents of rain crashed down against the roof of the tree house. The sound was deafening.

And it was then that I remembered Rhuger was outside, sleeping in his hammock. Shit, he was going to get soaked and sick and possibly get hit by lightning if he didn't get indoors! I bolted from the bed, legs not quite working yet, and threw open the door. My furtive gaze landed on where he swung lazily in his hammock without his shirt or vest, hands locked behind his head, face tilted up to catch the rain.

I couldn't breathe at first. All that green skin limned in the flashes of lightning and dripping with the cool rain had my brain blanking as I stood stupidly in the torrential downfall. After a moment, he tilted his head towards me and opened his eyes. They glowed silver in the near-dark, his whole body screaming predator.

He blinked a few times before abruptly recognizing I was standing in the downpour, in nothing but my thin nightdress and shivering. Though I wasn't shivering from the cold. He rolled out of his hammock, bare feet slapping the floorboards of the porch before stalking to me and grasping me by the upper arms.

"What are you doing out here? Get inside. You're going to catch a chill!" He hollered above the rain. Then his eyes slipped from mine and drifted down to my breasts, where my nipples were clearly on display through the soaked fabric. A tic worked in his jaw as he gritted his teeth, the line of his mouth going flat.

"It's raining! Come inside before you get sick or struck by

lightning!" I cried, shoving my drenched hair out of my face before grasping his forearms.

"That is not a good idea, pearl!" He shouted, angrily.

"Why? I don't want you getting hurt!"

"You ask me that looking like this?" Rhuger railed, gesturing to my night slip and how it stuck obscenely to my body, to my curves and soft rolls, leaving nothing to the imagination. "You're inviting me, a male orc, into your home in the middle of the night, looking like every male's wet dream! Storm or no, that's implying something, pearl!"

A flush crawled up my chest and neck, threatening to make my face implode. Color riding high on my cheeks, I scowled at him.

"Fine! If you'd rather be out here where you'll drown in your sleep like a damn turkey staring too long at the storm, be my guest!" I doubted he knew what a turkey was, but holy hell, the deluge was enough to cause harm and I was genuinely concerned.

"That's not what this is about, and you know it!" Rhuger hollered, ushering me back towards the door.

I huffed out an angry breath and stood in the doorway, shoving hair out of my face. Ready to chew him out for being such a pain in my ass. Lightning struck somewhere in the city and thunder rolled over us, tight on its heels. The whole tree shuddered under its force. I squeaked as I was pushed back farther into the house, enveloped by Rhuger.

As if he could protect me from the wrath of the storm with his own body.

We stood there, clutching one another and breathing hard for a few moments, realizing that we weren't dead. That the thunder had passed. Then he shoved me out at arm's length, face a flat angry mask.

"Well, at least you're inside now," I growled, pulling free and stalking towards the door. I grasped the handle and slammed it. The sounds of the storm were still deafening, but at least I could hear myself think. Whirling on him, I pointed outside. "You thought it was safe to be out in that rather than just staying in here with me until the storm passed?"

"I'd rather face the storm, honestly." He muttered. I jerked as if he'd slapped me.

"Well, I'm sorry I'm such horrible company." I snapped and stomped for my bed.

"You're not." He said thickly. He got a face full of pillow for his efforts. Rhuger caught it and looked at me in shock. I just handed him a blanket.

"You could have fooled me." I hissed. "I wish I'd never gotten drugged with the luibh gaoil. It's ruined everything."

"You regret last night. What we did." It wasn't a question.

"Only if you're going to treat me like this after! You've done nothing but avoid me and be an asshole! I couldn't help that I'd gotten drugged!" I yelled, hurt. "No one explained what the luibh gaoil was!"

"I know, pearl. I'm not blaming you for that." Rhuger sighed heavily.

"Then what are you blaming me for?" I demanded, desperate for clarity.

He was quiet for a moment. "You don't know what you're doing. What this looks like."

"Oh." I scoffed. "So I can't know my own mind either?"

"Rìgh Thorn will not approve and-"

"I don't care!" I nearly shrieked. "I don't *care* what the clan thinks or my grandfather thinks, or anyone else, for that matter! I only care about-" Snarling, I ran my hands over my face in irritation, wishing I could shake some sense into him.

"What?" The word was quiet, demanding. I waved one of my hands over at him, flapping it to show I meant him. "Use your words, pearl." His voice was oddly flat and barely above a whisper.

"YOU!" I nearly growled, eyes going wide. "I only care what *you* think about me, okay?"

His expression softened as he stood there holding the pillow and blanket, dripping water all over my floor.

"You need to care, pearl. It looks like you've taken me as a mate when you bring me into your home at night." Rhuger spoke softly, every word clear as a bell.

My ears nearly sang with how hot they were. Would that be so bad? I could barely function without this orc in my thoughts. I wanted him, badly. Since that first day when he found me in the cave if I were honest with myself.

"And?" I snapped.

"Is that what you're intending? To take me as a mate?" He asked. I looked at him and his face was shuttered and haunted-looking. It made me pause, and re-evaluate. Why did he look like that?

"You say that like you wouldn't have a choice in the matter. You have a choice, you know. I won't force you." I murmured above the sounds of the storm.

Rhuger went absolutely still.

"I don't want anyone else," I told him honestly, anxiety riding high. "I *have* to find a mate before Rìgh Orok claims me as *his* mate or risk *war*. There's no choice for me. If you don't feel the same, I understand, okay?"

It's like those words snapped something inside him because

Rhuger threw the bedding aside and stalked to me, getting all up in my face.

"You could have any orc you wish as your mate out there. You are young, you are hearty and brave, and you are beautiful." He practically snarled at me, pointing out the window. Lightning flashed to punctuate his words, followed by thunder that shook the tree again. "You could demand whoever and whatever you wanted and get it."

"Why would I want them?" I asked, honestly confused by this odd change in direction. Didn't he say he wanted me last night? Go into very vivid detail about how he wanted to fuck me once the herb was out of my system? Didn't that mean he wanted to be my mate?

"Why would you want me?" He countered, frowning at me, gruff, nearly to the point of anger. His chest was heaving, and I had a hard time thinking past the urge to lean forward and lick the rainwater off of his pectorals.

"Why?" I asked breathily.

"Yes. Why."

"Because you've been kind to me, protected me. You haven't... taken... from me or hurt me. I'm more than just some prize to you." I told him. "Because of everyone, *you* are the only one to make me *feel* like this. *I can't stand* thinking of anyone else touching me. I trust you. I feel safe with you."

"I am not as good as you paint me to be, pearl." He growled, grimacing in pain as if my words hurt him. "Don't let the orgasms I gave you cloud your thinking! You didn't understand what you drank, what it meant, and what would happen. Last night was not of your clear-minded consent as it should have been! Now my intentions are anything but pure and there are far better orcs for you here than *me*."

Ah.

That's why he'd been in a foul mood all day and was so gotdamn grumpy.

All he saw in what happened last night was that I didn't know what I'd drank, that I would have taken anyone to my bed because of it, and that he was doing his duty to protect me. And he felt guilty for enjoying it. Guilty for stepping past that line of friendship into fuck buddy territory. Despite keeping his word not to mate me.

What this giant fucking *gumby* didn't seem to grasp was that if I *had* known what the luibh gaoil did... I would have drank *more of it*. Or, more accurately, I would have told him how I truly felt and learned how he felt first. *Then*, if everything was copacetic, I would have drank every fucking cup on that table.

"You're perfect, Amelia." Rhuger's voice cracked on my name and I froze.

"Have you ever thought to stop and consider maybe *I* think *you're* perfect, you gumby?" I asked him, incredulous. "I still can't fathom what you see in me, I'm fat and weird and opinionated and from a completely different planet. But I'm not stupid enough to let my self-worth issues impede having you in my life. You're more important to me than that."

"Pearl, I'm not a good male. I've killed, slaughtered, and *enjoyed it*. I'm a broken mess and I don't know if I'm capable of giving you what you deserve." His words pained him as they whispered past those damnably kissable lips. And suddenly, I was angry.

"You *absolute gumby*!" I bit out, getting up in his face. "Why the *hell* would I want what you're unwilling to give me? Why the *fuck* would I expect you to accept all of my faults and shortcomings but not accept yours? I want you for who and what you *are*. The good, the bad, the ugly, and the beautiful. *ALL OF IT*. I already *know* that you thrive in battle. It's been clear as day to me since we met. I may not thrive in battle like you do, but I admire it. I admire you."

I took a deep breath and watched his expression soften.

"I already *know* that you have your own nightmares and ghosts from your past that haunt you, that's obvious to me. I have my own nightmares and monsters. There's no way for me to know how you've built me up in your head, but I'm here to tell you that you've got it wrong."

He was quiet for a minute, processing. Finally, he swallowed and asked me in a soft voice, "What's a 'gum-bee'?"

I paused, then huffed a laugh, "Gumby is a… Story character who is tall and green and often silly."

"I kind of like it." He said and that lovely mouth that made me want to sin quirked up in a brief smile.

"Then I'll call you 'gumby' just like you call me 'pearl'. How about that?" Rhuger nodded at me, his expression was soft. And then, I got a little wicked idea. "Use your words, *gumby*. I need to hear you say it."

"Yes." He hissed as a shiver stole over him.

Oh, he liked getting a taste of his own medicine. But now wasn't the time to play, to test the limits of what we both could bear. I needed to clear the air, to make sure there weren't any more misunderstandings. I sighed and looked him in the eyes.

"Look, Rhuger. All I know is what you've shown me," I told him honestly, and quietly. Finally ready to admit to him what was in my heart. "I fell in love with you a while ago. On that very first day you found me if I'm honest. I would have taken you to my bed *without* the luibh gaoil in a heartbeat if I'd known you felt the same. I haven't sought a mate because, for me, there's nobody else but you."

He froze at that.

"You're handsome and kind and you have the females in a tizzy over you. You must have a sweetheart or lover among the males, as you said happens. I... shouldn't have assumed last night meant something. Shouldn't have assumed you might feel the same way I do. I'm sorry." I ducked my head, attempting to hide my shame and heartache.

The yawning, black emptiness was threatening to swallow me whole again. I felt cold—like it was snatching away what small warmth I'd regained this past week. I don't know why I'd hoped this would be different. That maybe Rhuger might cherish me instead of being doomed to a lifetime of being used by guys like Orok.

Suddenly, the need for air and space was overwhelming, and I darted toward the door. Monsoon be damned. In a blink, he stood before me, face shuttered. Frozen, I shivered as he lifted one large hand and cupped my face in its warmth. His thumb traced my bottom lip, and I realized he was watching the tears that were falling from my damnable eyes.

"It meant something." He whispered.

The silence stretched out between us as the rain battered the roof overhead. I took a breath to speak, but he rushed into the silence.

"There isn't another, either." The words tripped over themselves on their way past his lips. "You're like a dream, pearl. I'm afraid I'll wake and you'll be gone."

Well, that wasn't what I'd expected.

It must have shown on my face because he raised his other hand so he could cup my cheeks. His thumbs skirted them, wiping away my tears. I lifted my own hands and rested them on the outside of his. Wanting to press his palms against my cheeks, but refraining.

"What do you want, Rhuger?" I whispered into the quiet between us. His thumbs paused as his eyes bored into mine. Turned to molten silver rings as his eyes dilated.

"What do *I* want?" His voice was low, brushing against my skin like velvet.

"Yes."

His expression shifted into something fierce as his gaze devoured me. Rhuger started breathing heavier, and his hands trembled against my cheeks as if he was barely restraining himself. He swallowed hard before he spoke.

"I want to drown in those uisge-beatha eyes of yours. I want to feel these lovely neamhnaid hands all over my skin. I want that tiny pink tongue of yours on my cock." He growled like some feral beast. As if his words were conjuring things he'd only imagined in his mind. And here I stood, his willing prey, already in his clutches. "What I want is to wrap myself up in all of your softness for the rest of my days, pearl. I want to fall asleep with my cock buried inside you each night and awake to your smile every morning. I want you for my own. As my mate."

He took a step closer to me. Close enough now that I had to tilt my head all the way back to hold his gaze as he towered over me. Something about being a big woman and having a guy be bigger and taller than you, so, for once, you felt dainty... Well, it made me fucking *weak.*

He made me weak and willing to surrender completely for the first time in my life.

"The moment I found you within the Croabh na Beatha, I lost my heart. Stolen, yet kept safe, by the only person who has ever bothered to truly see me. All of me. You." His words came out in a rasp. "I have never been more grateful for anything else in my life."

My heart cracked for him at that. They should have seen him for who he was all this time. Understood and cared for him. Not feared and shoved him into a persona that fit their narrative. So many people in his past treated him like the devil, and eventually, he believed them. I hoped I could someday show him how I saw him.

As my battle-worn, scarred, and magnificent champion. As someone who never let the darker parts of his life win, no matter how brutal the struggle. Someone who shone brilliantly like the North Star amongst the star-flecked heavens, unable to see his own light because it shone brighter than any other. The one person I could call *home.*

"I thought I'd never have a mate. But since I found you, all I can think about is making you mine. I can't breathe, I can't sleep, I can't even eat without you plaguing my thoughts and dreams." He shuddered, his words mirroring my feelings. "You should fear me for how much I want you, pearl."

Rhuger was so close that I could feel the heat of him and his breath whispering against my lips.

"I see you Rhuger. And I am not afraid." I murmured, our lips nearly brushing as his eyes opened wide in surprise. Some broken, strangled sound caught in his throat. Pressing his forehead against mine, he let out a shuddering breath.

"If you don't want this, say so now and I will leave." He was shivering from restraining himself, gentle and thoughtful of me even now. "If you want another, tell me and I will leave. If you give yourself to me, I won't... I won't be able to share." His throat bobbed as his voice cracked on those words. "Once I fully taste you, I won't be able to live without you."

And it wasn't even a question. Of course, I wanted all of that from him. And of course, I didn't fear him. He'd never given me a genuine reason to be afraid. I wanted him. There was no one else I'd ever wanted more than Rhuger. Even if I could go home to Earth, I sure as hell wouldn't go without him, live without him.

So, with a small noise, I closed the distance between us, kissing him fiercely. Showing him I wanted this. Wanted him.

He froze in surprise, but with a lick of my tongue against the seam of his devilish mouth, he growled and opened for me. Our lips and tongue and teeth were a whirlwind of hunger as he hauled me against him. With a snarl, he pulled away and I was left breathless.

"This isn't the herb still in your system, pearl?" His breathing was ragged, hands fisted in my wet hair. The hard planes of his body felt so damnably *right* against the soft curves of mine, and my pussy throbbed relentlessly as more than just rainwater dripped down the insides of my thighs.

"No, I'm sober. You're the... the Rìgh mo cridhe. And I'm not into sharing either. Just shut up and kiss me, Rhuger." I hissed, fingertips trembling as they explored his chest. The answering rumble beneath my fingertips, a heated growl, made my toes curl against the floorboards.

"As you wish." He whispered against my lips. The kiss he gave me then wasn't the devouring of just moments before, but sinfully, delectably slow. It didn't take long before I was moaning into his mouth, my arms wrapped around his neck. My body pressed as close to his as I could get.

He reached down without breaking the kiss, grasped me by the backs of my thighs, and easily hoisted me up so I could wrap my legs around his hips. *Fuck* he felt so damned good where the length of him pressed against the apex of my thighs. Rhuger groaned into my mouth as he walked us to the bed.

Our bed.

CHAPTER 48

RHUGER

Gods, I'd been such a *thrice damned idiot.*

To think all this time, she'd already been in love with me, and I'd been too blind to see it. Too unwilling to believe someone would find me worthy of being their mate, their lifelong partner. And when she'd said those three words... *Rìgh mo cridhe.* The last of my self-doubt and denial, my defenses, just crumbled away.

To her, I was the king of her heart. Her cridhe as much as she was mine. Why had I waited so long? Every reason I'd had seemed trivial, shallow, and stupid now.

Knowing her mouth on mine, her perfect little hands sinking into my hair, and her thick thighs wrapped tightly around my hips was all of her own choosing, nearly made me take her right there on the floor. But she was my cridhe and deserved the downy plushness of a bed beneath her as I fucked her into it. As I pushed myself as deeply into her softness as I could go.

So I walked towards the bed, *our* bed now. The way the luscious curves of her hips and ass overflowed my hands, and her weight pressed against me was heaven. She'd called herself *fat*. As if she'd thought herself too heavy, too plump, for me to hoist or carry as I saw fit.

Foolish female. It'd been a habit I was bound to break her of. Just as I was bound to watch her break and fall apart beneath me. As often as she'd let me until the stars went out.

When we reached the bed, I unhooked her ankles from behind my back and flung her onto the bed like a sack of grain. She let out a delightful squeak as she bounced on the mattress. I paused, watching all of her pillowy curves jiggle and ripple with the movement beneath her soaked night dress.

Unable to hold back any longer, I pounced atop her. Amelia laughed, a heady sound that I couldn't help but grin over. Source, her laughter was contagious and melted the moment from pure fiery passion to something far more intimate. Something I'd only share with her.

Amelia's strange smile, with its blunted teeth, drew my gaze as she giggled beneath me. Her cheeks were rosy, and she looked genuinely happy. The realization that I caused her joy took my breath away. To think I'd one day not only find my cridhe but be a source of happiness to her was beyond what I'd ever hoped for.

I felt the smile fall from my face, and Amelia looked up at me with those enormous, trusting, uisge-beatha eyes as her smile softened and her cheeks stained pink. Slowly, I dipped my head and brushed my lips against hers. My braid slithered over my shoulder to drape against the pillow next to us as she wound her arms up around my neck. Pulling me down to her in a gentle command.

And like any good penitent, I obeyed.

AMELIA

The feel of Rhuger pressing atop me, into me, as I wrapped my legs around his waist was enough to melt me into a puddle of bliss. I'd never known until now how much I'd ached for him my whole life. He was the missing piece, the other half of my being. And I devoured him greedily.

Our mouths met and parted and met again. Our breath intermingled as our tongues and teeth intertwined along with our limbs. Rhuger braced himself on his forearms on either side of my face, kissing me as if I were a delicacy he wanted to savor.

Shifting his weight, he skimmed a hand along my side, down to my thigh. He slipped his long, thick fingers under the hem of my wet night dress and skirted his palm against the curve of my hip. My mind swam, so drunk with him I could barely think.

There was one thing I wanted to do. *Needed* to do. To let Rhuger know how much I loved and desired him. So that from now on, he'd have no more doubts.

"Wait!" I cried and put a hand on his chest.

Rhuger pulled back slightly, rumbling incoherently, his expression as intoxicated as I felt. Before I could question it, I sat up and rolled, shoving him back, so he was lying down. Surprise lit Rhuger's expression and a haunted sort of hunger when I kneeled between his sprawled legs.

I reached for his kilt, but he'd already read my intention and was unbuckling it. He was impatient and started having trouble getting his shaking hands to cooperate. My heart swelled with emotion, and I gently batted his hands away.

With a few tugs, I had his kilt undone. Before I could blink, he'd ripped it out from under himself as if it burned him, tossing it as far from us as he could. Like I might change my mind and cover him back up with it. I couldn't help the giggle that escaped me. His gaze snapped to mine, where I had a hand clamped over my mouth.

"What?" He growled.

"Eager, are we?" I laughed, my hand dropping to curl against the front of my wet night slip. "I won't change my mind, you know."

"Of course, you won't." He said with a sinful, smug grin before flopping back on the bed, and tucking his arms behind his head.

It caused the planes of his chest and stomach to stretch and elongate, still glistening from the rain. And if my attention, and my gaze, wasn't already trailing down the utter perfection of him, the teasing bastard pulled up one of his massive legs and tipped it outwards. Posing just to put himself on display for me.

Bringing all of my attention to the very erect, very thick heft of his cock where it jutted proudly from his groin above his large sac. I couldn't help the heat that rose to my cheeks or how my thighs squeezed together at the sight of him. How my heartbeat and breathing quickened at finally seeing him up close.

My tongue darted out to wet my lips. He stilled.

I looked up at him, and his gaze was intent on my mouth. Teasing him, I flicked out my tongue to lick at my lips again. His cock bobbed hard, pre-cum beading at the pronounced head. He hadn't lied about wanting to see my tongue on him, then.

The poor guy was trying to play it off like I wasn't affecting him so badly. And it was then I realized I really held all the power with him. He was letting me lead. Afraid I would stop and desperate for me to continue doing to him whatever I wanted.

It was... *heady*, the power I had over him. I couldn't help the grin that split my face. Both at my own mental pun and at this sweet male. He looked at my expression, confused. *Adorable.*

I just winked and blew him a kiss before turning my attention back to the beast nearly in hand.

I'd seen plenty of human dick. None of it was that impressive, to be honest. Especially to someone of my size. But Rhuger?

The orc was fucking *hung*. Definitely a shower. His cock wasn't as big as the womb-splitter orc from the day I came through the portal. No, not that big. But holy shit, I was doubting he would even *fit*. He was thick, long, and curved up towards his stomach, nearly to his navel.

Not only that, but his anatomy was a bit, well, *different*.

It looked relatively close to a human cock from a distance. Sac, shaft, head—the basics.

His coloring was the obvious difference. The dark sage green of him down at the base of his shaft, fading to pale cucumber along his length. The foreskin was dusky pink, and the tip that peeked past was a bright ruby red, flushed with blood.

But up close, there were some more definite differences.

For one, his shaft, instead of looking like one cylindrical unit, appeared like it had four connected lengths, with four vertical grooves between them. There was a bulge towards the center of his shaft that I couldn't understand the function of yet. He was ribbed, both top and bottom. And the veins stood out in sharp detail, even against the ridges.

He made some of the more outlandish sex toys I'd purchased back on Earth look tame.

The head of his cock came together and looked more like a human tip, flared and slick with one deep divot that seeped pre-cum like a fountain. The difference came in that those four grooves were only less defined than on the shaft and only slightly visible underneath his foreskin.

I could feel his eyes on me as I studied him and learned his differences visually. Finally, I drummed up the courage and touched the length of his shaft with my fingertips. Rhuger made a noise in his throat, and his cock bobbed so hard it nearly smacked into my palm.

Looking into his eyes, they practically glowed as his mouth hung open, watching as my fingers traced the veins and the grooves in his cock. He moaned when I slid an index finger into a groove along his shaft.

Startled, I looked up to gauge his reaction, and his chest was heaving, eyes heavy-lidded with pleasure. It seemed those grooves were sensitive. Curiosity piqued, I used both hands to explore him. My fingers couldn't wrap completely around his thick shaft. And that knowledge alone made my pussy clench on nothing, hungry to be filled.

Moving my hands lower, I cupped his sac. Rhuger hissed as I gently massaged first the right side, then the left. He seemed to have two testes like human men, only larger, and I gently rolled them and cupped them as I inhaled his musky, sweet scent. I skimmed both thumbs into both underside grooves as I took his shaft back into my hands.

"Dammit, pearl, what are you doing?" He hissed, hips bucking slightly.

"I'm sorry. You're so different. I was exploring. Did I hurt you or make you uncomfortable?" I asked him, snatching my hands back.

"No!" He shouted, holding out a hand. "No, quite the opposite."

"You... like what I was doing?" I asked hesitantly, looking him in the eyes. He swallowed thickly and jerked a nod. I looked down. His cock was practically squirting pre-cum at me, and that bulge in the center of his shaft had gotten bigger.

"I need you to say it, gumby," I whispered as I looked up at him from under my lashes.

"Naughty lass." He growled, but his lopsided smirk betrayed his tone. "Yes, sweet temptress, I very much like what you were doing to me."

Hearing him talk like that was so fucking sexy. I licked my lips. Settling over him, I laid down between his spread legs and propped myself up on my elbows. Taking him into my hands again, I tilted him where I wanted him and watched as pre-cum slid from his slit, down his shaft to the mattress.

Rhuger's breathing hitched, and I flicked my gaze up to his before I slowly lowered my head. I paused an inch above him, breathing on the ruby-red tip of his crown. Rhuger's cheeks flushed a vibrant green, and his eyes were heavy-lidded as he panted at the sight of me hovering over his dick.

I gave the tip a feather-light kiss, and he made a strangled sound in his throat. Pre-cum pushed past the loose seam of my mouth and that's when I had my first taste of him. My shoulders slumped and my eyes rolled back into my head as I downright *moaned* against his cock at the taste. Creamy and sweet and ever so slightly salty, with a hint of male musk.

He was fucking *delicious*. Like homemade salted caramel.

Ducking my head, I tipped it to the side as I licked at his sac and dragged my tongue up his shaft in long, luxurious strokes. I didn't want to waste a drop of this. He was so damn *tasty*. I braced my elbows on either side of his hips and settled myself in to swallow him whole.

Rhuger began a hitched litany of Black Tongue as his black-clawed hand came down to run through my hair. When I licked my way up to his crown, I glanced up at him from under my lashes. I let my pink tongue show before I began my lick at his frenulum, dragging it up his head, and letting the tip of my tongue slide into the deep slit that dripped for me.

Rhuger gasped hard, hips jerking up against my chest where I had his thighs pinned beneath me. His eyes were locked on my face, so I smiled. And then I tilted my head and slipped him into my mouth.

"Amelia!" He cried my name as he bucked beneath me. I loved how he reacted to me, but I wouldn't let him face fuck me, though. I wanted to savor his flavor, and that meant he had to stay where he was. "That's right, pearl. Take my cock in that tight little pink mouth of yours." His words cracked as they ground out between his teeth.

I obliged. He was thick enough that I was straining my jaw wide so as not to use my teeth. I was damn thankful I didn't have sharp teeth like the orckin. I wrapped my lips over my teeth and began dragging my mouth up and down his length. Tonguing every ridge and groove as I suckled his massive cock.

My hands massaged his balls and ran up and down his base, fingertips trailing in the creases and along the veins on his shaft. I moaned around him as I worked him as deep into my mouth as I could get him. It was only a little more than halfway before he hit the back of my throat.

Every time I stroked my lips or fingers over that bulge in his cock, cum would rush out into my mouth. Delighted, I milked him as I drank him down like the luibh gaoil. Rhuger hissed. I flicked my gaze to his face, and his black and silver eyes were wild as he slid his hand down to cup my cheek.

I moaned against him again, releasing him from my mouth with an audible *pop* before lapping at the pre-cum leaking a steady stream from his slit. Gods, I loved the way he tasted, loved how he responded to me, how I pleased him. My panties were already soaked, and not from the rain.

"Shit, pearl, that little pink tongue of yours is going to be the death of me." He groaned.

I loved the sounds he was making. The moans, hisses, groans, and heavy breathing. All intermingled with words I had yet to learn in Teanga Dhubh. I was getting *really* wet listening to how good I was making him feel.

Pulling back, I let my lips drag against his head. I licked his head in one long stroke, so he could see how my little pink tongue gathered his slick before I swallowed it. Showed him all the small ways I'd been fantasizing about him since we'd met.

"Shit." Rhuger rasped before switching to a litany of moaning Black Tongue. Hand cradling my head as he kept himself propped up on his elbow to watch. I slid his length inside my mouth again, and he flung his head back with a hissing growl.

"Oh gods, pearl. You're so fucking beautiful, sucking me like that." He groaned, and I chuckled with his length in my mouth. He cried out and tried to buck up into my mouth again. Unable to do so, he rocked against my chest as if unable to control his hips.

"Stroke my knot. Lick it like a *good lass*." He crooned, and I did as I was told. I was rewarded with a ragged moan. "Och, just like that, pearl. *Just like that...*"

His hips kept thrusting against me with growing urgency as I continued to suckle and stroke him. Breathing ragged, he fisted my hair in his fingers, and I could tell he was close. With one last dive as far as I could take him, I sucked *hard*. Rhuger roared as I milked him with my mouth and tongue. His hot, delicious cum shot down my throat, and I gulped it.

My mouth created a tight seam, so I was able to carefully swallow it all. I kept teasing him with my tongue, and I could feel his cock throb and jerk in my mouth as he released more than any human I'd ever gone down on. His orgasm lasted a hell of a lot longer, too. Rhuger's rough moaning nearly sent me over the edge as he caressed my face.

RHUGER

Once I fell back onto the bed in a limp tangle of limbs, I watched as she pulled her mouth gently from my cock. It popped free from between her lips and listed to the side, only half-hard now. She gently pointed it back toward her mouth. There was still a droplet of cum on the tip and, with a feather-light lick, she swept the bead from my crown onto that delightfully wicked pink tongue. I shuddered underneath her, little aftershocks of pleasure rippling over my body at her touch.

"You... you swallowed it all," I whispered, jaw slack with awe.

Mating was often a messy business. Orckin males came quite a bit, and it was often too much to swallow. It was common for it to rush out of our mates or pleasure mates' mouths to dribble down their chins. Or for them to pull free as soon as we hit climax, milking us to splash on their bodies instead. It wasn't often they could swallow it all.

"Yes. Of course. You're delicious." She said as if it were the simplest, easiest thing in the world. Shrugging one shoulder, she kissed my crown and got to her hands and knees, releasing my hips from her hold.

I watched her movements with rapt, predatory intent. With a brazen hand, I reached down and cupped her dangling breast. They were lush, my cridhe's breasts. Full enough to overflow my hand, yet small enough to readily play with. I kneaded it, marveling at the silkiness of it, and flicked the nipple with a claw. Her hips bucked backward, and she sighed a needy moan.

So sensitive, my mate. I loved it. Loved that she responded to my merest touch or breath the way she did. Her gaze, when it met mine, was lust-drunk, and she bit her full bottom lip between her blunt teeth. She'd lavished me with her attention. Now it was my turn.

"I liked what you said earlier." I breathed, lifting my knees behind her thighs in silent demand that she crawl up to where I could kiss her. She did, and I claimed her mouth with mine. When I released her, I continued, "What you called me."

"What?" Amelia asked as she crawled up my body like some lithe nocrys female in heat. Watching her hips and ass sway behind the face that I loved so much left me lightheaded as my knot flooded with cum again.

I guided her up to where she could straddle my hips with my hands, the tips of her breasts brushing against the bottom of my chest through her damp nightdress. Pressing my hands gently against her shoulders, I pushed her up, so she braced herself with her hands against my chest, her ass still slightly in the air. Baring my teeth, I let my hands wander up and down her hips, thighs, and stomach. Marveling at the feast before me.

Gasping at my touch, she watched as I devoured her with my gaze. When I locked eyes with hers under my brows, I reached up to the neckline of the dress and pulled. A small cry escaped her as the fabric ripped. I shredded it to ribbons between my claws as I tore the slip from her body.

Amelia's tiny claws sank into my flesh and the slight pain mingled with the pleasure of seeing her atop me. She still wore her undergarment that hugged her generous ass, and though I wanted to be mindful of her belongings, I'd waited far too long for this. Groaning, I curved my broad palms down her low back to cup her ass roughly. She panted and wiggled against me. I jerked her down so her mound pressed and ground against my cock. Only the lacy fabric of her undergarment between us.

So I slipped my hands under the black lacy thing and yanked. The fabric gave just as easily as her nightdress and I tossed the scraps aside. She now sat atop me, bare and lush and beautiful. Free of the undergarment, her wetness slid against my cock and I hissed at the slick feel of her, the heat of her.

The tip of my cock peeked out from underneath the soft swell of her belly, her warm softness pressing down and around it was sweet torture. I rocked up against her, holding her hips right where I wanted them. Amelia gasped out a breathy moan at the friction. Gods, I loved the erotic expression on her face and the sounds she made for me.

I sat up, propping my elbow on the mattress, and slipped my hand up into her soft waves. I grasped her hair between my fingers and clenched my fist. Just hard enough to bare her throat to me. The lovely curve of it made my mouth water, made me want to sink my sharp teeth into it to taste her in all ways. To mark her as *mine*.

She liked it when I did this to her. So I pulled a little harder, and she ground into me, coating my cock with her juices. Her breath came faster and her nipples hardened to little pebbles before my eyes. She stared down at me, and the look in her gaze stole my breath. Drawn to her beauty like a moth to a flame, I sat up fully and grazed my lips against hers.

"I liked it when you called me the Rìgh of your heart," I whispered against her mouth. Her lips quivered against mine and a small, needy sound escaped her. "I want you to call me that when we are together like this. Call me your Rìgh."

"Yes, my Rìgh." My pearl's voice turned sultry, her body going loose-limbed and pliant. She enjoyed this, my dominance. Almost as much as I craved her submission.

My breathing grew ragged as she breathed those words against my mouth. I'd never cared much for titles. But hearing the title I would have had, fall from her kiss-swollen lips? *Absolute perfection.*

My erection swiftly became thick and throbbing against the sensitive flesh of her core. I rolled my hips up to meet her precisely where we both wanted to be. The ridges along the bottom of my cock grazed against her clit as I thrust. She cried out exquisitely into my mouth and I nearly lost my mind.

"Pearl, will you let me fully mate you? Will you give your Rìgh the greatest of gifts of being inside you? Of being your mate? Of filling you with my seed until you swell with our child?" I groaned against her trembling lips. My leash was about to snap for good.

"Yes, my Rìgh." she shuddered against my hold. And a rush of fresh wetness coated my cock as her pussy quivered against me. The moment Amelia had spoken those words and ground her need against mine, I flew into action.

Every ounce of me roared in unrelenting, primal need each time she called me her Rìgh. The words were like luibh gaoil in my blood. Singing and drawing forth an irresistible desire to stay knotted within her until she conceived. No matter how long it took.

All rational thought fled as my leash well and truly snapped. All I could think of was planting my thick cock inside her soft cunt. Of thrusting into her until we both came, just to do it all over again. But I was her Rìgh. And like any good Rìgh, I had to see to her needs before my own.

So when I flipped us over, rolling so that I was on top of her, my cock pressing at her entrance, I didn't sink it into her as my instincts demanded. Instead, I made my way down her lush body. Kissing and licking and caressing every inch of the lusty goddess I was about to call my mate.

My mate.

Despite her calling me her Rìgh, I would grovel and beg and

debase myself before her. Because what was a Rìgh compared to a goddess? Just another worshiper. And oh, how I would worship at the altar of her body. From now until the day I died.

I parted the damp curls of her seam with my long black tongue. Her slick honey coated my tongue and the taste of her exploded in my mouth. Sweet and musky and all Amelia. Her hips jerked as I growled against her core, her taste and scent invading my senses. Wrapping my arms under her ass and over her hips, I pulled her tight to me.

Her moaning and panting was the sweetest symphony as I lapped at her pussy, slipping my tongue as deep inside of her as I could. No matter how hard she squirmed, I held her firm to my mouth. With a lewd sound, I pulled my tongue from her and replaced it with my fingers, claws retracted. My tongue found her clit, and she cried out as I laved it and fucked her with two of my fingers.

Gods, she tasted like heaven as she writhed beneath me. I could lick and suck and drink down her juices every day for the rest of my life and still crave more of her on my tongue.

Memories of the night before crowded my mind. Of the night spent wringing every last cry of pleasure from her as the luibh gaoil flooded her system. A night that was seared into my memories. Only tonight, I'd finally get to do what I'd been fantasizing about since I'd found her.

I slipped a third finger inside of her and began rubbing the pads of my fingers along that sweet spot inside of her I'd discovered. That delightful place that made her come undone so quickly. She screamed then, pussy clenching hard against my fingers, tiny claws sunk into my scalp as she shoved and rubbed my face against her orgasm. I growled in fierce pleasure at causing her release, my face buried in her pillowy softness.

Her juices spurted against my chin and hand. I grinned to

myself as I pulled away from her. She lay there, thick thighs and hips twitching as her juices leaked from her pussy. She was the most exquisite thing I'd ever seen.

My cock throbbed hard, and I could deny myself no longer. I leaned over her and captured her mouth with mine. Letting her have a taste of her own sweetness.

"Are you ready, my goddess?" I crooned against her lips, my cock rubbing up and down her clenching core. Oh, she was more than ready, but I wanted to hear her say it. Needed to hear it.

Because no matter how much I took control of this, it was her commands I was following.

"My Rìgh…" she breathed, sending me hurtling towards madness. "Oh yes! Please. I need you inside of me!"

"Good lass. Such lovely manners should be rewarded." I growled.

Shuddering at her delightful pleas, I slowly angled myself, cock in hand. I'd never done this before, sunk my cock into a female's sheath. I was nervous I might hurt her, as I was much larger than all three of my biggest fingers, longer.

Steeling my nerve, I went slow. If she whimpered or cried out in pain, I would stop. Even if it killed me to do so.

"Tell me if it hurts, pearl," I growled, and she nodded. Unable to think past my warring needs to be careful and to be inside her—I couldn't demand her to voice her consent beyond her nod.

With a gradual and deliberate press of my hips, I pushed the tip of my cock inside her wet hot heat. She gasped and threw her long, juicy thighs around my waist, clutching me to her as her pussy clenched around my cock.

Source, she was so *tight*.

I grit my teeth against the onslaught of sensations. Her heavy breathing caused her breasts to press against my chest. The painfully pleasurable tightness of her pussy, the marvel of her slick heat, and how gods damned *good* it felt to push inside of her. To have her flesh give and stretch and clutch at the hardness I drove into her waiting cunt.

"Oh, Rhuger, oh gods, you're so big!" she gasped into my ear, breathing light and heartbeat fluttering against the heavy thumping of my own. Her words sank in and I paused, the crown of my dick now firmly planted inside of her.

"Am I hurting you?" I asked between gritted teeth. It wouldn't do to come when I wasn't even fully inside her yet.

"No! You feel so fucking good, my Rìgh." Amelia gasped, whimpering her desires into the shell of my ear. "More, I need more! I need all of you inside me!"

With a snarl and a blinding surge of lust that nearly made me reach release, I pressed into her again. So tight, my pearl. My love. My *mate.*

After decades of searching for her, I'd finally found her. Was finally claiming her. The female I'd spend the rest of my life with. The female I'd seek day and night to please and sire orclings upon. To care for and protect. The female who was impatiently drawing me further inside of her by using her heels against my ass to press me deeper. Her desperate desire matching my own.

In an exhilarating rush, I felt my testicles clench, my slick thickening with seed. I stilled above Amelia, my cock not even halfway inside of her, and resisted her demanding heels against my ass. Shudders wracked my body as I resisted the pulse of my knot as it sought to spend.

I couldn't call myself an orc, couldn't call myself her Rìgh, if I couldn't ensure she reached the apex of her pleasure before me. But she wasn't making it easy.

CHAPTER 49*

AMELIA

"Hold still, pearl." He hissed above me. Surprised, I looked up to see that his face was contorted.

"What's wrong, Rhuger?" I asked, breathless. Wanting to make sure he was okay.

"You're tight, my love. If you move now, I -" He clenched his eyes shut, and a shudder wracked him. I realized then that he was so close to coming, one clench from me and he'd go over the edge.

I knew he didn't want that. He was struggling so hard not to. But I didn't want him to think I'd be disappointed if he came early, either.

So, I reached up and cupped his cheeks with my hands. His eyes shot open, oceans of black with slim rings of silver. All I could do was smile up at him with all the warmth I possessed.

"It's okay if you come now. It's okay." I murmured, willing my body to calm. To let him choose and lead. He shuddered, his expression turning fierce before he turned his head to kiss my palm.

"Not for me." He whispered, voice raw.

"Why?" I asked, rubbing his jaw and distracting him with my words and my hands. Allowing him a diversion so he could regain the control he was fighting so hard for.

"I've had a long time to think about what I would do and how I would do it if you ever let me into your bed." He whispered, eyes shuttered and hungry. "I was a fool. Thinking that I'd be the one masterfully taking you. Making you shiver and come undone at my touch."

"Well, you did that yesterday." I chuckled, and he smirked wickedly before turning solemn again.

"I never knew how hot and tight and *wonderful* you'd feel. How it would be to be buried not even halfway between your thighs, your long soft legs wrapped around me." His hand skimmed my thigh where it was hitched up over his hip, and I shivered. "Your arms holding me like this. So sweet and lovely, my pearl. You're a goddess. More than I ever wished for."

A soft smile curved my lips as he spoke. His words were so much a male's outlook, yet so indescribably loving. I'd never felt more beautiful in my whole life than I did at this moment. Who thought a rough rogue of an orc from a whole other planet would be such a sweet talker?

"I'm overcome." He rasped above me, eyes open, vulnerable. "I'm lost... Yours as surely as you are mine."

"Yes," I murmured as he kissed my palm again. "Yours. Your pearl. Your love. Yours."

That haunted, hungry look stole across his face. And it hit me then that he still thought I'd disappear like a dream. So I pulled him down to me and kissed him with every ounce of love in me. Every bit that I had left after wasting it on someone who didn't deserve it. Tears slipped free as I not only gave him my body, but my heart, too.

What was left of it.

"You're mine, Rhuger. My love." I whispered against his lips. He moaned my name and sunk himself into me, both between my thighs and between my lips.

I shuddered and gasped, back arching as he slid in to the hilt. He was so thick that accommodating him skirted that edge of pain. He began murmuring a lilting string of Black Tongue as he kissed my neck, and my cheek, sinking his hands into my hair until I moaned his name into the shadows between us.

Then his mouth found mine, his tongue slipping deep and sure and gentle against mine. And as our mouths met and parted and met again, he rocked against me gently. So careful and restrained as he worked me to fit the slide of his cock.

He pulled back then to look at me. And a thousand words were written in his eyes as he gently brushed my hair away from my face. I turned, my eyelashes fluttering, and kissed his palm, lips dragging against his skin. I looked up at him from under my lashes and his mouth parted before he pulled out of me.

I moaned and clutched at the sudden loss of him. But a moment later, he slid back inside of me with a smooth thrust of his hips, and I cried out for him. It registered then, as he began a measured rolling rhythm, that he hadn't broken eye contact.

He was watching me. Watching me writhe and moan beneath him like a starving man and I was a feast. Like if he looked away, I would break. He would break. A shattered dream.

I *loved* the way he was being so tender and sweet with me. How beautiful this kind of lovemaking was. And I didn't want him to think he would break me with his passion.

I wanted him. I wanted all of him. He could break his passion against me and I would take it like the shore took the pounding waves. Gladly. I wanted to watch him lose his control. Wanted him to let go with me and give in to what was building between us.

So I pulled my legs from around his waist, to his surprise, and planted my feet on the bed. Before he could stop, with an undulating arch of my body, I rose to meet his thrust. His careful control seemed to shatter then.

His breathing hitched as I rose to meet each of his thrusts with my own. By now, I was openly moaning, not caring if the entire clan outside heard me. He felt so damn good. Rhuger shifted, grasped my hip in one large hand, and began pounding into me in earnest.

His size and power became overwhelming, and I felt my orgasm build in waves from my slowly curling toes to my shaking thighs. The sharp slap of flesh against flesh, the hiss of Teanga Dhubh as he growled above me, and the slick sounds of our joining, our ragged breathing, were the most erotic symphony. My hands roamed his chest and shoulders, unable to drag him close enough to sate me.

My cries hit a new pitch as I felt the orgasm climb towards its peak, my walls quivering around him. His breathing grew shallow and his thrusts erratic. He canted his hips just right, and every thrust slicked his head *hard* against that sweet spot inside of me.

Before I knew it, I was screaming his name, dragging my nails across his back, and splintering into a million shards of light as the orgasm crashed over me. Drowning me in wave after wave after wave of pleasure.

He roared my name into my neck, his teeth scoring the tender flesh there and causing me to buck against his wild thrusting as he nearly crushed me into the mattress. Heat flooded inside of me, and I swear I could feel each spurt of his seed as it filled me. The knowledge and sense of him coming inside of me sent me right over the edge again, and I cried out as I milked him for all he was worth.

With a shaky moan, Rhuger slumped above me, his forearms bearing most of his weight. We lay tangled together, twitching and panting with the aftershocks of our lovemaking. I left soft kisses on every part of his skin my mouth could reach.

I realized at that moment that not only did I have a submissive streak and a praise kink, but I also had a breeding kink. It seemed my orckin blood ran through my veins far stronger than I could have possibly guessed. Because, gods, his possessive need to make a baby with me left me *weak*.

"Like I said," Rhuger chuckled as he rolled to the side so as not to crush me beneath him, pulling me with him so he was still sunk inside of me. "I was a fool."

"For giving me the best sex of my life?" I panted, legs shaking as I tried to remind them how to, you know, be *legs*. His chuckle was all dark, sensual, satisfied male as he smirked at me.

"No, my mate," he said the words with such love and reverence, I nearly cried. "I was a fool for thinking I was in charge of our mating. One moment I'm in control, the next you become a hungry she-cat in heat and I barely last long enough to get to see you come undone beneath me."

I laughed then. Loud and long and hearty. "Oh, you poor thing. *SUCH* a hardship."

Rhuger just chuckled. "Och, the greatest of hardships to satisfy a lusty goddess."

"I'm only lusty for you. And I'm far from a goddess, Rhuger." I snorted. It was sweet that he thought of me that way and kept telling me so. It filled some need I didn't realize I had. To be thought beautiful by my partner. My *mate*.

"You are *my* goddess. And I'm blessed beyond all to be the one to bury my face between your sweet thighs." He said with finality as he began kissing my throat, tongue laving where his teeth hadn't quite bitten me but had come close. The longer his tongue was there, the less it hurt, strangely enough.

"You utter *scoundrel!*" I cried in mock outrage.

"Mmmmmh. But you knew this already, och?" He chuckled into my ear as his large warm hands began roaming my breasts and my backside.

"Good thing you're good at that," I said blandly.

"What?" He asked, pulling away enough to look at me.

"Having your face buried between my thighs?" I grinned at him and he growled, rolling me over onto my back until I squealed and laughed. Before the laughter died, it turned into a moan as he hardened inside of me, filling me full of him as he panted in my ear, nipping the sensitive point.

"Again?" He breathed into the shell of my ear and I shuddered, nipples pulling taut. I nodded, blushing furiously. "Use your words, my pearl."

"Yes, Rhuger," I whispered.

"Yes, what?" His tone was teasing, mocking my attempt to consent that wasn't the way he wanted.

Bastard.

So I looked up into his black and silver eyes and let all the lust I felt for him show on my face.

"Yes, Rhuger my Rìgh. I want you to fuck me blind. I want you to fuck me so hard, and so good, you ruin me for any other cock for the rest of my days." Repeating what he'd said to me the night before. As he'd spanked me and then finger fucked me until we'd both come.

The pure shock and lust that raced across his face were better than chocolate. I could see the moment his own words registered and the memories of spanking me lit his eyes. His half-lidded gaze turned hot while a slow, devilish, lopsided grin spread across his delectable mouth in a way that made my cheeks heat.

"Who would have thought that a pearl would spill such filth from such a tiny pink tongue?" He crooned as he slid his hands up to lace his fingers with mine over my head.

"Considering this tiny pink tongue was wrapped around your cock not that long ago, I'm worried that you're so surprised," I replied dryly.

Rhuger laughed then, head tilted back, hair spilling over one shoulder. He was so good-looking; he was *devastating*. My pussy throbbed so hard around his cock in carnal response to him that his eyes rolled back in his head. He groaned and thrust hard, laughing expression turned lusty.

"Maybe I should laugh more often if it arouses you so, *mate*," Rhuger rumbled. The pure seductive masculine expression on his face had my breath catching.

"You're dazzling when you laugh," I confessed.

"And you give me a reason to laugh." He whispered, devilish mouth quirking up in the corners. I saw something spark in his eyes and his smirk turned devious. "Come!" He demanded, sliding out of me. Grasping my hand, he yanked me to my feet.

"What are you doing?" I asked, confused and slightly alarmed as I tried not to fall on my face. Good sex making my legs shaky.

He looked down at me as he led me to the door. His shuttered black gaze was piercing and full of heat. Reaching the door, his large black-clawed hand grasped and held it. The rain was still pounding outside, a torrential staccato that matched the beating of my heart.

"Did I not tell you how I'd claim you, pearl?" That wicked mouth of his quirked up into a lopsided grin the devil would be jealous of.

"Yes." I swallowed, thickly.

"And how was that?" *FUCK*. His words rasped over my bare skin like velvet, making me shiver.

"You told me you'd bend me over the railing and fuck my brains out in front of all the clan." My soaked pussy clenched, sending a flood of our mingled juices down my thighs.

"Och, you remember. Such filth from your mouth is a symphony, pearl." He smirked and wrenched the door open.

"In the rain?" I asked, startled.

"I didn't think you'd be afraid of a little water living next to an ocean." He was baiting me, eyebrow cocked. The challenge and dare hung heavy in the air between us. Rhuger didn't drag me outside or close the door. He waited for my decision. For my consent. Then he whispered, "I can't get the sight of you in that slip in the rain out of my head. It's burned into my mind."

It was his fantasy.

He'd already fulfilled my fantasy just by existing. The least I could do was indulge him.

It wasn't like anyone would be out in this downpour. And it would be harder for anyone to hear us over the sounds of the storm. If I was honest with myself, the memory of him slicked with rain was heating my very blood.

"Let's do it." Smiling at him, I squeezed his hand and the smile he gave me in return was thrilling.

I was going to fuck my mate in the middle of the night in a gotdamn thunderstorm. Primal delight threaded through me as he walked back into the rain, tugging me forward. The cold of the rain hitting my skin was fleeting, my body already too hot to even mind.

The bruised clouds overhead allowed little light from the moons to cast their glow upon our surroundings. Even the lanterns had gone dim. But it was enough to see Rhuger by.

The rain was running down the planes of his bare physique in enticing rivulets. Lightning flashed above us, snapping through the dark underbelly of the clouds and lighting the strong planes and valleys of Rhuger's form in stark contrast. His erection strained up towards his navel and a fluttering began low in my belly.

"You're a vision, pearl." His voice cracked, his silver gaze visible in the low light. A predator with his willing prey in his sights.

I couldn't speak. Overwhelmed by the sight of my naked mate before me. Looking like a wet dream come to life, literally. My feet moving on their own, I stepped up to him, reaching up to tug free his wet braid. The long strands of his freed hair lay plastered all over his chest and shoulders. Making him look like some god of dark desire.

He shivered as my smaller hands skimmed his chest, his collarbones, and his jaw. Without breaking eye contact, he tilted his hand, taking my fingertips into his mouth and nipping the sensitive pads with his sharp teeth.

A shudder wracked my body as the sensation went straight to my core.

He roughly turned me around, my back now plastered to his chest. His erection settled in the valley between the globes of my ass. I moaned out loud at the feel of him there. With those deft, long, thick fingers of his, Rhuger began roaming the most sensitive parts of me. He teased my nipples, rolling them between his fingers and scraping them gently with his sharp claws.

Sliding his cock back and forth against the crease of my ass, he let his hands roam lower, over my soft belly, as his mouth nipped at my ears, my neck, and my shoulder blades. I could feel his lips dragging against my skin and I tipped my head back, moaning, the rain kissing my face and sluicing down our bodies.

"I want to take you roughly." His voice was so dark and gravely with need, I could barely make out the words. When they registered, I nearly came with how badly I needed it.

"Please!" I panted, wanting him to do just that.

I'd loved our sweet mating before, but gods, I just needed my brains fucked out of me. I needed to hand control over to someone. And I knew he was just the male to do it, to take that control. To keep me right where we both wanted while honoring the trust I was giving him.

"Such pretty manners. You truly are a good lass." He growled into the shell of my pointed ear, hands grasping my hips hard.

Rhuger's hand came between us, sliding up my spine and pushing me forward at the same time. His fingers gathered my wet hair at the base of my neck and jerked. I cried out and ground my ass back into his groin. One hand to my shoulder, the other fisted in my hair, he herded me forwards to the railing with his hips.

Reaching forward, he took each of my hands with his free one and placed them on the railing, arranging them to his liking. Satisfied, he kissed my rain-slicked shoulder. His free hand slid up and down my spine as his other pulled my head back, baring my throat.

I was already panting as he roughly kneed my legs apart, widening my stance and forcing my ass up in the air. Rhuger's hand slid up and down the contours of my ass, gently kneading it and slipping his hand brazenly between my thighs. I wasn't just wet from the rain, and his dark chuckle rubbed against my skin like velvet. I shivered.

Without warning, his free hand left me. As a flash of lightning cracked open the sky above us, his hand landed so hard against my ass that I could feel my flesh shuddering from the impact. I moaned loudly, bucking under his hand, rubbing myself shamelessly against his cock where he was rubbing the dripping length between my ass cheeks.

"You're perfect." His snarl ripped through the air as the thunder rumbled around us. The vibrations from the sound waves set the water on my flesh to hum and made me clench hard against the shaft of his cock. "You're so *fucking perfect*."

His hand came down on my other ass cheek and I cried his name into the storm. I could hear his ragged, near-unhinged breathing behind me. It was like he was so close to losing control.

"You're *mine*, do you understand?" He snarled. The sudden possessive streak didn't alarm me. It turned me on even more. I nodded vigorously against his hold on my hair.

"Say it!" His demand was a rough bark.

"I'm yours, Rhuger!" I screamed into the night, into the sheets of rain and the roiling clouds.

"*Good girl*." He rasped. Hands suddenly tender again, he reached around to palm one of my breasts, flicking one hyper-sensitive nipple with his claw. My wail was long and desperate, and I couldn't grind my ass against him hard enough.

"I'm going to fuck you now." The growl sent shivers up and down my spine. He gripped my jerking hips, steadying them as he pulled back. The tip of Rhuger's massive cock slicked up and down my pussy and I moaned shamelessly at the feel of him so close to being where I needed him most. I attempted to scoot back, to maneuver, so he'd slide inside of me instead of everywhere but.

He jerked his hips to the side, narrowly missing my opening. The snap of his massive hand on my thick ass made me yelp. He tsked at me and allowed me to look over my shoulder at him, despite his death grip on my hair.

"Are you going to behave? Be my good girl?" He demanded. "Or am I going to have to punish you?"

I had no idea what a punishment would be, but I was in too much need to be patient enough to find out. Nodding and writhing with need where I stood, he chuckled as he set himself against my opening. His hips snapped forward and he sunk into me completely to the hilt. I wailed in ecstasy as the crack of our wet flesh rent the air like a latent rumble of thunder.

And gods, the wild pounding rhythm that overtook him as he slammed his cock into me repeatedly sent me sky high. Screaming his name into the wind, I heard him roar behind me, not in release, but with feral male satisfaction. My body shuddered and clenched around his cock, but he never faltered at his ruthless pace. The erotic sounds of our rain-slicked flesh meeting and our combined cries of pleasure drowned out the sounds of the rain.

Snapping a wicked hand against my ass again, I jerked and moaned. I knew I was going to have at least some form of marks on my ass tomorrow. Knew sitting down would probably be off the table with how hard he was spanking me and fucking me. But gods, it felt so damn good. My skin and my blood were singing with the thrill of it.

Chancing a look behind me over my shoulder, I could barely see the feral look on his face. His blown-out pupils left thin rings of glittering silver that were riveted on my ass. On how every demanding thrust left my flesh quaking and rippling. Rhuger's snapping thrusts and rasping moans were proof of how much he truly enjoyed the show.

I'd never been so glad for a fat ass in my entire life.

His eyes snapped up to meet mine then, and I nearly came undone. I throbbed with how his gaze affected me, hands scrabbling for better purchase on the railing. How the utter perfection of his powerful form rutted me with such lithe, feral grace. Baring his teeth at me, eyes wild and animalistic, his grip on my hip shifted up to my shoulder. Nails digging into the flesh around my collarbone, I felt them pierce my skin—the pain mixing with the pleasure and turning into something infinitely sharp.

Leaning over me changed his angle, and the flared tip of him, the ridges along the underside of his cock, rubbed against that sweet spot inside of me without mercy. My mind blanked, the pleasure overwhelming and so intense I couldn't stop screaming. I couldn't tell if it was one orgasm or a thousand overlaid end to end.

Fuck. I'd never thought being used so roughly would feel so *gotdamn good*.

His breathing grew more erratic behind me, his thrusts losing rhythm, though losing none of their primal urgency. Rhuger was close. His calloused hand moved from my shoulder to cup my bared throat. He didn't bear down on my throat with his powerful fingers, just held it there. The unquestionable power and control of holding my very breakable neck in both hands while he pile-drived me from behind built my pleasure higher than it'd ever been before.

"Come for me, mate. Come, pearl. Show me how beautiful you are screaming my name." Rhuger snarled into the rain-slicked space between us. He didn't have to tell me twice. I immediately capitulated with his command.

"*RHUGER!*" I wailed his name out into the fading lightning, my death grip on the railing scoring the wood deep. I shattered then, into a million suns as waves of pleasure pounded my mind into oblivion.

Distantly, I heard Rhuger roar my name. Felt him buck deep

inside of me, hitting my womb as his release rolled over him. His hips ground into me in fitful jerks and again, knowing he was filling me with his seed, straight to my womb, sent me over the edge. Climax long and low and rippling. His hips twitched, and he hissed, the sound ending in a strangled moan.

CHAPTER 50

RHUGER

My cridhe was perfection incarnate.

Sweet, loving, lusty, kind, wickedly intelligent, with a body that would make the stars weep with want. And she willingly, wantonly, craved my dominance and my touch. She enjoyed the thrill of being roughly fucked and handled just as much as she did the soft caresses and gentle kisses I rained on her silky flesh.

Separate, we were off. Difficult to tame and understand by others. Too rough or too soft for our worlds. But together? Together we were an incomparable balance. Truly, she was my cridhe in every way that mattered. Mating marks be damned.

All the careful control I'd built up over the years, the longing for a mate that might never come, fled as her gorgeous ass took my feral fucking and turned it into something exquisite. Her lush curves rippled and shuddered with each snap of my hips as I drove myself home inside of her.

The skies overhead shook and rattled the world in bright flashes of lightning. The storm was an echo of the passion between my cridhe and me. And when she screamed my name into the torrential storm around us, her sweet cunt squeezing down hard, milking my knot, my cock, for all it was worth, all I could do was roar her name as I shattered into a million stars.

Once we drifted back into our bodies as the rain lightened, and the lightning and thunder rolled away into the distance, Amelia went limp and slumped towards the slick floorboards of the deck. I caught her and held her upright until my knot eased enough to pull free from her without causing her pain. Gods, I doubted I'd ever come so much in my life, if the thick rivulet of my seed dripping down the insides of her thighs was any sign.

Amelia's legs were trembling and couldn't hold her weight as she slumped against me, panting as she caught her breath. So I bent down and scooped her up into my arms. She squeaked and wrapped her arms around my neck. Still so certain I'd drop her if she didn't.

I carried her over the threshold of *our* house. There was something so right about carrying my cridhe into the house I'd made for her. The house she'd made into a home. It warmed a part of my heart I didn't know was there.

Kicking the door closed behind me, I carried my cridhe, my princess, my mate toward the bed.

"Wait!" Amelia cried, and I paused, looking down at her rain-slicked form. "I need to use the toilet..."

Her cheeks had flushed that pretty pink again. As if her using the toilet in front of me was embarrassing. Smiling at how adorable she was, I carried her to the bathroom. I gently set her down on her feet and she wobbled on her shaky legs.

"Alright, come here," I murmured, helping her by holding her waist as she tottered to the toilet.

"I can go by myself!" She protested with her cheeks puffed out.

"I know you can, but you're having trouble walking, pearl. I don't want you to fall and get hurt." The smile in my voice had her pouting up at me. Her brows furrowed and her bottom lip poked out.

She didn't argue, but made some frustrated noise in the back of her throat. I got her seated, then went at waited with my back turned at the door, to give her the privacy she obviously wanted. When she was finished, I helped her to her feet and led her out of the bathroom.

"Jeez, what did you do to me? I couldn't walk straight if my life depended on it!" She groused, holding onto my forearms for dear life as she tried to get her legs to cooperate.

"Nearly fucked you blind and ruined you for anyone else's cock but mine." I chuckled darkly at our little inside joke. "Now let's get you dried off and into bed. I don't want you to get sick."

"You have to get dried off too!" My little pearl insisted, and I smiled. She was amazing, thinking of me and my comfort, too.

"*We'll* get dried off."

"Can..." she began and ducked her head as I sat her down on the edge of the bed and grabbed a towel. I cocked my eyebrow, waiting for her to continue as I knelt in front of her and started drying her hair.

"Can what, pearl?" I asked, feeling my lips twitch and fighting back a smile. She was so cute when she was flustered and I loved it.

"Can we maybe... Cuddle?" Her shoulders were near as red as her ears as I dried her hair. Pausing, I pulled the towel back to look at her face. Amelia's freckles stood out against all that pink in her cheeks. She finally braved a glance up at me and did a double take.

"I'd love to, pearl," I whispered, a broad grin on my face. How was it this female could always find a way to make me smile?

I hadn't had any physical closeness with anyone for years now. Until meeting Amelia, I hadn't really missed it. I was too busy proving myself to Rìgh Thorn, fighting other clans in battle, or building our tree home. But from the moment I'd laid eyes on my cridhe in her strange clothes in the Craobh na Beatha, I'd hungered for it. From her.

"Okay." Amelia's smile was soft and her eyes glittered. I'd made her happy. With something so small that we both needed so badly.

I helped her dry off, taking extra care where she was sensitive from my attentions. Then she insisted on drying me off. It was a shock to have someone treat me so gently and tenderly. She even re-plaited my hair for me.

Once we were done, I tucked her into bed and stood up.

"Where are you going?" She asked as I walked away, a slightly nervous tone in her voice.

"I'm getting us something to eat and drink," I replied over my shoulder.

In the kitchen, I grabbed two mugs, a pitcher of water, and a plate of fruit, bread, and hard cheese. Her look of surprise as I carried over my finds was precious. And the way her uisge-beatha eyes were drawn to my swaying cock as I moved toward her made me crave her with a fierce and sudden need.

But that would have to wait until she was fed. I couldn't have my cridhe go hungry. So I sat down on the edge of the bed and placed the platter of food on the bed between us, then poured her a mug of water and handed it to her.

"Thank you," she murmured and downed the water in long swallows. I paused, watching her throat work, and wondered if she'd swallowed my cum like that. Shaking my head, I took the mug from her when she'd finished. Amelia snuggled down into the bed under the covers and patted the mattress next to her. "Come cuddle with me?"

Precious. Absolutely *fucking precious*.

I downed my own water and set the mugs on the floor next to the pitcher. I lifted the blankets and crawled under them with my mate. Shifting the platter to balance on my hip, I scooted closer to her. Once I'd settled so our legs were intertwined, I picked up a dearc ruadh and held it to her lips.

"Gonna feed me like a baby bird, huh?" She chucked and opened her mouth wide enough for me to pop the berry between her teeth.

"I have to make sure my mate is satisfied in all ways," I murmured, brushing her bottom lip with my thumb as she chewed. She blushed furiously and tried to hide her face in the pillow. Chuckling, I brushed back her hair and tucked it behind her delicately pointed ear. "Still so shy?"

"I'm not used to this." She whispered. As if saying it aloud were a sin. "Being taken care of like this. Having any form of aftercare."

"Aftercare?" I asked, picking up another berry and holding it to her lips until she took it in her mouth.

"It's when partners take care of one another after sex. Sometimes things can get emotional or they try something and it's overwhelming. Aftercare is what you do to help your partner get back to normal in the ways they need." She explained after she swallowed the berry. "I was shocked the other night when you got me water and food."

"You mean human males don't always provide this?" I asked, frowning. "Did your ex-husband not do this for you?"

Amelia looked down, pulled her arms in tight, and shook her head no. Rage and sorrow warred in my breast as I looked at the love of my life. My guiding star. I swore that I would always provide her with this aftercare. Show her how she should have been treated all along.

I lifted her chin so she would look me in the eye. When she did, I leaned in and placed a chaste kiss on her berry juice-stained lips.

Pulling away, I saw silvery tears gather along her lashes, threatening to spill onto the pillow.

"Why are you crying, pearl?" I asked softly, cupping her lovely rounded cheek in my hand.

"I feel... Ashamed that I've never had this before. Like I did something wrong to not deserve it." Her voice cracked on her words and my heart cracked with it.

"Oh, pearl... It has *never* been your fault and you've *never* done anything wrong to keep you from getting treated with care after mating." I told her, cupping her face in both hands and wiping her tears away. "It just goes to show that Rìgh Thorn's Academy really is the right path. And that your ex-husband was a Source damned fool."

"Academy?" She asked, looking up at me with glassy eyes. If it were my will, she'd never cry from pain or sadness ever again. Only from joy.

"Och. Rìgh Thorn, when he returned from your world, Earth, he designed and built the Academy." I began, pulling my hand free to snag a nut for her to eat. When she took it in her mouth, I kept talking. "There are classes on plants, the stars, language, arts, and more. But it's the Mate School that was central to the whole endeavor. He told us he learned a lot while he was in this other world. That he wanted to design classes for males to take. To train them about female pleasure, how to care for them, and how to care for orclings. There are even classes on pregnancy, which are very informative. There was never anything so detailed and educational amongst the Oc'Turin."

"Did... Did *you* take the classes?" She asked me with such an open naivete.

"Och, I did," I told her with a cocky grin. "Got top marks too."

"Ah, seems I thought I was getting a warrior but you also play instruments and are a dedicated scholar. My warrior poet." Amelia teased, scrunching her nose. "Seems like my mate's the total package."

"How else was I supposed to learn the language of my mate's body and desires?" I whispered against her lips with a grin.

"I mean... Practice makes perfect. You could have just fumbled about and I would have still loved you senseless." Her smile was warm and teasing as her words hit home in my heart. That she would have taken me as her mate and loved me still, even without the training. That I would have been good enough as I had been, made my eyes sting from unshed tears.

"And not be able to give my cridhe the best I could possibly give her?" I asked thickly. "Clearly you have a lot to learn about me, mate."

Amelia paused, recognition sparking in her eyes, her brows rising and expression softening. I mentally kicked myself. I hadn't wanted to tell her yet that we were cridhe. It seemed like a big step to take for someone who'd only been on my planet for a few weeks. And she'd taken so many leaps so far.

I wanted to wait for a better time. So instead of just telling her just how deep our connection went, I pushed another berry between her lips to stop her from asking. Frustration showed in her expression, but she went with it and started feeding me tidbits from the platter, too.

It startled me at first, but I quickly melted into the sweetness of her care for me. When the platter was empty, I set it on the floor next to the mugs. When I turned back, Amelia was wiggling her way closer to me. Smiling, I wrapped my arms around her and pulled her against me. Her head pillowed against my shoulder, she nuzzled my chest and left a few kisses before quickly falling asleep.

But not before she murmured, "I love you, Rhuger."

"I love you too, Amelia," I whispered, emotion choking me once more. So I pulled her in tight and sank my face into the brown waves at the top of her head. Following her into slumber.

⚔

AMELIA

"I never knew it would feel this good," Rhuger mumbled against my hair, sleepily. We'd just woken from a nap and he was spooning me. Feeling so wrapped up and safe with him was a wondrous new experience. I'd never felt so safe or so loved as I did right then. With the memories of our lovemaking and the possibility of doing it again with the male I loved, I felt warm and fuzzy.

"What would?" I asked, voice hoarse from screaming.

"Being with a female. It's—well, different from what I've been told. Could be because you're mostly human." He murmured, sliding his hand across my belly absently. Not in a sexual way, just skimming my stomach with his fingertips, tracing invisible lines into my flesh.

"You've... never been with a female...?" I asked, turning to look at his face, shocked. He gripped me tighter and nuzzled the back of my neck.

"Mmm no." came his sleepy reply. "Few males long ago. There weren't many females to offer. Ones that did, I didn't like."

"You mean to tell me you gave me mind-blowing, world-altering sex... and you've never been with a female?" I asked, incredulous. I didn't give a shit if he'd banged a few guys in the past. He was mine now. It's just that he was so *good* at it—at making me, a female, come undone at the seams. Repeatedly.

Fucker, *how?*

"Mmm." His shit-eating, sleepy grin was damn sexy. "Why do you think I had a hard time lasting?"

I laughed. I couldn't help it.

"Give me time and I'll have you coming five times to my one." He mumbled and kissed my head again.

"Your stamina, as it is, is remarkable, love," I told him and he smiled into my hair, pleased at my praise. Honestly, I was surprised he'd been so eager after I'd given him a blow job, let alone the two rounds after that. "Is it really that common to make a female come that many times compared to a male's one?"

"Yes. The more orgasms a female has, the more fertile she is. Long ago it was just for pleasure-seeking or when a couple wished for orclings. Now it's for survival." His tone had turned pensive, and he released a sigh.

"How was it different from what you heard? Being with me, I mean." I asked, attempting to turn the conversation from something so grim. I couldn't help my curiosity. Was it because of my human blood? Or was it just a cultural thing?

"You're more sensitive. Doesn't take much touching to get you aroused." He murmured, stroking my stomach, now in a *very* sensual way. My belly fluttered and, well, he wasn't wrong. Really, that small touch was all it took to get me ready to go. "You're so wet, my slick isn't needed. And your cunt—it—*mmmhhh.*"

He growled into my ear, and I felt him stiffen against my ass. Already getting hard just by thinking about it. It was... it was hot, dammit. He pulled the covers back and lifted my thigh. The obscene amount of cum from the both of us made them almost stick together. With a kiss on my neck, he shifted and slid himself deep inside in one smooth thrust.

I gasped and groaned, my walls clutching hungrily at him already. I was sore, admittedly, but my horniness *heavily* outweighed any sensitivity I had. He hooked my thigh up and back, over his leg, so he could have both hands free. And with him at this angle, my mind nearly blanked from how he slid against that sweet spot. His hand pressed hard into my belly as if he was feeling himself fuck me from the inside and out. His other arm he slid under my neck so he could reach down to fondle my breasts as he rutted me.

"*MMMMhhhh....yes that.*" He growled as he began a punishing rhythm. "I love it when your cunt clenches my cock like a fist. Like you're trying to milk me and suck me deep inside your womb."

Soft cries escaped my lips with each of his thrusts. The wet slap of skin on skin and how he kept pressing that sweet spot between his hand and his cock had me bucking wildly back into him, desperate for more. And my mate didn't disappoint.

He growled and snarled against my neck, his sharp teeth scraping against my fluttering heartbeat. I couldn't stop myself from sinking my claws into his forearms as my climax built. My cries grew louder and his hand left my breasts to cup my throat as he gently bit down on my shoulder. His other hand drifted from my belly down to my clit and he flickered his fingers over it rapidly.

I was *so close*!

"That's right, pearl." He panted into my ear as his hips slapped against my ass.

He spread his legs so mine would spread too, and I moaned long and loud. It felt so vulnerable, being railed like this, spread wide and bared. And it sharpened the edge of my swiftly climbing orgasm.

"That's right, sing for me, my cridhe." He nipped at my earlobe and I shuddered.

There it was. That word again. The one that meant 'heart'. The one Hisouk told me meant the orckin equivalent of a soulmate. Rhuger had insinuated it a few times now, let it slip in moments of vulnerability, but this was the first time he'd come right out and called me his cridhe directly.

Tears threatened as my heart broke open, bursting with emotion. Rhuger thought of me as his *soulmate*. His cridhe. His one true match in all the universe. Even if he wasn't ready to openly call me his cridhe, fearful perhaps that what we had was still so fragile, I was alright with that.

I could wait.

But this fucking orgasm sure as hell couldn't.

Between one thrust and the next, the orgasm shattered me and I wailed Rhuger's name into the pillow. He groaned gutturally behind me, but kept going. I was a shaking sobbing mess in his arms as he rolled us. Without slipping free from where my pussy was still clutching at him from the aftershocks of my orgasm, he knelt with his knees far apart behind me. My thighs flung wide, back over his hips, my knees resting on the backs of his calves, and my face buried into the bedding.

"I love it when you scream my name when you come, pearl." Rhuger rasped as he bent forward, gathering my hair at the nape of my neck and pinning me to the bedding like a spread butterfly. He curved his other hand around under my tummy and began stroking my clit as he started a slow, rocking cadence.

"Rhuger..." I whimpered, arching my back so my ass stuck up further into the air. The slow gentleness was a stark contrast to how hard he was fucking me just moments before, and my pussy shuddered and clenched around his cock.

"What was that, pearl? What did you call me?" He asked darkly, thrusts slow and smooth so I could feel every gotdamned ribbed and flared inch of him. So I could feel the pressure and release of his swollen knot from my opening.

"Rhuger, my Rìgh..." I gasped as his fingers tightened around the strands of my hair, tugging it slightly.

"That's my *good lass*." He snarled in satisfaction and kept up his deliberately slow pace.

His breathing grew more ragged as he fought his control. Hearing him so close to losing it was like that luibh gaoil. It set me to writhe beneath him as his thrusts lost their rhythm and became more erratic. Trying to keep that slow, smooth pace but occasionally slipping so he'd thrust hard and deep enough to make me cry out.

There was something so damned erotic and electrifying about being so prone and so dominated. I'd laid my heart bare and now my body, too. And he was giving me more than I'd ever thought I'd get. I wanted to tell him, wanted to say how I felt in a way he'd understand. Then it came to me.

"My Rìgh," I panted as I looked at him over my shoulder, his fist still pinning my hair to the bedding. "I'm yours... I submit and surrender..."

The change in Rhuger's expression was immediate. It slid from open lust to a paused surprise, to savage, primal need. He bent further forward, wrapping his free arm around my waist to hold me where he wanted me, and pressed his chest against my back, whispering in my ear a litany of Teanga Dhubh as he picked up his pace. And again, that change in angle nearly blanked my mind from how *wonderful* he felt, hitting me where I needed him most.

"Then do as I command, my cridhe." He growled, panting into my ear as I moaned beneath him, now truly pinned and defenseless and loving every second of it. Hearing him call him his cridhe setting every nerve alight. "Take my knot and milk me dry with your sweet, hot, tight little cunt."

His pace intensified and I fought to breathe as I obeyed, the pleasure overwhelming. My eyes rolled back in my head and my toes curled as he pounded into me against my sweet spot. Bucking in his firm grip, I came *hard*. So hard I almost pushed him out of me, locked him out.

But he wasn't having that. With one final hard thrust that pushed his knot back into me, filled me entirely with his cock. He made me see stars as I scrabbled my hands for purchase in the sheets. Rhuger roared his orgasm against the back of my neck and I swear I could feel the pulsing of his knot as it released spurt after spurt of his seed as his hips ground into my ass.

And still, I clenched and spasmed down hard around him, causing the both of us to moan as he claimed my mouth with his. Rhuger's orgasms definitely lasted longer than a man's, and I was all about it. Especially as he continued to rock against me, tempering the hard edges of our orgasms and bringing us gently back into our bodies.

As his cock popped free from my still clenching pussy, a rush of his cum sluiced out of me. He released my hair and propped himself up on that arm as he held my still-twitching body. I couldn't help but hum as the sensations left over from my orgasm shook me. Gently, he helped me turn and lie down on my back on a clean stretch of bedding. Looking up at him as he leaned over me, I bucked, an aftershock of pleasure making me tremble.

"Are you alright, pearl? Did I go too far?" He rasped, his brows drawn together. What a fucking *cutie pie*.

"No, gumby. I'm alright, I think. I'm not used to having sex that good." Chuckling, I curled my hands over my chest as my body slowly calmed. Rhuger laid down on his side next to me and propped his head up on his elbow.

"Is this normal, then?" He asked, concerned. "For human females?"

I laughed then, grinning like an idiot. I got my arms to work enough to reach up and cup his perfectly sculpted cheeks. Shaking my head at his sweetness, I gazed at him with all the love in me, and he took a hitched breath.

"Only normal for females who have excellent partners," I murmured. "And somehow, I feel you have all of those excellent partners beat hands down."

Rhuger smiled and kissed my palm before I brought my hands back down to my chest. He looked down at our mingled juices on my twitching inner thighs. He ran his fingers down the inner curve of one thigh, gathering the wetness there on his fingertips. Bringing them up onto my stomach, he skimmed his fingers over my soft belly with sure, steady strokes.

Confused, I tilted my head and watched as he rubbed the slickness into my skin. Then he went for more, bringing those long, thick fingers of his up to massage the reddened tips of my breasts. Into the love bites and hickeys that littered my neck and shoulders.

"What are you doing?" I asked him, sleepily.

"Painting you in my scent." He replied softly, onyx and silver eyes meeting mine. "You're my mate now. Until it's widely known that we are exclusive, or until you carry my child, this will let the others know you are spoken for. That way, the other males will leave you alone."

"You know, you could have just put a ring on it." I chuckled, strangely not embarrassed by the idea of the folk in the clan smelling how well he'd fucked me.

"What?" He asked, eyes dilating and brows cocked in surprise.

"Wedding rings? Like my Grandpa wears." I mumbled, wishing I'd kept my mouth shut.

"You mean to take you as my mate *and* my wife?" He asked me softly, almost shy.

"Yes?" I asked, looking up at him. "Is there something wrong with that?"

"Marriage is usually for those who produce orclings. A way to celebrate a mated and fertile pair." Rhuger murmured, fingers still painting my body. It was adorable that he was taking his task into overkill territory.

"So if a mated pair decide they want orclings but cannot have them together... do they separate and mate with others?" I asked. Orckin mating culture was far more complex than I'd initially thought.

"Sometimes," Rhuger said, eyes downcast. "Sometimes they will take additional mates and only marry the ones that produce orclings."

"That sounds..." I trailed off, unable to find the words.

"Barbaric?" He asked. "Yes. It's why I left my clan, the Oc'Turin. Well... one of the many reasons. Often males will share a female or females long-term until they become pregnant. Unlike the Oc'Dellor, where it's often only short-term, if at all. The Oc'Turin females rarely have a choice in who they bed. Once they become pregnant, they'll then marry whoever the father is in hopes of more orclings." He told me, voice cold.

"How can they figure out who the father is if they're fucking multiple people?" I asked, alarmed for the females and pretty sure the orckin didn't have paternity tests.

"Scent." Rhuger sighed as he flopped back on the bed, pulling me close to him and nuzzling his face into my hair.

"What if she hates him or doesn't want to marry him?" I asked, angry on the female orcs' behalf.

"She has no choice but to." He told me, eyes flat like a shark's. "The Oc'Turin aren't as enlightened as the Oc'Dellor or some of the other clans. I was always uncomfortable with how things were done. When I came here to visit and saw how cherished the females were, how one didn't have to share mates, it became a big reason why I left my clan."

"But Sharn said the females are expected to take multiple males to their beds?" I asked, confused.

"Multiple males yes. But not mates."

"I have the confusion," I said flatly. "What's the difference?"

"Taking a male to one's bed can just be a one-time thing. Mates show long-term commitment and within the Oc'Dellor, it means both parties agree."

"Oh. So, she meant taking multiple males as in having multiple one-night stands versus having a bunch of boyfriends. Well, that's a relief." I sighed, "But it's shitty that the Oc'Turin females aren't allowed that. Is there any other way for them?"

"Och. There are two. If a pair finds one another and their mating marks appear, it means they're matched in every way. They will be lifelong partners, cridhe, and are the most fertile if the pairing is male-female." He was playing with my hair as he explained.

"What do they look like?" I asked him.

"It's been a long time since matched mates were around. Ruksala's the last in Oc'Dellor with the mating marks over her chest. Her mate passed many years ago." He sighed. I recalled the marks he mentioned. I thought they'd been faded tattoos.

"The second way would be if we stabilized the Geata on our planet. Then we could create offspring with those similar to us and survive as a people that way." His gaze met mine, and he smiled. "It would be a feat, but trying to fix the Geata and get to your world through the Craobh na Beatha is unlikely."

"Why?" I asked.

With how well most of the orcs I'd met treated their ladies, I was sure most of the single women I knew, and some of those in unsatisfying relationships, would leap at the chance for a loving partner. Well, at least the orcs in the Oc'Dellor clan.

"Why my world?"

"Well, I'm not sure. The orcs in Oc'Veltas and their citadel might know. But they've isolated themselves since the plague. If I had to hazard a guess, it would be because your kind is so like ours that we could bond, mate, and love one another."

It was so romantic it made my heart want to rip in two. "What happened to the Geata?"

"War. I don't know the entire history, but war and greed turned our kinds against one another. The Geata were destroyed or damaged. And now it is rare that they even work at all. For Rìgh Thorn to not only go through to *your* world but to *return* hasn't happened in generations." Rhuger kissed my head again and pulled the blankets higher over us. "It would be a miracle to stabilize a gate."

A miracle.

The idea seemed to slip into my blood as I settled against Rhuger, eyelids growing heavy. I'd love to go home. I wouldn't leave Rhuger, though. But maybe we could get it working again. And maybe there could be love again between our two peoples.

"So... What's a 'boi-friend'?" Rhuger asked, cocking an eyebrow at me.

"Oh, hmm how to explain? For people we take to bed once, humans call that a one-night stand. People we agree to have an intimate relationship with we call boyfriends or girlfriends or date-mates. Those who we commit to getting married to are fiances or fiancees and those we marry are husbands, wives, or partners. Usually, only husbands and wives or partners seek to have children. At least that's the convention." I explained as I played with our fingers, intertwining and releasing our hands, running my fingers against the muscles and ligaments, exploring our differences.

"Ah." He said. "So, does that make me your 'boi-friend', then?"

His smile was small but warm.

"I'd like to think you're more than that." My face flushed hotly as I murmured the words I'd kept in my heart. I couldn't look at him. But I could feel his eyes on me.

"Hmmm. Does that mean I'm your 'fee-ahn-say'?"

"You're my mate," I muttered and ducked my head into his chest so he couldn't see my face.

"Och, but what am I in human terms?" He asked, chuckling at my embarrassment.

"You're my mate," I said louder.

"But what does that mean in human terms?" Rhuger was relentless, and he attempted to lean back to see my face, but I buried it deeper into his pectorals. "What does 'mate' mean to humans?"

"... Well..." I hesitated. How could I tell him that in nature, mated pairs were endgame? That husbands and wives rarely had that? That I definitely hadn't... but that with him... I felt like I did.

"Tell me, sweet pearl." Rhuger's rumbling murmur, and his patience while I worked up the courage, helped me gather my thoughts. And I was thankful he held this space for me.

"Back home on Earth, there are many species of animals that mate for life," I murmured, pulling back.

"And humans don't?" Rhuger asked, searching my eyes.

"It's not as common as people would want." I shrugged, looking down. A stab of shame that I'd failed to have that hit me. But it faded as I remembered that I'd sought it with the wrong person. That the right person was now in my arms. That I now had a chance to claim what I'd been searching for all of my life. "Most married couples don't last. It's hard to find someone you feel so compatible with that it's like you can't breathe without them. And even when you do, it doesn't always last. And it's not always romantic either."

"So you see me as higher than your ex-husband." His voice was whisper soft and full of awe and emotion. I nodded into his chest. He laughed. I looked up finally and found his face alight with joy. "You see yourself with me for life, then?"

"Yes," I whispered, nodding like an idiot in the face of how gorgeous he was smiling like that. My heart felt like it would burst out of my chest, it was beating so hard.

"You bring me so much happiness, my mate, my pearl," Rhuger murmured as he bent down to place a soft kiss on my lips. "I see myself with you for life, too."

And like an overemotional dumpster fire floating down a flooded street during a hurricane, I started bawling my eyes out.

"What's wrong, pearl? Amelia?" He asked, suddenly concerned. But all I could do was blubber and wail like a child, so he just held me close. Rocking me in utter confusion. When I finally calmed down to just hiccups, he pulled away enough to look down at me, wiping my sticky cheeks and brushing my damp hair from my face.

"Is this bad?" He asked softly, an ache in his voice.

"No!" I cried and trapped his face between my hands. Startled, Rhuger just waited while I caught my breath. "I just... never thought I'd have this with anyone. Ever. I was worried you might not feel the same."

Rhuger's expression changed from one of worry to something so tender it wrecked me.

"How could I not feel the same? You are as necessary for me as air and water and food. As light and sleep." He slipped one of my hands from my face and kissed my knuckles before twining our hands together.

Emotion exploded in my chest and I took a deep, shuddering breath and held it. Trying to keep the flood of emotion from bursting forth. His soft smile nearly did me in. So I gulped it down and curled into him, instead. Rhuger snuggled closer, and it wasn't long before we fell asleep, tangled up together.

TO BE CONTINUED IN...

Turn the page for an excerpt from:

RHUGER'S CRIDHE

ORC MATCHED 1.5

Coming 2023!

AMELIA

Feeling for him, I knelt down next to him and tackled him to the ground. Surprised, he laughed and set the fruit and knife aside. He rolled so I lay on my back in the grasses, staring up at the cloudless sky, the hazy impressions of two of the moons lighting a big part of the sky.

"Am I too soft for you?" I whispered the question as I lay there, looking up at where Rhuger was propped up on his side.

"How do you mean?" His silver eyes focused on me, brow furrowing.

"Well, you're a warrior and though you're exiled, you're still a prince. You still have so much opportunity stretched before you." I began, letting the words slip past my lips, worries I'd held so close to my chest. Worries I hadn't realized had existed until now. "I know some martial arts. I can fight, but not to the degree you can."

"Okay." He murmured, waiting for me to continue.

"Are you sure I'm a good match for you? I'm worried I won't be able to keep up. That I'll fall behind." An old wound, this was. I'd always strive to keep up with my peers and yet still fell to the wayside.

Either too far ahead or too far behind.

"I don't need you to keep up with me." He replied, tone soft and sure. "You give me what I need."

"What's that?" I asked.

"A safe place to rest. Somewhere I can let my guard down. Where I can bury myself in softness and forget the rest of the world exists for a little while." Rhuger murmured as he laced his fingers with mine. "You won't fall behind. You can't. Because I'll always come home to you. You are my home. And I'll always take you with me."

Maybe it was from being emotionally neglected by romantic partners. Maybe it was because this was all new to me and I had trouble regulating my emotions. Hell, *maybe* it was because of all the baby hormones that were being dumped into my system so suddenly after insta-baby-sex. Regardless, my feelings were running rampant and I felt like I would burst from them.

So I distracted myself.

I looked down the powerful column of my mate's throat with its whirling black tattoos to his torque. A wicked thought entered my mind and I grasped it as if it were a tie. I tugged Rhuger down to me so we were nearly nose to nose. His reaction was immediate, shifting from relaxed guard to dominant predator in the blink of an eye.

"Naughty little pearl." Rhuger's voice dropped into a deep, rolling rumble that crackled with desire. "Don't you know that if you grasp a male's torque or his belt, like that..." His mouth curved into a sinful smirk. "...you're bound to find yourself in all sorts of trouble..."

"Oh?" I asked, voice gone high and breathy in the face of such masculine power pinning me within the wildflowers. Even though I'd caused this problem myself.

"Oh, yes." He murmured, drawing out the s-sound around his

sharp teeth. "A male can't be held responsible for what he does to such a bold female. It's as clear a signal as any that she's ready to mate. Immediately."

I didn't waste a moment and tugged on his torque again. This time, he rolled on top of me, pinning me to the ground with all of his weight. I squirmed beneath him as he ground his hips between my legs. Grasping my wrists, he pinned them above my head with one hand, his other trailing along my jaw, my throat, the ties at the front of *his* shirt...

"I like it that you're wearing my tunic..." Rhuger growled, teeth flashing as his pupils blew out his silver irises until his eyes looked like glittering pits. "... That you willingly wear what's mine, wear my scent..." He slipped a clawed hand up under the tunic to scrape gently against the underside of my breast.

"That's because I'm yours, my Righ," I whispered, squeezing my thighs around his hips to punctuate my point. "Just as you are mine."

I was a thirsty ass bitch, who could only think about stuffing as much of his cock inside of me as I could get. Pulling my shirt up to my armpits, I exposed my breasts for him and he growled as he claimed my mouth. Rhuger's hand slipped from my breast to curve over my soft tummy, as if cradling the child growing there, before drifting down to slip his fingers under the waistband of my pants. Releasing my wrists and my mouth, he leaned back on his knees, tugging my pants from me. I eagerly lifted my hips so he could tug them down, and he made a sound of approval as his gaze trailed along my exposed skin.

Gods, he couldn't get my clothes off of me fast enough. I wasn't even willing to wait for him to take off his kilt and planned to lift the swiftly tenting leather and spread myself wide for him so he could rut me in the sunshine. But he had to get my pants off first and my boots were getting in the way. I whined at the idea of being completely naked while he was still clothed, kilt lifted so he could fuck me into the ground beneath us, the wild woman he claimed. Needing it to become our immediate reality with a vicious desire.

A branch cracked somewhere within the treeline, and Rhuger froze above me. He took a deep breath and then was off of me like a shot. I sat up, pulling my shirt down and my pants up. Rhuger was standing in front of me, swords already drawn. In the next breath, I lunged for his knives and palmed them.

If we were about to be attacked, I wasn't about to let my mate face it alone. I wasn't about to let my child come to harm without fighting with every ounce of blood in my veins, either.

As I got to my feet and readied my weapons, I saw a good dozen orcs stalk from between the trees and out into the tall grasses. I felt the blood drain from my face. One orc was the giant womb-splitter who had hunted me when I first arrived on Talam.

"Give us the female and you can leave unharmed, Fògradh." A short orc bristling with knives called.

"Do you really expect me to let you just *take* my mate?" Rhuger's voice was low, even, and it bit like sharp steel.

"Our orders are to take her alive. You? Not so much." The short orc shrugged like it wasn't a big deal.

"Who are they?" I whispered behind Rhuger. He didn't move.

"And what does Rìgh Orok of the Oc'Turin want with Leanabh Banrigh Amelia of the Oc'Dellor?" Rhuger asked.

"That's not our business. Or yours." The orc replied with a sleazy grin that spoke of what Orok wanted from me. I felt panic flare and flap against my vision, darkening the edges like black wings. Suffocating and horrible.

I'd been mated. I'd even gotten pregnant. All before the date and time Rìgh Orok was slated to come for me, just like I was supposed to. I should have been safe, should have been free from the cruel future everyone had painted for me if I became Righ Orok's mate.

But it looked like Righ Orok couldn't care less if I had a mate or not. Was pregnant with another male's child. Come hell or high water, it seemed he was determined to take me as his mate for whatever nefarious purposes he had.

"Then come and take her from me," Rhuger growled, head dipping to his chest, arms spread wide, with his blades held high. If we weren't in mortal danger, I would have *severely* appreciated his words and how gotdamned hot he looked.

The short orc glowered and gestured to the orcs at the far ends of their line. The four orcs that left the line and stalked towards us were jacked like bodybuilders, and I felt my mouth go dry. If they were Oc'Turin and trained in war just like Rhuger was... We would not stand an ice cube's chance in hell.

My mate, my cridhe, stepped forward a few feet to meet them. I stayed where I was in a defensive crouch, knives at the ready. And I made the hardest decision of my life.

Whatever was about to happen? Whatever the outcome of the battle we were facing. I was going to survive it all for our child.

And then I was going to take my revenge.

INDEX &

PRONUNCIATION GUIDE

Online Pronunciation Guide With Audio:

https://www.authorcarlottahughes.com/orc-matched-pronounciation-guide.html

ALL VOICE CLIPS SOURCED WITH PERMISSION FROM
https://learngaelic.scot/

Please note that not all words have a pronunciation guide or a link to the audio. These words are pronounced phonetically and are the creation of the author.

EVERYDAY WORDS

<u>NAMING:</u>

Cridhe (p. Cridheachan): [/krʲi.ə/] Heart; the title of an orckin's soul-bound partner and mate

Daonna: [/dɯːNə/] Human

Fògradh: [/fɔːgrəɣ/] Exile

Gaiseadh: [/gaʃəɣ/] Blight

Taobh A'Muigh: [/tɯːv/ /ə'muj/] Outsider; usually what someone is called if they are not part of a clan

Neamhnaid: [/Nʲãũnɪdʲ/] Pearl; often a nickname for a princess or female of royal blood or someone with a pearly sheen to their skin

Duhb'Oidhche: [/ duh/ /ɤçə/] Black Night; a rare night that is both moonless and starless, the dark all-encompassing. A nickname given to the Orclings of Neit, the god of war.

FAMILY:

Màthair: [/maːhərʲ/] Mother

Athair: [/ahərʲ/] Father

Piuthar: [/pju.ər/] Sister

Bràthair: [/braːhɪrʲ/] Brother

ROYALTY NAMING:

Rìgh: [/Riː/] King

Banrigh: [/bãũNRɪ/] Queen

Leanabh Rìgh: [/Lʲɛnəv/ /Riː/] Prince

Leanabh Banrigh: [/Lʲɛnəv/ /bãũNRɪ/] Princess

Fear a Chì (p. Feadhainn a Chì): [/fɛr/ /ə'/ /hee/] Spiritual leader of each clan. They are conduits to the Source and are often caretakers of the orphaned orclings; often female

ROYAL ITEMS:

Seud Iteach: [/ʃiad/ /ihdʲəx/] A feathered ornament that Leanabh Rìgh wear in their hair

Seud Neamhnaid: [/ʃiad/ /Nʲãũnıdʲ/] A pearl ornament Leanabh Banrigh wear in their hair

SPIRITUAL PLACES:

Craobh na Beatha: [/krɯːv/ /nə/ /bɛhə/] Tree of Life

Gàrradh: [/gaːRəɣ/] A circle of trees interwoven like a protective cage with a fire pit and resting places for weary travelers; a holdover from when Talam was first created

Geata: [/gʲɛhdə/] gate, the carved gate within the Craobh na Beatha and the sea cave at Orc Rock Farm

Neach-gleidhidh: [/Nʲɛx/ /gleː/] Sentinel, one of the giant beings that look as if they're made of stone. It is an ancient tale regarding the birth of Talam and how if ever a time came when the planet would be ruined by the orckin, the Sentinels would come alive and wipe the planet clean to start again

SPIRITUAL ITEMS:

Chleoc: [/klɔːxgə/] An ancient type of ring that cloaks the appearance of orcs to look more human-like, a common item left over from the ages past when humans and orcs traveled to one another's lands

Clach Grèine: [/kLax/ /ˈɟɾʲeːnʲə/] sunstones; stones that absorb the heat of the sun during the day and expel the heat at night

Frith-rathad: [/frʲi/ /Ra.ad/] Path; often regarding one's life path or destiny

Tog Taigh: [/tog/ /tɤj/] The building of a house for the express purpose of impressing a potential mate. The urge to build a home for a mate is strong amongst males, but can also occur amongst females, though this is rare. This urge and creation of a home is something revered amongst the orckin as a rite of passage and often has to be earned by acts of service within the clan.

LEGENDARY PEOPLE:

Banrigh na Gealach: [/bãũNRɪ/ /na/ /gʲaLəx/] The Moon Queen who fell in love with the Night King. She gave up her celestial position and came to Talam to be with him. He fell to her knees, love-struck and she was the only one he ever bowed to. Their love spawned the cridhe bond and began a new age of prosperity for the orckin.

Rìgh na Oidhche: [/Riː/ /na/ /ɤçə/] The Night King who fell in love with the Moon Queen who came down from the stars out of love for him. He fell to his knees and swore fealty to her alone. Their love spawned the cridhe bond and began a new age of prosperity for the orckin.

LANGUAGE:

Common: English

Teanga Dhubh: [/tʲɛŋgə/ /ɣuh/] Black tongue, the primary orckin language

HEALTH & WELLNESS:

An'sgudal: [/əN(ʲ)/ /sgudəL/] The wasting illness that strikes the orckin, predominately affecting females and orclings; accompanied by the Dorcha'aon, it is unknown how they are connected

ANIMALS:

Buabhall: [/buə.əL/] A fluffy, bison-looking creature that wanders the plains within Oc'Turin territory

Cnuimh: [/krũĩv/] Worm

Cuileagan: [/kulagan/] Flies

Dorcha'aon: [/dɔrɔxə/ /ũːn/] An apex predator with six legs, six glowing eyes, and a maw filled with sharp teeth; they come with the an'sgudal and eat the males and their nocrys

Eun'bogha-froise: [/ian/ /bo.əˈfrɔʃə/] A large bird whose plumage is the colors of the rainbow; they like to fly amongst rainbows after a storm

Iolaire'lasair: [/juLɪrʲə/ /Lasɪrʲ/] Fire eagle or phoenix

Moileasgan: [pronounced similarly to mollusk] Enormous mollusk that is carnivorous and will lie under the sand in wait then snap closed around their prey; neamhnaid are found within the Moileasgan

Nocrys: Large felines which act as steeds and guardians to the orckin; they have black or dark grey fur and scales and choose their rider

Fuar Nocrys: [/fuər/] Nocrys that are found in the snowy mountain ranges of the Oc'Blyre; they are white and grey to blend in with their surroundings

Seillean: [/ʃeLʲan/] Bees specific to Talam. They are notoriously difficult to hive as they often will have two queen bees per swarm

FOOD:

Luibh Gaoil: [/Lɯiv/ /gɯːL/] Whiskey spiked with an herb that triggers a state similar to the cridhe frenzy

Uisge-beatha: [/ɯʃgʲəˈbɛhə/] very strong whiskey distilled by the orckin

Fìon-math: [/fiən/ /ma/] A floral wine that's lighter on the palate than uisge-beatha

Cofaidh: [/kɔfɪ/] A drink similar to coffee

Dearc Ruadh: [/dʲɛrxg/ /Ruəɣ/] An edible red berry the size of a cherry that grows on a bush with black leaves; has a tart taste similar to cherries

Tiùbar: [/tʲuːbər/] Edible tubers with a mushroom-like stalk that looks like a dildo. All parts are edible but need to be roasted

A'crathadh Cnòthan: [/ə/ /krahəɣ/ /krɔ̃ː.ən/] Nuts from the tree with the waving noodle-like spikes on the trunk; the nutmeat tastes like pumpkin seeds and peanuts

Aran: [/aran/] Bread

Càise: [/kaːʃə/] Similar to cheese, it's made from the hardened sap of a tree

Fighe Inntinn Bog: [/fi.ə/ /ĩːNʲdʲɪNʲ/ /bog/] Similar to marijuana but a lot stronger

Caraiceag: [/karɪgʲag/] Pancake-like food stuffed with nuts and honey

PLANTS:

Folach Vines: [/fɔLəx/] Long trailing vines that are found growing over the entrances to Baile Coille within the Fàinne Sleagh. They have broad, spear-like leaves and their flowers bloom on the underside of the leaves. The flowers have a pleasant odor and the pollen has properties connected to the dorcha'aon.

ITEMS:

Concrait: [pronounced similarly to concrete] A building material similar to concrete

LOCATIONS & CLANS:

EARTH:

Earth: The planet where Amelia is from

Orc Rock Farm: A dilapidated farm that Ruth buys and transforms, with Thorn's help, into a Tolkien-inspired bed-and-breakfast based on Hobbiton

TALAM:

A planet with three moons that orbits twin stars in a solar system across the universe from Earth. There are many continents, but none have been explored outside of the primary continent in which the orckin reside.

Talam: The planet on which the orcs live, also the continent on which they reside

Muir Sgàil: [/mur ʲ/ /sga:l/] The Shadow Sea, is a large body of water that is a host to all kinds of monster-like creatures that make sailing across it impossible

OC'DELLOR:

A clan of orckin who reside in the forested lands of Talam. They tend to have grey coloring to help them blend in with the shadows, teeth similar to a wolf's, and live in tree homes built into the giant trees.

Leader: *Rìgh Thorn Oc'Dellor & Banrigh Ruth Dellor*

Baile Coille: [/balə/ /kʁLʲə/] The forest city of the Oc'Dellor

Daingneach: [/daiŋʲgʲNʲəx/] The fortress where the Oc'Dellor rulers live

Eun'bogha-froise Market: [/ian/ /bo.ə ˈ frɔʃə/] A large winding market lined with vendor stalls and colored brightly like a rainbow.

Craobh Bean Glic: [/krɯːv/ /bɛn/ /gliçgʲ/] The wise woman tree where the Fear a Chì and the orphaned orclings live

Craobh Brathaidh: [/krɯːv/ /brahəɣ/] The traitor tree where traitors are hung for their crimes; is located next to the fortress Daingneach

Fàinne Sleagh: [/faːNʲə/ /ʃlʁɣ/] The stone ring of the caldera that juts up through the trees surrounding Baile Coille as a natural fortification

Noc'tal Forest: The wide forest surrounding Fàinne Sleagh that borders Oc'Sentan and Oc'Turin lands

OC'TURIN:

A clan of orckin who reside in the steppes and rolling hills of Talam. Their coloring leans more towards greens and browns to blend in with the grasses and stones of the steppes. Their teeth have large, sharp canines and flat molars. They live primarily in stone homes with living roofs, blending into the environment. They are often considered the harshest of the orckin as their training is brutal and starts early and they are rigid in their views of females.

Leader: *Rìgh Orok Oc'Verna & Banrigh Sagra Oc'Byrne*

Clach-tholl: [/kLax/ /tɔuL/] The stone capital city of the Oc'Turin built into the sides of a gorge over a river.

Cìp Carragh: [/kʲiːhb/ /kaRəɣ/] The stone keep where the Oc'Turin rulers live; there are many caves dug into the hard rock of the steppes that are connected to it

Feurach Clachach: [/fiarəx/ /kLaxəx/] The name of the steppes and stone grasslands of the Oc'Turin that borders the Oc'Dellor and Oc'Blyre lands

Carrachan Neach-gleidhidh: [/kaRəxan/ /Nʲɛx/ /gleː/] A Sentinel surrounded by a unique ring of standing stones; cairns are erected for the dead here in a spiral pattern

OC'VELTAS:

A reclusive clan of orckin who reside in the isles on the eastern coast of Talam. Their coloring leans more towards blues and sea greens to blend in with the waters that they often swim in. Their teeth are narrow and sharp. They live primarily in The Citadel in homes made of stone and glass. They have isolated themselves for generations and have technologies far beyond the other clans.

Leader: *Banrigh Aria Oc'Veltas*

Tòrr Chathair: [/tɔːR/ /kahɪrʲ/] Oc'Veltas city, also often called The Citadel

Geodha Corranach: [/gʲɔ.ə/ /kɔRanəx/] The crooked coves, channels, and islands that are scattered between The Citadel and the mainland

OC'SENTAN:

A clan of migrating orckin who reside in the jungles and desert of northern Talam. Their coloring leans more towards dun and orange colors to blend in with the rock and sand. Their teeth are the most human-like with prominent canines. They are the most difficult of the clans to track down as they migrate with their mobile homes following the rains. They are excellent trackers and hunters.

Leader: *Rìgh Pàdruig Oc'Sentan & Banrigh Ealasaid Oc'Druim*

Fras Raonach: [/fras/ /Rɯːnəx/] The rain wilds are a mix between plains and desert, the monsoon rains come seasonally and replenish the wildlife

Òrdha Beinn-sheilg: [/ɔːrɣa/ /beiNʲ //] The jungle in which the Oc'Sentant do most of their hunting and gathering with lots of wild edible plants

Fàsach Coinnich: [/faːsəx/ /kɤNʲɪç/] The circular plain within the jungle where the caravans meet up each triple moon cycle to trade

OC'BLYRE:

A clan of giant orckin who reside in caves carved into the mountains in the south of Talam. Their coloring ranges from brows to greys to whites to fit in with their cold, rocky climate. Their teeth are sharp with tusks and can reach over eight feet tall. They are well adapted to the cold and mine the mountains for ore and sunstones.

Leader: *Rìgh Frang Oc'Blyre & Ruairidh Oc'Roideach*

Niomhair Abhainn-deighe: [/Nʲivɛrʲ/ /a.ɪNʲ/ /dʲejə/] A giant glacier that snakes like a river through the mountains

Neulach Callaid Bheann: [/NʲiəLəx/ /kaLadʲ/ /bjauN/] The mountain range along the south of Talam with peaks so high they're obscured in the clouds

Creagan Speur: [/krʲegʲan/ /sbiər/] A cliff city carved into a mountainside where the Oc'Blyre live

CONTENT AWARENESS*

I have sought to be thorough in identifying potential triggers, both explicit and mentioned, including kinks and mental health awareness. This is for the comfortability of readers who are sensitive to triggering content and because I believe in the informed consent of my readers. If you find any mentions of triggering content that I have not included, email me at *authorcarlottahughes@gmail.com* so I can address it within reason.

*Please note that chapter titles marked with an * mean there are explicit scenes. I've included mentions of triggering content below, though they are not specially marked in the chapter titles. Some triggers are generalized throughout the book and aren't specifically identified in the chapter breakdowns (i.e. misogyny). I do not write rape scenes. However, characters have that as part of their backstory and there are questionable consent moments (immediately stopped, addressed, and resolved).*

List of General Triggers: Misogyny, Extinction, Gaslighting, Societally Expected Pregnancy, Fear of Plague

List of Explicit Triggers: Attempted Sexual Assault, Explicit Violence, General Violence & Assault, Violence with Weaponry, Corpse Mutilation, Pregnancy, Harassment, Dubious Consent (addressed, and resolved)

List of Mentioned Triggers: Mentioned Sexual Assault, Mentioned Abuse, Mentioned Family Loss, Mention of Drowning, Mentioned Drug Use

List of Kinks: Praise, Knotting, Pleasure Dom, Breeding, Exhibition, Voyeurism, Primal, Marking, Tandem Masturbation, Masochism, Spanking, Hair Pulling

List of Mental Health Awareness: PTSD, Anxiety, Depression, Panic Attacks, Autism, ADHD, General Neurodivergence, IED

Chapter 01: Mention of escaping an abusive marriage, mention of types of abuse, mention of drowning, mention of family loss, mentioned drug use

Chapter 02: Mention and description of depressive episode

Chapter 03:

Chapter 04*: PTSD, Panic Attack

Chapter 05*: Enclosed Spaces, Panic Attack

Chapter 06:

Chapter 07: Fall from heights, ankle injury

Chapter 08:

Chapter 09*: Exhibitionism / Voyeurism

Chapter 10: Mention of a past abusive partner, mention of plague

Chapter 11: Mention of death in childbirth, mention of death in battle, mention of orphans, mention of abusive past, triggered rage (no one injured and brought under control swiftly)

Chapter 12:

Chapter 13:

Chapter 14*: Overstimulation, Crowd-Induced Panic, Autistic

Shutdown/Meltdown, mention of spousal loss in childbirth

Chapter 15:

Chapter 16*: Attempted Sexual Assault, Explicit Violence, PTSD Flashback, Panic Attack, Corpse Mutilation (Disembowelment, Malehood Removal, Hanging Corpse in a Tree by Intestines)

Chapter 17*: PTSD Flashback, Witnessing Post-Corpse Mutilation

Chapter 18*: Neurodivergent/Autistic Shutdown

Chapter 19:

Chapter 20*: Crowds in Tight Spaces

Chapter 21: Mention of war, mention of kidnapping, mention of family loss, mention of SA, mention of violent justice

Chapter 22*: Masturbation

Chapter 23:

Chapter 24*: Teasing, Attempted Bullying (called out), Coming Out (heard and accepted)

Chapter 25*: Blood, Hand Injury, Autistic Shutdown/Meltdown

Chapter 26*: Autistic Shutdown/Meltdown

Chapter 27:

Chapter 28: Interaction with a lecherous creepy person

Chapter 29:

Chapter 30*: Discussion of Forced/Arranged Relationship, Propper Pronoun Use Discussion, Discussion of Breeding Kink

Chapter 31: Getting bucked off a steed

Chapter 32:

Chapter 33: Mention of murdering a ruler

Chapter 34: Facing a monstrous creature

Chapter 35*: Kidnapped by a Monstrous Creature, description of physical shifting into another form, Panic Attack

Chapter 36: Arguing

Chapter 37*: Dub Con (kiss offered as a prize)

Chapter 38*: Explicit & General Violence: Tournament

Chapter 39*: Explicit & General Violence: Tournament

Chapter 40*: Explicit & General Violence: Tournament, Dub Con (kiss offered as a prize)

Chapter 41*: Discussion of Forced/Arranged Relationship, Autistic Shutdown/Meltdown, Panic Attack

Chapter 42*: Depressive Episode, Clan-Sanctioned Orgy, Dub Con (FMC unknowingly drinks aphrodisiac), General Violence

Chapter 43*: Dub Con (aftermath of drinking aphrodisiac), Spanking, Hair Pulling

Chapter 44*: Dub Con (aftermath of drinking aphrodisiac), Tandem Masturbation, Emotional Release

Chapter 45: Physical soreness post sex, public bathing

Chapter 46*: Mention of murder, General Violence (including kick to the groin)

Chapter 47*: Description of Past Sexual Assault, Arguing

Chapter 48: Thunderstorm

Chapter 49*: Exhibitionism, Spanking, Rough Sex, Thunderstorm, Throat Holding (NOT choking)

Chapter 50:

Excerpt from Rhuger's Cridhe: Pregnancy

ACKNOWLEDGMENTS

A huge thank you to YOU for reading my book! Thank you so much!

First and foremost, I have to give a major shout-out to my fellow Trash Cats, podcasting buddies from Smut Tea Podcast, writing comrades, and overall besties Jenifer Wood and Jersey Konlyn. You guys kept me sane, kept me going, and bribed me into completing Rhuger's Pearl, the 'orc bible', with coffee and flowers. Lastly, to Tiffany Roberts for DM-ing me about dialogue tags and saying you liked my quotes from Rhuger's Pearl. I fangirled for like a damn week. Bless.

An incalculably enormous thank you to Connor for just being himself. I wrote Rhuger before I ever met you and it's like, by doing so, I wrote you into existence. I hope you know Rhuger's Pearl is my love letter to you. You've inspired more courage in me than I thought possible and held the shattered remnants of my heart in your hands while I slowly healed myself. You haven't been my knight in shining armor, but the battle-worn warrior who had my back as I saved myself. A far greater hero, in my opinion. I hope the miles that separate us won't do so forever. And I look forward to the day I can hold your hand in mine. No matter what, you're worth it.

I'd like to thank my writing group, The Degenerate Syndicate:

Maddie Syn, Chloe Parker, Brianna Everly, Krista Luna, Ursa Dax, Sara Ivy Hill, Ami Wright, L.A. Holloway, Jinx Layne, Victoria Aveline, Kimberly Lemming, Luna Wolff, & Matilda Vega. Thanks for the encouragement, help, alien peen jokes, and for letting me live-stream drawing alien peen during our hangouts. We do it for the science.

And I'd also like to thank my mom. Because nothing screams belief in your dreams quite like being whacked in the back of the head by a copy of the first draft, then given a hug. Also, for both my mom and dad, for giving me the out I needed when I desperately needed an escape route from my living nightmare. I would not be here if you hadn't. I would have ended it another way.

Thanks to all the thirst traps on TikTok, too. Because hot damn.

Also, I'd like to thank the real-life Jayne, Kaylee, and River. My fur babies. For all the floof bean cuddles.

ABOUT THE AUTHOR

Carlotta Hughes is a giant orc-like lady living with her four cats and an enormous book collection. She wrote a creation story with a polar bear at age five and has been writing ever since. When not reading or writing, she's often exploring, hyper-fixating on a new creative outlet, and generally being a bubbly goblin hermit. She loves snacks, being warm, weapons, and snuggles.

Carlotta writes thorny, corny, horny stories with sassy one-liners, alt-human love interests, sexually frustrated characters, lots of simping, and guaranteed HEA. Her stories explore the spectrum of humanity, including disabilities, gender, sexuality, kinks, and survivorship. You know, for science.

- Website: https://www.authorcarlottahughes.com/
- Amazon: https://www.amazon.com/Carlotta-Hughes/e/B09P9S6JVH
- TikTok: @authorcarlottahughes
- Instagram: @authorcarlottahughes

ALSO BY...

ORC MATCHED SERIES

0.5 THORN'S DOVE (2022)

1.0 RHUGER'S PEARL (2023)

1.5 RHUGER'S CRIDHE (2023)

2.0 SHARN'S HONEYBEE (Coming 2023)

2.5 RHUGER'S TINSEL (Coming 2023)

3.0 SIGG'S KITTEN (Coming 2023)